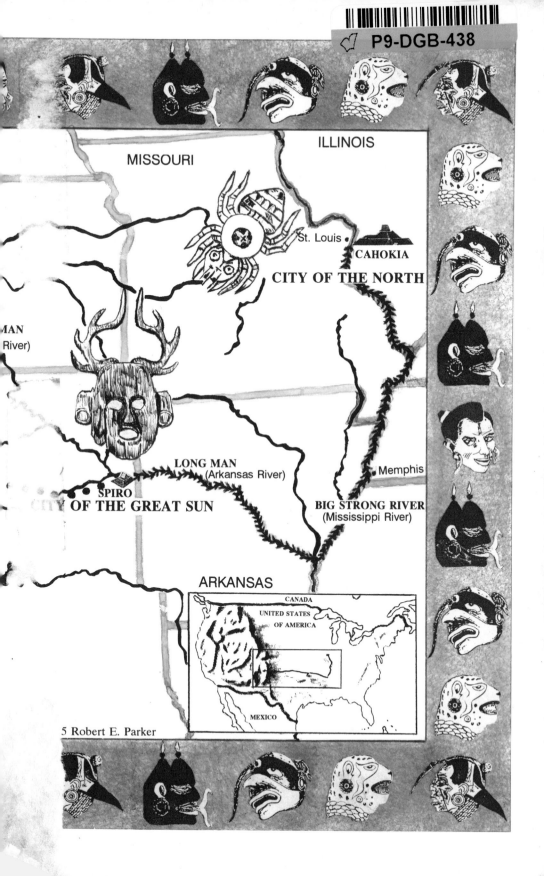

MISSOURI

ILLINOIS

St. Louis

CAHOKIA

CITY OF THE NORTH

MAN
(River)

LONG MAN
(Arkansas River)

Memphis

SPIRO

CITY OF THE GREAT SUN

BIG STRONG RIVER
(Mississippi River)

ARKANSAS

CANADA

UNITED STATES
OF AMERICA

MEXICO

5 Robert E. Parker

LET
THE DRUM
SPEAK

Other books by Linda Lay Shuler

She Who Remembers

Voice of the Eagle

LET THE DRUM SPEAK

A Novel of Ancient America

▲▼▲▼▲▼▲▼▲▼▲▼▲▼▲▼▲▼▲▼

Linda Lay Shuler

William Morrow and Company, Inc.
New York

Excerpt from *The Heights of Macchu Picchu* by Pablo Neruda. Translation copyright © 1966 and renewed © 1994 by Nathaniel Tarn. Reprinted by permission of Farrar, Straus & Giroux, Inc.

It is the policy of William Morrow and Company, Inc., and its imprints and affiliates, recognizing the importance of preserving what has been written, to print the books we publish on acid-free paper, and we exert our best efforts to that end.

Library of Congress Cataloging-in-Publication Data

Shuler, Linda Lay.
    Let the drum speak: a novel of ancient America / Linda Lay
  Shuler.
        p.   cm.
    Includes bibliographical references.
    ISBN 0-688-12834-3
    1. Indians of North America—Oklahoma—Fiction.   2. Man,
  Prehistoric—Oklahoma—Fiction.   I. Title.
  PS3569.H768L48   1996
  813'.54—dc20   95-33068
                                                                       CIP

Printed in the United States of America

First Edition

1 2 3 4 5 6 7 8 9 10

For Bob

▲ Author's Note ▼

A True Story

The history of the Spiro site and its principal earthwork, the Craig Mound, contains one of the more remarkable records of Pre-Columbian cultural achievement in North America north of Mexico.
. . . With a site of such stature it is understandable that there is more to its history than what archaeologists have been able to make of the record.
— PHILIP PHILLIPS AND JAMES A. BROWN
Pre-Columbian Shell Engravings

Trying to re-create the prehistoric past of a people with no written record is like reassembling the broken parts of a pottery jar. Pieces are missing, but the shape of a missing piece may be assessed by the contour of the jar as a whole.

Much is known about Spiro. For centuries, the "mounds," mysterious earthworks in eastern Oklahoma on the Arkansas border, lay undisturbed and even feared as the habitation of spirits. In 1832, when the Five Civilized Tribes were being dispersed into what eventually became Oklahoma, the Choctaw settled in what is now the Spiro area. It is said that their spirits linger.

The Civil War disrupted tribal life, a railway brought easterners, and all was changed forever—all but the mounds. They rose in brooding mystery as always, grassy flanks undisturbed.

Choctaw and Choctaw freedmen landowners held the mounds in superstitious reverence, especially Craig Mound, which was a large cone with three smaller ones attached. Tales of "haunts" and strange apparitions abounded. Attempts to dig by a few pot hunters were frustrated by landowners' adamant resistance. However, as time passed, secret digging revealed artifact potential. In 1933 new owners agreed to lease Craig Mound to a group of partners for the sum of fifty dollars each. And the digging began.

There was trouble from the beginning. The lessees were jealous of one another but united in their deeper suspicion of outsiders, especially city slickers and museum people. However, the lessees were stubborn and resourceful. When they needed help, they hired coal miners. It was the miners who dug crude tunnels and accidentally discovered a burial chamber in the main cone— with sensational results.

What they found stunned the archaeological world—sculpture so unprecedented that the authenticity of stone pipes, for example, was questioned. Diggers with wheelbarrows hauled out loads of pearls, shell beads, textiles of feathers and fur, embossed sheets of copper in fantastic designs, pottery, copper earspools, masks, tools, weapons, and jewelry and other adornments in abundance. Most incredible were the engraved conch shells, cups, and gorgets, elaborately designed and masterfully executed, illustrating people and events of an ancient time.

When word of the find became known, buyers from museums and collectors arrived hurriedly and bought treasures from wheelbarrows—what treasures were saved from trampling and catastrophic mishandling. Many are now in museums worldwide.

The lessees, still jealous of one another, decided they had all that was worth having, and set off a couple of black powder charges at the tunnel entrance to be sure nobody else got anything.

Eventually the University of Oklahoma, with financial help

from the Oklahoma Historical Society, the University of Tulsa, and many private donors, scientifically excavated the remaining portions of the burial mound and other mounds in the ceremonial complex, as well as the large city that surrounded it. Bit by painstaking bit, more pieces were added to the broken jar.

Subsequent excavations continuing to the present day revealed even more about the people who had lived there and their extraordinary culture. But, due to the unfortunate rape of Craig Mound, much is missing still.

How can a writer know intimate things that artifacts cannot reveal? Other mound sites in the Southeast, where no such devastation occurred, offer information about the culture as a whole—adding yet more pieces to the jar.

But what of the people themselves? What were their fears, their loves and aspirations? Were they much as we are, except that they did not have the accumulation of knowledge we possess?

As Pablo Neruda says in *The Heights of Macchu Picchu,*

> *There dwells within me a bird*
> *Imprisoned for a thousand years,*
> *The old and unremembered human heart.*

The drumbeat in your blood is the voice of your ancestors. Let the drum speak.

—*FAR WALKER*

PART 1

▲▼▲▼▲▼▲▼▲▼▲▼▲▼▲▼▲▼▲▼▲▼▲▼

THE CITY OF THE GREAT SUN

A.D. 1293

▲ 1 ▼

The all-powerful ruler known as the Great Sun stood on his dwelling terrace high on the mound and stared down at the commotion in the plaza below. He scowled. A thunder drum had boomed the usual warning; signals from lookout points announced the distant approach of strangers. But traders were always arriving. Why the furor?

Shading his eyes with a hand at his tattooed forehead, the Great Sun gazed north and east across fields and dwellings to the sacred river, Long Man, a giant whose head rose in the foothills of the mountains and whose foot lay far down in the lowlands. A great bend in the river encircled a peninsula where the City of the Great Sun rose in glory with its ceremonial center of soaring mounds and outlying villages. The Great Sun's view was partially obscured by trees crowding Long Man's flank, but he knew the river's embankment bustled with the usual activity of men drying fishing nets, women washing clothes, children playing, and guards patrolling the river's strategic bend to collect tribute from foreign canoes. But no foreigners appeared.

Again the thunder drum boomed, and more people scurried from outlying villages into the great plaza, eager to trade or to inspect new arrivals.

The Great Sun turned westward toward the plaza. He still shaded his eyes although it was morning and his spiritual brother, the Spirit Being, now shone low in the sky behind him. It was early summer, already hot although morning shadows lay long. Perspiration beaded his upper lip.

He was a tall man, broad of chest and shoulder, whose stance and every gesture and glance proclaimed a heritage of royal command. A crown of white swan feathers, eight inches high in front and four inches high in back, symbolized his royal status; each feather was tipped with a small red tuft and a tassel. The crown bore a scarlet diadem lavish with white pearls and conch shell beads intricately engraved. Only the Great Sun was privileged to wear such a crown. *And only the Great Sun knew that he who wore the crown concealed a secret in his spirit. A shameful secret that must never be discovered. Never.* Especially not by his brother, Striped Serpent, nor by Manimani, his sister, nor by either of his two mates. Not even by Patu, his beloved small son.

A breeze fingered the feathers, ruffled the tassels, and carried the sound of people gathering below in the plaza. He had discarded his cloak of scarlet feathers and wore only an ornate breechclout that hung to a point in front and dangled to his knees; it glistened with pearls and feathers and bright shell beads. An engraved conch shell disk upon his chest proclaimed his sacred heritage. Copper and shell earspools glittered, and moccasins of scarlet deerskin ornamented with pearls adorned his feet.

As each person approached the sacred mound where the Great Sun stood in all his splendor, that person was required on threat of death to bow three times and howl the required greeting, *"Hou! Hou! Hou!"* Nobles of lesser stature were acknowledged with one or two hous, depending upon lineage; only the Great Sun merited three.

The boom of the thunder drum, the excited exclamations of villagers, and the shouts of children mingled with the respectful howls of greeting and the yelps of tethered dogs.

The Great Sun gestured and immediately a slave appeared below. His head was shaved and he wore only a plain breechclout. "Hou! Hou! Hou!" he bellowed, touching his forehead to the ground, then he ran up the long flight of stairs on the mound's slope, passing the Great Sun's guards on either side, until he reached the terrace where the Great Sun stood. The slave howled again and prostrated himself on the ground, arms outstretched.

After a suitable pause, the Great Sun grunted and the slave lifted his head but did not presume to gaze at the holy one.

The Great Sun gestured. "Summon the *caddí.*"

The slave backed away, then ran down the stairs, shouting. When he reached the plaza he disappeared. He reappeared soon, followed by the caddí, a short, powerfully built man in a jaguar cloak. He was greeted by a loud chorus of "Hou! Hou!"—the two greetings his status as governor commanded. He ignored them and strode swiftly up the steps to stand before the Great Sun.

The caddí bellowed the required greeting and knelt with bowed head. He raised his right arm and awaited acknowledgment.

The Great Sun spoke. "I wish to know who comes."

The caddí lowered his arm and rose. "It is said to be Koko-pelli—"

The Great Sun snorted. "Impossible! He is too old. Long in the Afterworld with his ancestors." He turned away to conceal sudden apprehension. Could it be true?

"Of course." The caddí fingered a knot on his jaguar robe. Many moons had waned since Kokopelli last came and departed, but the Great Sun's jealousy of Kokopelli's magical powers and sexual conquests was no secret. He continued carefully, "It is said to be Kokopelli reincarnated. Chomoc is his name. With a mate, Antelope. The daughter of She Who Remembers."

The Great Sun gave a sharp exclamation and gestured dismissal. He watched the caddí bow respectfully, back away, and descend the steps to the plaza to mingle with the crowd.

The Great Sun gazed across green hills that would be known one day as eastern Oklahoma—a fertile land, rich with game. He strained for a first glimpse of the invaders. Far away two hawks circled high, watching for small animals or birds that travelers might flush. Smoke from the signal station at the Guardian Mound announced the approach of travelers, but as yet none could be seen.

The Great Sun turned away. Kokopelli! Could it be? And the

daughter of She Who Remembers! Did she possess her mother's powers? A cold finger jabbed his spine. *His secret, hidden so carefully from all, might not be hidden from one who possessed the powers of She Who Remembers.*

Something had to be done! Those travelers must never arrive. He would confer with the shaman.

The Great Sun signaled a guard to summon the litter bearers to carry him across the plaza to the Temple of Eternal Fire. There, in the sacred place atop the highest mound of the great ceremonial complex, he would await the shaman.

Antelope shifted the cradleboard on her back and tried to keep step with Chomoc and the rest of the men as they climbed another hill. The excitement of adventure in accompanying Chomoc on a great trading journey had long since faded to weariness.

The dogs strained under the heavy loads on their travois; they, too, were tired. Since leaving Cicuye (to be known one day as Pecos, New Mexico) they had traversed plains and forests, slogged through marshes, crossed rivers, waded streams, and passed occasional farms and villages during their travels. Now farms and dwellings were closer together, connected by a network of paths.

Antelope glanced behind her. Villagers from some nearby town followed silently in the distance, watching. People had never followed this way before.

"Are they friendly?" she asked their old guide, Horned Toad. She made her voice casual. Horned Toad had objected to her coming and was impatient with what he considered to be foolish female concerns.

"Of course. They are my people."

He spoke in Caddoan, the language of his people. It was quite different from Towa, the language of Cicuye, and he had been teaching Caddoan to Antelope and Chomoc during their journey. Chomoc was already proficient, but Antelope spoke it haltingly.

Horned Toad had told often of the City of the Great Sun; it was where he was born. He had gone with his mate to Cicuye long ago. When Chomoc asked the old man if he could be their guide and translator, he had accepted eagerly, but Antelope knew it had been a difficult journey for one so old. No wonder he was crotchety.

It was hot, and she was tired and sweaty. Her feet hurt in moccasins worn thin from their long journey, and she felt that if she could not bathe and wash her hair soon, she would wither and dry up like an empty bean pod.

When had they left Cicuye? It was too long ago for Antelope to remember. Lately she had longed for the comfort and security of home. Here on this journey she was a woman with a baby, a handicap slowing down everyone and everything. At home she was She Who Remembers—to whom eager young girls came to learn the secrets only women knew. A person of importance, revered. But she had loudly insisted upon coming against Chomoc's wishes and the advice of family and friends, so how could she admit she should have stayed home?

She brushed away a loose strand of sweaty hair from her cheek and watched Chomoc as he strode easily uphill, his strong, bronzed legs tireless. He had relished every step of this adventure; always, his moccasins refused to remain long in one place. She wondered if there might be a spell a shaman could cast that would make Chomoc and his moccasins stay home. With her.

Did he suspect the real, the secret reason she wanted to accompany him?

As they reached the crest of the hill the men paused, but only for a moment, to search for sight of the City of the Great Sun they had come so far to see. A place where men built mountains to honor their gods, a rich city for trading.

Antelope looked back at the crowd following; they, too, had stopped. She tugged at Chomoc's arm. "Why are those people following?"

He shrugged. "Who knows?"

Horned Toad said, "They are curious. They have not seen Towa travelers before." He gave Antelope a quick glance. "Especially with a woman and baby. They are harmless."

Antelope hesitated. "But—"

Horned Toad scowled. "Am I or am I not the guide for this party? Is not my knowledge to be trusted? I tell you they mean no harm." He jerked his staff in emphasis.

"We believe you," Chomoc said. "But we are not so weary we could not defend ourselves if necessary." He laughed. "Especially since most of them are women and children."

"Ha!" a man said. "It can be easier to defend oneself from a wild boar than from a woman."

There was loud agreement with laughter and ribald comment.

Dark clouds billowed on the horizon and a haze of smoke hung beneath; they should reach the city tomorrow. Antelope's unease faded and a surge of excitement banished her weariness. She turned to Chomoc, who always announced their approach to a city by playing his flute as his father had done.

"When will you begin to play?"

"When there is someone in the city to hear. We are still too far away." He gave her an amused glance.

"But they will hear. They always do."

"We will wait until we see a welcoming party."

"Why?" She flipped a dark braid.

Horned Toad scowled. "Why must you always question Chomoc—or any of us? It is not seemly."

Chomoc whirled to the old man and speared him with a look. "She Who Remembers may question anyone whenever she wishes to do so. Remember that."

Horned Toad flushed angrily and retreated into sullen silence.

Antelope sympathized with old Horned Toad, but just the same she wanted to give Chomoc a hug. She wanted to lie with him then and there. She had traveled long and endured much for that, but it would have to wait. Instead, she asked, "How will they know we come? I don't see—"

"They watch. See the puff of smoke on that distant hill? Look at the color; they burn both grass and pine needles. A signal. Someone will come."

What will they be like? Antelope wondered. *Will they welcome us?* A twinge of foreboding touched her. The baby. How would they react to Skyfeather's blue eyes? It was said by ignorant ones that a witch's eyes were blue. . . .

Antelope fingered her necklace of bright polished stones with its scallop shell pendant inlaid with turquoise in a mystic design, and was reassured. All would be well. It was the sacred necklace of She Who Remembers, bequeathed by her mother, Kwani. One who was She Who Remembers was protected by those who had been She Who Remembers before her, the Ancient Ones, all of whom had possessed the necklace in their day, and whose spirits possessed it still.

Antelope reached behind to touch Skyfeather in the cradle-board. Her beautiful daughter, born but two moons ago. Antelope felt a fierce surge of protectiveness.

Nothing would harm this child!

▲2▼

Horned Toad paused to rest.
He did not want to because others in the party grumbled impatiently; they were eager to reach the City of the Great Sun. But he was deeply weary. He sat down, easing his bony frame to the ground. The younger men stood around or squatted, while dogs sighed and lay down in their harnesses, grateful for respite from pulling the heavy loads. The people who had been following were out of sight; perhaps they had returned home.

It was morning, already hot. It had rained the night before, only a brief shower, and the moisture had been swallowed immediately by brush and grasses and soil grown thirsty by prolonged drought. A breeze swept over green hills from distant mountains, carrying the fragrance of brush and grasses and rich earth warmed by Sunfather.

Horned Toad hugged his knees and rested his head on his arms. He had come a long way to die; he was almost home. Too long he had waited to return to his birthplace after his mate entered Sipapu where ancestors dwelt. She was of the Towa tribe of Cicuye; as was the custom he had left his people to join hers when they mated. For years they had been as one. Soon he would be with her again.

Soon he would be home.

It was quiet but for the muttering of the nine men and that one woman, Antelope, he had guided all this way from Cicuye. It was Chomoc who grumbled the loudest, as always. How dare he presume to reprimand an elder, his guide and translator, as he had yesterday! Horned Toad flushed, remembering. Chomoc was too much like his father, Kokopelli, expecting always to be obeyed, to be consulted and admired. He and his flute.

It was Chomoc who had arranged this journey, promising riches, saying he wanted to follow his father's footsteps of long ago, to learn what had become of him; to play the flute and to trade as his father had. A good trader this arrogant Anasazi might be, but how could women want him—as they did in every village visited? How ugly he was, with that sloping brow and hawk nose and amber eyes; what did women see in him? It was a mystery.

Look at Chomoc's mate now. Antelope. Like, yet unlike, her mother. Beautiful but different. Kwani had refreshed the spirit like spring rain; Antelope seemed always on fire about something. Bossy, she was. But people loved her. Why? He shook his head. He had to admit Antelope cooked well and was a good mother, but that was what women were supposed to be.

The old man spat at a fly on his bare leg and missed; the fly buzzed away and Horned Toad watched the spittle trickle down his leg. He glanced at Antelope, who stood—like a man!—with hands on her hips, glaring up at Chomoc. They had been arguing—again—and now her clear voice rose in outrage.

"No, I will not enter that city riding a travois like a sick child or a crone. I have walked all this way. Now am I to sit to be hauled by dogs? Ha! No, I shall walk by your side, I and Skyfeather."

Chomoc looked down his beak nose. His amber eyes gazed into black ones shooting sparks at him. Full lips, down-turned at the corners, eased in a smile. "Very well. You may walk beside me but Skyfeather rides the travois. It is not suitable for the mate of Chomoc to carry a baby when dogs and travois are available."

"I have carried her ever since she was born. Over two moons ago. I shall carry her now."

"No. Important people come to meet us and escort us into the city. It is bad enough for the mate of Chomoc to walk, but to carry the baby would say that Chomoc is too poor, too stingy, to provide travois. That I will not allow."

Antelope and Chomoc glared at each other while the rest of the party stood about, mumbling impatiently, pretending not to notice. Horned Toad shook his head. These two argued often; they relished confrontation. It was not seemly. They behaved like two men rather than like man and mate. Except at night. Their lovemaking, overheard and whispered about, was discussed hungrily by men whose mates were far away at home— where Antelope should be, performing her duties as She Who Remembers.

Suddenly Antelope laughed, throwing back her head so that her long hair reached her waist. Chomoc laughed, too, and they stood close together while Antelope lifted the cradleboard from her back and handed it with the baby to Chomoc.

"Very well, irrational one," Antelope said. "Your daughter shall ride, but She Who Remembers will meet the welcoming party standing by your side."

She pressed her breasts against him. Beautiful they were, and she knew it. *It was not seemly.* But Antelope had never been like other women. It was because she was twins.

Horned Toad squinted into the past, remembering. Back in Cicuye. There had been much talk around the evening fire of how the Medicine Chief told Kwani the baby she expected would be twins. But Kwani pleaded to have one child only; twins were unnatural. So the Medicine Chief promised he would twist them into one in the womb. When Antelope was born, her Pueblo mark of birth at the base of the spine was shaped like a tiny penis! And did she not have two whorls of hair on her head instead of one? Horned Toad shook his head admiringly. What a Medicine Chief the Towa had! Making twins, boy and girl, become one child in the womb. How did he do that?

True, Antelope was a beautiful woman. But she had a man's strong spirit—her twin brother's spirit—unseemly in a woman. Yet Kwani had chosen Antelope to be her successor as She Who Remembers.

Again the old man shook his head. Things were not as they used to be, as they should be. When he had been young, traditions were respected. Look at Antelope standing there like a man, hands on her hips and chin high like that! Always she said whatever she chose to say, regardless of how it might make her mate appear in the eyes of others. And Chomoc allowed it. In fact, he seemed to consider it an enjoyable challenge. And she with a baby, and a blue-eyed baby at that. Blue eyes! But nobody seemed to realize what those blue eyes might mean.

What was the world coming to? How must the Creator regard these wayward creatures? Well, soon he, Horned Toad of the Hasinai, would be back where he belonged, in the City of the Great Sun, home of his ancestors. He would join them there.

Ah, how weary he was!

As they reached the crest of another hill, the party stopped to rest under the trees. Antelope and the men exclaimed in surprise. Ahead, a flat-topped, pyramid-shaped mound, tall as ten moccasins, was surmounted by a building with an extended entryway five moccasins long. To one side, smoke rose from a signal fire.

"Who dwells there?" Antelope asked Horned Toad.

The old man did not reply. He stood with legs apart, staff overhead, gazing at the mound. A figure appeared from the entryway—a man with a conch shell horn hanging from a cord around his neck; he saw the party, turned, and shouted to someone within. In a moment, a smaller figure emerged and they conferred briefly.

Horned Toad held his staff in both hands and raised it up and down, then from side to side. The smaller figure spoke, and the man lifted the conch shell to his lips and blew. Antelope winced at the sound. Her father, long in Sipapu, had possessed such a horn; hearing its cry was a poignant reminder.

Horned Toad turned to the group. "That is the guardian station at the city's border. We may come, but we must be accepted by One Who Watches before we may enter the city center."

"Why?" Antelope asked.

Horned Toad jerked his staff in irritation. "Why must you always ask why?"

Chomoc said sharply, "Because she wants to know, and so do I."

Horned Toad scowled. "It is customary. When we enter the city we shall observe the customs."

"Who is One Who Watches?"

"The one who determines if we may enter the city." He gestured ahead. "Come."

As they approached the mound, two more figures emerged,

carrying bows and arrows and tall staffs with banners. Two large, shaggy dogs stood beside them, barking warnings.

"Guards," Horned Toad said. "They will meet us."

Antelope was uneasy, but she tried not to show it as the guards ran down steps on the sloping side of the mound and strode toward them, dogs following. The men were not tall but they were broad and muscular, with tattoos or painted ornamentation on every inch of the body not covered by a woven breechclout. Their hair, worn in two buns on top, was elaborately adorned with fur and feathers. A beaded forelock hung over the forehead and dangled between the eyes. As the guards drew near, their sharp black eyes scrutinized each person and each dog and travois. Blacktail and the other dogs growled warnings as the two guardian dogs approached.

They stopped a short distance away; one of the guards ordered their dogs back and spoke loudly to Horned Toad. He answered. The guards spoke again and beckoned.

Horned Toad turned to the group. "We go to meet One Who Watches. It would be wise to be respectful."

Chomoc snorted. "We are traders, good traders. It is they who should be respectful." But he quieted the growling dogs, and joined Antelope and the others as they approached the mound.

Antelope gazed up at the two figures on the mound. The man with the shell horn was dressed like the guards, but the other was not. As she grew closer to the mound, Antelope saw the smaller person was a woman wearing nothing but a brief fur pelt fastened at the waist by a fringed belt. Necklaces nestled between generous breasts with nipples encircled by ornate tattoos. She was neither young nor old; her round face was ageless. Her eyes, shadowed by brows that met in a continuous line, were expressionless. She gazed at the party in silence, then spoke to the man with the horn. He raised it to his lips and blew again; the sound shuddered in the air.

The dogs reacted violently and were restrained by Chomoc's men, who led the animals and their travois a distance away, reassuring them. Naked children appeared from among the trees, staring and jabbering. Antelope became aware of silent villagers, hiding in the shadows, watching.

The guards stopped at the base of the mound and spoke to Horned Toad. He translated, "I alone must speak first with One Who Watches. Wait here."

As he climbed the steps with effort, the woman stood waiting. Her gaze flicked Antelope and rested upon Chomoc. A fleeting expression lit her eyes and vanished.

The man with the horn led Horned Toad to the woman and introduced him. They spoke for some time, gesticulating and glancing at the group below. Finally, Horned Toad called down, "One Who Watches wishes to speak with Chomoc."

Chomoc stepped forward and Antelope followed.

"No!" Horned Toad said. "Chomoc only."

Antelope said with a calm she did not feel, "I am She Who Remembers, mate of Chomoc. Where he goes, I go."

"If you wish to enter the city you will do as One Who Watches requests."

Antelope's black eyes snapped. She turned to Chomoc. "Who does that woman think she is? I—"

"One in authority." He gestured impatiently. "Humor her so we may be on our way."

"Very well." Pause. "If that is your wish."

"It is." He strode up the steps and, ignoring Horned Toad and the man with the horn, he bowed deeply to One Who Watches. Removing a fine turquoise-and-shell bracelet—one that Antelope had given him—he offered it with a flourish. As she reached to accept it, he took her hand and slipped the bracelet over her wrist with a lingering gesture, subtly caressing.

The woman smiled and her shadowed eyes gleamed. She stepped closer. Full lips parted and her tongue emerged from between beautiful teeth, tasting his presence. Gleaming eyes locked into his. It was as if only the two of them were there.

Antelope stared up at them. She knew well how women reacted to him—and he to them—but this was too much.

How dare he give that woman the bracelet I gave him! How dare he!

She darted toward the stairs of the mound, but the guards pushed her back. She stood in stony dignity until the conversation on the mound ended and Chomoc and Horned Toad descended the steps.

Antelope confronted Chomoc in cold rage. "That is *my* bracelet. I want it back."

He assumed a regal stance. "You gave it to me. Therefore it was mine to do with as I chose, and I chose to use it to buy safe passage into the city for us all." Amber eyes burned as he leaned close. "We are watched. Do not disgrace us with childish jealousy, foolish one."

Antelope glanced at the silent villagers moving closer among the trees. The guards regarded her with amusement; they had not understood her words but they knew well what was happening. One Who Watches looked down at her, fingering the bracelet. She smiled.

Horned Toad jerked his staff. "What are we waiting for? Come, let's go!"

The men murmured with impatient agreement, glancing about them with unease.

Antelope swallowed her rage. Maybe she *was* being childish. She said with dignity, "I am ready." She would settle the matter with Chomoc in private. Indeed she would.

They took one of the many paths through the trees; children tagged behind and Antelope glimpsed women and a few men following. Antelope saw that the women, short and sturdy, wore only short skirts fastened at the waist with woven belts; the men wore brief apronlike breechclouts. All were tattooed with strange patterns.

Finally, Horned Toad stopped. "We wait here."

"For what?" Chomoc asked.

"For the greeters. The welcomers." Braced by his staff, he lowered himself to the ground. "We wait."

The men removed their packs and sat down. They were weary and ill at ease, Antelope knew, and so was she. She sat with her legs crossed, rested her arms on her knees, and inspected the surroundings. They were on a ridge encircled by the bottomlands of a river. Many plastered dwellings with steep thatched roofs and extended doorways stood in groups surrounded by garden plots. A network of worn paths connected the dwellings and led down to the river—and to what seemed to be a vision, a dream, far ahead.

Antelope shaded her eyes with her hand, gazing through the trees into the distance. Surely those mountains, with buildings on top, were not man-made!

The men talked excitedly, pointing to the great mounds. "What is that place?"

Horned Toad said proudly, "The heart of my home city. The dwelling place of the Great Sun."

Chomoc looked about him, at the many, many houses and

fine garden plots, and at what must be a great ceremonial center ahead. This was a big, wealthy city!

"Good trading," he announced with satisfaction.

The men agreed. Some eyed the women venturing closer. A man said, "I will trade for one of those."

There was loud laughter. Skyfeather whimpered, and Antelope lifted the cradleboard and held it in her arms. "I know you are hungry," she said, and brought the tiny face to her breast. Miniature lips clasped the nipple and sucked hungrily.

Chomoc sat beside them, watching. He had been gentle and solicitous since their confrontation. They had, indeed, received safe passage; already she had forgiven him. Almost.

He leaned close and whispered, "I am hungry, too."

She laughed.

A distant sound rode the breeze. Many flutes and a drum.

"They come!" Chomoc shouted.

There was a commotion as villagers scurried away, herding dogs and squealing children into dwellings or among the trees. Chomoc and his men jumped to their feet, reached for their shields and quivers, rearranged their breechclouts and necklaces, and ordered the dogs.

Horned Toad rose with effort. He must continue to fulfill his responsibility as guide and interpreter. He reached for his staff with its feathered insignia of rank, and stood to face the welcoming party approaching in the distance.

Meanwhile, Antelope watched Chomoc fasten Skyfeather's cradleboard securely on the travois of the most trustworthy dog. The baby began to cry. Antelope reached to unfasten the cradleboard.

"She doesn't like that dog."

Chomoc pushed Antelope's hands away. "Blacktail is the best, as you know. Skyfeather will get used to him."

"She is too young; she needs to be with me, to feel *me*, not a dog." What did Chomoc or any man really know about Skyfeather or any baby? "I want to carry her."

The sound of flutes grew stronger as figures appeared through the trees. The baby cried loudly, her tiny mouth stretched wide.

Antelope faced Chomoc, her chin high. "Give her to me."

"No." He bent close, whispering. "They come. Every man will stare at you; they always do. If you carry the cradleboard they will look also at Skyfeather and see her blue eyes. But if she is in the travois, they will pay no attention."

He was right. Now was not the time for confrontation with witch-hunters. Why did Chomoc have to be right so often? Why was he smiling that smile at her when he knew it would make her agree to anything he wanted?

"Very well," she said graciously as if Chomoc had quietly asked her permission. "I shall allow Skyfeather to ride on the travois. But only until I decide she must be with me."

If the men were amused, they took care to hide it. Only old Horned Toad snickered, not even taking the trouble to cover his mouth with a scrawny hand.

Antelope watched the figures approaching. They were still too far away to be certain, but could it be that *all* of them were playing flutes? It sounded like it—a shrill cry wavering on the breeze with a drum throbbing the beat.

She turned to Chomoc. "Play!"

"Not yet." He gestured to the men. "We go to meet them."

As they grew closer, Antelope stared.

The flutists—there were at least ten of them—were followed by a very tall man, a giant, wearing a deer mask with antlers and shiny shell teeth surrounding the mouth hole. He walked alone. Behind him, marching in time to the beat of the drum, came a large group of warriors, shields in hand. Some held lances; others carried bright banners that flapped in the breeze.

"Who are they?" Chomoc asked Horned Toad.

"My people." He stood as straight as he could, holding his staff aloft. "I shall greet them." He turned to Chomoc. "I shall need a gift. It is customary."

"I gave a gift already. To One Who Watches."

"Another gift, a better one, is necessary for the Great Sun."

"Very well." Chomoc removed his handsome necklace of turquoise, bright shells, polished stone beads of many colors, and eagle claws. He handed it to Horned Toad. "See that our welcome is suitable."

The old man accepted the necklace with a sardonic glance. "That is why I am here, is that not so?"

"Of course. See that you do it well."

Antelope heard only the cry of the flutes and throb of the drum. She stared unbelievingly at the giant who marched with steps so long everyone else had to hurry to keep up.

"Who wears the mask of the deer?" she asked Horned Toad.

"The most feared shaman of all." Horned Toad did not conceal his pride.

Antelope swallowed with foreboding. Why was a shaman coming to meet them? She wanted to snatch Skyfeather from the travois and hide her somewhere, somehow.

As the group came closer, Antelope swallowed again. All but the shaman wore breechclouts and sandals; their bodies were fearsomely painted and tattooed. Some wore their hair rolled in a bun; others had shaved their heads on each side but for a tall crest from brow to neck, embellished with feathers and ornaments, a tail hanging down in back. Each wore a forelock in front, stiffened with bear grease and hanging at the brow by two large shell beads; the forelock dangled between the eyes and swung back and forth over the nose. Each eye was surrounded by painted markings of a falcon's eye, fierce and compelling.

But it was the shaman who made Antelope's heart jerk with alarm. The man was tall as seven moccasins, and the deer mask with its antlers made him even taller. He towered over the others, a nightmare figure. A necklace of large copper beads held a portion of a conch shell suspended from its slender throat and elaborately engraved. Along with it were so many necklaces of bear and cougar teeth hanging to his waist that only glimpses of tattooed torso could be seen. Large copper earspools glistened on either side of the mask, and shimmering pearls encircled his arms, knees, and ankles. Beneath the necklaces a great copper gorget on his chest held an engraving; Antelope could not see what it was. A woven belt at his waist supported an ornate breechclout with a pointed end embellished with a long tassel; the tassel dangled between his legs and swayed as he strode to the *boom, boom, boom* of the drum and the cry of the flutes. One long arm swung free; the other held a large rattle that hissed with each step.

The dogs in their harnesses hesitated, growling, as the party grew near. Chomoc spoke calmly, quieting them.

The warriors stopped an arrow's flight away. The drumbeat ceased; the flutes were silent. The flutists parted as the shaman stepped forward, warriors on either side. He stood in terrible majesty, waiting.

Horned Toad raised his staff and greeted them in Caddoan. Holding Chomoc's necklace in his outstretched hand, he stood with surprising dignity for one so old and weary.

The warriors glanced at one another. The shaman raised his rattle overhead and shouted a reply.

"He invites me to come forward and speak with him," Horned Toad said.

Chomoc gestured. "Then do so. Tell him we come in peace to trade."

Antelope watched Horned Toad approach the shaman. The necklace swung in splendor from his hand, glistening.

The warriors watched with falcon eyes, bows in hand. The shaman gestured with a finger; immediately warriors surrounded Horned Toad and led him to the shaman.

A warrior poked Horned Toad in the back. "Kneel."

"I am one of you. I do not kneel." He stared up at the deer's head towering above him; black eyes behind the holes in the mask stared back. "This is my home. I return at last to die."

"Die you shall," the warrior said, and poked him again. "Kneel."

A voice spoke from behind the mask. "It would be wise to obey." The voice had an odd inflection, as though a rattle hissed in his throat.

Again, a finger lifted. Two warriors snatched the necklace, handed it to the shaman, and forced Horned Toad to his knees. They stood over him, lances in hand.

Antelope gasped in alarm. She turned to Chomoc. "What sort of welcome is this? I thought we had safe passage."

Chomoc did not reply; he gazed at the shaman as though to penetrate the giant's mind with his own. Chomoc spoke, and the weary men with him snatched their bows and arrows. They did not draw their bows but held arrows at the ready.

Antelope tensed. One old man and a few weary travelers were no match for such a group. She fingered her necklace and pressed it to her, seeking reassurance from its powers.

The shaman nudged Horned Toad with his foot and spoke loudly. Horned Toad leaned on his staff to stare up at the figure looming over him and answered with angry gestures. They spoke too rapidly for Antelope to understand the language she was still learning.

Again the giant prodded Horned Toad, and again the old man answered, shouting his reply in outraged fury. He pointed at Chomoc's necklace, demanding it back.

Skyfeather began to cry again, her shrill little voice piercing the air. Horned Toad rose to his feet, babbling in that strange tongue, and pointed to the baby in her cradleboard on the travois.

The giant nodded at one of the warriors, who strode forward, gesturing in sign language. Antelope knew sign language well by now, having traveled far with Chomoc, trading at villages all the way. The warrior wanted to see Skyfeather.

"No!" Antelope shouted. She bent to unfasten the cradleboard from the travois.

"Leave her there!" Chomoc said softly. "Let Blacktail take care of him."

As the warrior came closer, the dog hunched low, growling. The baby still screamed, her eyes closed tightly, her face turning from side to side.

If the dog attacked, Skyfeather would be whipped about in the travois; she could be killed. Antelope bent again to snatch the baby.

"Wait." Chomoc held her back. "You will see."

Blacktail inched forward, preparing to attack. The warrior peered at him from falcon eyes.

"Hold your dog," he signed.

Chomoc stepped forward. "Stay back."

"I wish only to look at the child."

"Why?"

"The shaman requests it."

"Inform the shaman that we refuse."

"One does not refuse the shaman."

The warrior turned and signaled to his group. Immediately, bows were raised, arrows pointing at Skyfeather.

Antelope screamed and threw herself upon the travois, covering the baby. Her heart squeezed in fear and for a moment her spirit left her body. It returned, and with it a total calm, her every sense acutely alert. She felt the stir of air as Chomoc's men leaped forward and surrounded the travois. She sensed rather than saw their raised bows and arrows. Glancing up, she glimpsed those arrows pointing at the giant.

Death was near.

She closed her eyes and waited. Calmly, as if she were already in Sipapu with Kwani and all who had been She Who Remembers before her.

There was a sound, one she knew well! Chomoc's flute. A sound the warriors had heard before, long ago. It soared like a hawk, like an eagle among clouds, demanding, commanding.

Kokopelli!

The warriors murmured, glancing at one another and at the shaman who stood motionless as a stone. Again, he gestured with a finger and bows were lowered.

Chomoc strode to face the warrior who had come for Skyfeather. Approaching, he swayed forward and back, amber eyes afire, while Kokopelli's voice sang through the dancing fingers of his son.

Kokopelli! The shaman and warriors stood with motionless unease, listening.

Antelope unfastened the cradleboard and held it close, front side against her so that the tiny face was pressed to her breast. Skyfeather quieted in her arms, but Antelope's heart still pounded and she trembled. What had Horned Toad said to make the shaman demand to see Skyfeather? What had they argued about? Antelope looked at the shaman hidden behind the mask, and at the falcon warriors waiting for Chomoc. Horned Toad stood defiantly, bracing himself with his staff.

What had the old man done after guiding them safely all the long way?

Had he betrayed them?

▲ 3 ▾

Chomoc confronted the sha-
man and Horned Toad with a final soaring trill on his flute, then
replaced it in the deerskin pouch at his side while the warriors
watched every move. The unease and uncertainty he felt were
not usual for him. What could he say to these people who should
be welcoming him as everyone else did wherever he went, eager
to experience his flute, his storytelling skills, and his trading expertise?

What did these people fear?

He stared at the deer head looming above him. Who was the
man behind the mask? Whose eyes were they that pierced his
own?

He said, "I, Chomoc, son of Kokopelli, greet you."

No sound came from the round mouth hole encircled by
shell teeth.

A warrior stepped forward, brandishing a lance. "Kneel."

Chomoc assumed an arrogant stance. "The son of Kokopelli
does not kneel. However"—he bowed deeply—"I am honored,
we are all honored, to be greeted by these excellent flutists, these
noble warriors, and by the most powerful shaman of all." He
gestured to the five dogs and loaded travois. "We come in peace

23

to trade. One Who Watches granted us entry."

"Kneel!" The warrior thrust the lance at Chomoc so that the sharp point touched his belly.

But again the shaman lifted a finger and the lance was lowered. From behind the mask an arrogant voice spoke. "You and the others are not welcome here, but I will allow the woman and her child to appear before the Great Sun. He alone will decide whether or not they may remain. The rest of you will leave."

Chomoc suppressed the anger and concern that surged in him. He said, "We come in peace to trade. We are but few. The famed shaman and these many warriors have no reason to fear us."

The warriors laughed angrily at the implication of fear. Chomoc spoke directly to Horned Toad in Caddoan. "Why do they not welcome us?"

A warrior jerked Horned Toad away and pushed him among the other warriors turning to depart. The flutists raised their instruments preparing to play.

"Hear me!" Chomoc shouted. "One Who Watches granted us safe passage. My mate has powers you would be wise to respect. If you refuse us, you refuse her as well. Consider this." Command was in his voice but his heart thumped against its cage.

The shaman's rasping voice behind the shell teeth spoke again. "The powers of She Who Remembers are well known. But those of the Great Sun are stronger. As are mine."

He gestured. Two swaggering warriors approached Antelope—casually, as though retrieving a wayward child.

Immediately, Chomoc's men surrounded Antelope and stood with drawn bows. But Antelope motioned them aside and strode forward. Still holding Skyfeather to her breast, Antelope marched to face the shaman, head high, while the two warriors followed on either side, pushing her along as though she were their captive.

Antelope ignored them and faced the shaman, who stood gazing down at her from behind the mask. Her knees trembled, but she met his gaze defiantly. She spoke slowly, remembering each Caddoan word.

"I am Antelope, She Who Remembers, sister of Acoya, Medicine Chief and City Chief of Cicuye, he who possesses the robe of the White Buffalo. I am daughter of Kwani, who was She Who Remembers before me. We know the secrets. We have good medicine. We call the deer. We call the buffalo." Let him know who he was dealing with!

A reaction like a small wind stirred among the warriors and the flutists who glanced at one another and at the shaman.

Suddenly, as Antelope gazed into the eyes behind the mask, she had a flash of insight. No buffalo had been seen for many days on their journey. *This shaman could not call buffalo!* And his warriors were well aware of that.

Exultation flooded her. "We are not pleased at the reception you have given us. However, I may choose to call the buffalo for the Great Sun if we are given the reception that we of Cicuye expect." She paused, noting their attempt to conceal sudden interest. "Many, many buffalo."

Chomoc cast her an appreciative glance. Antelope had never called buffalo. But Kwani had. So why should not Antelope do so also? An admirable adversary, this mate of his, whose travel-stained robe clung to her beautiful body like a royal ceremonial garment as she stood before the shaman, small beside him, fierce and defiant, but with an aura not lost on the giant with his mask and horns and shell teeth.

The shaman gestured, his large hands with long fingers slashing the air. "Show me the child."

For a moment, Antelope hesitated. But only for a moment. She turned the cradleboard around so it faced the shaman. Sky-feather's eyes were closed. She slept soundly, dark lashes on round little cheeks, feathery fringes of black hair soft on her head.

"My daughter, Skyfeather, who shall be She Who Remembers after me, as were our ancestors. I shall teach her what I know."

Chomoc said proudly, "Our daughter shall also know to call the buffalo." He turned to the warriors and flutists pressing close. "Wherever we choose to stay, there the buffalo will come."

He hoped fervently that would be so, but something must be done to get them to the city. He and Antelope and his men were bone weary; they must have food and rest and the comfort women provide.

Unexpectedly, the shaman turned away. He muttered a command. Horned Toad made his way through the crowd of warriors and flutists to Chomoc. "You and the others will follow." He did not seem gratified.

Chomoc waved to his men who sheathed their bows and arrows, commanded the dogs, and followed Chomoc and Antelope as a drum began to speak and the flutists shrilled in chorus.

"Well done, my love," Chomoc said softly to Antelope.

She smiled. "At least it will get us there."

"We hope."

Together they marched to the flutes and the drum toward a haze of smoke hovering over the place they had come so far to see.

Ahead, the shaman strode more swiftly than dignity dictated. His spirit was in turmoil. What would the Great Sun do when he learned that Kokopelli's son and his mate, She Who Remembers, had been brought to the City of the Great Sun? When smoke signals had announced that One Who Watches— the respected head of the powerful Cougar Clan—was granting them entry, the Great Sun had not expressly forbidden them to come; that would imply weakness on his part—which, of course, was inconceivable. Rather, he had suggested that it could be dangerous to the powers of the shaman for the son of Kokopelli and his mate to come among them. He said no more; it was unnecessary. The shaman knew too well of Kokopelli's powers. Perhaps his son had the same.

But it was true, too true, that he, the greatest and most feared of shamans, could not call the buffalo. He had tried, many times, in shamed secret, but the buffalo remained far away. Hunters had to travel vast distances for the prized meat and robes and all that buffalo provided.

If . . . if it was true that the woman could, indeed, call the buffalo, perhaps he should allow her to do so—and then take the credit! The valuable prizes buffalo offered would be nearby, easy to obtain and easy to bring home. He, the famed and feared shaman, would make it possible.

Best of all, he could supply the Great Sun with a suitable sacrifice for the Green Corn ceremony, when the New Fire began a new year. The infant of She Who Remembers would be well received by the gods.

Yes, this woman, Antelope, would serve him well. As for Chomoc, he could be eliminated easily should it be required. A shaman had the means.

Swinging his rattle, the shaman stepped buoyantly to the drum's throbbing beat.

The party approached the city with a flourish, the shaman striding at the head. His antlers soared above all but the banners flapping in the wind. Behind him, encircled by warriors, came Horned Toad, Chomoc, and Antelope with the baby, followed by Chomoc's men and the dogs with loaded travois. The drum boomed and the flutists played, but Chomoc's flute soared above them all, following the melody as if Chomoc had known it always.

As the city grew near, Antelope could barely keep up with the others as she gazed in astonished amazement. Surely these soaring mountains were not man-made! There were a number of them surrounding a plaza; some mounds were tall and others smaller. On top of one great mound stood what seemed to be a temple. Another had what looked like an elaborate dwelling; steps rose from the plaza up the flank of the mountain to the crest. Upon each step a warrior stood motionless and ready, weapons in hand.

But it was the people—the strange people—thronging the plaza that gave Antelope an eerie feeling of unease. So many strangers! How foreign they looked, with elaborate tattoos on chests and arms and legs, including the women! Even the dogs were strange, shaggy and with sharp-pointed noses. And how fearsome were the men's painted faces, some with heads shaved but for a tall crest stiff and straight up from front to back, and with a beaded forelock hanging down between the eyes! So many ornaments, necklaces, animal skins, odd headdresses! Who were these people, really? Were they trustworthy?

Would Skyfeather be safe here?

Where was—what did Horned Toad call him? the "Great Sun"?—who would determine their fate? What would happen when she was brought before him?

Antelope felt the touch of the necklace and was reassured. She had given four of the beads to Kwani so their spirits would be close while they were apart. Kwani had returned to the House of the Sun to die; she must be with ancestors in Sipapu now. Did she sense her daughter's fear?

Antelope glanced at Chomoc, who strode jauntily, head

high, fingers dancing on his flute. He was enjoying himself! He relished the challenge of facing new people in a new city—a different world.

Antelope's unease faded. If Chomoc could do it, so could she! She quickened her pace and began to sing a wordless song accompanying the melody. Her voice, high and sweet, soared with Chomoc's flute, drifting like a cloud sped by the wind.

The Great Sun sat alone in his royal dwelling and gazed toward his doorway, which faced east to greet his spiritual brother each morning. To the right of the doorway was a luxurious sleeping place, a bed of reeds covered with fine furs and blankets of cotton in a bright design woven with feathers. Another sleeping place was in an adjoining room where his two wives were permitted to come when summoned. The Great Sun was tempted to lie down and force disquiet from his mind, to drink the black drink and allow his mind release. But sounds from the plaza below and from the approaching party made it obvious that he must remain alert and in total command.

The flutists were certainly in fine form today. Better than usual. Listen to that flute with a special trill! It sounded like—

The Great Sun rose abruptly and strode to the doorway. That flute had to be played by Kokopelli—or Kokopelli's son. And the woman's voice soaring over all! Whose? Never had he heard—

But he knew. It was the voice of She Who Remembers. He had listened to tales of it since childhood.

The shaman had allowed these dangerous foreigners to come. Why?

Was Striped Serpent responsible? As brother of the Great Sun he took every opportunity to cause trouble. Or was the decision the shaman's alone?

Anger, and something more, welled up. If it were anyone else but the shaman, that man would die! Now. Flung from the top of the Great Sun's mountain, down the stairway to the plaza with warriors stabbing him at every step on the way.

But it was the respected and honored shaman who dared to bring these people to the City of the Great Sun when he knew very well the Great Sun did not want them here. The shaman—whose powers he, the ruler, needed and depended upon.

The Great Sun gripped his stomach with both hands where

pain sneaked a sudden attack. From below came excited shouts, barking, conversation. The foreigners had reached the plaza and were being greeted by the War Chief as was customary. Trading would follow.

"Hou! Hou! Hou!" One of the guard warriors knelt outside the door.

Only his family, servants, and members of the nobility were allowed inside the Great Sun's residence. The Great Sun stepped through the doorway and stood before the warrior. "Speak."

"Hou!" The warrior lifted his head but took care not to look at the Great Sun. "The shaman brings She Who Remembers and her infant girl child for you to determine whether or not they are to remain or be sent elsewhere. She Who Remembers claims to be sister of Acoya, Medicine Chief and City Chief of Cicuye, who possesses the robe of the White Buffalo." The warrior paused; such momentous news merited emphasis. He continued, "The shaman wishes permission to bring them before you now."

The Great Sun stepped to the terrace that commanded a view of the plaza. As he did so, there were shouts of "Hou! Hou! Hou!" and a commotion as people crowded for a glimpse of the holy one standing high above them. It was permissible for his people to see him en masse, so he stood there a moment in majesty, searching. Trading was already under way with much excited bargaining. Where were She Who Remembers and Kokopelli's son?

As if summoned, the shaman appeared from the crowd with two warriors leading a woman. One look told the Great Sun who the woman was. Only such a one would carry herself with that royal air. He would show her what royalty was!

He gestured, and the warrior backed away with another "Hou!" and ran down the stairs to the shaman. The Great Sun stood waiting while the shaman led the woman up the stairway past the guards. She carried her baby in a cradleboard on her back, but she climbed the steep steps as lightly as a doe on a hillside.

The closer she came, the more startling was her beauty. Lustrous dark hair framed an oval face with brows hovering over the deep, dark pools of her eyes—eyes that penetrated his as she gazed up at him. Presuming to look at him, against all rules! Fearlessly! She should die for that.

He watched her climbing the steps toward him because he

could not stop watching. Each movement, graceful as a cougar's, displayed an inviting body maddeningly hidden beneath a soiled garment. He would rip that garment away, see those swelling breasts thrusting. . . .

No. She must die.

The baby began to cry and Antelope stopped where she was to remove the cradleboard; she held it close in her arms. Sky-feather snuggled against her mother's breast and quieted.

The shaman prodded Antelope up the steps. As they approached the place where the Great Sun stood, the shaman removed his mask.

For the first time, Antelope saw the shaman's face. It was long and lean with deep-set eyes and a thin, aquiline nose. Forehead, cheeks, and chin were elaborately tattooed; it was as if he wore another mask, secretive and subtly ominous.

He prodded her again and signed, "Kneel."

He knelt and pulled her down with him. He howled a greeting with bowed head, held his mask under one arm, and gripped Antelope with the other.

Held fast, Antelope knelt but did not bow her head, nor did she howl a greeting. Rather, she stared up at the man standing several steps above them whose cinder-black eyes stared back. It was a handsome, arrogant, magnificently arrayed man who stood gazing down at her. Under that gaze Antelope felt as if she were being held on her knees by an unseen force, as if the man standing above them had somehow pushed her down. It was an intolerable feeling, and she pulled herself loose from the shaman's grip and stood up.

"I greet you," she said politely.

He gestured, and the shaman again took her arm and led her up the few remaining steps to the terrace where the Great Sun stood, arms folded, gazing at Antelope with hooded eyes.

"Hou!" the shaman cried in his strange, rasping voice. "I bring you daughter of Kwani, She Who Remembers, and her girl child, Skyfeather."

He reached to take Skyfeather from Antelope's arms, but she held the cradleboard to her more tightly and refused to relinquish it.

The Great Sun spoke sharply. Two guard warriors stepped forward to take the cradleboard. Antelope fought fiercely, but the men wrenched the cradleboard from her arms, yanked out the naked baby, and handed the screaming child to the Great Sun.

"My baby!" Antelope shouted. "Give her to me!" She struggled to be free from the warriors holding her.

The Great Sun ignored her and held Skyfeather in outstretched arms as one might hold a pot for inspection. The squirming, shrieking child was perfect in every respect. An ideal offering for the gods.

As he held Skyfeather, turning her this way and that, abruptly she stopped crying and stared at him. He was suddenly conscious of her gaze. Blue eyes, large and luminous, locked into his with surprising intensity for one so young. Her round little face with sweet, small mouth and nubbin of a nose was a baby's, but those eyes . . .

Blue! It was said that witches' eyes were blue.

A breeze ruffled the soft down on Skyfeather's head. How very beautiful she was. Already.

"Give me my child!" Antelope said, her voice suddenly demanding and cold. "Remember who we are."

Instantly, warriors surrounded Antelope with lances. Such a sacrilegious display of arrogance toward the holy one merited death. They waited for their ruler's sign.

The Great Sun stood immobile for a moment. He should give the death signal. But something about this baby, about Antelope . . . What was it?

An inner warning like the clank of ax on stone echoed in his mind. This woman had powers; perhaps the child did, also. He glanced at the shaman who stood aside, mask under one arm, pretending uninterest. He must be cautious; this woman's brother was a Medicine Chief who possessed the sacred robe of the White Buffalo, which bestowed mighty medicine; he could be a very dangerous adversary. He would discuss this with the shaman in private.

The woman's eyes bored into his. Searching for his secret?

Yes, he must be cautious—for the time being. He gestured and the warriors surrounding Antelope withdrew, all but the two holding her.

"Release her," the Great Sun said, and handed the baby to the warriors holding the cradleboard. "Give her the child."

The warrior obeyed with obvious reluctance. Antelope took Skyfeather and tucked her back into the cradleboard, taking her time doing so, ignoring the Great Sun and all the others.

The Great Sun fumed inwardly. How insolent she was! He would teach her humility. Ah, yes.

From below came the soaring song of Chomoc's flute, teasing, laughing, inviting all who heard it to laugh, too.

The Great Sun scowled. "Take this woman and Kokopelli's son to the village of Yala. They are to remain there until I decide otherwise." He turned toward his dwelling and signaled the shaman to follow.

Yala was the most distant of the villages clustered along the river, and the poorest. The lead warrior grinned, took Antelope's arm, and shoved her toward the stairway leading down to the plaza.

Antelope jerked her arm loose. She signed, "I know the way." She speared him with an imperial stare and descended the steps with a dignity and grace covertly relished by the guards on each step who watched one slender, moccasined foot follow the other and a beautiful body move under a soiled robe as if to music unheard.

Another watched from the crowd below, staring up at Antelope descending the stairway—the aged midwife Waikah. She pursed her lips over toothless gums and hobbled closer. As the warrior and Antelope reached the plaza, Waikah brandished a skinny, wrinkled arm.

"Go away!" she yelled at Antelope. "You do not belong here!"

Antelope met the fierce old gaze. For a moment she was pierced with a premonition that what the old woman said was true.

But no. She and Skyfeather and Chomoc would be safe here. Of course they would.

▲4▼

Horned Toad looked about him with satisfaction. Little had changed since he left as a young man to be with his Towa bride in Cicuye. The mounds still stood in splendor, even the small ones beyond the plaza, which were ancient and no longer used for ceremonies. Children clambered on them now, playing warrior and captive, even as he had done years ago.

Upon the highest mound, the Temple of Eternal Fire stood in glory. He, Horned Toad, had been one of the countless laborers who hauled basketful after basketful of earth to build this mountain that stood forever in majesty. He gazed up at it, remembering the long moons of his labor, and feeling that part of himself was forever enshrined in a holy place.

Yes, little had changed. Across the plaza, another mound was topped by the dwelling place of the Great Sun. Before him was an ancient plaza, used now as a ceremonial ground where games, dances, and less important ceremonies took place. Nearby were homes of the nobility. In the clear light of late afternoon, their square houses, with steeply pointed thatched roofs and doorways extended like an arm outthrust, stood sharply outlined against the bright sky. Horned Toad experienced a pang of

33

envy. Only the nobility dwelled here among the gods; all others lived in villages along the river terrace.

The newer plaza lay between the great mound and a smaller one to the north. This plaza was for the chunkey games of the nobility, for sacred events, and for the all-important trading. Behind the great mound, closer to the river, was the burial mound for holy men. From where he stood, Horned Toad could not see it, but he felt its proximity in the place where his spirit dwelled.

How good it was to be home! He breathed in the smells: the fragrances of earth and stone and thatched roofs, delicious odors from cooking pots, the familiar—and almost forgotten—aroma of body paint mingled with good sweat, and the fresh, tantalizing breeze wafting across the river. It made him feel young again. Looking around at women gorgeously ornamented with beautiful tattoos on lovely bare breasts, he decided that, although he had come home to die, there was no need to be hasty about it.

He had watched Antelope and Chomoc being led away to a village somewhere with their dog and travois. Good riddance! Now he could enjoy being among his own kind again. There must be many grandnieces and -nephews and cousins of his lineage here. He would inquire. Chomoc's men and their dogs and travois had been left to shift for themselves as best they could; most were planning to return home as soon as the dogs were rested. Trading had been good and more was to come.

People still crowded the plaza, talking about the travelers, speculating, whispering, gloating over prized objects already obtained in trade from the son of Kokopelli and his men. Turquoise! And cotton cloth! Here, cloth was woven from buffalo hair and plant fibers. Fine, of course, but not as soft nor as pliable and washable as cotton.

Horned Toad watched women kneeling beside trading goods displayed on mats and blankets spread upon the ground. Those who had obtained cotton cloth or turquoise were besieged with trading offers. He could hear the murmur of their voices and their occasional laughter or vigorous arguments, mingled with the sounds of the holy place—drums, chants, turkey bone whistles, rasps, and rattles—all blending with the distinct sounds from busy villages. Horned Toad swatted a mosquito on his neck. He had forgotten how many stinging insects lived near the river.

But it was the river, Long Man, that bestowed power and prosperity. The city's location at the river's bend allowed control of the water trading route from the mountains of the north to the sea of the south. Many villages stood upon Long Man's flanks. Because the river also connected with the highlands of the west and the mountains and valleys of the southeast, the city also controlled traffic between the western Plains and rich markets beyond.

Horned Toad sighed. He knew this powerful city, his birthplace, held storehouses of untold wealth. He smiled, glimpsing the possibility of a leisurely, luxurious future—should he decide to live a while longer.

If only . . . but he would not think about that. Surely the Towa he had brought with him from Cicuye realized their awkward unimportance in a place such as this and would not stay long. The nobility would not be annoyed by their presence. Nor with him for bringing them here.

People passing by stared at him covertly. As if he were a stranger, an outsider who did not belong here! Wiping his sweaty face with a dirty sleeve, Horned Toad left the plaza for the village of his former home on the rocky terrace overlooking Long Man.

He would find his kin and begin life anew.

Who was that old woman who had been following him about, peering at him from beneath a shawl? He seemed to remember. . . . Ah, yes, the midwife Waikah. She had aged a great deal since he left, but then so had he.

Why was she following him? Curiosity, perhaps.

Antelope and Chomoc stood on a village path surrounded by a gaping crowd. Naked children shouted and stared at the travois and its mysterious treasures covered by a buffalo hide. Women poked at it and were warned by a growl from Blacktail. Chomoc carried the most valuable things in his pack, but clothing, blankets, and other personal objects, as well as more trading goods, were in the travois—Blacktail's responsibility, which he took seriously.

It was afternoon and hot for early summer. The warrior had brought them past many dwellings strung out along a terrace overlooking a river where farmers tilled the rich bottomlands. Antelope had traveled a long way from home to be here, but this final trek, surrounded by staring, tattooed, babbling strangers with no welcome in their eyes, seemed to be the most difficult. And dangerous.

She turned to Chomoc, who was ordering people to stay away from Blacktail; he might attack.

"Why are we standing here?" Antelope asked. "What do we wait for? Do you know?"

Chomoc indicated a warrior who stood at one side talking with a stocky, middle-aged woman who shook her head as she glanced at them. It increased Antelope's unease and she moved closer to Chomoc. "What is happening? What will they do to us?"

He looked down his nose. "Chomoc's mate and Chomoc's child are safe with Chomoc. Have no fear."

Black eyes snapped at him. "Fear? So I am without courage? How far have I come, how long have I traveled strange lands among strange people to be with you in this—this place where *you* wished to be?" She flipped a braid. "How many men would do the same, eh?"

"I know of but few, those who came with us." He smiled, enjoying the confrontation, as usual. "You are not afraid. I apologize."

She did not respond. She was too tired. Her feet hurt, her back hurt, she hurt all over. She needed a bath, she was hungry and thirsty, and she wanted to lie down and nurse her baby and dream of home.

The warrior still argued with the woman, who glanced again at them, frowning. In spite of herself, Antelope felt a prick of fear. She reached behind to touch Skyfeather asleep in the cradleboard. *Nothing would harm this child.*

At her mother's touch, Skyfeather woke. A woman nearby saw the baby's blue eyes. She gasped. Jabbering excitedly, she turned to others, pointing at Skyfeather. People crowded close, staring. A baby with blue eyes! Blue!

The warrior heard the commotion and whirled to investigate. Falcon eyes under a gleaming copper headplate swept the crowd; a jeweled arm gestured them aside.

Antelope's heart jerked in alarm. She lifted the cradleboard from her back and held it close, the baby's face against her breast—where the necklace lay, the necklace of the Ancient Ones. "Help us!" she prayed.

She sensed no response, but her heart quieted.

The warrior grasped the arm of the woman with whom he had been arguing, and led—dragged—her to Antelope and Chomoc.

"This is Red Leaf, mate of Many Bears," he said. "You will remain with her in her dwelling until the Great Sun decides what to do with you."

Waving the crowd aside with a rattle and clank of bracelets, the warrior strode away, copper ornaments agleam.

Red Leaf faced Chomoc and Antelope with a sullen gaze. Antelope experienced a twinge of sympathy; she would not like being forced to take foreigners into her home either. She said, "We shall appreciate your hospitality."

"You shall be paid well," Chomoc said authoritatively.

The sullen expression remained. Red Leaf said, "Come with me."

Antelope noticed that the backs of Red Leaf's stubby fingers were tattooed in a pattern to match the red-and-black ornamentation on her arms and breasts. A different pattern in black marked her forehead and chin. As Red Leaf turned to lead them away, Antelope saw the swirling design was repeated on Red Leaf's back. She wore a woven knee-length skirt fastened at the waist by a handsomely fringed deerskin belt that swayed with each step. Buckskin moccasins, beaded and painted, reached above her ankles. Her long black hair was fastened in back by a cord with copper beads. She walked with an air of command, head high, swinging her arms. A person of importance.

A murmuring crowd followed Chomoc and Antelope as they made their way along the path, followed by the toothless old woman who had yelled at Antelope to go away. She was silent now, hobbling after them, peering from beneath her shawl. Antelope felt a twinge of unease. Who was she?

They passed several houses with roofs like thatched tepees, and extended doorways that required one to bend low to enter; the dwellings squatted on a terrace overlooking the river.

The first time Antelope saw the river she paused to stare. It was the widest river she had ever seen; an arrow could not fly from one bank to the other. It was swift and busy with dugout canoes, women washing clothes on the rocky bank, fishermen mending nets, children playing, and many people digging in the banks at river's edge.

"What are they digging for?" she asked Chomoc.

"I don't know." He turned to a man nearby. "What are they doing?"

"Digging for mussels," the man answered, surprised at such

ignorance. "Good to eat. Sometimes there are pearls."

Antelope was puzzled. "Pearls? What are they?"

The man beckoned to a young woman who stepped forward timidly. A necklace of shining white beads glistened on her bare breast. He gestured, touching the necklace. "Pearls."

Chomoc gazed at them, his eyes alight with trading joy. "Ah!" he sighed. He turned to Antelope. "This is why we are here—to find new things like this. Pearls!" He beamed with excitement. "I knew we would find riches, but I did not know about pearls. Think of the trading in Cicuye! Ha!"

He removed his flute from the pouch at his side and began to play a triumphant song of joy. The crowd grew bigger as more people heard and came running. Antelope had to devote all her attention to Blacktail to keep him under control.

No one noticed Far Walker, the young Healer, following. He gazed at Antelope like one dying of thirst, as if only her beauty would quench his longing, as if the spider tattooed on his back had enmeshed him in its deadly web.

The Great Sun sat in his royal dwelling upon a platform raised on four carved legs, and looked down at the shaman, who sat cross-legged upon a floor mat. They had been talking for some time.

It was hot and still. Flies buzzed and a mosquito explored the Great Sun's muscular bare arm; he slapped it away. The shaman sat with head bowed. He wore the necklace of woven snake-skin in several colors and patterns that only shamans could wear. The Great Sun noticed that the stiff black crest on the top of his head had been flattened by the mask, which fit over the head and rested on the shoulders. The mask with its antlers and shell teeth lay beside him on the floor, another presence.

They sat in silence. No decision had been reached about Kokopelli's son and his mate, Antelope. The Great Sun wondered if the shaman was thinking of Antelope's brother, Medicine Chief of the Towa, who owned the robe of the White Buffalo—powerful medicine. He wondered if what was said about Kokopelli's son was true. Did he have his father's magical skills? And Antelope . . . No, he must stop thinking of her. Of the robe to be torn away so he might see . . .

She had defied him. She must die.

But the powers of She Who Remembers and her brother

were known. Their gods could take terrible revenge. He had had dreams lately—ominous dreams. Warning him? He must be cautious.

He said, "Is it true that the son of Kokopelli—what is his name?—can communicate with animals?"

The shaman did not look up. "Chomoc. His name is Chomoc. It is said he communicates with animals, but this has not been proven."

"It is also said that"—the Great Sun would not speak her name—"the mate of Chomoc calls the buffalo." He crossed his muscular arms and looked away, pretending uninterest.

The shaman raised his head and shot him a glance from deep-set eyes. His long, lean face was expressionless. "So it is said."

"But you do not call buffalo."

"No."

The shaman's left eyelid closed, then opened again like an owl's eye—an annoying habit that made the Great Sun uneasy. He suspected that was why the shaman did it.

"Why not?" His voice was gruff.

The shaman removed a small pouch hanging from a cord around his neck and withdrew a crystal the size of his little finger. It glittered as he held it to the light. He said, "My crystal warned me it was dangerous to call buffalo here."

The Great Sun looked into the shaman's tattooed face. Something was hidden there. He stretched his own handsome legs, consciously comparing them with the long, bony legs of the shaman. "It is dangerous to send hunters so far for what we need that buffalo provide. Perhaps Chomoc can persuade them to come closer."

A glint appeared in the shaman's eyes and was concealed. He replaced the crystal in its pouch carefully. "If it is your wish that buffalo be called, I obey, holy one. I shall call the buffalo."

The Great Sun gazed out the open door into green-and-blue distance. Unease squirmed in his stomach. Something was amiss here. How much did the shaman know that he did not tell? How much of what he did say was true? Why did he, the Great Sun, tolerate this uncertainty?

"You can call the buffalo? Then do so."

The nostrils in the shaman's thin nose flared, and the tattoos surrounding his thin-lipped mouth seemed to quiver. His hooded eyes flicked the Great Sun as he asked, "It is your decision to allow Chomoc and his mate to remain here?"

"I shall confer with the Spirit Being and with other gods. Until then, Chomoc and his mate are to remain in Yala."

The shaman did not conceal his gratification. "I obey, holy one."

The Great Sun gestured dismissal. The shaman took his mask and rose so that he towered over the Great Sun. He bent low, his snakeskin necklace swinging. "Hou!" he growled in his rasping voice, and folded his lean frame sufficiently to back out the low doorway.

For a time, the Great Sun sat there, brooding. Foreboding seeped into his spirit. He wanted to confer with the High Priest, to ease his mind, but he was away on pilgrimage.

The Great Sun rose and strode about the room. Again he saw the Towa woman climbing the steps to him, drowning him in the pools of her eyes. Seeking his secret?

She must die. Yes. And the child, too.

But not yet.

What about Chomoc? If, indeed, he had his father's powers, he would be dangerous, too.

Kokopelli had been a Toltec nobleman-turned-trader who cast magical spells with his flute. His expertise with women was legendary; in every village women had eagerly sought his attentions. The Great Sun strongly suspected that the women of his royal household had not been immune to Kokopelli's spells when he passed this way long ago.

Chomoc could be like his father. Something must be done to dispose of him, but what?

He pondered for some time, resting his chin on his hand. Finally, he jerked upright.

He knew!

At last he knew. He summoned slaves to carry him in a litter across the plaza to the Temple of Eternal Fire. There he would make a sacrifice of thanks to the gods.

▲5▼

Antelope and Skyfeather lay beside Chomoc on the floor of the loft in Red Leaf's dwelling. Nearby, piles of corn were stacked like firewood, and tall jars held other supplies. In the sweltering darkness Antelope could not see the thatched roof overhead, but she could smell the smoky, musty residue of past fires that permeated it. A small fire burned now in a large urn on the floor below, providing smoke to discourage mosquitoes and other bothersome insects. The smoke swirled up to the loft and its occupants, then drifted out through vents between roof and walls.

Antelope felt perspiration trickling down her body. She covered her mouth and nose with her hand, trying not to inhale the smoke. She hated this place! Closing her eyes, she visualized her beautiful home in Cicuye, high on a ridge swept by clean winds and cool breezes. She thought of Acoya, her brother, and her mother, Kwani. A pang of longing squeezed her heart.

Kwani.

Antelope reached for the scallop shell pendant of her necklace, seeking communication with the Ancient Ones, and with Kwani, who possessed a necklace of four beads that Antelope

41

had removed from her own so they would be close when they were apart.

"Help me. I am far from home in a strange, foreign place. I am afraid. . . ."

Antelope strained to sense a reply. Was it a whisper she heard? "Be strong," it said.

Tears stung her eyes. Was it Kwani speaking?

"I will be strong," she whispered silently, "as I have been during all this long journey. But I know now I should not have come. I . . ."

Could she admit it?

"I came because I did not want Chomoc to leave me. . . ."

Tears trickled down. She wanted Chomoc to be with her, only her, and not women in every village who wanted him. As they had wanted Kokopelli, his father . . .

It was true. Chomoc was like his father. He always would be.

Kwani had longed always for a home and people of her own, and a mate to love and protect her, and children. . . .

Perhaps I am more like my mother than I thought.

Darkness grew deeper. Outside, night sounds faded. Antelope drifted into sleep.

She was wakened by an old woman's snores from below, mingled with the unmuffled sounds of Many Bears and Red Leaf enjoying one another. Red Leaf's occasional sharp exclamations made Antelope wonder how vigorously Many Bears might be enjoying himself.

Many Bears and an old woman and a great, shaggy dog had met Antelope and Chomoc at the door when they arrived the day before. The dog growled at her and Blacktail but was quieted by Many Bears. The man's small eyes under thatched eyebrows had darted at her, swallowing her in a gulp. He was short, squat, barrel-chested, and reeked with body paint and something he may have applied to discourage insects. The smell of it drifted up now, with the smoke.

Antelope yearned for the stars and for the clean, cool breath of the plains. She wondered if she could climb down the ladder and slip outside later, after everyone was asleep. Old Poqua, Red Leaf's mother (or was it grandmother?), was a bundle of ancient bones held together by hide so wrinkled that her tattoos seemed jumbled together. She snored convulsively in wheezing gasps. Bobcat and Ringtail, Red Leaf's small sons, slept quietly, ignoring familiar sounds in the room and the restless sounds of night outside. The family dog and Blacktail were tethered outside.

Chomoc lay on his back, arms overhead. Antelope could not see him in the thick darkness, but his breathing was deep and slow; he slept. The sounds from below quieted at last, until only Poqua's wheezy snoring was heard.

Was everyone asleep now?

Carefully, so as not to disturb Skyfeather or Chomoc, she rose and groped her way to the ladder. Halfway down she gave a startled cry. Many Bears had reached up to lift her the rest of the way down; she felt his grip on her thighs. She jerked herself loose and climbed back up.

Chomoc met her at the top of the ladder. "What happened?"

"I wanted to go outside. Many Bears grabbed me while I was on the ladder."

A moment of tense silence. "Next time, tell me so I can go with you. I will climb down first."

"Maybe he just wanted to help me in the darkness. . . ."

"Maybe."

They lay quietly together, both with their own thoughts, each wondering what the future held. What would the Great Sun decide to do with them? His power was such that he could do anything he wished. Would he drive them away to face the long, arduous journey home?

Would he harm Skyfeather?

Antelope remembered the dark eyes piercing her own. Something about that look warned of . . . what?

Danger.

He could have them killed with the lift of a finger.

She saw again the old woman with the wizened, malevolent face and toothless mouth saying, "You do not belong here!"

Who was she?

Again, Antelope clasped her necklace.

I will be strong.

Antelope woke with a start. Outside, loud howls echoed and re-echoed; the entire city was alive with "Hou! Hou! Hou!" Dogs barked; in the distance a drum throbbed.

She jerked upright. Chomoc had taken his pack and was gone; faint morning light shone through the vents. She crawled to peer through one of the openings. Every man, woman, and child faced east, arms raised, greeting Sunfather with respectful howls. Only one voice sang, a strong male voice soaring. Chomoc's. His song continued:

> *Your long life,*
> *Your old age,*
> *Your waters,*
> *Your seeds,*
> *Your riches,*
> *Your power,*
> *Your strong spirit,*
> *All these to me may you grant.*

Where was he? Antelope could not see him, but she knew he must be by the river; he bathed before sunrise whenever water was near. The thought of a swim in a cold, swift river after a sweltering night was wonderful; she would join him. Skyfeather was hungry, as always, so Antelope nursed her, listening to the busy sounds of a strange city, visualizing a clean, clear river swirling about her naked body, revitalizing her.

It was quiet downstairs and the smoke was gone. Cooking smells drifted in from outside through the vents; cooking was done outdoors. Antelope found she was hungry—ravenous, in fact—but she would bathe first. She changed Skyfeather, noticing that the supply of cedar bark diapering in her pack was nearly gone. There were many cedar trees about; she would obtain more bark today. She needed it for her moon-flow padding, too.

She tucked Skyfeather in the cradleboard, lifted it to her back, and climbed down the ladder. The room was empty. Sleeping mats were rolled up and placed against the wall. Ropes of dried squash and corn and bundles of herbs dangled from two posts supporting the loft and the roof. Baskets and tall jars stood about; clothing, hunting gear, and other objects hung from pegs along the walls. In a corner, Chomoc's empty travois stood upright; on the floor beside it contents from the travois were carefully arranged and undisturbed. This was a neat, orderly dwelling where the belongings of others were respected.

Sounds of activity and wonderful cooking smells drew her outside. Red Leaf and old Poqua squatted beside a shallow cooking pit, poking coals around a bubbling pot. Bobcat, two winters old, whined to be nursed. Antelope saw that his eyes were crossed, indicating a future as a feared shaman. He tugged at his mother, who pushed him gently aside as she poked coals with a stick. Ringtail, four winters old, jumped up and down, shrilly demanding breakfast. Many Bears and the dogs were gone.

Red Leaf glanced up at Antelope but did not speak. Her long hair fell loosely around her bare shoulders. Poqua peered at Antelope from within the folds of her wrinkled face and poked the coals more vigorously.

Two women approached, returning from the river with jars of water on their heads. They stared at her and paused at Red Leaf's fire. A muffled discussion in their strange tongue followed, with furtive glances at Antelope and Skyfeather.

I must show I am one of them.

She went back inside, found a large jar like those the women carried, lifted it to her head, and without another glance at the women by the fire she followed one of the worn paths to the river, encountering other women on the way. They stared, but Antelope gave them friendly glances and continued on her way, head high, as if she had lived there always.

The path Antelope followed led to a mass of tall reeds at river's edge which had been cleared away sufficiently to allow access to the water. Evidently this was the spot chosen by women to wash clothes; several women slapped wet garments upon large stones while naked children splashed about, squealing. The women saw her, glanced at one another, and continued working as if she were not there.

As Antelope looked up and down the river she saw that many paths led to the water, each to a spot where certain activities took place. From where she stood the river was wide and seemed shallow; children played far from the bank. At another spot, women and girls dipped bowls into the water and lifted them to their heads with easy grace. Beyond, men and boys dug for mussels, or worked on boats or nets on the sandy bank. Across the river another village could be glimpsed through the reeds at water's edge. Similar activities took place there, with gestures and bellowing shouts from one side of the river to the other. Canoes glided swiftly by, some with fishing nets aboard; some with trading goods. All seemed intent on navigation as they followed the river, disappearing around the bend.

Antelope stood with the bowl on her head and the baby in the cradleboard on her back. She felt the hot sun and smelled the fresh river smell and listened to strangers talking in words she did not understand. Behind her, beyond the trees and encircled on three sides by the river, the great mounds of the ceremonial center rose. Where the Great Sun dwelt. He who held their fate.

Where was Chomoc?

A path meandered along the rocky bank and Antelope followed it. She yearned to bathe, but she knew she must find the bathing place; to bathe in the wrong spot might besmirch the river in the eyes of these people, these strangers. She must be careful.

Water birds darted from reeds and wheeled overhead. The sun grew warmer, and Antelope felt perspiration beading her body. The breath from the river was cool. Perhaps she could splash a little water on herself and Skyfeather, just enough to refresh them a bit. A tall stand of reeds lay ahead. She would hide there while she cooled off.

She lifted the bowl from her head and set it on the ground beside the reeds. She removed her moccasins, lifted the cradleboard from her back, and took out Skyfeather, who wriggled with pleasure at the feel of freedom and the sun on her bare little body. Placing cradleboard and moccasins beside the bowl, Antelope parted the reeds and stepped among them. They swayed and rustled, then closed overhead.

Water lapped at her feet, wonderfully cool. She bent, scooped water in her hand, and splashed it on Skyfeather. The water was sandy, but Skyfeather cooed and waved her arms. Antelope splashed water on herself; it felt good, but the sand had to be washed off. Perhaps the water would be more clear deeper into the river.

The reeds rustled as she pushed against them and stood near the edge, knee-deep in cool water flowing softly by. But for the distant sounds and the inviting voice of the river, all was still. She peeked through the reeds to see up and down the river; no one was in sight.

She dipped Skyfeather in the water, up and down. The baby loved it and wanted more.

I want it, too.

Again Antelope looked to be sure they were alone. Then, tucking Skyfeather under one arm, she slipped off her soiled robe and sat down in the water with Skyfeather in her arms.

The water swirled about them, infinitely refreshing. Antelope splashed handful after handful upon them both, washing away the sweat and weariness. She swished the dirty robe back and forth to get it a little cleaner, and wondered what Chomoc would say if she told him she may have bathed where she wasn't supposed to.

A sound. At first, Antelope did not know what it was; but as it grew louder, she realized it was a man's voice, chanting. He might discover them! Carefully, so as not to disturb the reeds any more than necessary, Antelope eased back, holding Skyfeather with one hand while trying to quiet her as she wriggled and kicked and made baby noises. The other hand held the robe against the tug of the river. She drew it closer and peered through the reeds.

A man approached and paused downstream at the riverbank. He stood with his back to her as he gazed downstream, chanting. His rich, resonant voice rose and fell and rose again as if pulled forcibly from deep within. From a pouch at his side he withdrew something and tossed it into the river. He was not tall, but he was muscular, wide of shoulder and slim of hip. His bare back held a strange tattoo—a giant spider. An ornate headband held a tall copper ornament at his forehead; Antelope wondered what it was. Bright feathers dangled from copper earspools and from his rope of hair hanging down in back. A raccoon pelt was fastened to his right arm above the elbow; the tail waved as again the man withdrew something from the pouch and tossed it into the river, chanting, chanting.

Antelope stared, trying to quiet her wriggling baby, trying to quiet her thumping heart. Something about the man out there gave her pause; he had innate power. Who was he?

Skyfeather jerked and her wet body slipped from her mother's grip. Antelope grabbed the baby with both hands. The robe, released, swirled into the river and drifted toward the spot where the man stood. Skyfeather began to cry.

The man whirled, saw the robe, saw the reeds astir. He snatched the robe, strode to where Antelope crouched hidden, and jerked the reeds aside.

Antelope gasped and stared up at the face whose eyes, encircled with black and red markings, gazed down at her with stunned surprise . . . and something more.

She held Skyfeather close; nothing would harm this child!

The man stood motionless, staring down at her with an intensity that made her suddenly afraid—and acutely conscious of her nakedness. She rose and thrust out an arm with an imperial gesture.

"Give me my robe."

He did not speak but threw down the robe, whirled, and strode swiftly away, the spider on his back stirring.

·6·

Far Walker could not sleep. He stirred restlessly on his sleeping mat. What he had seen today when he pushed the reeds aside seemed to have been a magical vision—glimpsed but unreal.

He had beheld the foreign woman before when she entered Yala with her blue-eyed child. It was as though flowers were strewn in her path, as though thunder drums announced her coming. Radiance enveloped her, sensed but unseen.

Today at the river when he pushed the reeds aside, his world convulsed. He, Far Walker, a Healer, one of the Great Sun's esteemed Honored Men, smoldered with inner fires that consumed him. No longer could he discern which spirits brought illness to those who came to be healed; the burning within him made him blind. Nor could he comfort those who sought his wisdom. His *kia*, his being, had become ashes.

She Who Remembers and Chomoc had been taken to the dwelling of Red Leaf. Was the beautiful foreign woman sleeping now? He had visualized her lying upon a sleeping mat. Now he remembered, ah yes, the lovely body in the river, discovered that morning. . . .

* * *

49

The day after her arrival, with the first pale light of dawn, he had followed the path to the river, tossed his breechclout aside, and plunged into the water. Floating downstream he gazed up at fading stars, seeking relief from his burning, but Long Man's cold embrace could not quench the inner fire.

The Spirit Being rose and began his journey. Hours passed, but the inner torment continued. In desperation Far Walker entered the door of his old teacher and beloved mentor.

Peg Foot was sorting herbs and glanced up as Far Walker stood before him.

"Welcome." He smiled his toothless smile and gestured Far Walker to be seated.

They sat in silence, waiting for words to find themselves. The pungent fragrance of herbs enveloped them. Outside, children shouted in play, dogs barked, and women's voices floated in as they passed by.

Peg Foot sat cross-legged and Far Walker saw that the peg replacing his old teacher's missing foot was worn and soiled, and so was the strapping that held it in place. Usually, the carved and painted peg shone polished and bright, but Peg Foot's vision had faded and he could no longer care for his famous peg as once he could.

From a distance came the throb of a drum—Earthmother's heartbeat. Far Walker felt words rising from inside him.

"My kia . . ."

They sat in silence for a moment, not gazing at one another, while Far Walker found his words.

"The woman from Cicuye, She Who Remembers, has stolen my kia. . . ." He paused. *She Who Remembers is not a witch; how could she steal my inner being?* It made no sense. Miserably, he added, "I burn."

"Ah." Peg Foot nodded and busied himself with the herbs. He loved this young Healer, the best student he had ever had. "You seek my counsel?"

"I do."

"Very well." He gestured to a mat. "Lie down."

Far Walker stretched out on the mat and Peg Foot bent over him. He examined Far Walker's eyes, lifting each lid, and poked a finger into the mouth and peered down the throat. He pressed his cheek against Far Walker's chest and listened to the beating of his heart. He prodded and poked the stomach and abdomen, intent upon what his fingers told him.

Finally, Peg Foot nodded. He selected a twisted root from a jar and diced it with a flint chopper. From bundles of herbs he extracted several flowers and buds and put them and the diced root into a pouch.

Far Walker sat up and watched with interest. He knew Peg Foot was preparing a spell but the combination was an unusual one.

Peg Foot handed the pouch to Far Walker. "Prepare a tea with these and drink it all. Save the residue, give it to Long Man, and pray the kia chant. Do you remember it?"

It was a long and difficult chant, but Far Walker nodded. "I remember."

"Very well. Long Man will wash the burning away and return your kia to you. Then you will return the pouch to me with a thumb's length of salt in it."

That was fair payment. Far Walker gestured agreement. "I thank you, honored Teacher."

They sat in silence again for a moment. Finally, Peg Foot said, "I hear that the Great Sun sent all the foreigners home except the son of Kokopelli and his mate and baby. Maybe he will send them away also, and your kia will no longer be assailed by the beauty of She Who Remembers." He shook his grizzled head. "The powers of Kokopelli were well known; if his son possesses them also, the Great Sun may feel challenged."

He paused and glanced out the doorway to see if anyone might be listening. "She Who Remembers, like her mother before her"—he lowered his voice to a whisper—"has been accused of witchcraft. But never proven. It is her beauty that casts spells."

"She has my kia."

"Do as I counsel and she will have it no longer."

"I shall do as you say, honored Teacher."

Far Walker rose, bade a respectful farewell, and strode outside. It was a fine summer day with puffs of cloud in a turquoise sky and hawks riding the wind. As he approached his lodge, his mate hurried to meet him. Lako was a placid, round little woman who enjoyed her prestige as mate of a Healer but who did not welcome the responsibilities. She preferred the company of women friends, gossiping and working together, rather than accommodating those who came to her mate to be healed. She feared the spirits that caused illness; she did not want them in her home. She complained often in her querulous voice, and Far Walker had thought more than once of divorcing her according to custom, but he needed a mate and none in his village interested him. None, that is, until She Who Remembers appeared.

Lako met him breathlessly. "Word comes that my clan in Three Hills plans a feast and celebration with Women's Dances and they want me there so I am going today and I need the canoe and somebody to go with me and I'll be taking corn and venison." She paused for breath, her face alight. "You will take me."

"I cannot."

"But I want you to be there. I will dance—"

"I cannot." He indicated the pouch. "I must prepare a brew—"

"Always a brew!" Her mouth twisted. "Always something that smells bad. Very well. I shall ask Beaver Tail to go with me and I shall take the canoe." She turned and ran back to the lodge.

Far Walker did not follow. Beaver Tail was known to be more than willing to accommodate other men's wives. Let him take her, Far Walker thought. He wanted to be alone. To prepare the brew and cool the burning.

When he knew Lako was gone, he returned to his lodge. It was in disarray with the haste of her leaving. No matter; he was in disarray also. He emptied the contents of the pouch into his brewing pot, added water from the water jar, and placed the pot upon coals still glowing in the fire pit outside. Because he wished to be alone he placed crossed sticks at the extended doorway; no one would enter now.

He busied himself with rearranging the objects on the household altar: a finely carved pipe with a bird on the stem; a small crystal in a beaded pouch; a collection of rare pebbles from Long Man, each with colors corresponding to the colors of the Sacred Directions; and an assortment of objects whose powers were known only to him.

He prayed, "Heal me. Return my kia." But the face of She Who Remembers, her lovely body, her voice, remained with him—and the burning.

Pungent odors from the boiling pot drifted in. The brew was ready. He removed the pot, praying while it cooled. Then he drank it all and poured the soggy bits of residue into a carrying pouch, fastened the pouch to his waistband, and headed for Long Man, the river. People spoke as he passed, but they saw his intent look, knew he was on a quest to Long Man, and did not expect a reply. One did not interfere with things sacred.

Far Walker reached the place by the river where he conducted healing ceremonies. Now he must heal himself. He knelt, scooped water in both hands, and drank. Then, facing east, chanting the kia prayer, he followed the bank upriver toward the Healing Place as he tossed bits of boiled root and buds and flowers to Long Man.

The Healing Place, the most sacred spot on the river, was near the bend where a tall stand of reeds marked the spot. As he neared the reeds he continued to chant.

> *Accept my offering, holy one.*
> *Cleanse with your sacred spittle*
> *My kia. Quench my inner fires!*
> *Heal me. Heal me.*

Upstream, near the reeds, something caught his eye—something inconceivable. A woman's robe drifting in the water! The reeds stirred; someone was there.

With an exclamation of outrage at the desecration of a holy place, Far Walker strode to the reeds, pushed them aside with both hands, and stared. She Who Remembers crouched there, holding her child, her wet body gleaming like a pearl in a mussel shell as she enveloped him with a gaze so deep and dark he felt he was falling into an abyss.

Groaning at the memory, Far Walker sat up on his sleeping mat and pressed his face to his knees. Peg Foot could not heal him and he could not heal himself.

Only she, only the shining pearl woman, could quench the burning, and she was mate of Chomoc. Forbidden to him.

▲ 7 ▼

Amid loud hous from bystand-
ers, the Great Sun stepped from the litter at the base of the high
mound and climbed the wide steps to the sacred Temple of Eternal Fire. Each step was accompanied by shouts of homage and
the thump of the homage drum.

At the door of the temple the Great Sun paused while the
elaborately carved drum sounded a final beat—like the beat of
his own heart, steady and strong. It needed to be if he was to
accomplish his objective here. Chanting to the spirits of former
Great Suns, he bent to enter the low extended doorway.

A priest was there, one of eight whose only duty was to take
turns attending the fire night and day to make certain it never
died. The fire was child of the Spirit Being, now high on his sky
trail. To allow the fire to die would destroy their world and everything in it. The priest knelt on one knee, bent low, and howled
his greeting.

The Great Sun gestured. "Summon the shaman."

The priest rose, backed out the door, and disappeared.

The Great Sun gazed at the four cedar logs that lay in the
form of a cross with a small fire burning in the center. He closed
his eyes in silent communication with this child of his spiritual

brother. All was still but for the fire's whisper and the distant sounds of the city far below. Around him the inner walls of the temple rose in splendor, draped with heavy strands of pearls gleaming against fur and feathers and copper and shining shell gorgets incised with sacred symbols. More symbols were inscribed on the High Priest's star wall—symbols only he understood. Another wall held the carved stone mace of each former Great Sun, with an empty place to hold the present Great Sun's when he was in the Afterworld.

Not yet. Not for a long time.

Unless . . . unless his secret was discovered.

He twisted his hands. Why had it happened—the unpardonable thing that remained secret? Until he knew of it, he had been the Great Sun, all-powerful, and only the High Priest was more holy. Strength and pride flowed with the blood in his veins. Now truth stalked him, hounded him, leered from the shadows, and mocked him in the night.

But no one knew except himself. Unless the shaman . . .

Was that why he feared the shaman? Because he might discover the secret?

Was that why he wanted Antelope, She Who Remembers, whose powers were known? Her powers could be useful to him. If she learned the truth, he could have her killed instantly before anyone else knew.

No. He did not want to kill her. He wanted . . .

He would seek help from his spiritual brother.

The Great Sun reached for a carved stone bowl that lay on an altar nearby. Chanting, he dipped his fingers into the bowl and removed a pinch of corn pollen. Still chanting, he tossed it into the fire.

"Accept this sacrifice, holy one. Grant me your wisdom. Grant me your seeing eye."

He must see into the mind of the foreign woman, must see *her*. The lovely body hidden . . .

Would she discover his secret?

Footsteps approached and the doorway darkened as the shaman entered. He bowed low with a rattle of necklaces. "Hou!"

The Great Sun sat on a pedestal beside the altar and gestured the shaman to sit on the floor beside him. Even when the shaman was seated, his head was nearly level with that of the Great Sun. The shaman arranged his long legs and rested his elbows on his knees. He did not look at the Great Sun but gazed into the fire, his long, thin face expressionless under the tattoos.

The Great Sun stirred uneasily and a small frown creased his regal brow. Why was he always uncomfortable in the shaman's presence? At last he said, "I have decided."

The shaman's expression did not change; he waited in silence, eyes averted, long thin hands folded.

The odor of cedar smoke perfumed the room and drifted upward. The fire whispered. The Great Sun watched its flickering light reflected among the pearls on the walls. How could he tell the shaman that She Who Remembers was not to die? At least not yet. He pushed bracelets up and down one muscular arm as if words could be found there.

"Moons must pass before the Green Corn and New Fire ceremonies when the blue-eyed child will be sacrificed. Therefore, the foreign woman and her child are to remain in Yala. For the time being." He watched the shaman from the corner of his eye to see his reaction.

The shaman's expression did not change. He nodded briefly.

The Great Sun continued, "The son of Kokopelli is an expert trader. As was his father." He cleared his throat to ease the words. "Our conch shell supply requires replenishing. Chomoc will take four canoes, with slaves to man them and valuables to trade, and return with filled canoes."

The shaman shot him a sardonic glance from hooded eyes, but said nothing.

The Great Sun realized that his shaman knew that traders from the southeast often brought conch shells to the City of the Great Sun for trading. In fact, such traders were expected soon. Rarely did the Great Sun have to send traders on a hazardous journey to the far southeast for shells, and of course the shaman knew this as well as he. But the shaman was the shaman, and he was the Great Sun.

He continued, "Until you call the buffalo, more skins and other buffalo products are needed. Our stores are low, as I assume you know." He paused, and the fire sparked; was it listening? "However, the journey will be for another reason."

He rose abruptly and stared down at the fire. The shaman remained seated, his tattooed face expressionless, but his thin hands stirred restlessly, clasping and unclasping. Today his black hair was fastened with a copper headband from which a shell fringe dangled; the tiny shells swayed in agitation.

For a time the only sound was the fire's soft voice.

The Great Sun gazed at the High Priest's star wall covered with powerful medicine—diagrams proclaiming the seasons. Could they also divulge the future? He continued, "It is said that the new rulers of the southeast desire conquest. Information is traded as well as goods on trading journeys. Chomoc will learn who is now in power, what that ruler desires, and how it may affect me and my city. He will report back to me personally." *Let him know I expect to be completely informed.*

The shaman smiled thinly, his eyes hooded. "What do you wish of me, my lord?"

The Great Sun scowled. He disliked the shaman's hissing voice. His chin jutted from his square face as he said, "Must I inform you of your duty? Intercede with the gods and spirits to assure the success of Chomoc's journey. Inform the caddí of my wishes; he will arrange it all."

The Great Sun gestured dismissal and the shaman rose. He glanced at the Great Sun and bowed so that his beaded forelock and necklaces swung forward with a rattling sound.

The Great Sun added, "You will call the buffalo. Because they are far away it will take a long time for them to come close. Call them immediately."

Buffalo products were a primary source of the Great Sun's wealth and that of the city. Until recently, traders from buffalo country had come often; it was usually unnecessary to send hunters on a distant journey. Was that the real reason why the shaman had not called the buffalo before? Or were there other reasons, unexplained? He added dryly, "I assume you *can* call the buffalo?"

"Of course." The shaman's hooded eyes flicked briefly at the Great Sun's chest where a large shell gorget lay engraved with the sacred sun symbol of authority, the symbol only a Great Sun could wear. "Hou!" Still bowing, he backed out the door.

The Great Sun watched with satisfaction as the shaman bent low in the doorway to accommodate his height, so low that his headdress ornaments scraped against the roof of the entrance and were knocked askew. He looked ridiculous and the Great Sun was gratified to note his embarrassment. A little humility would do him good.

When the shaman had gone, the Great Sun sat by Red Man,

the fire, probing with his spirit to assimilate Red Man's wisdom. Because the fire, like himself, was brother to the Spirit Being, Red Man and he were brothers. The Great Sun sat there for some time, gazing at the small blaze.

Did the shaman suspect the true reason he was sending Chomoc away? Did he know how the Towa woman haunted him in the night?

Could it be that She Who Remembers was a witch after all? Never before had a woman's beauty and mystery assailed him this way. His two wives were young and comely, of course, but they lacked what She Who Remembers possessed—power and mystery.

He rose and paced the room. He wanted her. His body demanded it. He was the Great Sun; no witch could match his power. He would have her. Then she would die. When he was sated at last. Yes. He would order the shaman to provide the Towa woman as his mate.

He, the Great Sun, would possess her. All of her.

Again he sat before Red Man. The fire was low.

"You are hungry?" he asked politely. Even the Great Sun must revere Red Man.

He took a thin cedar log from the pile nearby and added it to the flames. "Here, I feed you. I, the Great Sun, your brother."

A puff of fragrant smoke billowed, floated upward, and disappeared through a smoke hole in the eaves. The fire crackled.

The Great Sun nodded. "It is good, is it not? Very well. I shall send the son of Kokopelli away. His mate and their child shall be your gifts for the Green Corn ceremony. Until then, I shall have his mate for myself. This is my decision. However, I fear that both the son of Kokopelli and his mate possess dangerous medicine. They have powerful gods. . . ."

Would she discover his secret?

He removed his crown of white swan feathers and his embroidered scarlet moccasins inlaid with pearls. Thus humbled, he chanted praises to Red Man while flames devoured the cedar. Then he extended his hand in a gesture of royalty to royalty.

"I seek your assistance."

The fire burned quietly, little more than embers.

Word sped through surrounding villages that She Who Remembers and her mate, Chomoc, son of Kokopelli, and their blue-eyed baby had been in Yala five days at the home of Red Leaf. This was astounding news. No one of such importance had been sent to Yala before.

"Why are they here?"

"Horned Toad brought them. To trade."

"Those that came with them have left. Why are these others still here?"

"Yes. Why is She Who Remembers here? At Red Leaf's dwelling?"

"No foreigners have been sent to her dwelling before. Why—"

"She is beautiful, they say. Maybe the caddí wants her."

Smiles behind hands. The caddí's appetites were well known.

"Who is she?"

"You know. A Chosen One—"

"Who teaches young girls the women's secrets."

"We teach our girls all they must know."

"Of course. But—"

"I wonder what she tells them. . . ."

"Yes. I wonder also."

"Did you know the baby has blue eyes?"

Whispers. Meaningful glances.

Waikah shouldered her way to the fore with bony elbows. The aged midwife was respected and the crowd made way for her. Wisps of scraggly gray hair had escaped from a single braid and clung to her tattooed cheeks. Under shaggy white eyebrows her small, black eyes darted from person to person like a bumblebee. When she was assured of attention, she waved a scrawny arm.

"The Towa foreigners must go! We want no blue-eyed children here. My kia tells me they are witches. Give the foreigners to Long Man!"

The crowd murmured uneasily. Drowning was a last resort in disposing of evildoers, and only after the shaman determined that Long Man agreed to accept them. People shook their heads, murmuring.

"A Chosen One who teaches women's secrets is not a witch!"

"It is said they are son of Kokopelli and daughter of She Who Remembers."

Waikah stood immobile, her toothless mouth twitching. "I warn you all. They are dangerous. They do not belong here. Send them away!"

The babble increased. Some agreed with Waikah; others did not.

Word continued to spread. Curiosity mounted. For several days, all remained the same. Chomoc and Antelope and the baby remained with Red Leaf and her family. Chomoc spent much time in the plaza trading, but Antelope seemed hesitant about mingling with the other villagers.

Then one day Antelope uneasily found herself surrounded by an inquisitive crowd, mostly of women and children. She was going to the ceremonial center to join Chomoc at his trading, but before she reached the plaza the crowd pressed so close she had to stop. She stood uncertainly, reaching behind to touch Skyfeather in the cradleboard.

Nothing would harm this child!

What did these people want? They did not appear to be un-friendly. At least, not obviously.

She said, "I seek my mate, Chomoc. Allow me to pass."

She pushed ahead, but the crowd pressed closer.

She spoke sharply, a little more at ease now with Caddoan words. "Allow me to pass."

A little girl reached up to touch Antelope's necklace.

"No!" Antelope drew back. "No one touches the necklace of She Who Remembers but she who wears it."

People crowded closer. Never before had they seen a neck-lace of polished stone beads of many colors—and with a scallop shell pendant inlaid with turquoise in a mystical design! It was whispered that the necklace of She Who Remembers had mag-ical powers. They stared in awe.

Antelope noticed an old woman at the edge of the crowd, the one who had confronted her when she first arrived with "You don't belong here!" Beady black eyes pierced Antelope's with ma-levolent impact.

She hates me! Antelope thought. *Why?* A small warning bell chimed in her mind. *I am a stranger here; I must be careful.*

With people pushing close, Antelope felt closed in. These people could turn hostile any moment. With both hands she pushed people aside. Then she lifted the cradleboard from her back to hold Skyfeather close, and elbowed through the mur-muring crowd. For a moment she thought she glimpsed the man who had discovered her among the reeds, but he quickly disap-peared.

Who was he? she wondered—as she had wondered often since that time when he stood gazing down at her in the water. Something about him . . . She saw him, sometimes, in dreams. He stood looking down at her among the reeds, his eyes looking deeply, deeply into hers. Who was he?

He lingered in her memory.

It was midsummer now, growing hotter. Chomoc sat on his trading blanket in the plaza and inspected his bulging pack with satisfaction. Trading was excellent. A buckskin bag was heavy with pearls. He had bought many other valuables with his rainbow flint and with his cotton cloth and belts of Anasazi and Towa weaving. His jewelry of turquoise and shell bought many pearls, which would be easy to carry on a journey. They would buy much more than what was traded. Chomoc thrust his hand into the buckskin bag, savoring the cool touch of his pearls. How wise it had been to come here!

Traders still crouched at his trading blanket, fingering his wares. Their black eyes glittered between dangling forelocks, and their bracelets rattled as they gestured in bargaining. Chomoc's own turquoise bracelets slid up and down his arms, and his rings flashed with each movement.

Horned Toad sauntered by with three comely women in his wake. The old guide still used his staff as he walked, but his step was amazingly sprightly and his posture erect—as he might well be elsewhere, Chomoc thought, smiling. For one who had come home to die, it looked as if it would be a while yet.

Horned Toad saw Chomoc surrounded by eager traders and paused. He glanced at Chomoc's bulging pack. "Getting rich, I see."

"Of course. And are these your mates?"

"Of course." He gestured grandly. "One more at home. I buy them." He smiled broadly, flashing what teeth he had left.

Chomoc laughed. "Maybe I should consider doing that."

"Better not tell Antelope. Here she comes."

Chomoc turned to see Antelope hurrying, with Skyfeather in the cradleboard clutched in her mother's arms. Traders made way for them as Antelope came and squatted beside Chomoc. Her mouth was grim and her eyes sparked. "What do they want?"

"Who?"

"All these people. They crowd me, stare at me and at Sky-feather. I don't like it."

"Of course they stare. We are foreigners, and you, my love, are something to stare at."

Horned Toad said, "Maybe they stare because they don't know how to tell you what they want you to know."

Antelope shot him a hot glance. "And what might that be?"

Horned Toad gestured to a woman standing outside the ring of traders. Hesitantly, she stepped forward, and Horned Toad spoke to her quietly. The traders glanced at one another, their dark eyes expressionless among the tattoos.

Horned Toad and the woman talked for some time. Finally, Horned Toad said, "They want to know the secrets of She Who Remembers."

Antelope lifted her chin. "I tell no secrets."

"They have no She Who Remembers here."

She looked at the woman who met her glance and then lowered her eyes. Antelope laughed briefly. "You don't mean they want *me* to teach *them*?"

He shrugged. "Maybe."

Antelope glanced about her. These women and children were from another world than the one she knew. Their strange tattoos and expressionless gaze, their language, their robes, their dwellings—everything was totally foreign. She gazed across the plaza at the great mounds soaring to unknown gods, and listened to strange city sounds, and smelled sharp city smells so different from those of home.

What that old woman said is true. I do not belong here.

Longing for Cicuye welled up in a flood. "I want to teach my own people. I want to go home."

Chomoc snorted. "I am having the best trading of my life. I do not intend to leave. We are *not* going home. No. Not yet."

Antelope swung the cradleboard to her back and faced Chomoc.

"I came all this way to be with you. Our daughter was born in a stony gully, remember? With no women to help me." Antelope wrapped both arms around her stomach in recollection. "Skyfeather has had no naming ceremony, she has no protection from the gods. How can she enter Sipapu?" She shook her head. "We live now in a stinking, smoky loft in someone else's dwelling. I am going home to *our* dwelling, *our* people, and you will take me."

There were loud snickers from traders relishing the confrontation. Women and children who had been following Antelope watched and listened avidly. They did not need to know the Towa language to recognize a domestic dispute.

Chomoc's face flushed clear to his slanted brow. His amber eyes burned as he said softly, "Think how you are making me and yourself and Skyfeather appear before these people. Are we to be laughed at, derided in secret, despised?" He glanced at the men surrounding them whose tattoo-ringed eyes watched every move as a cougar watches a fawn. "You endanger us all."

The toothless old woman who always seemed to be near shouted, "You do not belong here!" Wrapping her shawl more closely around her, she hobbled away.

Suddenly, Antelope knew the old woman was right. A cold hand clamped her heart.

▲ 8 ▼

Antelope sat with Red Leaf and old Poqua at the outdoor cooking fire. Because Antelope had been there only a few days, she was acutely conscious of being an uninvited and unwelcome guest. She wanted to help but was not sure her contribution would be welcome. Poqua stirred a pot of venison stew, while Red Leaf chopped tubers to be added.

Antelope said haltingly, "I want to help. May I get water?"

Red Leaf replied, "The water jar is full." If she was amused at Antelope's language efforts, she concealed it.

Antelope felt rebuffed. She wished Chomoc were there, but he was trading again in the plaza. She would find him and see more of the city while doing so. She picked up Skyfeather, who slept peacefully, and lifted the cradleboard to her back.

She said, "I go to find Chomoc."

The boys, Ringtail and Bobcat, were playing with a neighbor boy. When Antelope started down the path toward the plaza, four-year-old Ringtail came running.

"Where are you going, Antelope?"

She gestured toward the plaza.

He indicated he would go with her, but she said, "Ask your mother."

He called to Red Leaf, who shrugged indifferently, and the boy skipped along beside Antelope. Ringtail was a miniature of his father, but a likable child nonetheless, with sparkling black eyes under a thatch of black hair that hung to his shoulders. His pudgy little body was bare but for a tiny breechclout that was more ornamentation than garment. His round face beamed as he said, "I will take you where you want to go."

She smiled. "Thank you."

They passed farmhouses with extended doorways and neatly tended gardens. Most activities took place outdoors, and women were busy in the gardens or grinding corn or tending to other domestic chores. They saw Antelope and Ringtail and called greetings. Children and dogs came running, and soon Antelope had a covey of naked children accompanying her, with yapping dogs trotting along.

They passed a house being built, and Antelope stopped to watch. The houses here, like everything else, were very different from those of home. She would have much to tell at evening fires when Chomoc finished his trading and they returned to Cicuye.

Children hopped about impatiently as Antelope studied the house. It was constructed of poles set upright in the ground, with cane woven between the logs and plastered with clay. A man and a woman were on the pointed roof, thatching it with thick bundles of grass. They were intent on their work and ignored her.

The dogs investigated the base of the house and lifted their legs, establishing territory. The woman shouted down at them, ordering them away, but the children paid no attention. Ringtail and the other children stood silently, staring at two old men who approached slowly, leaning on staffs.

Antelope regarded them covertly. How strange they were! Their tattoos were sparse and different in design from any Antelope had seen before. No forelock dangled between their eyes. Their heads were shaved on either side, leaving a long hank of stiffened hair on top swept up and back in a tall, arched crest. They leaned forward slightly as they walked, heads thrust out, eyes darting this way and that, like giant birds. As they came closer, Antelope saw that their hands resembled claws with long, curving, black-dirty fingernails.

The children huddled together, watching the men approach, then turned and ran away, dogs following. Ringtail remained, but he stood close to Antelope, hiding behind her as the men passed, leaving a whiff of bad odor in their wake.

"Who are they?" Antelope asked.

"Bone Pickers." Proud of his knowledge, he tugged at her. "I will show you."

It was a warm morning in midsummer with clouds billowing over distant mountain peaks. As they approached the plaza, people stared at Antelope and Skyfeather, and whispered to one another. The city bustled with activity; there were shouts and laughter, the throb of drums, singing, chanting, the pound of poles on mortars, and an underlying hum of conversation.

Ringtail took Antelope's hand and led her across the plaza toward a great mound thrust against the sky—one large mound to which three smaller ones were attached, one after another. To Antelope, it looked like a mythical creature hunched and waiting.

"What is that?"

"For dead people."

A peak-roofed structure stood near the mound, and as they approached, Antelope had to cover her nose. The stench was overpowering. Ringtail and the others did not seem to notice.

Ringtail said, "Dead bones are in there."

Dead bones? There had to be more than a few bones to create such an odor, Antelope thought, but she did not want to discuss it. She wanted to find Chomoc and talk to him about going home. Home to her clean, sweet-smelling city high on the ridge. Home to her people.

Chomoc was already shouldering his pack when they found him among the traders whose wares were spread before them on the ground—pots, bowls, flint implements, gardening tools, bone needles, corn, venison, fish, nuts, seeds, tubers, furs, copper, jewelry—a bewildering array.

Chomoc beamed as they approached. "Good trading today. Very good."

Ringtail said proudly, "I showed her."

"Thank you." To Antelope, he asked, "What is he talking about?"

"Bones. A building with smelly bones."

"That's the mortuary house. Bones are put in baskets and

stored there until burial." He gestured to the great mound sprawling behind them. "That's where important people are buried." Chomoc was proud of his ability to learn about places where he traded. It was good business.

"Just their bones?"

"Except for royalty—the Great Sun and his family. They are buried whole."

"But the bones . . . what happens to the rest? The flesh, I mean."

"The Bone Pickers scrape it off and burn it." He took Ringtail's hand. "Come. Let's go home."

Ringtail withdrew his hand; he was too big for that. But he marched proudly beside Chomoc as they followed the path back to Yala.

Antelope remembered the old men with long, black fingernails. Revolting. She would be glad to leave this place.

She hurried to keep up with Chomoc's stride. She knew he was eager to be back in Red Leaf's dwelling and spread the contents of his trading on the floor to be examined and admired. Surely he had enough by now.

"When will we return to Cicuye, Chomoc?"

"Soon."

"How soon?"

He flashed her a glance. "When I am finished trading."

Several days passed. Chomoc rearranged everything in their packs, and in the bundle to be carried by Blacktail on the travois. Blacktail and Many Bears' dog were mutually antagonistic, so Chomoc took Blacktail to Horned Toad to look after until the dog was needed.

Meanwhile, Antelope stayed close to Chomoc, accompanying him on his trading sessions. Being with him gave her a feeling of security. She needed that here.

Soon they would return home.

BOOM, boom, boom. BOOM, boom.

It was the moon of midsummer. Antelope and Chomoc joined the crowd on the path by the river. The trail meandered through fields of pumpkins and corn where bean vines climbed the corn stalks. Naked children shouted and ran, and women working in the fields dropped their buffalo bone hoes, adjusted the woven waistbands that held their skirts, and joined the crowd, chattering excitedly. Men practicing a ball game in the plaza deserted the field and hurried toward the river, their short breechclouts flapping.

The booming drum and smoke signals from the Guardian Mound had summoned warrior canoes to meet the visitors. Surely, this was an unusual and important arrival! The canoes sped upstream, the strong arms of warriors swooping forward and back in a paddling motion as fluid as the river.

Again the signal drum sounded. It was answered by another drum, one with a high, throbbing beat, accompanied by a piercingly shrill whistle. As Antelope and Chomoc rounded the bend, Antelope stopped to stare.

An exotic procession approached. First came a long wooden canoe paddled by eight nearly naked, brilliantly ornamented and tattooed men towing a long, ornately carved and painted canoe covered with a canopy. The heads of the paddlers were almost completely shaved but for a long hank of hair that hung like a tail from a circular spot on top of each head. A ninth man stood at the bow beating a strangely pitched dual drum; in his mouth was a long whistle like a pipe, which he blew as accompaniment to the high two-tone drumbeats by which the men kept time, their muscular arms moving in perfect unison and their long tails of hair swinging.

Antelope stood with villagers thronging the riverbank as the wooden canoe with its tasseled canopy swept by majestically. Inside, a solitary figure, a woman, reclined against lush furs. She was partly hidden by a swaying curtain of glistening shells, but Antelope had a tantalizing glimpse of her as the canoe passed. She was dark and extraordinarily beautiful and was surrounded by baskets and jars. She glanced neither left nor right at the gawking crowds lining the riverbank, but gazed straight ahead, her dark body aglow against pale furs.

The splash of the paddles, the cry of the whistle, and the shout of the two-tone drum mingled with excited murmurs of the villagers. Warrior canoes sped by. With military precision they formed a blockade on the river and ordered the foreign canoes to stop. The lead warrior directed that his canoe be brought alongside that of the visitors. With a piercing whistle accompanied by drumbeats, the foreigners obeyed. The lead village warrior and the drummer stood eye to eye, signing.

Antelope watched with interest. Different tribes had different tongues and they communicated expertly in sign language. It was rapid and a bit different from what she was accustomed to, but clearly the two men understood each other.

After it was completed, the drummer called in his language to the mysterious woman behind him. A jeweled hand emerged from the shells and gestured the canoes to shore. The drum sounded and the whistle shrilled once more as the canoes were expertly maneuvered to the bank. The paddlers, big men all, lined up as the drummer, still carrying his drum and whistle, approached One Who Watches and the man with the shell horn, who had hurried from their mound to assess the visitors.

More signing ensued. The visitors were ordered to pay tribute to the Great Sun before being allowed to pass and enter the city.

Antelope turned to Chomoc. "What if they refuse to pay?"

"They will pay. Watch."

The man with the drum and whistle gestured to the paddlers, who parted the strings of shells. A bare jeweled foot emerged, followed by another, and the woman stepped out to the bank.

The crowd murmured. She was tall for a woman, darker than most, and majestically beautiful. A robe of fine white cloth, intricately embroidered with shell beads, clung to a gorgeous body and was tied at one shoulder leaving the other shoulder and one breast bare. Raven-dark hair hung in three long coils, each entwined with shell beads. Hands and arms displayed ornaments of shell, turquoise, and glittering stones aglow against red-brown skin.

Antelope experienced mixed emotions. Admiration and envy mixed with a pang of unease. She turned to Chomoc. "I wonder who she is. Do you know?"

He did not reply. He stared, amber eyes gleaming.

The woman approached One Who Watches and stood in regal silence.

One Who Watches signed, "Our Great Sun demands tribute. Where is it?"

The woman gestured and a paddler reached into her canoe and removed a small basket. Carrying it in both outstretched hands he offered it to One Who Watches, who accepted it, opened it, inspected the contents, and handed it to the man with the shell horn.

"You may pass."

With an arrogant toss of her head, One Who Watches turned her back and strode away, followed by the man with the horn and two big dogs.

"What was in the basket?" Antelope asked Chomoc.

He shrugged absently. "Who knows?"

His gleaming eyes never left the woman, who gestured again. The paddlers reached inside her canoe and removed a litter covered with furs. They carried it to her and lowered it, kneeling in reverence. With consummate grace she sat, stretched out her long beautiful legs, crossed her jeweled bare feet, and reclined against the furs.

Again, unease touched Antelope with a clammy hand, but the crowd sighed, entranced.

Four men removed baskets and jars from the woman's canoe and four other men lifted the litter. The man with the drum pounded a marching beat and blew his whistle as he led the way for the litter bearers. They were followed by the other paddlers, who walked in single file behind the litter, their long ropes of hair swaying, black eyes watchful and alert as they carried jars and bulging baskets in outstretched arms, stepping in time to the beat of the drum.

Agog bystanders made way for the procession. Antelope glimpsed Horned Toad with his wives in the crowd; she elbowed her way to him. "Who is she?"

"The queen from the powerful City of the North. Her name is Tima-cha. She has not come here before. An important occasion!" He beamed with pride. This was his city; he shared the honor.

"Why is she here?"

He cast her a disdainful glance. "To see the Great Sun, of course. Important matters to be arranged."

Tima-cha and her procession were halted momentarily by the pressure of the crowd. An older boy, demonstrating fearlessness to his companions, jerked hard at the arm of one of the paddlers to see what was in a basket. Infuriated, the man kicked him away and the boy fell groaning, clutching his stomach.

Outraged exclamations followed. An angry crowd pressed closer, blocking the procession. A thrown stone missed Tima-cha and hit a litter bearer.

In the cacophony that followed, Antelope stood frozen. Harm to these ambassadors from a powerful empire would surely result in war; already they had suffered irreparable insult—a stone thrown at Tima-cha.

With a shout, the drummer whirled, laid down his drum and whistle. He yanked aside the furs on the litter, revealing a cache of bows and arrows. The men carrying baskets and bowls set them down, snatched weapons, and stood surrounding their queen with drawn bows. Tima-cha sat upright in stony dignity, her face expressionless, as she gazed ahead, ignoring the crowd.

Confronted with drawn bows, the crowd growled—a dog-pack-sounding growl. The situation was explosive. Antelope reached behind her to touch her sleeping baby. Where was Chomoc?

Suddenly, over the growls of the crowd came the soaring song of a flute, teasing, laughing, singing of happiness and wondrous joys yet to be known. Antelope saw Chomoc dart to the front of the litter, playing his flute as he bent forward and back, coaxing the litter bearers to follow him, coaxing the people to make way.

On and on the flute sang its merry, teasing trill. Slowly, the crowd drew back. Slowly, the men lowered their bows, replaced them on the litter, and picked up their burdens.

Tima-cha looked down at Chomoc; her lovely lips curved in a smile. She spoke, and the procession resumed.

Men, women, boys, girls, dogs—all ran ahead or followed behind or lined the path, watching as the man with the dual drum pounded a beat, Chomoc's flute soared and sang, and the whistle added staccato accent.

Antelope stood aside as the crowd followed the procession. She watched them—women with babies in cradleboards, excited boys, dignified elders, farmers, coppersmiths, fishermen, young girls giggling—all listening intently to Chomoc's flute.

The crowd's sullen mood melted away, and children danced to the merry song. Chomoc's flute had worked its magic again.

He is like his father. He can achieve whatever he desires with the sorcery of his music.

Tima-cha's smile at Chomoc was not impersonal. Was it an invitation?

If so, what would Chomoc desire?

She knew. Yes, she knew, and she burned hot with the knowledge of it.

* * *

The Great Sun stood on the terrace of the temple and watched the procession approaching among the distant trees. Again he examined a message shell the caddí had brought him, a conch shell engraved with the pictured announcement of the visit of the northern queen, Tima-cha, for the purpose of arranging trading agreements; a runner had brought it a few days before.

He turned the shell over in his smooth, strong hand that was spared labor; bracelets and rings gleamed in the sunlight. Straight dark brows met in a frown over his straight nose. What did this ruler want? Hers was a powerful empire. Was she threatened by marauding tribes, perhaps? It was said that her city was surrounded by strong walls and a moat. He felt a tinge of envy. A moat! In all his thirty-nine winters, never had he seen a moat. His younger brother, Striped Serpent, had seen one during his many diplomatic journeys, and had described it with admiration.

The Great Sun gazed over his city to the river surrounding it on three sides. That was all the moat he needed. That, and his famed warriors, protected him and his domain.

What did she want? He needed no more trading agreements; his was a rich city. Perhaps she wanted a military alignment. That he would not allow; she could fight her own wars.

Well, she was a woman. It would be no problem to control her and whatever situation might arise; his two wives had taught him that. They were down there now, gawking with the others. Frankly, he had tired of them. It was time to take others. He wondered if Striped Serpent would take them; he wanted everything else the Great Sun possessed.

He wondered what this woman looked like.

He wondered what she wanted.

There was Chomoc's flute again, soaring over the drum and that absurd whistle. The Great Sun's grim lips relaxed in a smile, and his black eyes glittered. Chomoc was due for a surprise. And would his skill with the flute not be useful in negotiating trade deals during his coming journey?

The procession reached the plaza accompanied by a huge crowd. Every one of his villagers must be there, as well as those from neighboring areas. Now would be a good time to allow them to view the Great Sun in all his splendor greeting a ruler from another important city who had traveled far to confer with him.

She Who Remembers would be impressed. As well she should. It would facilitate his plans. . . .

He gestured; the litter bearers waiting at the foot of the mound snapped to attention.

"Hou, hou, hou!"

Howls of homage were repeated by people thronging the plaza who waited in tense anticipation for the meeting of their Great Sun and this ruler from a distant realm. They jabbered excitedly, children yelled, dogs yapped, the drum shouted, the whistle shrilled, and Chomoc's flute soared over all, increasing expectation with wonderful promises.

Slowly, the Great Sun began his descent on the great mound. Now the thunder drum took over, booming with each step, drowning out the other drum and the whistle and Chomoc's flute. The drummer, watching from a nearby signal post, beat the great drum with mighty blows making the very air vibrate.

At the foot of the mound, slaves unrolled a royal mat for the Great Sun to walk upon to meet the visiting ruler. Women rushed to fill baskets with petals to be strewn in his path, and warriors brandished lances to keep dogs and people at a proper distance. Slowly, the Great Sun descended, pausing briefly at each step as the drum boomed. A breeze stirred his cloak of scarlet feathers and his swan feather crown with its red tufts and tassels; sunlight glistened on his scarlet diadem and carved shell gorget and the thick strands of pearls and other jewels that hung to his waist. He was a magnificent sight, and he knew it.

Majestically, the litter bearers entered the plaza with their queen, followed by the men in single file bearing gifts. Tima-cha sat upright, gazing at him. She was still too far away for the Great Sun to see her clearly, but there was no doubt that this was a beautiful woman.

As he neared the bottom of the stairs, the Great Sun paused, allowing all to see him in his glory while the women with flowers lined up at each side of the mat, waiting to strew blossoms as he approached. His two wives emerged from the crowd and climbed the remaining stairs to stand proudly beside him. They were young and beautiful, of course. But compared to this queen . . .

Would this ruler propose to join their realms? If so, he might take her as another wife. A pleasant thought. He would get closer for a better look.

Where is She Who Remembers?

He glimpsed her in the crowd standing beside Chomoc. His flute was silent now. He stared at the queen as though Antelope were not there.

To the final booms of the thunder drum, the Great Sun descended the rest of the stairs and stepped upon the mat.

The drum stilled.

The silence was electric.

The queen descended gracefully from the litter and stood waiting for him. Her beaded robe and her many jewels glistened against the sheen of her dark skin. Her eyes, shadowed by thick lashes, regarded his approach.

The Great Sun strode slowly, crushing the flowers and releasing their fragrance. He gazed at this ruler, this tall, dark woman of formidable beauty, and he desired her.

He signed, "My people and I welcome you."

Her glance was enigmatic. She spoke in Caddoan with a bewitching accent. "I thank you."

What color are her eyes? Not brown, not blue.

She gestured and the men with baskets and bowls brought them to him and placed them at his feet. A quick look revealed they held carved pipes, copper, salt, and other treasures.

Again the woman gestured and a man brought her one of the furs from the litter, a perfect jaguar skin. She offered it to the Great Sun with jeweled arms outstretched.

Ah, how delicious those arms would be in my embrace!

He accepted the skin and handed it to one of his wives, who exclaimed over it, caressing the silky fur.

From around his neck the Great Sun removed a glowing pearl necklace of many strands. Stepping close—how enticing she smelled!—he looped the necklace over her head. It circled her neck three times and fell to her lovely thighs.

The crowd murmured. Surely, a most lavish gift! Their Great Sun made them proud!

The queen slid her fingers lightly over the pearls. "Your generosity is well known and proven. I thank you."

Are her eyes green?

He replied, "Your generosity overwhelms us all. I invite you to dine in my dwelling."

He and Tima-cha turned to their litters to be borne across the plaza to the Great Sun's dwelling mound. The Great Sun's wives prepared to follow but were waved back by their spouse; this was state business.

As the bearers proceeded, Chomoc's flute began to sing again. Tima-cha gestured him to her side and he strode beside her, his music serenading her beauty.

The Great Sun scowled.

Chomoc must go. Now.

▲9▼

The dwelling mound of the Great Sun soared in splendor on the north side of the plaza. Countless basketloads of stomped-down earth had created its sloping sides, which were covered with soft green grass to prevent erosion. Wide logs, smoothed and shaped, formed steps leading to the royal dwelling at the summit where slaves worked feverishly preparing for guests. Striped Serpent, in regal array, strode about, ordering the slaves to make haste or be flogged.

At each step a warrior stood, legs parted, lance in outstretched right hand, waiting to greet the Great Sun when he arrived. A breeze swept from the river and stirred their fur-and-feather headdresses but did little to cool their tattooed bodies glistening with sweat. Sounds floated up from the approaching procession—howls of greeting to the Great Sun, the babble of voices, excited yells of children, dogs barking, and the music of a flute soaring over all—while slaves dashed up and down the stairs of the mound with baskets and bundles of food for a feast.

The procession had nearly reached the mound when the caddí, accompanied by four warriors, made his way through the crowd. The Great Sun saw them approaching and beckoned the caddí to him. They spoke briefly and the warriors strode to Chomoc. The procession halted.

"Come with us," a warrior ordered.

Chomoc stopped playing his flute. "Why?"

"The Great Sun wishes it." Falcon eyes peered at him.

Chomoc glanced up at Tima-cha, who sat regally on the litter. "Is it *your* wish that I leave?"

"No."

Chomoc lifted the flute to his lips and began to play again.

The caddí gestured, and the warriors grabbed Chomoc. The Great Sun spoke sharply. "Wait."

Chomoc jerked himself loose angrily. "I am Chomoc, Anasazi, of the Place of the Eagle Clan. I am your guest."

"As am I," Tima-cha said. "It is my wish that this musician accompany me." She glanced sharply at the Great Sun. "His music may enable me to overlook the insults inflicted upon me by the people of your city."

The Great Sun concealed his concern and anger. He gestured the caddí to his side.

"Wait," he whispered. "Ambush Chomoc tonight." The queen would be occupied, come darkness. The Great Sun felt a stirring in his loins at the thought. She would forget the thrown stone. Ah, yes.

And he would forget, for a while, the beauty of She Who Remembers—whose spirit stalked him in dreams.

Did she suspect his secret?

The Great Sun sat on his carved chair and looked down at Tima-cha and her entourage seated on the floor around him. Since his was the only chair, it was necessary to seat the queen on furs. She sat regally, her face expressionless, as slaves carried in bowls and baskets of choice foods. The Great Sun had not invited her men to eat with them, but she had insisted. Now she sat as if on a throne, her head high. The Great Sun was nagged by conflicting emotions—both admiration for and resentment of her royal demeanor. She was, after all, in the presence of the Great Sun.

The slaves, heads shaved and naked but for breechclouts, carried each bowl and basket to the Great Sun first, for him to approve and to help himself. He examined each item, smelled it, helped himself, and waved it away. Then each container was placed on the floor before him, and the Great Sun shoved it at the men with his foot.

Tima-cha was ignored.

The men glanced at one another. Babbling in outrage, they jumped up, spilling corn and venison and berries upon the floor. A man signed, "You insult our queen again! Why is she not served first?"

The Great Sun swallowed shocked surprise. Women were never served first no matter who they were. Men and boys—all males—ate first, always. Even a baby boy was served before his mother. But these barbarians did not know that, and now their queen was insulted again. The men scowled threateningly. This visit could result in war, not lucrative trading deals. Something must be done.

From outside came the sound of Chomoc's flute. He had followed Tima-cha up the steps to the Great Sun's dwelling but had been refused admittance—to the queen's obvious displeasure. Now his flute sang again, hinting of intimate joys yet to be savored.

Suddenly, Tima-cha rose, preparing to leave. "I shall not allow myself to be insulted again."

An alarm sounded loudly in the Great Sun's brain. *Something must be done.*

He rose, facing the queen. "It is our custom to serve men first. But that is because we have never before been honored with your queenly presence. Permit me to make amends. You, honored monarch, shall be served first in a room of your own with a musician to entertain you."

He signaled a slave. "Prepare to serve the woman in my sleeping quarters. Seat her on my bed. Take all other food to her first, then bring it to me." He could hardly believe what he heard himself saying, but this was an emergency. Besides, he would have her later. On his bed.

He turned to another slave. "Bring Chomoc to me."

The slaves could not conceal their astonishment. One left to summon Chomoc, and the others scooped up food spilled on the floor.

Chomoc entered with aplomb as though he had expected to be invited. A look passed between him and Tima-cha that was not lost on the Great Sun; he fumed inwardly. Tima-cha spoke to her men and they sat down sullenly, dark eyes watchful.

The Great Sun rose. "I shall escort you. Come."

The slaves gawked in stunned astonishment as the Great Sun led Tima-cha to an adjoining room, followed by Chomoc. The arrogance the foreign ruler displayed deserved instant death—her decapitated body flung down the stairs and her head impaled on a lance and displayed in the plaza. The few warriors accompanying her would be easily dispatched. Burned alive, probably. The implacable fierceness of the great city's defenders was legendary; it was amazing that this ruler came with only nine men as protection. But more amazing was the Great Sun demeaning himself by escorting this arrogant woman to his sleeping quarters and demanding that she be served first! The slaves peered at one another fearfully. Could it be that this foreign ruler was a witch?

The Great Sun returned to his seat. The slaves filed in and out of his sleeping quarters carrying more baskets and bowls and bundles of food for her selection. Chomoc's flute sang of intimate pleasures, of joys to be savored that only he could provide. The Great Sun helped himself to food offered, then shoved it with his sandaled foot at the warriors, who ate sullenly.

The flute played on, seductive, enticing. Then it stopped.

The Great Sun waited for the music to begin again, but there was only silence.

What was happening in there?

Antelope trudged back to Red Leaf's dwelling. Many villagers remained in the plaza, relishing the excitement, but she had watched Chomoc seducing—yes, seducing—the foreign queen with his flute, and now he was with her in the Great Sun's dwelling. She, his mate, She Who Remembers, was left behind like a frayed basket while he feasted with royalty.

Antelope blinked back furious tears. It was always like this. There would always be another. . . .

The queen was beautiful. And she had responded to the magic of Chomoc's flute; that was obvious.

Antelope bit her lip. How well she knew the seductive power of Chomoc's music! Since childhood he had charmed and bemused her, comforted her, captivated her with the songs of his flute. He was the only man she had ever loved.

How many women had Chomoc loved?

That foreign queen had seductive powers of her own. What was happening up there in the Great Sun's dwelling?

Antelope clasped her necklace to her, seeking communication with Kwani and with all who had been She Who Remembers before. She sought to see her mother's face, to hear her voice.

"My mate is with another. I fear I am losing him. Help me."

There was no answer.

"Help me!" she pleaded.

The silent voice spoke. "He loves you. But he is son of Kokopelli. . . ." The voice faded away.

Was it her mother's voice that she heard like a whisper in her brain?

"Speak to me!" she cried.

Silence.

Antelope brooded about this as she followed the path by the river. A pang of loneliness for her mother and brother and her beautiful faraway home made her stop and close her eyes, remembering. Windwoman's afternoon breeze touched her cheek in a gentle caress. Skyfeather stirred in her cradleboard. She would be hungry soon.

"I have you, small one," Antelope said. "We shall go home soon." But a vague fear lingered. Was she doomed forever to be a stranger in a strange land?

The path to Red Leaf's dwelling followed the river's bend. The area was nearly deserted as people remained in the plaza. Ahead, the queen's royal canoes rocked gently at the river's edge while two of the Great Sun's warriors stood guard. Antelope felt their falcon eyes probing her as she passed.

She reached Red Leaf's dwelling and was greeted by suspicious growls of Hoho, the dog. Poqua, the old grandmother, sat outside in the shade of an oak with Bobcat, the two-year-old, asleep on the ground beside her. She was notching a stick with a flint knife and paused to speak sharply to Hoho; he quieted but watched Antelope with wolflike eyes.

"I greet you," Antelope said.

Black eyes under gray brows darted a glance at her, then returned to the work at hand. Her thin gray hair, in two scraggly braids fastened by bits of dyed buckskin, swung a bit as she worked. Several beautiful necklaces dangled on her shriveled breasts, partly obscuring faded tattoos. Antelope watched as bony hands expertly notched a stick already rounded and smoothed. Another stick, unnotched, lay nearby.

Skyfeather awoke and began to cry. Antelope lifted the cradleboard from her back and sat beside Poqua. The old woman seemed to ignore her, but Antelope was hurting because of Chomoc; she needed the comforting this woman of many years might give. Antelope removed Skyfeather from the cradleboard and held her to nurse.

For a time, Poqua bent to her work. A breeze stirred the leaves of the oak tree making little shadows dance on the ground. A bird called.

Suddenly, Poqua reached a clawlike hand to touch Skyfeather's downy head. Antelope almost drew back, but Poqua's eyes met her own with unexpected woman-to-woman communication, and Antelope smiled. This old one could be a friend, and she needed a friend.

She said, "What are you making?"

Poqua stood the notched stick on end, then took the unnotched stick and rubbed it up and down upon the notches in a rasping rhythm. She began to sing in a high, wavering voice, rocking to and fro.

Bobcat woke. He sat up, his crossed eyes looking at Antelope and Skyfeather with surprise. After a moment he snuggled against his grandmother and began to sing with her, his sweet child's voice blending with her cracked one, the two of them rocking in unison.

Antelope looked at them, and at Skyfeather whose hungry little mouth tugged at her; she watched the shadows dance on the ground and gazed up into leafy green. A squirrel was there.

Chomoc could talk to squirrels.

Suddenly, Antelope began to cry. Heaving sobs tore from inside her. Helplessly, she tried to stop but could not.

Skyfeather whimpered. Holding the baby in her arms, Antelope jumped up and ran into Red Leaf's dwelling. Blindly she climbed the ladder to the smoky loft and sprawled on the sleeping mat, clutching Skyfeather to her as though she, too, would be taken away. Heartbreak, humiliation, anger, fear, homesickness—all gushed in great, gasping sobs.

Someone touched her ankle. Antelope jerked away, remembering Many Bears, but a soft voice spoke, crooning. Old Poqua stood on the ladder, reaching for her. Her wrinkled face was suffused with concern.

Still sobbing, Antelope grasped the old woman's hand and helped her climb into the loft. The three of them lay close together while Poqua's crooning voice, in a foreign language but understood nevertheless, soothed the sobs away.

It was late; the moon had set and only starlight flickered on the river. Chomoc followed the path to Red Leaf's home, stumbling now and then in the darkness. He was weary, but elated. The queen had questioned him sharply about trading opportunities in the west. She was obviously impressed with his knowledge. But of course. He, Chomoc, son of Kokopelli, knew the trails, the villages, the trading opportunities better than anyone, and his flute opened doors; it spoke the language of the heart.

His flute had spoken ardently to her. How beautiful she was!

Chomoc smiled, remembering. She had responded, but only with the power of her glance. Her dark eyes caressed him, but she refused his touch. What she wanted was his knowledge, and that he gave her. One is willing to pay for beauty.

Tomorrow his flute would speak to her again. She would long for more than his trading expertise. . . .

He felt his man part thrusting against his breechclout. He had not had a woman other than Antelope for a long time and his manhood was hungry.

Clouds drifted, covering the stars; it grew darker. Chomoc bent low, following the path. He thought of Antelope and Skyfeather waiting for him and hurried his steps; soon he would be home.

Home was where they were. Home was refuge, and comfort, and Antelope—whom he loved dearly, of course.

He remembered Tima-cha's smile and lingering glance, and felt a stirring again.

He did not see the dark figures looming ahead until they were upon him. They threw him facedown to the ground. He smelled dank earth; pebbles bit into his skin. The men bound his arms and legs and covered his head with a blanket. He struggled, cried out. The blanket was smothering him; he gasped for air and fought to free himself.

Was this what the Great Sun wanted—to dispose of him? He would not do it easily.

With all his strength, Chomoc twisted and yanked at the blanket, which was gripped by unseen warriors. Moons of foot travel had hardened and strengthened him; it took three of his assailants to lift him and carry him away, still thrashing.

Water. He smelled water. He was jostled and wet as they splashed into the river and heaved him into a canoe.

For a moment he lay there, struggling to free his arms and legs, trying to breathe through the blanket.

"Release me!" he shouted.

A lingering touch. A fragrance. Slowly, the blanket was removed—as if he were being undressed. There was a soft laugh in the darkness. A foreign voice spoke—in Caddoan, with an accent.

"I take you home to be one of my consorts."

The queen! How dare she!

"I refuse."

Soft laughter again.

Fury at being captured like a slave, thrown to the ground, and whisked away in a foreign canoe was eased by the tantalizing fragrance. Tima-cha reached close to touch his arm. Her fingers trailed down his arm to his stomach, lingered a moment, then sought his man part. Against his will, his manhood rose to her touch. She purred and withdrew her hand.

Chomoc was stabbed with sudden excitement. If this was what the foreign queen wanted, he was the one to supply it. Indeed yes. He smiled in the darkness and waited for her to touch him again.

The men who had attacked him joined the others in the lead canoe. Quietly, they slipped midstream and sped swiftly, silently, away.

"Where is Chomoc?"

The Great Sun stood in his dwelling and scowled down at the caddí, whose square face flushed under the copper headband. "What do you mean you could not find him?" The Great Sun waved an arm so that his many bracelets rattled. "He became a feather and Windwoman blew him away?" Sarcasm seared his voice. "My feared warriors and my *esteemed* caddí could not find one lone man in the dark, a foreigner unfamiliar with our trails? Perhaps I should order a woman or a child to do it. Yes?"

Striped Serpent, who had spent the morning with one of his brother's wives, gestured with authority. "Answer!"

The caddí cleared his throat and fumbled with his necklaces. "It is said . . ." He paused miserably. "Far Walker says he thinks he heard paddles on Long Man last night. Going upstream. She Who Remembers thinks Chomoc may have gone on a trading journey with the foreign queen. Or so it is said."

Striped Serpent snickered. The Great Sun stared down at the caddí for some time. "The queen has departed?"

"She and those who came with her."

"When?"

"During the night. It must have been just before we were to ambush him. If, indeed, he did go with her."

The Great Sun turned abruptly away. Tima-cha had gone! She had obtained all she wanted in trading agreements and was to spend this night with him alone. He had prepared for it. . . .

She was gone.

With his back turned, the Great Sun waved the caddí dismissal; with vastly relieved hous the caddí backed out the door.

The Great Sun paced the room. He paused at the altar and picked up a favorite ceremonial pipe; he ran his fingers over the smooth carving without seeing it.

The queen had taken Chomoc? When she could have spent a wondrous night with the Great Sun?

No. Of course not. Never. Something else had happened to him.

Had he left to return home?

No. He would not leave without his mate and child, and they were still in Yala.

Ah, yes. Chomoc was gone, no matter how.

She Who Remembers was alone now.

From the depths of the distant forest came a low, guttural howl. The voice of the jaguar.

▲ 10 ▼

"**M**ore," Many Bears said.

He thrust his bowl at Red Leaf with one hand and wiped his mouth with the back of the other. Red Leaf scooped up rabbit stew with a gourd dipper and emptied it into his bowl. He and the two boys, Bobcat and Ringtail, slurped loudly, holding the bowls to their mouths and scooping out the meat with a finger. Now and then they would toss a rabbit bone to Hoho, who snatched it midair, chomped, swallowed greedily, and waited for more.

Antelope, Red Leaf, and Poqua sat on their heels around the fire pit, waiting for the males to finish so they could eat what was left. It was early evening. The sky had faded from pink to purple and birds flocked noisily in the oaks and cottonwoods. Antelope listened to their raucous communication and wondered what they were saying.

Chomoc would know.

Antelope bit her lip. Where was Chomoc now? And with whom? She was alone here, she and Skyfeather, in this foreign, faraway place with no man to protect her, no man to hold her in the night. . . .

Last night she had dreamed of home. She saw Kwani, her

mother, teaching the young girls, heard her mother's voice.

"Men can protect us and make beautiful things, but only we hold the mystery of life within. Only we can give birth and make the tribe grow."

As she turned to look at Antelope, Kwani's face blurred, then dissipated into mist. The mist swirled and another face emerged—that of a malevolent old woman whose toothless mouth opened wide, shouting, "You don't belong here!"

Antelope had wakened, haunted, filled with foreboding. Now she sat in this foreign place with the only friends she had. Although she had been there but two moons, it seemed like forever. How much longer must she remain?

"More," Many Bears said again.

His unexpectedly high voice contrasted with the rest of him. Antelope watched him covertly; she was afraid of him. He was short, squat, with thick fingers and toes. Tattoos embellished muscular arms and legs and a barrel chest adorned with a necklace of bear claws. They reminded her of the Bone Pickers' fingernails. More bear claws dangled from copper earspools; the claws swung menacingly. Oiled black hair was coiled in a large bun on top and hung in a tail in back. Small eyes in a pudgy tattooed face darted at her as she looked at his necklace.

He patted the long, curving claws. "I am the best hunter," he said, grinning over his bowl. "I know the animal spirits, the *asgína* and the *talí*."

Bobcat and Ringtail squirmed excitedly. "Tell us, Father! Tell us again!"

Antelope was learning the language gradually and understood many of the words. His lingering glances made her uncomfortable and she looked away without reply.

"Tell us, Father!"

Many Bears scooped out the last bit of rabbit with his finger, belched, and settled himself comfortably.

"Very well. I will tell about animal spirits. When I kill a bear or deer or any animal, I am respectful. I ask forgiveness and I handle it properly. Then the animal gets a new life and can be killed again, maybe seven times, because the animal spirit did not die. Do you understand?"

"Yes!" Ringtail wriggled impatiently. "Tell the rest!"

Many Bears belched again. "Why don't you tell it, eh?"

Ringtail beamed. "I will tell it. Asgína is the spirit of the animal after the first time it is killed. Talí is the rest of its lives."

"That is right," Many Bears said. "You learn well. Remember that every animal has its own number of lives to live, and if it is killed before then, its body takes shape again from the blood drops. When all its lives are lived, the animal's body decays and its spirit goes to the Night Land. Do you know what happens if you are disrespectful to the animal's bones or bowels?"

"It is angry." Bobcat's crossed eyes were aglow as he displayed his knowledge.

"And it takes revenge," Ringtail added authoritatively. "It makes the hunter sick. His bones hurt. Maybe he dies, too."

Many Bears grunted with satisfaction. "You will be good hunters one day. Like me."

Smoke drifted with talk and laughter from neighboring dwellings as families sat around their fire pits. Antelope looked at the peaked roofs of the houses and their long extended doorways like arms outstretched, and she yearned again for her home in Cicuye, and for her life and her people there. When would she return? Uncertainty lay heavy on her heart.

Remembering her dream, she turned to Red Leaf.

"Who is that old woman who watches me and says I do not belong here?"

"What old woman?"

Poqua laughed. "She means Waikah. I've seen her watching Antelope. She doesn't like foreigners."

Many Bears scratched his stomach. "That old sow doesn't like anybody."

"She is respected," Red Leaf said, "and she is of the Cougar Clan, the same clan as One Who Watches. She does not have to like people for people to like her."

Poqua nodded. "True. But do not allow her withered spirit to concern you, Antelope. She is not as she used to be. Something has changed her kia, her inner being. She is wounded inside. Wounded people, like wounded bears—"

"Attack," Many Bears snorted with satisfaction.

He finished his bowl and left to join a game somewhere. The boys ran to play with Hoho and other boys and their dogs. Red Leaf filled the bowls again and handed one to Poqua and to Antelope, and slurped from one herself. She was a good cook; the stew was delicious, what was left of it. Antelope watched Red Leaf's tattooed finger scooping out the meat and poked her own finger into her bowl to scrape out the last bit.

Poqua laid her bowl aside and crossed her arms as she did when she was being firm about something. "I shall tell you," she said, looking at Antelope. "I have sung the ancestor songs with my singing stick. My ancestors speak to me."

Antelope and Red Leaf listened respectfully. Poqua, an esteemed grandmother, was highly regarded for her age and her singing stick revelations. She peered at Antelope from within the fine mesh of wrinkles surrounding her eyes, and continued.

"I have decided to adopt Antelope and Skyfeather into this family. My ancestors wish it. Many Bears will announce this at the Talking Place. You, Red Leaf, will take Antelope as sister and Skyfeather as niece in the clan ceremony. Then we shall have three days of feasting."

Antelope was speechless. She gazed at Poqua in astonishment.

There was a moment of stunned silence, then Red Leaf babbled at Poqua too rapidly for Antelope to follow. Poqua sat back on her heels and regarded Red Leaf calmly. Then she rose and came to stand by Antelope, who sat with bowed head.

Antelope swallowed a lump in her throat. She was not sure she wanted to be adopted; she had a family of her own back home.

Poqua placed one gnarled hand on Antelope's head. "I, Poqua, grandmother of the Beaver Clan, take Antelope, she who is She Who Remembers, as my daughter, and her child, Skyfeather, as my granddaughter. This my ancestors desire and I desire also. She Who Remembers will be adopted as a member by all those of the Beaver Clan, and will teach our young girls the women's secrets. Skyfeather will grow up as one of us."

Poqua removed one of her fine necklaces of conch shell beads and draped it over Antelope's head.

"For you, Daughter."

Antelope swallowed mixed feelings. It was a beautiful necklace and she was touched that Poqua wanted to adopt her and Skyfeather, but all she really wanted was to go home to her own family. But until Chomoc returned to take her . . .

Maybe he will not return.

Meanwhile, it was true that she should do what she was destined to do—teach as She Who Remembers.

If Skyfeather is Poqua's granddaughter, she will be protected.

She looked up at Poqua solemnly. "I am honored." Antelope was surprised to discover her eyes blurred with tears.

The Talking Place stood high on a terrace where the bank plunged steeply down to Long Man. The moon, sister of the sun, the Spirit Being, poured silvery light upon the people of Yala gathered there. Children of the sun and moon glittered in an ebony sky where pale clouds drifted one by one.

The villagers sat around a fire whose light flickered upon faces gazing at Antelope, who sat between Poqua and Red Leaf, holding Skyfeather in her arms. For some time, Many Bears had been speaking. He continued in his high voice.

"I have told you of Antelope's family: of her mother, She Who Remembers, who appointed Antelope as her successor, and of her brother, Acoya, City and Medicine Chief of Cicuye, who possesses the robe of the White Buffalo. I have told you of her mate, Chomoc, son of Kokopelli. . . ."

He paused, glancing briefly at Antelope, who sat with eyes averted, biting her lip. Many Bears' oratory was accompanied by florid gestures and posturing like those of a small boy showing off—both irritating and ridiculous. How could she live in the same house with this man? But she must. She made herself listen to him. She was acutely uncomfortable, surrounded by staring strangers with whom she must live until Chomoc returned.

If he returned.

She clenched both hands as Many Bears continued.

"Chomoc, as all know, has departed, leaving his mate and child in our keeping. Our esteemed elder, Poqua, and my esteemed mate, Red Leaf, have adopted Antelope, also known as She Who Remembers, and her daughter, Skyfeather, into our family." His small eyes darted at Antelope. "She Who Remembers is now my mate's sister."

There were murmurs. The sister of a man's mate was expected to perform wifely duties on the sleeping mat from time to time, especially if she lived in the same dwelling.

Antelope had not understood all he said and wanted to know. She turned to Poqua. "What is he saying?"

"I will tell you later. Listen now." She spoke to Many Bears. "Speak more slowly so my daughter will understand all that you say."

Many Bears paused in his posturing and cast her an annoyed glance.

"Very well," he said. "If it is your wish." He gestured grandly. "Now it is the pleasure of Many Bears, he of the claws"—he fingered his necklace—"he of renowned hunts, mate of Red Leaf, who is daughter of Honored Men and granddaughter of the matriarch of the Beaver Clan—" He paused and his high voice rose dramatically. "It is the pleasure of this hunter to announce that our fine citizens of Yala now include two new members, Antelope, also known as She Who Remembers, and her daughter, Skyfeather."

"No!" Old Waikah jumped up, waving a bony arm. "These foreigners cannot become citizens of Yala. I, Waikah, protest! Send them away!"

"They are members of my family," Poqua said firmly. "They are citizens now."

"No!" Waikah screeched. "They do not belong here! I demand that they leave!"

"Sit down, old one, and be silent!" Many Bears commanded.

"Yes!" the crowd cried. "Be silent!"

Waikah shrank inside her robe, pulled her shawl over her head, and hobbled into the shadows. But Antelope felt her fierce gaze like a thrown lance.

Why does she hate me? I must become a citizen for my child's protection, but that old one is an enemy.

Fear slithered up her spine.

Many Bears continued with ostentatious authority. "The initiation shall now take place. We are honored that the caddí, governor of our City of the Great Sun, has come to conduct the ceremony."

Many Bears gestured to the caddí, who was surrounded by three musicians and two warriors. With an ostentatious bow to the caddí, Many Bears sat down.

To the accompaniment of hissing rattles, the caddí rose. As Antelope looked at him in the firelight, he was a formidable figure in his jaguar cloak and ornate copper headband with fur and feathers in his coiled hair bun. He was short and broad-chested with arms and legs surprisingly thin for his thick body. Bracelets slid up his arm as he raised it in an imperious gesture. Again the rattles spoke.

Antelope shivered at the sound. She felt vulnerable and intimidated by this man and by Many Bears and the crowd of strangers, surrounding her in the shadows, whose faces she could see but dimly. One face she thought she recognized, that of the man who had found her in the river. She gazed through the haze of smoke. Was it he?

The rattles quieted, and the caddí's voice rose in a tone of accustomed authority. "Our esteemed shaman comes."

A flurry of drums and whistles announced the approach of the shaman. The crowd parted as he strode to the fire, his tall figure topped by the towering deer mask, his conch shell and copper ornaments agleam, and his feathered staff thrust upright.

For some time the shaman had been consulting with his power objects in a futile effort to determine how to obey the orders of the Great Sun to provide him with She Who Remembers as a mate, and at the same time persuade her to call the buffalo for him in secret. He had made another spirit quest to call the distant animals but with no success whatever. If Antelope became mate of the Great Sun, she would not call buffalo under any circumstances; that was his responsibility as shaman, one he must fulfill on pain of excruciating humiliation and lingering death.

He was desperate.

Now, as he stood in firelight at the Talking Place, surrounded by villagers, he knew he was expected to initiate She Who Remembers into the tribe. But once she was one of them, she would belong to the Great Sun. Hope of calling the buffalo would be lost forever.

He fingered the medicine pouch that held his crystal. Perhaps its strong powers would assist him in this emergency. But first, he must conduct the preliminaries.

Holding his staff aloft, the shaman faced each of the four directions, pausing at each one to chant the ancient words of the ritual. The firelight illumined his mask with its great horns and shadowed eyes and open mouth where mystic words emerged from between shell teeth. He towered above them, a supernatural divinity in the haze of smoke and firelight.

Antelope stared up at the shaman, and her stomach cramped. He seemed the embodiment of evil, yet it was he who communed with gods. When he finished chanting, he began to speak to the people, who listened respectfully, glancing at her now and again. The shaman's voice rose and fell with dramatic cadences.

She whispered to Poqua. "I can't understand him. Tell him—"

Poqua shook her head. "He is the shaman."

Again the shaman raised his long feathered staff and swept it in a circle. Then he pointed it at Antelope and spoke in a commanding voice.

"Antelope, come forward."

Antelope drew back. She whispered to Poqua, "I don't want to."

Poqua pushed her. "Go. You must. It is necessary."

Antelope was holding Skyfeather in her arms. She handed the baby to Poqua and rose. Her heart thudded and her knees felt wobbly, but she stood proudly and walked to face the shaman.

He waggled his staff and spoke sharply.

Antelope said, "I am learning your language, but I do not understand it well yet. Please speak more slowly."

Shadowed eyes in the mask towering above her glittered as he stood in silence for a moment. Then his large, thin hand gestured a command, and the caddí stepped forward.

The shaman and the caddí spoke briefly. The caddí turned to Antelope, who stood with as much dignity as she could muster when her knees shook.

The caddí turned to Antelope. "The shaman says that after you are accepted into the tribe, the Great Sun may decide to take you as mate. Provided, of course, that you prove worthy."

Antelope gasped. People looked at one another in disbelief, exclaiming. Tribal law demanded that the Great Sun's mates be commoners, but a Towa newcomer! It could not be.

Antelope remembered the tall, fiercely handsome man with the cold gaze. She knew instinctively he was dangerous. The thought of being his mate was frightening. Again, her stomach cramped. She said, "I am mate of Chomoc."

"No longer. Chomoc is with Tima-cha in the City of the North." He smiled meaningfully, glancing around.

Antelope's eyes flashed. How dare he! She took a deep breath. "Chomoc is a trader. He travels. He is *my* mate and he will return to me and to Skyfeather—bringing riches, as always."

She smiled briefly. "If he enjoys Tima-cha while he is there, who can blame him? But he is a trader first and always. And always he is mate of She Who Remembers. He will return."

She paused and looked at the villagers, who returned her gaze with rapt attention. This was a confrontation to be included in tribal history, retold endlessly at evening fires.

Antelope continued. "Also, I must remind the Great Sun that I am She Who Remembers. My duty to all of you is to teach young girls the women's secrets handed down from generation to generation by those who were She Who Remembers before me. Could I do this as mate of the Great Sun?" Again she paused, gazing from person to person. "Never."

She turned to look at them all, men and women and children gathered around the fire, staring at her as though they had not seen her before. As if in response, her body answered with the unmistakable moisture of a moon flow. As she felt it ooze between her thighs she stared up at the mask looming above her.

Deliverance!

She signed, "I depart for the women's hut now."

Amid murmurs the shaman jerked back and turned abruptly away from the contamination of her woman's bleeding. He spoke sharply to the caddí, who speared Antelope with a look.

"The shaman wants proof."

Antelope speared them with a look of her own. She reached under her garment, then thrust her hand at the shaman, who glanced at it and waved his staff before him to eradicate contamination.

Antelope turned away, chin high. The crowd parted to avoid her as she lifted Skyfeather from Poqua's arms and headed for the women's hut on the outskirts of the city. There she would stay until the flow ceased, avoiding all contact with men and with the life of the city. Red Leaf or Poqua would bring her food and water, and mosses or cedar bark, until the flow ceased and she was purified in the river, thus no longer a danger to the city or its people. It was the women's way.

The shaman swept his staff in a circle around him, chanting purifying incantations. Then he gazed through the mask holes at the villagers huddled close together, whispering among themselves, fearful that their shaman was contaminated. A bad omen!

The shaman announced loudly, "I go to fast and purify myself. I shall inform the Great Sun that the woman he desires as mate may be available at a later time." He flung his cloak about him and strode down the path followed by a hiss of rattles.

There was a babble of talk. Women who had spent many days in the hut nodded among themselves. It was something She Who Remembers had to do; it was unavoidable. But how exciting to have her flow begin while in the presence of the shaman and while *refusing the request of the Great Sun*! To refuse his request meant certain death. But She Who Remembers was not like other women. . . .

The excited babble continued. No one noticed Far Walker slip away into the shadows.

Back in his dwelling, the shaman smiled. Antelope's comment about being She Who Remembers had solved his problem. Why had he not thought of it before? If the Towa woman was officially She Who Remembers, she would not be a commoner; she could not become mate of the Great Sun. She had been adopted into the Beaver Clan whose esteemed matriarch, Poqua, accepted her as She Who Remembers. Therefore, an official ceremony establishing her as such must occur. The High Priest should officiate but he had not yet returned from his pilgrimage. Therefore, it was the shaman's responsibility.

But the Great Sun would be furious! Dangerously so.

I must be cautious. I shall wait for the High Priest.

Even the Great Sun must accept a decision of the High Priest. But what if the High Priest did not return in time?

Meanwhile, a way must be found to force the Towa woman to call the buffalo in secret.

He removed a crystal from its pouch. The crystal was as long as his little finger; the holding end was wrapped with fine threads of many colors. He pressed the sacred power source to his forehead and felt the crystal's cool touch.

"Show me the way," he prayed.

·11·

There was no moon. In murky darkness the narrow, twisting path to the women's hut was obscured among the trees. Antelope had been to the hut before, but she was not at all sure of the path. She held Skyfeather close and placed one foot carefully in front of the other, finding the trail.

For the first time in her life Antelope was glad of her moon flow. Remembering the shaman towering above her and his eyes glittering through the mask of the deer, remembering his demand that she be mate of the Great Sun, she felt her heart thudding. Her moon flow had saved her—but only for the moment.

If Chomoc were here, she would be safe.

Chomoc, come home. Please. I need you.

Is it true that he is with Tima-cha?

An owl suddenly swooped by with a rustle of wings. Startled, Antelope stumbled. She twisted her body to protect the baby and in so doing fell hard against a boulder.

A sharp pain.

Nothingness.

* * *

Something cool lay on her head and the side of her face. She reached to touch it.

"No!" A man's voice. Someone pushed her hand away.

Her head hurt. Her cheek hurt. She opened her eyes. By the light of a torch thrust in the earthen floor she saw she was in the women's hut. A man squatted beside her, his face in shadow.

A man in the women's hut! What was he doing here?

She tried to sit up but a hand gently pushed her down.

Antelope reached for Skyfeather. The baby was not there. She jerked upright; a soft pad fell away from her face.

She shrieked, "Where is Skyfeather? Where is my baby?"

The man bent close and she saw it was he who had discovered her bathing in the river. Deep, dark eyes commanded hers from under black brows. He said, "Your baby is with Red Leaf and Poqua. She is safe."

He lightly but firmly pushed her back down. He reapplied the pad to her cheek and readjusted the bandage around her head. His touch was calm and professional, but Antelope sensed power in him, both reassuring and intimidating. His face, with its prominent cheekbones, straight nose, and wide brow, bore tattoos on cheeks and chin in an oddly flattering design. Copper earspools glowed in the torchlight, and an ornate belt held an apronlike garment with a long point in front. His hair, in two coils on top with a long tail hanging behind, was entwined with strange objects. Medicinal? An engraved copper gorget lay on a broad chest.

Who was he?

He said, "You are hurt, but I will heal you. Here."

He lifted her head and held a bowl to her lips. It was a bitter brew, and she turned her face away. He pulled her to a sitting position with an arm around her, ignoring the pad, which fell from her face again.

"Drink," he said.

She looked up at him, at his warm gaze and unexpected half smile, and she drank it all.

"Who are you?"

"I am Far Walker. A Healer. I found you and your baby and brought you here." His voice was calm and deep.

Antelope looked into his eyes. This was a handsome man—disturbingly so. His arm remained around her, supporting her.

But in the women's hut? No male entered here, ever.

He seemed to read her mind. He said, "I do not fear the bleeding. I am a Healer and will purify myself. There is a matter I must discuss with you. But first—" He laid her down again and reapplied the pad to her sore, swollen cheek. "It will hurt for several days but it will heal. There is a cut. Here." He touched a bandaged place and she winced.

Antelope lay on the sleeping mat—the only furnishing the women's hut provided—and gazed up at this astonishing man who leaned close, his dark gaze enveloping her in a way that made her suddenly conscious of her womanhood.

He touched her hair. "Beautiful."

She felt herself reacting physically in a way she had not since Chomoc left. "Is that what you wished to tell me?"

He laughed, his teeth white in torchlight. "Yes. Often. But there is more."

He sat back on his heels and regarded her. "It is said that you have special powers."

"Yes. I am She Who Remembers. The Ancient Ones speak to me. I teach young girls what they must know—if I am allowed to do so here."

"It will be decided by the council. You are a Caller also?"

"I do not know. My mother called the deer. At Punamé. I have not tried."

"Ah." He looked away as if searching the shadows for words. "Soon the Green Corn moon will bring the time of New Fire. That is when the Great Sun may take a new mate, a commoner. And that is when the sacrifice takes place."

"What sacrifice?"

"A slave, usually. A child sometimes." He glanced at her, then looked away.

Antelope gasped in shocked disbelief. Human sacrifice! She had heard of it, of course, but surely that could not take place in a city such as this.

Far Walker continued, "Your child might be considered a suitable sacrifice."

Antelope jerked upright with a choked cry. Again, the pad fell away from her bruised cheek. *"No!"*

Again he gently pushed her down. "If you were mate of the Great Sun, your daughter would become a noble. No harm would befall her." He replaced the pad carefully.

She stared up at him, her head throbbing. "I want to go home. Take me home."

He shook his head. "I cannot. But there is another way. If you have powers, you are not a commoner. Demonstrate your powers after a spirit quest, and I will suggest that you receive honored status. Your child will become an honored one, also. Both of you will be commoners no longer. Unless"—he gave her a glance—"unless you wish to be mate of the Great Sun."

"No! I am mate of Chomoc."

"What if he does not return?"

"He will return."

"Perhaps. Perhaps not. My mate has gone and may not return. . . ." He rose abruptly. "I go now. I will come again to treat your wounds. But one more thing I must tell you. Jaguars have been seen downriver. Do not leave this hut in darkness."

He took the torch and slipped out the door, closing it behind him.

Antelope glanced around nervously. Coals from a small fire Far Walker had built to make the brew cast a faint light upon the walls and ceiling. The room was empty but for sleeping mats, a frayed basket of moss, and a shriveled strip of deerskin with leather thongs that someone had discarded. Antelope stuffed a handful of moss on the deerskin and tied it around her waist, wishing she had her own moon-flow strap. Wishing another woman were there with her. Wishing she were not alone . . .

She wished Far Walker were still there.

How strange he was, with those tattoos, and his apronlike garment, and the things he wore in his hair! But she did not fear him. To the contrary. Remembering how he had held her, how he had looked at her, remembering the timbre of his voice, the strength of his arm, she wanted him. She wanted him.

Too long she had been a woman alone.

The coals faded and darkness swallowed her. A wind rose, snuffling around the hut, nudging the door.

Is it really the wind?

Her head hurt more, and she had lost the pad for her sore cheek. She fumbled for it in the darkness, found it, and pressed it gently to the swelling. It smelled of an ointment.

Is that the wind outside?

Cold fear seeped into her.

Would jaguars smell her blood?

Antelope held the scallop shell of her necklace with both hands and pressed it hard against her breast. With all her being she strained to reach the Ancient Ones.

There was no response.

When she had been a child, sometimes she could see what was happening far away. Could she do it now?

"Mother, come to me!" she cried, her voice trembling.

Nothing.

"Chomoc!" she moaned. There was no reply, no glimpse of him.

For a long time Antelope lay in the darkness, clasping the shell. Fear squatted like a vulture on her chest.

Have I lost my powers?

·12·

The Great Sun regarded his royal family assembled in a circle in his dwelling. They faced the altar and the Great Sun himself, who stood before them gazing sternly over their heads. However, he was acutely aware of each of them—his sister, Manimani; his arrogant younger brother, Striped Serpent; his two mates; and his beloved young son, Patu. Patu, who would never become the Great Sun because the rank was inherited through women. A tragedy.

The Great Sun pushed the thought from his mind. He had assembled his family to make an announcement, but the words refused to come. He glanced at his mates: plump Kala, who had given him Patu, and small, pale Lipoe. Clan law decreed that all Great Suns marry commoners and his mates looked the part. Ordinary.

I tire of them both. It is another I desire. I shall tell them now.

But he hesitated. Great Suns did not take foreign women as mates. He would be the first.

Striped Serpent gestured with a rattle of bracelets. His small eyes peered sharply from under a copper headband from which bright feathers dangled. "Why are we here, my brother? Speak!"

The Great Sun scowled. His brother was a burr in the moccasin. He cleared his throat. "My ambassador in the City of the North sends word that Chomoc, son of Kokopelli and mate of She Who Remembers, is now mate of Tima-cha, the queen. She Who Remembers has a mate no longer."

Kala and Lipoe glanced at one another.

"Send her away!" Striped Serpent said. "Her child's eyes are blue—"

"She may be a witch," Manimani said with the authority of the Great Sun's sister. "Suitable for sacrifice."

"Exactly," the Great Sun said. This was the opening he needed. He continued, "The child of She Who Remembers will be a suitable gift to the gods at the Green Corn ceremony and will bring our city good fortune, which, as you all know, is needed. Our stores dwindle. It is important to protect the sacrifice meanwhile. Therefore"—he paused, but only a moment—"I have decided to take Antelope, called She Who Remembers, as mate so that her child will be protected in my household."

There was a babble of shocked astonishment.

"She is a foreigner, a Towa," Manimani said, her voice trembling with outrage. "It is forbidden."

"Of course. So the shaman will initiate her into the tribe. As a commoner."

Again Kala and Lipoe exchanged glances. Lipoe said, "I have no child. Give the baby to me and I will care well for her."

"No. A child needs its mother," the Great Sun said.

"But I will be—"

Striped Serpent interrupted. "The beautiful Towa woman has no one now to share her sleeping mat. A pity, I would say. My brother is being charitable."

Manimani snorted. "You judge others by yourself. Our brother speaks wisely. She Who Remembers is alone now, living with Red Leaf and Many Bears. We know something of Many Bears, do we not?"

"We do," the Great Sun said with a surprised and pleased glance at his sister. "She Who Remembers and her child will not be safe there."

"True," Manimani said. "Therefore, I agree that the child be given to Lipoe and the foreign woman be sent home. Horned Toad and a few warriors will take her. No harm will come to her, and her clan will be grateful for our protection and generosity."

"They will not be grateful for the loss of the child," the Great

Sun said sharply. "Remember that their City and Medicine Chief, Acoya, is brother of She Who Remembers. He possesses the robe of the White Buffalo. The Towa of Cicuye have powers we shall do well to respect. No, the Towa woman will remain here. The sacrifice will be protected."

Striped Serpent rattled his bracelets again. "What happens after the sacrifice is made? The child will be dead. As you say, the Towa will not be grateful for the loss." He snickered.

"They won't have to know," Manimani said.

"Of course they will know. The mother—"

The Great Sun spoke. "Enough! I have decided. You may go now." He was not sure he could maintain his composure any longer. He was the Great Sun; whatever he desired was his. He desired this woman; he would have her. He flung his feather cape aside, strode into his sleeping room, and yanked down the buffalo hide curtain in the doorway. How dare they question him! If they were not Suns, members of his family, they would be executed. He visualized Striped Serpent decapitated and tumbling down the steps of the mound leaving a bloody wake, and was gratified.

Manimani and Striped Serpent strode angrily through the extended doorway, talking. Kala and Lipoe huddled close together. In sharing their mate, they had become sisters.

"What will happen?" Lipoe whispered nervously. "Will he— discard us?"

"No. We will find a way to get rid of her."

"And I may have the child?"

"Yes."

They looked into each other's eyes and clung together, trembling.

More days passed and Chomoc did not come.

When Antelope left the women's hut, Far Walker brought healing ointments to the home of Red Leaf and applied them to Antelope's wounds. In doing so, he was the calm professional; there was no hint of the man he had been in the women's hut. Secretly she wished for that man again.

Each day Antelope listened for Chomoc's flute. Each night she lay in smoky darkness with only Skyfeather at her side. She struggled to ignore a persistent inner voice.

Chomoc has deserted us.

Then why had he not taken his trading goods? Most still remained in Red Leaf's dwelling, stacked neatly against a wall. His pack was gone because he had it with him for trading when he went to the plaza. Could he have left the valuables in Red Leaf's dwelling for her and for Skyfeather to sustain them after he had gone? A balm for his conscience?

Gone with the foreign queen.

It was nearly dawn and she had not slept. She turned fitfully on her mat. She felt as if something inside her was broken, as if her spirit oozed away like water from a cracked jar.

She must heal herself.

She clasped her necklace, pressing the scallop shell pendant to her with both hands. She pressed the shell hard to her bare breast, desperately seeking her powers.

There was no response.

Have I lost my powers?

She felt herself trembling and tried to control it. Without her powers she could not be She Who Remembers. She would be but an empty pot, broken.

Because I left my home, my heritage, and the dwelling place of my gods; because I have stayed long in this foreign land with fearsome customs and strange gods, have I become unworthy of the trust of the Ancient Ones? Have they abandoned me?

Again she trembled.

Am I now unworthy of the necklace?

Sobs welled up but she swallowed them down; she did not want to waken the sleepers below.

Again she clasped the necklace, pleading. There was no response.

I am abandoned. First by Chomoc, now by the Ancient Ones. Even Kwani no longer comes to me. . . .

She was bereft. Alone, but for Skyfeather.

What have I done to my daughter? If I am no longer She Who Remembers, how will I teach her?

Again, she swallowed sobs. But she could not swallow despair.

I must pray. But I cannot do so here. I must find a holy place.

In the room below all was still but for Poqua's feeble snores. Dear Poqua, who had befriended and comforted her and prompted Red Leaf to make her welcome. Many Bears was away on a hunting trip with the dog Hoho; Red Leaf and the boys slept.

Antelope tucked Skyfeather into the cradleboard and lifted the baby to her back. Quietly, quietly, Antelope climbed down the ladder and slipped out the door into the darkness of pre-dawn.

My spirit needs a high place, a place of solitude.

An ancient mound, long unused, rose on the outskirts of the city. No one would be around at this hour. That was where she would go—if she could find her way.

The path shone palely in starlight. Antelope followed its twists and turns through the sleeping village. Dark windows stared like shadowed eyes; doorways gaped open. Dogs barked at her passing; one ran at her, snarling, but did not attack as she moved quietly away. Her heart thudded. Damp heat enveloped her like a wet blanket. Mosquitoes swarmed, and the baby whimpered.

"Don't cry. I will protect you."

Antelope removed Skyfeather from the cradleboard and tucked the wiggling little body inside the garment close to her breast. She cradled the baby with both arms.

"There, little one. Mosquitoes can't reach you now."

The path left the river and turned toward the ceremonial center where gods and holy men dwelt. As she made her way among the trees, Antelope felt that the trees watched, listened, murmured about her. Tree spirits talked to one another, she knew. What were they saying?

"I greet you," she said politely, remembering her Towa manners. Leaves from a trailing branch touched her, as if in acknowledgment.

The path left the trees and entered the ceremonial center. Antelope stood gazing. The sky paled; soon Sunfather would fling his golden mantle across the horizon.

The great mounds soared in awesome majesty, looming against the wakening sky—the mound where the Great Sun dwelt, and, beyond it, the massive burial mound for holy men. Nearby, a wisp of smoke curled from the sacred mound of the Temple of Eternal Fire; Antelope knew a priest kept watch over the flame there.

This was a holy place. Foreign and strange, but gods dwelt here.

An ancient mound lay hunched across the plaza. That was where she would go. Antelope walked swiftly, feeling the eyes of the unseen upon her. At the base of the mound she stopped and gazed up at the flat top, empty of temple now.

"I seek permission to enter your presence."

She stood very still, every sense alert to response. She reached out and touched the grassy flank, pressing her hand upon it. The grass, damp with dew, seemed to stir against her palm. Antelope felt an awareness, a communication.

She was welcome here.

Holding Skyfeather to her closely, Antelope climbed the old steps, which had crumbled here and there over the centuries. In predawn light the steps were hard to see, and once she stumbled and nearly fell. But at last she reached the top.

For a time she stood gazing over the plaza and through the trees to the river beyond, the river that had taken Chomoc away. Loneliness overwhelmed her, and grief, and anger.

Chomoc deserted us.

As if sensing her distress, Skyfeather began to cry. Antelope lifted her from under the garment and held her in outstretched arms toward the river.

"See Long Man who took your father away."

Skyfeather stopped crying. She looked at her mother and the blue eyes in her solemn little face seemed to understand. Suddenly she smiled—a bewitching, toothless smile.

Antelope hugged her, and felt comforted somehow.

On this high place away from the river, the mosquitoes were fewer. Antelope tucked Skyfeather back into the cradleboard and set it down beside her. Again she stood, gazing across the river and to the mountains beyond.

Mountains were the abode of gods. Could her spirit fly to them like a bird to its distant nest and be healed?

No. These were foreign gods, unknown. She closed her eyes, visualizing the beautiful mountains of home. She *needed* her home; her brother, Acoya; and her gods, especially now. She felt the touch of the scallop shell upon her breast and thought of Kwani—who possessed four beads from the necklace so they might be together when apart.

"Come to me, Mother."

All was still. A raven swooped low, circling, and soared away.

Was it Kwani?

"Come to me!" Antelope cried. "Help me. My spirit dies."

Silence. The raven did not return.

My powers are gone. I am She Who Remembers no more!

With a cry of despair, Antelope crumpled upon the ground. Sobs wrenched themselves from deep within, shaking her like a predator.

Chomoc left me, my mother ignores me, and the Ancient Ones refuse me. I am nothing.

Gradually, she became aware of Earthmother's touch.

"Help me, Earthmother!"

Antelope stretched out, pressing all of herself upon Earthmother's grassy breast. She was welcome here. Comforted. Her sobs ceased, and she lay there until the stars began to fade.

Skyfeather had drifted off to sleep. Antelope turned on her back to gaze up at the great sky dome. The Seven Sisters stood in a different place than at home, but there they were, eternal.

Eternal. Like the Ancient Ones—who would be there always. Would they come to her again?

A morning breeze swept from the river, bringing a cool caress. A raven rode the breeze, circling.

Was it Kwani?

The raven called, and called again, then flew away.

Antelope watched the bird disappear. As she gazed after it, awareness rose in her, and her heart filled. Had Kwani sent the raven to reassure her?

Am I She Who Remembers still?

Antelope pressed the shell of her necklace hard to her breast. With closed eyes she visualized Kwani's face.

She saw it! Close and dear, her mother's blue eyes gazing into hers.

The vision wavered, seemed to blend with many faces.

"Mother!" Antelope cried.

A voice, like many voices blending, spoke.

"You are one of us, you are She Who Remembers. Be strong."

Antelope felt a wild surge of joy. She had not lost her powers!

She spoke to the Ancient Ones. "I am alone in a foreign land. Abandoned . . ."

Voices of all who had been She Who Remembers became a single one, soft and insistent.

"We are not of one clan, one people. We are of all womankind and must endure much. It is struggle that strengthens and makes

us aware, that tempers the spirit and opens the mind's eye. You are She Who Remembers, a Chosen One, a Teacher. Assume your rightful place."

"I will. Oh, I will."

"You have another duty. Our people are in danger. Terrible beings from the Sunrise Sea will come one day—to kill, enslave, steal, rape, destroy. Warn our people and their children, and their children's children. . . ."

The vision faded and the voice was gone. Antelope opened her eyes. Sunfather unfurled his golden mantle. The sky blazed in glory, and suddenly Antelope's spirit blazed with it. She flung her arms wide. "I am She Who Remembers, now and always. A Chosen One. I will return home and warn my people."

Yes!

And she would teach again!

She lifted Skyfeather in her arms and climbed down the mound, visualizing the young girls gathered around her. There was much she could give those eager ones!

Without warning, the old, malevolent face thrust itself into her mind again, and black eyes under shaggy white brows flashed with hatred. The toothless mouth opened. Antelope covered her ears with both hands so she would not hear what she knew Waikah was going to say.

I am She Who Remembers. I belong wherever I am.

Far Walker watched her go. He pressed his fists to his chest but could not quench the burning. Almost he wished the jaguar had come or that the shaman had sent a furtive stalker to snatch her for the Great Sun so that he might rescue her again.

He had followed her out of sight, watching. He knew she sought to heal herself, to cease her grieving. That was why he had forced himself to be impersonal when he treated her wounds, to give her time. One day she would come to him.

How radiant she was as she descended the old mound! How did she know to choose it? As a boy he had learned of its healing powers and had sought them often since. It was an ancient holy place, welcoming children at play, holding its healing potency deep within itself, and bestowing it on few—those who came with a searching heart.

▲ 13 ▼

It was the moon of late summer. Antelope sat under the old oak tree with Red Leaf and Poqua, grinding corn and preparing other foods for the winter. It was a fine day with singing birds and the rustle of squirrels and chipmunks among the trees and bushes, but Antelope's heart was grieving.

Chomoc has left me for another woman.

An aching, burning humiliation.

She thought of him and the years of their childhood. They had loved one another. What happened?

Tima-cha seduced him. The beautiful foreign queen with her long, beautiful legs . . .

Antelope swallowed her tears. She must make herself forget. But how?

She looked about under the tall old oak. This would be a nice place to teach. Teaching would ease her heart. She was waiting for permission to begin.

"When may I start teaching?" she asked Poqua, visualizing a group of eager young girls seated under the tree.

"When the High Priest returns to consecrate you in the temple."

"When will that be?"

Poqua shrugged. "Who knows?"

She bent to her work, and Antelope followed, listening to the sounds of a busy town.

The village of Yala, one of a number surrounding the ceremonial center, lay cupped in a small bend of the river. On this late-summer morning women tended their gardens, covertly compared their corn and beans and squash and pumpkins with those of their neighbors, and made it a point to display their choicest samples in loaded baskets placed casually near a path.

Preparation for winter was already under way. Much had to be done: drying squash, drying persimmons into cakes, crushing nutmeats to extract oils, drying berries to be stored away, and drying grasshoppers to be pounded and used in stews. Maize was parboiled, roasted, and pounded with bean ashes. Tubers and chestnuts dried in the sun for the long, cold months ahead. Meat and fish were smoked, then packed with bear oil, or coon or possum oil, and covered with buffalo tallow.

It was a busy time, and Antelope welcomed the work; it made her feel almost as if she belonged, especially since she was coming to understand the language better. Skyfeather lay beside her in the cradleboard. The baby's bright blue eyes seemed to drink in everything around her, and she made happy little noises. It was pleasantly cool, with a breeze from Long Man and homey sounds from the village: talk and laughter, shouts of children, yapping dogs, whistles, flutes, and the intriguing sound of copper being hammered into tools and ornaments. Antelope had never seen copper before and there was much of it here—a rich-colored substance from Earthmother's domain, highly prized and made into sacred objects and ornaments.

From the distant plaza came shouts of men playing chunkey. Antelope had watched them rolling a small stone disk while two men ran after it and threw long poles. The man whose pole landed closest to where the disk stopped won that round. It was an exciting, noisy game with bystanders cheering their favorite players. Today, Many Bears was with them—to Antelope's relief. Something about him, the way his opaque black eyes crawled over her, the way he found excuses to be close and touch her in passing, made her increasingly uneasy.

But now he was gone for a while and it was pleasant here. She leaned forward and back, pressing the mano stone on the metate. Red Leaf used a mano stone and metate also, but Poqua preferred the hollow stump method, pounding corn with a pole. Her withered old arms heaved the pole up and down upon the corn in the stump with surprising force. Sometimes she would sing a tune, her thin, high voice keeping time with the thump of the pole.

For a time they worked in silence. Antelope's thoughts returned to Chomoc. Perhaps he would come back. She swallowed again; she would not give up hope. But if he did not return, maybe old Horned Toad would take her and Skyfeather back to Cicuye, her home high on the ridge.

Far Walker strode into her mind—with his hypnotic dark glance, his healing touch, and the sound of his voice. Perhaps, might he care for her a little? She *needed* to be loved. . . .

"They saw it again," Red Leaf said abruptly.

"Saw what?" Antelope asked, jolted from her thoughts.

"The Spotted One. They say it may be a witch in jaguar's form." She shook her head. "I fear for Many Bears when he goes into the forest. It is said the jaguar eats men."

"Not men. Dogs," Poqua said, leaning on her pole to rest. "People from across the river say three of their dogs are gone. One was found partly eaten." She gestured. "Jaguar tracks." She sat down and reached for her singing stick. "I will ask my stick where the jaguar hides."

"The stick cannot tell you, old one," Red Leaf said impatiently. "But perhaps your song will keep the jaguar away."

Poqua propped the notched stick between her knees and rubbed it up and down with the flat stick as she rocked to and fro, keeping time.

Antelope listened to the wavering voice and wanted to sing with her, but she did not know the words. Besides, this was a song to the jaguar spirit, and it was not proper to intrude in spiritual matters.

Suddenly, Poqua stopped singing and stared up the path. Antelope turned, and her heart jerked. A group of warriors marched toward them, led by the caddí in his jaguar robe. The robe swung as he walked, seeming to make the jaguar come alive.

Red Leaf gasped. "Say nothing," she whispered to Antelope. "I will speak."

The caddí and the warriors marched directly to Antelope. He pointed at her without speaking and gestured to the warriors. Two stepped forward and grabbed Antelope by each arm.

Red Leaf rose and faced the caddí, eye to eye. Her round face was flushed and her voice withering.

"What right have you to come here, bringing warriors, confronting my sister? I remind you I am of noble lineage. Antelope has been adopted into my family. You have no right here. Leave her alone and go away. Now!"

The caddí, unaccustomed to defiance, was taken aback, but only momentarily.

"I come at the request of the shaman. He wishes to speak with the Towa woman."

"Then let the shaman come here!"

The caddí ignored Red Leaf and gestured again. The warriors yanked Antelope down the path, nearly lifting her from her feet as she struggled.

Antelope's heart thudded hard against her ribs. *Why are they doing this? What does the shaman want of me?*

Poqua watched them go. Skyfeather began to cry and Poqua spoke softly. "Do not be afraid, Granddaughter. I am here." Again she sang with her notched stick. She looked at Red Leaf.

"All is not well. Something bad is going to happen."

Red Leaf nodded, frowning. "I know."

The shaman's lodge was smoky and dim; it smelled of potions and mysterious substances. Antelope sat on the mat where the warriors had dumped her before leaving her alone with the shaman. He towered above her, the eyes in his shadowed face lancing hers. Tattoos around his mouth squirmed as he spoke.

"You are fortunate," he said in his rasping voice. His long arm gestured. "I give you an opportunity to save your child."

Antelope swallowed. "Save her from what?"

"Sacrifice. At the Green Corn ceremony next moon."

"No!" Antelope cried. She jumped up to face him, but he still towered over her, a nightmare figure. "I am She Who Remembers, a Chosen One, a Teacher. My child will be also, one day." She tried to keep her voice strong, but it wobbled. "You cannot sacrifice a Chosen One."

He smiled briefly, baring white teeth in his dark face.

"Ah, but I can. I am the shaman and may choose whom I wish to honor the gods." One eyelid drooped, then opened again malevolently.

Antelope choked. Strength drained from her and she almost fell. "Why am I here?"

"I told you. To give you an opportunity to save your child."

She peered up at him, trying to see the place behind his eyes where his spirit dwelt, trying to know him. She would do anything, anything to save Skyfeather, and he knew it.

She made her voice steady. "What must I do?"

He shrugged. "Very little, as a matter of fact. Call the buffalo."

"But—"

"And tell no one. No one. If you tell, if anyone finds out, or if the buffalo do not come, your child will die." His long, thin hand slashed the air. "Do you understand?"

She had never called the buffalo, but she had said that she could. What should she say now? Her voice wobbled again. "It has been a long time since I called the buffalo. Maybe I have forgotten how."

He shrugged again. "Your misfortune, perhaps. And that of your child." Tattoos squirmed once more. "However, it is said that your mother, Kwani, called the buffalo. You will do so also." He leaned over her, his face close so that she smelled his fetid breath. "Call the buffalo. In the forest, on the fourth day of the new moon. Tell no one. If you tell or if you fail, the child will die." Again his hand slashed the air. "Leave me now."

Antelope stumbled outside. In brilliant sunlight, it seemed as if in leaving the shaman's lodge she had entered this world from the world below, the Land of the Dead. A hard lump burned in her stomach; the odor of his breath enveloped her still.

I have never called the buffalo. Why, why did I lie?

The buffalo were far away. Could she pretend to call them? No one would know the difference right away. In the meantime, maybe Chomoc would return and take her and Skyfeather home.

I will go into the forest. Because I must. On the fourth day of the new moon.

The forest. Where the jaguar dwelt.

Antelope made her way back, ignoring questions and curious glances from villagers who had seen the warriors dragging her along the path. Many Bears and the two boys, Bobcat and Ringtail, were at home when she returned, and stared as she approached.

Many Bears grinned. "Our sister returns."

"My sister, not yours," Red Leaf said tartly.

Antelope glanced at Red Leaf with gratitude. Her defiant confrontation with the warriors had been totally unexpected. For the first time Antelope felt that perhaps she did indeed have a sister.

"What happened?" Ringtail demanded in his shrill, four-year-old voice. "Did they hurt you?"

"No."

"What *happened*?"

"Antelope will tell us when she is ready to do so," Poqua said. "Do not question more."

Bobcat looked up at her with his strange, cross-eyed gaze. His small face was concerned and curious. "When will you tell?"

"When she is ready," Red Leaf said. She gestured to Sky-feather, who squirmed restlessly in her cradleboard. "Your daughter is hungry."

Antelope lifted Skyfeather from the cradleboard and carried her inside the dwelling that was now their only home. She climbed the ladder to the smoky loft and lay down with the baby at her breast. The small mouth tugged at her, drinking.

Can she taste my fear? Does she drink my desperation?

A scraping sound. Someone climbed the ladder.

She smelled him before she saw him.

Quickly, she laid Skyfeather aside and rose, crouching under the low roof. The grinning face of Many Bears was followed by the rest of him as he reached to climb into the loft.

Antelope pushed a foot at him. "Go away!"

He grabbed her foot and pulled her toward him. He was no longer grinning. "It is my right."

Antelope struggled to remove her foot from his grasp, and he teetered on the ladder. For a moment, he released his grip on her foot to steady himself. With all her strength, she thrust both feet at him, and he fell back with a hoarse cry, the ladder upon him.

Red Leaf stood there looking down at Many Bears with an inscrutable expression. "Remember, it is not your right unless she agrees. She does not agree."

Many Bears pushed the ladder aside and rose, his face

ablaze with angry humiliation. He shot Antelope a savage glance.

"We shall see about that."

He stomped out.

The Great Sun gazed down at the shaman, who sat before him on the floor. They had been talking for some time and the Great Sun was growing increasingly irritated.

"What do you mean, I should wait?" the Great Sun said, fingering the ornately engraved conch-shell gorget upon his chest. Its smooth, luxurious surface usually calmed him, but now it did not. "Her moon flow has ceased by now. It has been established that she is a citizen. A commoner."

The shaman's narrow face remained expressionless, but his rasping voice was tense. "My crystal informs me the omens are ominous. Red Leaf has adopted Antelope as her sister. Red Leaf's lineage—"

"I know her lineage. Minor." He thrust his face close to the shaman's. "Must I remind you of who I am? I want the Towa woman and her child. Arrange it."

A spark flashed in the shaman's eyes, and disappeared. "Very well, sacred one. It will be after the fourth day of the new moon. Omens will be more favorable then."

Perhaps the High Priest will return by then.

"Do it!"

The Great Sun waved dismissal, and the shaman backed out the doorway, bowing low.

The new moon rose in graceful choreography among the stars. People were careful not to look at Moonwoman through the branches and leaves of a tree because they knew it would make them ill—all but Antelope. She considered this to be another strange, foreign belief and gazed often at Moonwoman as she climbed from branch to branch in the oak tree.

Four days. Then I must go into the forest.

If only her mother were here. But Kwani had gone to the House of the Sun to die; now she was with ancestors in Sipapu where there was neither sickness nor pain.

Antelope touched the scallop shell of her necklace. Perhaps her mother would help her with the power of the four beads she had taken with her to Sipapu.

Maybe Kwani can keep the jaguar away.

▲14▼

Predawn; clouds concealed the new moon. Antelope woke as if someone had spoken.

This is the fourth day.

Foreboding poked cold fingers in her chest. All was quiet in the room below; outside, the city slept. The baby stirred, waking.

"I can't take you with me, Skyfeather. Too dangerous," Antelope whispered.

She nursed the baby and tucked her into the cradleboard to go back to sleep. Skyfeather was growing more active, and if she was not in the cradleboard she might tumble from the loft.

Antelope felt the touch of the scallop shell on her breast. It gave her comfort.

"Protect me!" she prayed.

Carefully and quietly she climbed down the ladder, taking pains not to waken the sleepers, especially Many Bears, who lay sprawled near the door, Hoho close beside him. The dog raised his head and regarded her suspiciously.

He is ugly as his master, Antelope thought, and tiptoed toward the door. Many Bears still slept, his naked chest rising and falling, his breath escaping with snorts and snuffles through slack lips.

Step by step, Antelope neared the open door. She was almost there when Hoho rose to follow her. In so doing, he nudged Many Bears, who jerked awake.

Frantically, Antelope ran the few remaining steps to the door and was nearly there when Many Bears grabbed her ankle. She stumbled but grasped the doorway beam, clung fiercely to it, and yanked herself loose from Many Bears' grip. Panting, she ran down the path, her heart thumping, glancing behind to see if he followed.

Many Bears did not follow. He lay in the darkness, smiling. Her fear of him was titillating. Where was she going? It did not matter; he would follow later. He, the greatest hunter in Yala, could track her easily. He would track her, find her, have her. Have her at last. It was his right.

It was nearly dawn when he slipped out the door.

Antelope breathed more easily. Many Bears had not followed. She made her way through the sleeping city and the surrounding farmlands, hesitating now and then in the darkness, trying to remember the way to the forest.

I must find a special place.

She was grateful for the darkness. No one must know if she was successful in calling the buffalo. The shaman insisted upon that. Otherwise, Skyfeather—

No. She could not even think of what he threatened. Somehow, some way, she would call the buffalo, and tell no one but the shaman. Her scalp prickled and she glanced about to be sure she was alone.

Is the jaguar near?

It was not an easy journey. The path twisted and turned, and sometimes Antelope did not know which way to go when the path forked. But at last the deep forest enveloped her as Sunfather's mantle lay across the horizon.

Trees surrounded her with a living presence. Clouds had disappeared and treetops caught the morning light, filtering it through silvery leaves to the forest floor. It was very still but for the whisper of Windwoman in the branches. Her cool breath touched Antelope.

Was it a warning?

Antelope glanced quickly around her. She was alone. Totally.

Maybe the jaguar hunts only at night.

Never had she felt so alone.

She clasped her necklace. "Help me! Please!"

Silence. But slowly her heart calmed and her senses became acutely alert. She smelled the grasses, the sweet scent of the trees, and Earthmother's pungent aroma. She pulled a blade of grass and chewed it to make its life a part of her. It tasted like summer's good-bye.

She listened with every pore. Windwoman sighed and a blue jay flew away, scolding. Distant birds answered. A rabbit darted across the path and disappeared under a bush.

With a pang, Antelope remembered her childhood and the pet rabbit that Chomoc had obtained for her.

She would not think of Chomoc now. She must find a place to call the buffalo. To try . . .

For Skyfeather's sake.

Resolutely, she rose and wandered among the murmuring trees. She must find a high place to be closer to the gods. It was some time before a hill appeared, topped by a tall hickory tree. It stood in solitary grandeur with outflung arms like a grandfather at prayer.

That is the place.

She scrambled up the rocky, grassy hill to the top and stood gazing around her. The forest, infinitely serene, spread in every direction. Antelope breathed deeply, inhaling the silence and the peace. Overhead, a hawk soared, riding the updraft. Somewhere, a bird called. What was it saying?

She sat under the hickory tree and leaned against the rough bark.

I must empty myself of myself to become someone else, a Caller.

She closed her eyes and opened her senses to the environment—the beauty, the silence, the peace.

Many Bears paused, squatted, and inspected the leafy ground. Yes, there it was, an indentation where a moccasin had pressed. He grunted in satisfaction and rose. She was nearby.

He felt a hunter's thrill.

*   *   *

Antelope sat under the tree for a long time, until all fear and grieving were gone and she was part of the grassy earth where she sat, part of the tree and the bushes and even the rocks and pebbles and the insects scurrying among them.

"Come to me!" Antelope pleaded to the Ancient Ones. "Make me a Caller!"

There was no response.

Or was there? Something seemed to tell her she must remove her garments and stand unadorned before the gods.

She rose and removed everything but the necklace. She stood under the sheltering grandfather tree and gazed up into its leafy heart. It welcomed her.

She wrapped both arms around the rugged trunk. She pressed her body hard against it so that the bark became part of her own skin. She pressed her cheek against the bark, too, and closed her eyes, concentrating.

"Tree, give me your strength. Help me call the buffalo. Help me!"

Many Bears stood gazing up at the hill where Antelope stood, magnificently, incitingly naked—hugging a tree! What mysterious rite was under way? He experienced a moment of unease; it was whispered that She Who Remembers knew witchcraft. He would be cautious. With infinite skill he circled the hill, watching, listening, waiting for his hunter's instinct to tell him it was time to attack.

Shadows lengthened, and still Antelope stood with the tree, her necklace pressed against her. Gradually, there came a soft drumming sound like a heartbeat. Was it her own or that of the tree?

With all her strength, Antelope strained to reach the Ancient Ones, those who had been She Who Remembers before her. The necklace was pressed hard against her by the tree.

"Mother, come to me! Help me become a Caller." Antelope's voice trembled. "Help me save Skyfeather . . . who has your blue eyes. . . ." She could say no more; tears dampened the hickory's rough bark.

The drumming sound grew louder.

Slowly, Antelope felt herself dissolving, as if in a dream. She saw a distant place, a great, rolling plain. She was there. She gazed into far distance. A vast herd of brown bodies spread over the hills.

Buffalo!

Suddenly, Antelope found herself chanting.

> *You of the great plains, you of the hills,*
> *Come to me!*
> *You of the wilderness, the forest, the mountains,*
> *Come!*

The chanting continued, sometimes in words Antelope did not know that she knew. Gradually, it seemed that she grew closer to the herd, close enough to see the great, shaggy bodies with heads hanging low, grazing while their short tails twitched. Dark clouds billowed and lightning flashed in the distance.

"Come!" Antelope called to them. "Come this way."

One big old female raised her head. To Antelope it seemed that the buffalo looked directly at her.

"Come!" Antelope cried.

Slowly, the big beast ambled forward. Others followed, a group at a time. Soon the entire herd was on the move.

Slowly, the vision evaporated and Antelope found herself dripping with perspiration, still clinging to the tree.

"I did it!" she cried. "I did it!"

She felt infused with a majestic, magical power she had not known before. Awed and exultant, she hugged the tree with both arms. She wanted to pray her thanks; a prayer was more potent when sung. She raised her head to gaze into leafy branches, and song soared from her throat.

> *Thank you, Ancient Ones;*
> *Thank you, Tree;*
> *Thank you, Kwani, my mother;*
> *I called the buffalo!*

She released the tree and saw the marks of the bark on her skin. The tree's essence was in her. A benediction.

She felt embraced, renewed.

How long she had stood there she did not know, but now her legs felt weak. She sat down, leaned against the trunk, and reached for her moccasins.

It was nearly dark.

Many Bears grinned in triumph. She was calling the buffalo! What news he would have to tell at evening fires! Ha! An urgency in his loins told him the time for attack was near. It had not been as easy to track her as he had expected, especially while keeping a lookout for the jaguar, but his legendary expertise as hunter rewarded him. There she was.

Naked.

In the fading light her body glowed like the inner surface of a conch shell. Beautiful breasts, swollen with milk, were tipped with bits of sunset sky and enhanced by the necklace she wore with the scallop shell nestled between them.

He swallowed.

The jaguar settled herself comfortably on a branch of an oak that hung over a game path. Her orange-tan body with beautiful spots of black blended with the tree, the leaves, and the shadows. From head to ringed tail she was four feet long, low-slung, thick-set, and powerful. Battle scars marked an aging coat.

It had been three days since her last meal and she was hungry.

Soon it would be dark. She waited.

Many Bears watched as Antelope rose to dress. Her long, dark hair flowed over her shoulders and stirred in the breeze. From full breasts her waist curved to a graceful swell of hips. There, a small dark triangle marked her woman part, hidden.

But hidden from him no more. He had his rights! How dare she refuse him! All day he had tracked her. Now his man part, hot and thrusting, demanded that he take what was his.

He scrambled up the hill, relishing her astonished shock and fear and the way she clutched her robe to her, great dark eyes ablaze.

"Go away!" she shouted.

He had expected her to turn and run, but she stood there, eyes flashing dark fire, a fire that fueled the blaze within him. He yanked off his breechclout and tossed it aside. Show her his famed manhood! Now she would know what it meant to refuse Many Bears his rights! He would take her and take her and then leave her naked and alone on the ground. He laughed with anticipation.

With both arms he grabbed her to him, crushing her soft breasts against his chest, pressing his man part hard against her. Let her feel his power outside as well as inside!

She fought savagely, scratching, clawing. She was strong for a woman, a worthy prize. His excitement grew. He threw her down and fell upon her. With wide-open mouth he tasted her all over, licked her, sucked savagely at her breasts, probed deeply with rough fingers into the silky realm of her womanhood. She struggled beneath him, a wild creature demanding escape. When she thrust fingers at his eyes, he held her hands down with both his own. He grunted and bit her lips and neck and wallowed his face upon her breasts, growling with pleasure.

How exciting she was! If he did not enter her soon he would lose his seed in a futile burst.

Suddenly, Antelope stopped struggling and just lay there.

With a snort of satisfaction, Many Bears raised himself, preparing to thrust. But without warning, Antelope opened her mouth wide with a supernatural sound that was not a scream, not a cry, but a terrifying, ululating combination of both—a voice from the world of spirits.

As if in response, from nearby came a deep, hoarse howl.

The voice of the jaguar!

Panic turned Many Bears' man part into a withered stalk. He jerked upright and stared into black night for a glimpse of glowing eyes.

Instantly, Antelope wriggled free, jumped up, and slipped away in the darkness.

Let her go. She is evil, like the jaguar. That cry! And the jaguar answered. . . .

Where is it? Where?

Poqua said something bad would happen.

Clammy with fear, Many Bears pulled on his breechclout and rose. Why had he not brought weapons with him into the forest? All he had was his hunting knife. Antelope had bewitched him, that was why. She was a witch, obviously. That cry!

Now she was gone. Maybe the jaguar would get her.

Swiftly and as silently as he could, Many Bears climbed

down the hill and headed for home. The jaguar was nowhere to be seen; it must have found Antelope. Good!

Once home, he would waste no time in informing everyone that Antelope had tried to call the buffalo using her witch's powers. She was a danger to all. If the jaguar got her, good riddance.

How dare that Towa woman, that foreigner, refuse Many Bears his rights!

The jaguar lifted her nose to the breeze. Something drew near. A human. Approaching at a distance, away from the game trail.

The jaguar leaped to the ground in one fluid motion. Crouching in the grasses, she inched forward, stalking. Occasionally she paused, motionless but for a twitching at the end of her ringed tail. No sound, no motion of brush marked her passing. Darkness hid her; only her golden eyes reflected starlight.

She heard him ahead. He smelled rank but she was old and hungry and he would be an easy meal.

With a mighty leap she was upon his back, raking him with razor-sharp claws. He fell facedown to the ground, screaming. His scream became a gurgle as she plunged long fangs into the jugular, clamped his neck in her powerful jaws, and shook him like a rabbit until bones snapped.

Then she feasted.

▲15▼

Antelope crouched among bushes that rustled and scratched her as she moved. Shock and outrage gripped her. She tried to control her trembling but could not. She felt icy cold. Numb.

Where was Many Bears? Was he creeping in the shadows to find her?

As quietly as she could, Antelope rose above the bushes. In the pale light of the new moon she saw him scrambling down the mountain, looking this way and that.

For her? For the jaguar?

He disappeared. Many Bears was gone. Now she was alone in the night forest, she and the jaguar. She told herself she should not fear the Spotted One. Had not her protectors, the Ancient Ones, sent the predator to frighten Many Bears away? But her trembling continued.

She was fouled. All over. The odor of Many Bears, the slime of his mouth, even the dirt from under his fingernails lingered in her pores. She yanked up handfuls of grass to scrub herself; she wanted to shed her skin like a serpent. It was useless; Many Bears still fouled her.

Suddenly, a scream pierced the air like a burning arrow, soaring, falling.

Antelope jerked upright. Wasn't that the voice of Many Bears?

The jaguar!

Antelope stood motionless, listening. Were the Ancient Ones exacting vengeance? She thrilled at the thought. His mouth, his tongue, his cruel fingers, the weight of his foul body . . .

She gagged and convulsed in vomiting. Spent, she crouched, listening.

Silence hung like mist in the shadows. For a long time Antelope strained to hear something in that silence, but no bird, no night creature made a sound. Where was the jaguar now? Unease slithered up her spine.

The jaguar had echoed her cry. Where had that cry come from? Never before had she made such a sound. Was it like that of Kwani, her mother, who had saved herself from the Medicine Chief who willed her to die? Or the sound Acoya, her brother, had made when he rescued Chomoc from the Pawnee? Perhaps it was a gift from her ancestors, a power in the blood.

Her trembling eased. Should she try to find her way back?

No. Not in darkness. She returned to the tree and found her clothes. She wished urgently to bathe before dressing. She remembered passing a stream nearby but she hesitated to try to find it now, in the misty shadows. She would wait until morning. Tomorrow she would cleanse herself and return to the shaman triumphant. She had called the buffalo and told no one.

Skyfeather was safe.

She spread her robe on the ground under the grandfather hickory tree and lay upon it. How could she sleep with the smell of Many Bears and the residue of his slime embedded in her skin? She wanted to roll in the dirt and leaves like an infuriated animal. Small night sounds, rustlings and whispers, rode the breeze.

Many Bears . . . the jaguar . . . her fouled, hurting body . . .

She escaped, at last, into sleep.

She dreamed of home. She stood on the highest point of the mesilla, the flat-topped ridge, where Kwani had initiated her as She Who Remembers. The city of Cicuye spread before her, tier upon tier, the beautiful city her father and brother had created. Beyond, the sacred mountain glowed in morning light. Far below, the river curled into the distance, trees and garden plots marking its path.

Home.

Kwani stood beside her, graceful as always in her white robe knotted on her right shoulder, leaving the other bare. Her deep blue gaze enveloped Antelope in loving embrace.

"You must be strong, my daughter. Remember we who are Chosen Ones must endure much."

"I shall remember."

"Danger awaits you. Danger—"

A sound woke Antelope. At first she did not know what it was. It came again—a voice calling her name.

Antelope jumped up. She knew that voice!

"I am here!"

A light appeared. It was Far Walker carrying a torch, holding it high. The flame zigzagged as he climbed the hill.

"I am here!" she called again, then realized she was naked. She grabbed her robe and flung it about her as Far Walker hurried toward her. Relief warmed her all over. Far Walker!

He held the torch high, gazing at her. "Are you all right?"

For a moment she could not speak. She looked at him, strong and assured, handsome and caring, and for no reason she knew she began to cry. She stood there, holding her soiled robe to her with both hands, and sobbed.

"Ah." He thrust the torch into the ground and tried to take her in his arms, but she pulled away. "You are hurt?"

"No. Yes." She wanted to lean against his hard chest, but she could not endure any man's embrace, not now.

"Come. Sit down."

He eased her to the ground and sat beside her, his arm around her. "Tell me."

In the flickering light of the torch, his face, close to hers, shone with concern. Her sobbing eased. He tucked her head against his shoulder and she was comforted for a moment. But there was something about being so close to a man . . . after Many Bears. . . . She withdrew her head and inched away from him.

He pretended not to notice. "Tell me," he said again.

"Many Bears. He followed me. He—" She shuddered. "He—"

"He is gone. The jaguar got him. Down there. I saw. . . ."

"Oh." She visualized the jaguar attacking Many Bears, and felt a savage joy. "My protectors sent the Spotted One to save me from Many Bears."

"Did Many Bears hurt you?"

"Yes. All over. The jaguar answered my cry—"

She stopped. How could she explain the sound that had exploded from some mysterious depth? "I gave a cry and the jaguar answered. Close. Many Bears was frightened, and I slipped away and ran into the bushes over there." She pointed. "Then he left."

"And the jaguar followed." He paused. "The hunter became the hunted." He glanced away. "Not much of him remains."

Antelope swallowed. It was a horrible death and she should be sorry. Instead, she was *glad.* But what would become of Red Leaf and Poqua and the boys? They would need her. "I must go back."

"In the morning." He took the torch and held it overhead. "I have my medicine pack. Let me see your wounds."

She clutched her garment to her. "There are no wounds, only scratches and bruises—"

"Let me see."

She could not reveal her soiled body. "No."

"I am a Healer, remember? I must see."

She sniffled like a child and wiped her nose with the back of her hand. "I want to bathe first." She had to cleanse herself of Many Bears before revealing herself to this man, this Healer. She had to become her real self again.

He gazed at her in silence for a long moment. He rose, thrust the torch back into the ground, removed his pack, and untied a capelike garment he wore knotted at both shoulders. He spread the garment on the ground and gestured for her to lie down.

"Sleep now. We shall both bathe in the morning."

Gratefully, Antelope lay down, covering herself with her robe. She thought for a moment he would lie beside her, but he tossed his pack nearby, used it as a pillow, and lay with the torch between them.

"Do not be afraid," he said. "The torch will keep animals away. Sleep well."

"I am not afraid." She lay in silence, gazing up into leafy branches tangled with stars. Finally, she said, "I am grateful to you, Far Walker."

He did not reply. Perhaps he slept.

*   *   *

Far Walker did not sleep. He lay awake, burning with long-ing. This woman he loved and ached for had endured the shock of a brutal attack; she must have time to recover before she could accept the lovemaking he yearned to offer. How long would it take for her to welcome him? How long?

No matter how long. He would wait.

What if Chomoc returns?

Far Walker lay restlessly on the forest floor. Questions churned in his mind. Why was Antelope here, alone in the forest, at night? Earlier that day he had found an excuse to visit Red Leaf's dwelling; there he learned of Antelope's disappearance. Red Leaf and Poqua did not know where or why she had gone, leaving Skyfeather behind in their care.

Many Bears was not there. Had he tracked Antelope? He prided himself on his hunting expertise, and bragged of female conquests.

Now he was dead. Tomorrow it must be known so that what remained of him could receive a proper burial. How would Red Leaf cope? And Poqua and the boys?

Will Antelope be blamed?

Far Walker sat up, hugging his knees. Newcomers, espe-cially those of other tribes, were suspect. If it became known that Many Bears had attacked Antelope, some would say she used her powers to summon the jaguar for revenge. The old accusa-tion of witchcraft would rise again, a demon spirit. Implacable.

They must not know.

He looked at Antelope asleep on her side with a hand under her cheek. His heart filled. If only she were his mate, he would protect her, love her always. Love her.

Why did she come to this hill? There is nothing here but a tree.

He lay back down and closed his eyes so he would not see Antelope so near. But he heard her breathing, soft and low.

Antelope woke to the sound of jays scolding a squirrel in the hickory tree. A brilliantly blue male and a drab female hopped from branch to branch after a squirrel who eluded them. He darted among the leaves, his bushy tail curved aloft, and re-garded the jays with contempt.

Antelope stirred and the jays flew away. It was a beautiful morning with sunlight filtering through the trees and white

clouds running with the wind. She sat up and looked for Far
Walker. He was gone but his pack was there, and the burned-
out torch; he would return.

Now she could bathe and try to become herself again.

As she wrapped her soiled robe around her, she saw the
scratches and bruised places on her body and felt again
the hands and mouth of Many Bears. . . . Ugh! She must find the
stream.

The soil was rocky, so she put on her moccasins and made
her way down the grassy hill. A deer bounded by, proud antlers
erect, white tail flashing. Going to the stream, perhaps. She followed as he disappeared among the trees.

She stood immobile, robe wrapped around her, and listened.

Birdsong. Rustles in the brush. Windwoman in the trees.
But no water sound.

Where had she seen the stream?

As she stood motionless, the deer returned, saw her, and
dashed away.

He must have gone to drink.

Antelope hurried ahead, watching for a flight of water birds.
There they were, swooping over the treetops! Eagerly, she followed a faint game path that led her to a wide, meandering
stream. Tiny fish darted in crystal water that reflected sky and
clouds and willows bending.

"Ah!"

Antelope removed her moccasins, tossed her robe aside, and
waded into the cold water. It felt wonderful. She sat down and
the water swirled to her shoulders. She took a handful of pebbly
sand and rubbed it over her scratches and bruises and all of her.
It hurt in places. Many Bears must be swept away, but no matter
how she scrubbed he was still there embedded in her skin like
an invisible crust, an oozing scab. She washed her hair and
scoured the inside of her mouth and reached to cleanse her
woman part where his coarse fingers had probed; she hurt there.

But the water felt good. She lay upon it, rocking with the
motion of the stream as it carried her gently beneath the willows
and cottonwoods for a little way. A fish nibbled at her toes, and
a turtle swam by, his snub-nosed head above the water, ignoring
her. She floated on, opening her wounded spirit to the cleansing
water.

As Antelope floated in the stream, gazing into trees and sky, she felt that perhaps the crack in her spirit, like a crack in a bowl, was being mended. Perhaps one day she would become whole again. In time.

She must return to Red Leaf and Poqua and the little boys. They needed her. Skyfeather needed her most right now; Antelope's breasts were tight with milk. She knew Red Leaf and Poqua would take good care of the baby, but they could not nurse her.

Where was Far Walker?

She stood and waded to the bank. The stream had carried her farther than she realized, and it was necessary to find her way back through brush and grasses to where her robe lay on the ground.

She rounded a bend, saw Far Walker bathing in the stream, and hid behind the trailing branches of a willow to watch.

He squatted in the water and used a fistful of fern or some other plant to scrub himself. He was lean and muscular. With body paint removed, his red-brown skin, wet and shining, glowed in the sun. He faced the opposite bank, and as he moved, the spider tattoo on his back seemed to come alive. What powerful deity did it command?

Far Walker flung himself full-length into the stream and swam with the current past the place where Antelope hid. He swept by, strong arms and legs at one with the water, male body agleam—a magical creature, a water spirit.

A Healer.

She needed healing. . . .

Her robe lay on the ground ahead, but it was soiled. How could she cover her clean body with a soiled garment?

Far Walker should be back soon. Meanwhile, should she wait, naked, for his return? Would that not seem more of an invitation than it was? What she wanted, needed, from him was not what Many Bears sought. She needed healing. Comforting.

A Healer prized cleanliness, and so did she. She would wash her robe in the stream. There would be a logical reason for her nakedness when he returned.

Glancing downstream to see if he was coming, she waded into the water, found a large, smooth rock protruding, and slapped the wet robe upon it. By rubbing it back and forth on the stone and rinsing the garment often, she made her robe clean.

Where was Far Walker?

The sun was high now and warmed her body, although the water was cold. She must return to the village. Skyfeather was sure to be hungry. She remembered how Chomoc liked to tease her nipples with his tongue and lick the drops of milk that oozed out. A wave of loneliness swept over her.

She wanted Chomoc to play his flute for her, warm her spirit as the sun warmed her body, to love her, ease her heart.

Chomoc, come back. I need you!

Far Walker did not return. On the opposite bank a skunk and three striped babies came to drink. Antelope watched them, amused. How could creatures so beautiful create such an odor when they chose to? A hawk swooped low, and the skunk hurried her babies into the bushes.

Downstream, a flock of crows made a commotion in a cottonwood tree. Something disturbed them. Could it be Far Walker?

She busied herself with washing the robe that needed no more washing, while straining to hear swimming sounds.

"Ho!"

Far Walker stood on the bank behind her. He wore his breechclout and carried twigs and leaves in both hands. His garment, upon which she had slept, lay on the ground.

"Come. I have the plants needed."

If her nakedness made an impression, he concealed it. Feeling—what? disappointment? relief?—Antelope wrung out her robe, carried it to the bank, and spread it to dry on a bush.

He gestured to his garment on the ground. "I am ready. Lie here."

She obeyed, feeling self-conscious. He built a small fire, removed a bowl from his pack, and filled it with water from the stream. He handed her an odd-tasting leaf to chew, then tossed small twigs and the rest of the leaves into the pot. He seemed intent on his work and gave Antelope hardly a glance.

When the contents of the bowl simmered, Far Walker inhaled the steam and began a chant in a strange language. He leaned over the pot, inhaled, and raised both arms overhead while his rich voice invoked the unseen. Finally, he removed the pot from the fire and set it aside to cool. He opened his pack, removed a small jar with a lid and a gourd rattle, and laid them on the ground beside Antelope. He squatted next to her and inspected her with a gaze not altogether impersonal.

How handsome he was! Antelope returned his gaze with mixed feelings. She did not want to be attracted to him or to any man, not anymore. She covered her face with an arm.

"Please get on with your healing. I must return to the village; my baby needs me."

"So I see." He touched a finger to a drop of milk oozing out, licked the milk from his finger, and nodded. "You have good milk. Your body spirits are in harmony."

Antelope peeked out from under her arm to watch as he opened the small jar and scooped out an ointment with his finger. He began to apply it gently to the bruises and scratches on her breasts and stomach. She flinched, but his touch was totally impersonal. The ointment felt good. He reached to part her thighs, but she removed the arm from her face and looked at him.

"Not there," she said sharply.

A glance said he understood; it was too soon after Many Bears. He reached for the pot and tested the temperature of the brew with his finger. Satisfied, he scooped out the leaves and twigs, discarded them, and handed the bowl of liquid to Antelope.

"Drink some of this."

She sat up. "Why?"

"Because I offer it."

"Why?"

He frowned. "If you wish to be healed, you do as I say. Drink."

She swallowed, made a face, and thrust the bowl at him.

"It tastes terrible. I don't need it. I feel fine now, and I want to return to the village." She rose, went to the bush where her garment was still damp, and put it on. She turned to face him defiantly. "I am ready to leave." She hoped he did not see how shaky her knees were.

He stood with the bowl in one hand and the gourd rattle in the other. Dark eyes commanded hers.

"Come here."

She hesitated, then came to stand before him.

He handed her the bowl. "Hold this."

She cupped the warm bowl in both hands as he dipped his fingers in the pot and flicked a bit of moisture upon her breasts and stomach, and then upon her forehead. The rattle clicked in rhythm while Far Walker chanted in a strange minor key.

Antelope had an odd sensation, a realization she was in the presence of something unknown, something powerful. She was not sure she liked it. She handed the bowl back.

"Here. Take it."

His black eyes warmed and he smiled suddenly. He accepted the bowl and drank the contents, tipping his head back so that his long hair, wet from the swim, hung loose down his back. As he drank, Antelope could see the swallowing-lump on his brown throat bob up and down. Anyone could swallow. What was it about Far Walker that gave him an aura of power?

He finished drinking and replaced the bowl and rattle and ointment jar in his pack. He faced her matter-of-factly. "We shall return to the village now."

He did not tell her what he had done. Why should she know that the brew they had drunk was a love potion?

·16·

Antelope and Far Walker were picking their way along a trail. It was nearly noon and Antelope's breasts were painful with milk. Antelope frowned in worry; Skyfeather must be starving.

Far Walker paused and gestured to a fallen tree. "Sit here a moment. There is something we must discuss."

"I cannot; Skyfeather needs me."

"A moment only. Sit."

Reluctantly, Antelope obeyed. She found this Healer to be a very persuasive man. He sat close; she moved away.

He gave her a level glance. "Tell me why you were in the forest."

"Why must you know?"

"There will be questions when the death of Many Bears is discovered."

Antelope looked away without reply.

He continued, "If it is known what Many Bears did, you may be blamed for his death."

She was shocked. "I? But—"

"Yes. Some will say you used your powers to summon the jaguar for revenge."

Antelope felt a pang of fear. What he said could be true. "The Ancient Ones protect me. Perhaps it was they who commanded the Spotted One."

He gazed at her in silence for a time. Finally, he asked again, "Why were you in the forest?"

He was persistent and it was none of his concern. She looked him in the eye. "A spirit quest."

"Ah." He watched a lizard scuttling over the leafy ground. "That is a good reply. You will say that when they ask. *But do not mention Many Bears.*"

She gestured to her bruises and scratches. "How do I explain these?"

"You do not." He flicked her a sardonic glance. "Maybe they will think it was I." He rose. "Come. Skyfeather waits."

Antelope followed him on the path. There was a hint of autumn in the air. The sky was brilliant, vibrant with hawks slicing the blue. Trees breathed their tree fragrance, whispering to one another. What secrets did they tell?

Antelope watched Far Walker's easy stride and the spider moving with the muscles on his broad back. What was the significance of a spider? How handsome he was! And kind. She had mixed feelings. She had wanted him once, before Many Bears. . . .

Could she ever want a man again?

Red Leaf sat in the shade of the oak tree and looked with satisfaction at the moccasins she was finishing for Many Bears. She had taken extra pains to make them handsome enough to do justice to his status as best hunter in Yala. She hummed as she threaded a bright bead on a bone needle. She pushed the needle through deerskin that he had brought her and that she had tanned and fashioned into moccasins. The beaded fringe was beautiful. She watched Poqua's gnarled fingers weaving a reed mat. Skyfeather slept fitfully beside them in her cradleboard.

Poqua said, "I still wonder where Antelope is. It worries me that she did not tell us where she was going."

"When she left it was too early in the morning."

Red Leaf did not mention that she had seen Many Bears grab Antelope's ankle; Poqua had slept through it and did not have to know. Poqua was too critical of Many Bears, who, after all, was a lusty man. Red Leaf appreciated lusty manhood—even though Many Bears had been lusting for Antelope, who was, unfortunately, a beautiful woman. Red Leaf was beginning to have second thoughts about the wisdom of Antelope's living with them now that Chomoc was gone. She would speak to the caddí about that.

Where was Antelope? Surely she would not have tried to return to Cicuye alone, leaving Skyfeather. All of her belongings and those in Chomoc's pack, which he had left behind, were still there.

Many Bears had departed at dawn without his hunting weapons. Where could he be? A thought nudged her. Could he have gone with Antelope somewhere? Had they planned to meet? Antelope had resisted his advances, but she had been long without a man. . . .

Red Leaf pricked her finger with the bone needle, and a drop of blood stained the soft deerskin. A bad omen. She licked off the red drop.

Skyfeather woke and began to cry, her small mouth stretched wide in distress. Poqua picked her up, crooning, and brought the baby to her withered old breast. Skyfeather sucked in ravenous frustration and screamed.

Poqua handed the baby to Red Leaf. "Take her to the midwife. Waikah will know who has milk to spare."

Red Leaf agreed reluctantly. Waikah was a gossip; now everyone would know that Antelope and Many Bears had disappeared without explanation. It was embarrassing. But Skyfeather must be fed. There were always nursing mothers in Yala, but some had more milk than others, and it was true that Waikah would know who could best feed a baby whose mother was away.

She took Skyfeather and was about to leave when Ringtail came running, followed by Bobcat and Hoho, who, as usual, barked for no reason except that he liked to bark.

"She is coming! Antelope is coming with Far Walker!" yelled Ringtail.

Red Leaf was surprised. Far Walker? What was he doing with Antelope? Where was Many Bears? She stood, waiting as they approached.

Antelope hurried to meet them. There was a look about her; she seemed changed somehow. Antelope reached for the screaming baby and held her close.

"I greet you, Poqua. I greet you, Red Leaf."

"Where have you been?"

Antelope did not reply but brought Skyfeather to her breast. Milk squirted as the hungry little mouth sucked greedily.

"Far Walker will tell you what happened," Antelope said and carried Skyfeather inside without a backward glance.

Red Leaf looked silently at Far Walker, who squatted beside her and Poqua. Apprehension jabbed her. Something was wrong.

He did not speak for some time, and then he said, "I was in the forest looking for medicinal plants and saw her footprints. And those of the jaguar."

He paused, not looking at them, and continued.

"She was on a spirit quest. It grew late, too late for her to return home in darkness . . . with the jaguar . . . so I found her and stayed beside her with a fire to keep the jaguar away."

Red Leaf clutched the moccasin in her hand. The bead fringe trembled. "Where is Many Bears? Did you see him?"

Silence. "Yes."

"Where?"

Far Walker looked at her, and Red Leaf saw the answer in his eyes.

Her voice cracked. "The jaguar!"

"Yes."

She screamed, a long, wavering cry. She rocked to and fro, clutching the moccasin to her breast. The cry became agonized, choking moans as tears streamed down.

Far Walker touched her shoulder. "We will bring him home for proper burial. His spirit will be safe and free."

Poqua bent over her singing stick and rocked back and forth, chanting a wail.

Ringtail and Bobcat stood by helplessly, staring at their mother and grandmother, not certain of what had happened.

"Where is he? When will Father come home?"

It was the fourth day after the burial of Many Bears. His spirit was safe now in Sipapu, and the time for discussing events leading to his death had come.

The house of the governor, the caddí, was crowded with dignitaries assembled for council. Present were head chiefs, Honored Men (including Far Walker), the *canahas* (esteemed elders), and citizens whose presence was requested, as well as Horned Toad. Also present were members of the Women's Council, including Red Leaf, Poqua, One Who Watches, and Waikah, the midwife. The shaman was in council with the Great Sun and would be summoned if necessary.

Antelope was not invited.

It was late afternoon; discussion had been going on for hours. The caddí was in charge. He stood before the altar of his too-crowded dwelling and looked at the people facing him. They sat in a semicircle, those of highest status at his right. Invited guests sat behind the semicircle near the door and spoke only when asked to. The others spoke in turn, beginning with the chiefs, while everyone else listened in respectful silence.

It had been determined, finally, that Many Bears and Antelope had been in the forest at the same time. The question now was why.

The caddí shifted uncomfortably; his bladder was full and painful but now was not the time to leave. He knew very well that Many Bears had been after Antelope; who could blame him? In fact, he, the renowned caddí, would have liked to have Antelope himself and had given the matter consideration. However, propriety and suitable procedures must be observed here.

He fidgeted with a knot on his robe and cleared his throat. "It is known that Many Bears was in the forest without his hunting weapons. If he was not hunting, why was he there? I ask the opinion of Badger Tail."

The wizened Hunting Chief sat with bowed head. He had spoken little thus far. Finally, he said with dignity, "Who can truly know the thoughts of others? Many Bears was the best hunter in Yala; his hunting methods were his alone. Perhaps he was seeking signs, observing, making hunting plans." He gazed up at the caddí. "He knew well the ways of the forest and those who dwell therein."

"Then he knew well the ways of the jaguar," the caddí said.

The War Chief nodded so that the beaded forelock hanging between his eyes bounced on his nose. "All hunters know the jaguar's ways. Perhaps Many Bears became careless."

Badger Tail flashed the War Chief a sharp glance. "He was courageous."

The caddí could ignore the demands of his bladder no longer. He said, "Let the pipe be passed while we consider the matter further." He reached for an intricately carved pipe on the altar and handed it to the youngest man present to light. "I go to relieve myself and to communicate with my kia. I shall return."

When he had gone, old Waikah said in her croaking voice, "We women know why Many Bears was there, do we not?"

Red Leaf said, "Yes, we know. He was planning a hunt. Unless—" She paused and glanced at the men passing the pipe.

Waikah interrupted with sarcasm, "Unless Antelope used her *famed* powers—"

Far Walker spoke quickly: "Antelope was on a spirit quest. She did not know Many Bears was there."

One Who Watches laughed and rattled the bracelet Chomoc had given her when she granted him and Antelope passage into the city. Black eyes glittered in her ageless, sensual face. "Who scratched and bit her? Was it you, Far Walker?"

The War Chief turned to give One Who Watches a withering stare. "Far Walker is a Healer, as we all know well. He does not inflict pain on anyone. Antelope's wounds are healing because of him."

Horned Toad removed the pipe from his lips and handed it to the man next to him. He had grown in social stature since he guided Chomoc and Antelope to Yala, and his new importance gratified him. He announced, "I have known Antelope since her birth. It is true that she has powers."

There was a stir. Far Walker prepared to speak again, but Horned Toad continued. "Powers were given to her by the Ancient Ones, all who were She Who Remembers before. They protect her. Also"—he paused for effect—"she is twins."

There were shocked murmurs. Twins were unnatural, as all knew.

The War Chief said, "It would be well for you to explain, Horned Toad."

The caddí returned and strode, amid muttering, to his place before the altar. He glanced about, sensing conflict and disorder. What had occurred while he was away? He gazed sternly at the people before him. "The discussion may continue."

Horned Toad spoke confidently. "I said that I have known Antelope since birth. She is twins."

The caddí was shocked. This was an important bit of information he had not known. He hoped he concealed his surprise. He said, "We wish to hear more."

Horned Toad beamed. "The Towa Medicine Chief discovered that Antelope's mother, Kwani, was going to have twins. Of course Kwani wanted one child only."

The women nodded. They well understood the stigma of an unnatural birth.

Horned Toad continued, "So the Medicine Chief said he would combine the twins into one. He formed a bracelet of black twine and tied it on her wrist. He made powerful medicine, and when Antelope was born she had two whorls of hair on her head instead of only one. Also"—again he paused, relishing the avid interest and attention—"the Pueblo mark of birth at the base of her spine was shaped like a tiny penis." He finished triumphantly, "She is twins, both male and female."

"She is evil!" Waikah croaked, shaking a bony finger. "She called the jaguar! She is responsible—"

"No," Far Walker said firmly. "The Ancient Ones protected her from the Spotted One. That is why the jaguar got Many Bears instead of Antelope—"

Red Leaf said loudly, "But for Antelope, Many Bears would be here. . . ." Her voice broke.

"She is evil! A witch!" Waikah shouted.

"No," Poqua said quietly.

Everyone turned to look at her. Her toothless mouth twisted with sorrow, and tears choked her voice as she continued, "My daughter is not evil. My daughter is not a witch. Have you forgotten she is She Who Remembers?" She shook her grizzled head at Waikah. "She was on a spirit quest. If the Spotted One took Many Bears instead of Antelope, it was not her fault. Many Bears was planning a hunt. It just happened they were in the forest at the same time—"

One Who Watches parted her full lips in a smile. "What spirit bit her breasts and scratched her body? Eh? If it was not Far Walker, who was it?"

There were embarrassed murmurings; men glanced at one another. The caddí was at a loss. He knew very well who had done it, but he was not about to say so. He knew better than to blame the Healer, who could put an evil spell on him for lying. What should he do? He could think of nothing and remained silent.

One Who Watches turned to look at Red Leaf. "I think we all know who did it." She licked her lips in a lingering gesture.

The caddí was astounded when Red Leaf rose and faced One Who Watches.

"It may be true that Many Bears found her. And maybe not." Red Leaf's voice trembled, but she held her head high. "Antelope is adopted into our family. She is my sister. As such, Many Bears had rights, rights that she refused to grant. What man here refuses to take what is his? Answer me that."

"Aye!" Waikah croaked triumphantly. "Many Bears found her, took her against her will, and she summoned the Spotted One for revenge. She is evil! She will destroy us all!"

"You lie, old one!" Far Walker shouted.

The caddí reached for his feathered staff; order must be restored. Sternly, he faced the babbling dignitaries and thumped his staff on the ground.

"I remind you we are in council. Let us consider what facts are known and make decisions based on wisdom."

The Great Sun stirred restlessly in the late-summer heat of his dwelling. His brother, the Spirit Being, had long since passed overhead, but the council in the house of the caddí was still in session. The Great Sun removed his crown of white swan feathers, laid it aside, wiped his tattooed brow with a ringed hand, and impatiently faced the shaman sitting on a mat beside him.

The Great Sun was eager to know the outcome of the session, but the shaman had come with something else on his mind. The shaman should be at the council, but here he was, seemingly in high spirits. His long, thin face glowed with animation, and the Great Sun noticed that he wore more necklaces than usual.

"I have done it!" the shaman said exuberantly. "I called the buffalo! Our runners and ambassadors send word that buffalo move this way. They come! A big herd!" His thin face flushed. "We shall have many robes, much meat, much pemmican! I have done it!" He gestured grandly, his long fingers slashing the air.

The Great Sun's dark brows met in a scowl. Buffalo were the last thing on his mind. The fourth day after the new moon had come and gone. Antelope should be here with him now instead of this shaman, babbling about buffalo; he should have called them long ago.

The Great Sun absently fingered the engraved conch-shell

gorget that hung on his tattooed chest. Where was Antelope? He visualized her lovely body beside him and felt the urgency of an erection. He rose and went to the door to gaze into the distance at the house of the caddí. What was happening there?

"I want a report on the council," the Great Sun said, with his broad back to the shaman. "And I want the Towa woman, Antelope, here with me this night." He turned and faced the shaman. His resonant voice vibrated with grim authority. "Do I make my wishes clear?"

The shaman's thin face was expressionless, his opaque eyes cold. One eyelid twitched and drooped. "You do, my lord."

The Great Sun gestured dismissal and the shaman bowed his way out. The Great Sun stood looking after him, his kia uneasy. Something was not right. What was the shaman hiding?

No matter. Antelope would be here soon. He would not allow himself to ponder the rumors that she possessed dangerous powers; he had powers of his own.

His secret was safe.

He summoned slaves to lay fresh sleeping skins on his bed and to gather flowers to envelop Antelope's beautiful nakedness with perfume.

▲17▼

The caddí wiped his brow and leaned on his staff to brace himself. He felt his years. It had been a long session, and the discussion had been heated. During all his many moons as governor, never before had the caddí encountered such a problem to be solved as that which he had faced this day, but at last a decision was about to be made.

He cleared his throat and thrust his feathered staff before him. Weary dignitaries and guests awaited his words. The crowded room was hot and reeked of sweat and body paint. Curious villagers were gathered outside, awaiting news; the sound of their voices drifted in with the buzz of insects. In the plaza, preparation for the Green Corn ceremony was under way with noisy construction and loud orders. Children shouted, dogs barked, babies cried, and somewhere a woman sang a lullaby. The caddí took a deep breath and began.

"It has been determined that Many Bears was killed because of the powers of Antelope, who may or may not have called upon her protecting spirits to summon the Spotted One. However, it is decided that inasmuch as she is responsible for his death indirectly only, she will not die in retaliation. That decision was made by all of you. Now her punishment must be determined. I

142

ask the War Chief to explain what punishments apply. Then a decision will be made as to which it shall be."

The caddí wiped his forehead again and sat down.

The War Chief had seen forty-two winters. He was not tall, but was broad and muscular with ornate tattoos on his face and body. Falcon eye markings embellished his own eyes. His black hair, in two buns on top of his head, was adorned with bright feathers; strings of animal teeth entwined a long hank of hair in back. His forelock, with two large turquoise beads, dangled between his eyes, and swung against his nose as he moved. His breechclout was pointed in front and back; each point held a handsome tassel of red deerskin. He was an impressive sight and he made it a point to take advantage of it. He rose to stand in the caddí's place.

"You know the rules," he began, his stern face solemn. "One who is responsible for the death of a member of our city or tribe must pay with his own life or by other means. In this case, the family of Many Bears may take Antelope as a slave for the rest of her lifetime. Or she may be ostracized and sent away to be refused access to any other city of our tribe. Or she may pay the family of Many Bears with objects of value enough to be acceptable to them. Or"—he shrugged—"Antelope may choose to give her spirit to Long Man in compensation for that of Many Bears." He crossed muscular arms in front of his chest and looked at Poqua and Red Leaf with a War Chief's authority. "Let us hear from Red Leaf's family. What is your decision?"

There was silence as Red Leaf and Poqua whispered together.

The caddí shifted uncomfortably. Of course he knew what Many Bears had done, and he could not bring himself to blame Antelope for using her powers—if, indeed, that was what she had done. But who was he to question the wisdom of these dignitaries? Justice must take its course.

Finally, Poqua rose and spoke, her voice quavering.

"It would not be wise for Antelope to live with us longer. We suggest that she and her child live elsewhere in Yala. We will accept payment of all the trading goods in Chomoc's pack that he left behind, and all that Antelope possesses except the robe she wears and her necklace. However—" Poqua paused wretchedly, glanced at Red Leaf, and continued. "However, we recommend that Antelope *not* be allowed to teach our girls as she has been planning to do. She will be She Who Remembers no more. That will be her greatest punishment. . . ." Her voice broke, and she sat down.

The caddí nodded. A wise decision. He rose to stand beside the War Chief and gazed at the murmuring crowd.

"Do you accept Poqua's recommendation?"

"No!" Waikah shouted. "If she stays in Yala, her evil stays with her! Give her to Long Man!"

Horned Toad shook his head. "I told you I have known Antelope since birth. She is headstrong and does foolish things, but she is not evil. She is twins, both man and woman. Her inner twin, her brother, may have summoned the jaguar, and she is being punished for it. It is my opinion that Antelope should not be punished at all, but the decision of this group must be accepted. I say let Poqua's recommendation be followed."

There were murmurs of assent.

One of the esteemed elders, a canaha, said, "We agree with Poqua's recommendation, but only if someone in Yala agrees to take Antelope and her child into their home." He looked over the group. "Who here is willing to do so?"

Stony silence was broken by a commotion at the door. The shaman entered and strode to stand with the caddí and the War Chief at the altar. His towering, bony frame in a shaman's mystical robe dominated the room. He did not wear a mask, but his face was painted in red and black with streaks of white, subtly ominous. He raised his right hand, palm out. A staring painted eye glowered from the palm.

He swept his hand from side to side so all might see.

"Behold the mighty eye of the Great Sun. He comes to look into your kia and know your heart. He wishes to learn what has transpired here."

The caddí bowed. "You shall know all."

Few paid attention as Far Walker quietly slipped out the door.

It was late afternoon when the shaman left the council and made his way toward the home of Red Leaf. Developments at the council elated him; it would be easy to fulfill the Great Sun's demands to give him Antelope. She would have to agree; nobody else had offered to take her. He made his way through the plaza where men were building temporary shelters for the New Fire ceremony next moon. They greeted him with two hous in honor of his rank, but they avoided him whenever they could, and that was gratifying. Fear was useful to a shaman.

The council had lasted most of the day and he knew the village buzzed with the news. Antelope was She Who Remembers no longer, and she and her child had no home. Nobody wanted them.

The shaman pondered. Were they afraid of Antelope? Probably. They had seen the mangled remains of Many Bears when he was brought home for burial. And Antelope was twins. Did the Great Sun know that?

I will give the Great Sun a complete report on the council meeting. She will wait outside while I tell him what happened, and then I will bring her to him.

It would be a job well done. The Great Sun would be impressed. Lately, it had seemed to the shaman that the ruler's regard for him had lessened. This was dangerous. The Great Sun could send the shaman's head bouncing down the steps of the mound and his body thumping after it.

I must be cautious.

When the shaman approached Red Leaf's dwelling, he thought at first that Antelope was not there because she was not outdoors, where most activities took place. But when Hoho erupted in a frenzy of barking, Antelope appeared in the doorway.

She did not greet him with hous; she was Towa. Ignorant. Rather, she stared in shocked surprise, then said politely, "I greet you."

The shaman stared back. He had forgotten how beautiful she was. No wonder poor Many Bears had been after her. No wonder the Great Sun burned with desire. She wore only a simple cotton robe tied at her right shoulder, leaving the other shoulder bare, but she glowed with an inner radiance that enhanced the loveliness of her face and the compelling allure of her body.

Her great, dark eyes met his. "Whom do you seek?"

The shaman extended the palm of his hand so that the Great Sun's eye confronted her. She glanced at it curiously, unimpressed.

He said, "The Great Sun's eye. He wishes to see you."

"Well, here I am." She seemed amused.

He was irritated. "I shall bring you to him. Come with me."

She shook her head. "I cannot. Skyfeather is sleeping and Poqua and Red Leaf are not here."

He glared down at her. "The Great Sun does not ask for Skyfeather. He asks for you. I shall take you to him."

The shaman reached out for her but she backed away. "I cannot leave my child."

"Indeed you can."

The shaman grabbed Antelope's arm, held it in a merciless grip, and dragged her after him. She fought to be free.

"Let go of me! Let go!"

Ringtail and Bobcat came running from where they had been playing at a neighbor's. Bobcat stared with his crossed eyes and flung his small self at the shaman's leg, where he clung. "Let her go!"

How dare he! The shaman shoved him aside.

Ringtail shouted, "Let go!" He reached to grab Antelope's arm, but the shaman kicked him. Ringtail clutched his stomach, doubled up, and fell to the ground.

Neighbors, gathered to watch, stared in silent fury. The shaman had ignored them, but now a growl came from the group, and they inched closer.

The shaman was unaccustomed to feeling threatened. He was, after all, the most powerful man in the city after the Great Sun and the High Priest, and it was he, the feared shaman, who did the threatening. A woman ran to Ringtail and knelt to hold the child while he moaned. She glanced up at the shaman with a look he would not forget.

Antelope jerked her arm free and faced the shaman. Her voice shook with contempt as she said, "I shall go to the Great Sun, and he shall know of his shaman's strength and great courage when attacked by two small boys defending a member of their family." She turned and strode up the path, head high, arms swinging.

A woman called after her, "I will care for Skyfeather until your return."

"I thank you," Antelope called back.

The shaman strode after Antelope and was relieved when the group did not follow but gathered around Ringtail. The shaman was furious, frustrated, and uneasy; his power to command was slipping. The Great Sun would not be pleased if the people of Yala lost respect for their shaman.

*   *   *

The Great Sun paced the room impatiently. He was ready. Slaves had carried him in his litter to his bathing place at Long Man where his kia as well as his body was refreshed, and his wives had rubbed his muscular body with sweet-smelling leaves and blossoms. They knew Antelope was coming. Whether they approved he did not know or care, and he had forbidden them to be present when Antelope arrived. Patu, his son of seven winters, was being instructed in military matters by the War Chief and would spend the night with warriors in their longhouse. So all was in order except for one thing, music. Women liked music, and as yet that was not provided. He would arrange for it at once.

He stepped outside to summon a slave, but stopped. Amid howls of greeting from bystanders, the shaman appeared with Antelope, and they began to climb the stairs of the mound.

Antelope was coming! He darted inside and looked around. All was ready: flowers, fruits, honey, corn cakes for nibbling. A feast would be provided later—much later. He sat in his chair, arranged his feathered cloak, assumed a regal air, and hoped his man part would be patient and not erupt too soon.

The shaman stood in the doorway, bowing low. "I request permission to enter."

"Where is Antelope?"

"Outside. You must know first what occurred in council, my lord."

The Great Sun flushed with impatience, but he had demanded to know, so he said, "Enter."

The shaman bowed again and bent to enter, his headdress scraping the top of the doorway. The Great Sun gestured him to a mat. The shaman sat, bent his long, tattooed legs in front of him, and rested both bony arms on his knees. He sat in silence, waiting for permission to speak.

Irritation creased the Great Sun's noble brow. His dislike for the shaman was increasing. He gazed over the shaman's head. "Speak."

The shaman rearranged his arms, adjusted his bracelets, and related what had happened in council. The Great Sun stared at him in shocked surprise.

"You say she is both man and woman?"

"So Horned Toad claims. She—"

"She has man parts?"

"I do not know. I have not seen—"

"Bring her to me."

Bowing low, the shaman backed out the door.

The Great Sun fumed. What kind of creature was she? He would soon know. Ah, yes.

A shadow darkened the doorway and Antelope entered. She did not bow, nor did she ask permission to speak. Instead, she stood there like a spirit being in her simple white garment and gazed at him steadily with great, dark eyes.

The Great Sun rose. "Come here."

She took a few steps, stopped a distance away, and stared at him with chilling intensity. Seeking his kia? How dare she!

A royal forefinger with its massive pearl-and-shell ring pointed to the seating mat. "Sit."

She gave him a regal glance. "I have something to tell you, and I wish to stand as I do so."

He was dumbfounded. Never had anyone, let alone a woman, spoken thus. She would die! But first . . .

He stepped forward and gripped the garment at her shoulder with his strong fist. Antelope staggered as he ripped off her robe and threw the torn garment to the floor. She wore no undergarment in the summer heat; she stood naked before him.

He caught his breath. She was more beautiful than he had dreamed. All woman, every lovely part. Excitement surged in him.

She backed away, eyes fearless. "Your shaman attacked two little boys who tried to save me. He kicked Ringtail in the stomach. The boy is four years old." Her voice was withering. "And now, the Great Sun, the all-powerful ruler, must attack me?"

That was too much. The Great Sun strode to the door to give the death signal to the guards outside. Then he stopped. Not yet; he would have her first. He picked her up, fighting and clawing, and carried her to his bed where blossoms lay. As he threw her down, she twisted and kicked him hard in the groin.

He doubled over in pain. She snatched her torn robe and ran outside. Holding the robe before her, she dashed down the steps while the guards on either side gawked in stunned admiration, surprise, and curiosity.

A guard snickered. "I wonder what happened in there?"

"What do you think?" another replied.

They glanced at each other. It would be a shame to decapi-
tate such a beautiful head and to hack such a ravishing body,
but if that was what the Great Sun desired, that was what would
be done.

They smiled.

·18·

$\mathbf{A}$ntelope ran wildly down the
stairs, her heart pounding. She clutched her robe to her with one
hand and tried to balance herself with the other as she flew down
the steps. At any moment she expected to hear the Great Sun's
shout to the guards, "Kill her!"

She ignored the sentinels on either side and the crowd
gathering below. She wanted only to run home to her baby and
her loft, and hide there. At last she reached the bottom and elbowed through the snickering, gawking mob reluctant to let
her pass.

"Here! Over here!" Far Walker's voice.

Antelope turned as he fought his way to her, grabbed her
arm, and yanked her through the crowd.

"Run! To the Temple of Eternal Fire. Hurry!"

"Why?" she panted, as he dragged her after him. To go to
the temple made no sense.

A shout arose from the Great Sun's mound and was followed
by shouts from the guards.

"That's why. Guards follow. Get to the temple, and you will
be safe. Forgiven forever. It is sanctuary."

His strong grip grew tighter and he ran faster, almost pulling her off her feet. Someone snatched the torn robe from her as the noisy crowd opened to let the Healer pass, then closed behind them. Shouting guards followed, but they could not shoot their arrows without hitting the people. Furious, they yelled for the crowd to disperse.

Now Far Walker and Antelope were nearly across the plaza, racing for the temple atop a great mound where a wisp of smoke rose to the Spirit Being. The crowd thinned and shouting guards grew closer. Arrows began to fly.

Antelope ran like a feral creature. She felt her lungs would burst and her heart leap from her throat. If arrows caught her, what would become of Skyfeather?

They had almost reached the mound when Antelope stumbled and fell. An arrow flew above her. Shouts grew closer.

Far Walker pulled her up. Perspiration glistened on his forehead and his face was tense with strain. "We are nearly there. You will be safe. Forgiven forever. Hurry!"

Antelope ran like a deer, hunted like a deer. The temple mound soared ahead. No guards were there. If she could make it up those steps . . .

Help me, Ancient Ones! Spare me from the arrows!

The steps were close now, wide and smooth. Arrows whizzed by, and guards called to one another in the chase. As Far Walker and Antelope reached the mound and leaped up the first steps, they were easy targets. An arrow streaked through Antelope's hair, pulling strands with it. Again, she stumbled and fell. Far Walker threw himself upon her; an arrow pierced his thigh.

Antelope lay facedown on the hard stone steps and felt the weight of Far Walker's body and his warm blood dripping upon her. She heard triumphant yells from the guards. She clutched her necklace.

Save Far Walker! Help me reach the temple!

Far Walker rose and pulled her upright. He waved her ahead. "Run! Don't wait for me. Run!"

Instinctively, Antelope zigzagged as she sped up the steps. Arrows sped close, and closer. Above, the Temple of Eternal Fire rose in splendor with its extended doorway reaching out, beckoning.

An arrow grazed her arm; another whistled by her cheek. Guards ran up the steps after her, shouting obscenities.

Antelope's breath came in wheezing gasps and her heart pounded against her ribs—a wild creature, frantic. Her strength faltered.

Help me!

Like storm water flooding a stream, strength surged into her. She darted up the last steps and flung herself through the doorway.

Safe!

At last.

It was dim inside and smelled of fire and smoke and sacrificial potions. She entered the sanctuary where a small fire burned, casting faint light upon a bent figure.

The ancient priest gazed in stunned disbelief as she staggered inside and collapsed, naked and beautiful, upon the hallowed floor.

Far Walker lay upon a mat in Peg Foot's dwelling and gazed up at the old medicine man who bent over him, examining his wound. Piercing dark eyes probed the wound as gnarled hands explored.

"You are fortunate. A flesh wound only."

Far Walker sat up, easing his sore leg. "Please attend to it, honored Teacher." How could he tell his mentor what he must? "I will obtain a robe for Antelope so she may leave the temple—"

"A robe? She has no robe? Why?"

"It was torn from her when she was with the Great Sun. Then someone snatched it as we ran to the temple."

"Ah." Peg Foot's wrinkled, leathery face was grave. "She refused the Great Sun, obviously." He shook his head. "She may have been redeemed by reaching the temple, but the Great Sun will not be denied revenge. He will seek a way." He pondered, rubbing his hand absently over the peg where his foot used to be. "We must seek help from Long Man."

"Yes, later." He would blurt it out now. "After Antelope gets her baby I must also find them a home. You are alone here. You need a woman to make your life easier and more comfortable—"

"Ha!" Peg Foot sat back on his one heel and the peg. "None of my wives made my life easier, and I had three." Sharp eyes peered into Far Walker's. "Something important happened in council, eh?"

"Yes."

"Tell me."

As Far Walker related all that had occurred, that Antelope was She Who Remembers no more and owned nothing but her necklace and the robe she wore, his thoughts were with her alone in the temple. Or was she alone?

"So you see," Far Walker said in conclusion, "she and Sky-feather need a home. You need a woman—"

"I do not. Why does she not live with you, especially since you—"

"I have a mate, as you know."

"But gone."

"She may return."

"I hear she is quite happy with Badger Tail." Peg Foot gazed with calm assurance at his favorite pupil. "What is your real reason for not asking her to live with you, eh?"

Far Walker felt his cheeks burn; this old Teacher was too wise. He stammered, "I made a potion."

A twinkle appeared in Peg Foot's eyes. "Ah. A love potion?"

"Yes."

"And you wait for her to come to you?"

Far Walker glanced away; the amusement in Peg Foot's eyes was disconcerting. "It was a good potion."

"Women wish to be wooed. Ask her."

Far Walker felt a surge of longing so powerful he tried to swallow it down. More than anything he wanted Antelope for mate, now and always. But after what happened with Many Bears, and then the Great Sun . . . he must be careful.

"I will think on it, honored Teacher."

Peg Foot nodded. "Ask Long Man."

Antelope lay trembling upon the floor of the temple. She was conscious of a shrouded figure nearby, but strain, anger, fear, and exhaustion enveloped her like a fog. For some time she lay there, feeling the hard floor against her bare body, feeling the sore place where an arrow had grazed her arm. Far Walker's blood was sticky on her back; he had taken the arrow meant for her.

Far Walker.

An emotion different from any Antelope had known before welled up in her. It was as if the Healer possessed a mysterious power that inexorably drew her to him. Never again could she give herself to a man. Yet she wanted him, needed him.

A soft voice spoke. "Who are you? Why are you here?"

Antelope looked up into dark eyes encased in a mesh of deep wrinkles. A hooded cloak covered most of the gray hair, but one thin braid swung forward as the figure bent over her and a gentle finger touched her back. "You are hurt?"

Antelope sat up. "Only a bit."

The priest peered at Antelope in silence. Finally, the soft voice spoke again. "Where is your robe?"

Antelope sat up and gazed into the ancient face shadowed by the hood and at the shriveled body seated before her. Something was . . . different.

Could it be? Was this priest a woman?

The old one smiled, revealing toothless gums. "I sense your confusion. I am Firekeeper, She Who Tends Red Man. Now tell me about the robe."

The quiet voice and calming presence enveloped Antelope like a balm. She looked into the shadowed eyes and saw compassion there, and wisdom.

Firekeeper smiled again. "Speak."

Suddenly, floodgates opened. Caddoan words, partly mastered, tumbled out in a torrent as Antelope related all that had happened from the time she left Cicuye with Chomoc and Horned Toad until the Spotted One took Many Bears. (Was it only three moons?) Antelope shook as she said, "I was *glad*!"

Firekeeper nodded. Her eyes were kind and her voice gentle. "Continue."

Antelope lived the events again as she told of the shaman's coming to take her to the Great Sun. Anger returned and grew as she related her story.

"The shaman, that tall, tall one, tried to drag me away, but my two little adopted brothers tried to save me. Bobcat has only two winters and Ringtail four—*little* boys. The shaman kicked Ringtail in the stomach"—Antelope's voice shook with outrage as she relived it—"and forced me to go through the village as a prisoner. Humiliating! Then he left me alone with the Great Sun up there on the mound."

Antelope visualized the arrogant and handsome ruler, magnificently arrayed, whose commanding eyes burned into her own.

"I saw—"

Antelope hesitated. What she had seen was a revelation. Should she tell?

Firekeeper sat silently, waiting. Her presence was comforting and reassuring. Helplessly, Antelope blurted the truth as if she were spewing out a poisonous substance.

"I looked behind his eyes to the place where his spirit dwells, and I *saw*." She leaned forward, whispering. "I saw a secret. He is not who he is supposed to be. *He is not truly the Great Sun.*"

Firekeeper gasped, covering her mouth with a thin hand. Her eyes darted about the room as if to reveal a hidden listener.

"And then," Antelope rushed on, "I was not afraid of him. I despised him only." Her voice shook. "That angered him and he tore my robe from my body so that I was naked. He picked me up and threw me on his sleeping place. I kicked him hard. Here." She pointed. "And then I ran. Someone snatched the robe from my hand as Far Walker brought me to this place, so I come to you like this. . . ." Her voice faltered.

Firekeeper turned aside as if she could bear no more. The fire cast small lights that darted here, then there, upon pearls and tapestries and bright feathers draped on the walls.

An altar stood in the center of the sanctuary. Firekeeper made her way there haltingly, as if she carried a heavy burden. At the altar she lifted an ornately carved pipe from which sacred objects dangled. Holding the pipe before her, she approached the fire.

"Red Man, you have heard," she chanted, waving the pipe back and forth over the flame. From a bowl on the altar, she scooped a handful of meal and tossed it into the fire. "Accept my gift, sacred one. Forget all you have heard here. Forget."

Antelope felt a prick of unease. Had her need for comfort, for understanding, and the urgent need to shed memories and confide in someone caused her to blunder? Should she have told?

Firekeeper returned the pipe to the altar and faced Antelope. "Rise," she said.

Antelope stood, conscious of her nakedness. Firekeeper removed her cloak and draped it around Antelope. "You may keep this until another robe is available; then return it to me."

Antelope's heart eased. She held the cloak around her with both hands; it smelled faintly of smoke and of mysterious substances. "I thank you, Firekeeper. I shall care for it well."

"Go now," the old one said. "But be aware of the danger of the secret you possess. Tell no one. *No one!* The truth will reveal itself." Her voice tensed with urgency. "Do you understand?"

"I do, honored one."

A warning, like the shrill cry of a hawk, echoed in far corners of her mind. Danger, indeed.

Who and where was the real Great Sun?

It was a cloudy day in late summer, hinting of a change of seasons. Peg Foot felt it in his aging bones and wished that he were young again and had his foot and could play chunkey. He stood with the bystanders, watching the players as they ran after the rolling stone ring and threw lances to see whose lance would be closest to the ring when it stopped. Shouted wagers and cheering rang in the air, blending with the sounds of preparation for the Green Corn ceremony soon due.

Temporary structures were being raised; ambassadors and many visitors would need shelter. Beyond, in the old plaza, trading was under way. Canoes from a village upstream had arrived with cotton and buffalo hides, and bargaining was lively. Children and dogs ran everywhere, as usual. Women carried jars of water on their heads and stopped to gossip with one another.

Peg Foot glimpsed Far Walker across the plaza. He carried a white robe that the women noticed and put their heads together to discuss.

Women.

Peg Foot snorted—and again wished secretly he were young again.

Far Walker hurried as fast as he could with his bandaged leg. He carried the white robe carefully; it was the most beautiful robe he had ever seen and had cost him dearly. But a special one was needed to ease the pain of what he must tell Antelope—that she had a home no longer and was She Who Remembers no more.

Ahead, the mound of the Temple of Eternal Fire glowed in green glory with grasses watered and cared for by slaves who clambered up and down the steep slopes like mountain goats.

As Far Walker reached the mound, he saw a figure in a priest's cloak descending the steps. It took him a moment to recognize Antelope. In a priest's cloak!

She saw him and ran eagerly down the steps to meet him, holding the cloak about her. She smiled as she approached.

Ah! How beautiful she was!

"Far Walker! I am glad to see you!" Antelope cried. She glanced at his bandaged leg, and her smile clouded. "You took that arrow for me." Her eyes embraced him. "Does it hurt much?"

"No."

He wanted to grab her and hold her close. Instead, he offered the robe. "For you."

Antelope released her hold on the cloak to accept the robe, and he glimpsed her lovely body clothed only in the necklace resting between her breasts. She held the new robe to her, crooning.

"Beautiful! See the wonderful colors of the beads and how they have been used in embroidery! Look at the lace! Who made this?"

"Someone from another village. You like it?"

"Yes! Oh, yes! I want to put it on."

Antelope ran up the steps and disappeared into the doorway. Soon she returned, adorned. The white robe, tied on one shoulder, glowed against her tawny skin and contrasted with the ebony of her long hair. Bead embroidery in vivid colors encircled the bottom of the robe and swept up one side in dramatic display. The robe flowed about her caressingly as she ran down the steps to him. Far Walker could only stand mute, gazing.

"It is beautiful, Far Walker! I thank you. I can't wait for Red Leaf and Poqua to see it." She smoothed a hand over the soft cotton fabric. "I must get Skyfeather now."

"There is something I must tell you first." Far Walker sat on a step and motioned her beside him. She brushed the step with both hands before she sat down. "A meeting of the council was held to decide who was responsible for the death of Many Bears."

A spark flashed in her dark eyes. "So?"

"They said you are to blame."

The spark flared. "Impossible! The jaguar—"

"They think you used your powers to summon the Spotted One for revenge. But they say you are responsible only indirectly, so you do not have to die."

Antelope stared with shock. "I had nothing to do with his death, but I am glad he is dead. He attacked me like an animal."

Far Walker nodded. "There is more. You do not die, but you must pay with all your possessions except your robe and the necklace you wear. That includes everything in Chomoc's pack—"

"That is outrageous! I refuse!"

"You have no choice, unfortunately. And there is more. You are no longer She Who Remembers, nor are you welcome to live with Red Leaf. You must find another home."

For a long time Antelope stared silently into the distance. Her hands were clenched but her face was expressionless, totally calm. Far Walker sensed the raging within her, however, and he yearned to comfort her.

Finally, he said, "I would be honored if you and Skyfeather came to live with me."

She faced him and he saw a shine of unshed tears. He put an arm around her and she did not pull away. "Live with me," he whispered.

Two little girls passing by saw them and ran to join them. They sat close to Antelope, giggling, fingering the quill embroidery, and peeking at Far Walker.

Antelope hugged them and sent them on their way. She looked deep into Far Walker's eyes for a long moment.

"I cannot live with you, because you have a mate."

"She is gone."

"But she may return. Where are your mother and sisters?"

He shrugged. "I have none. My mother died at my birth; I was her only child. Her sister raised me, but she is long in Sipapu. I am alone." He tightened his arm. "Make your home with me."

She edged away. "Not until it is known for certain your mate will not return." She lifted her chin in her old, defiant gesture. "Now I will get Skyfeather and find a place to stay until Chomoc returns." She rose and started across the plaza.

He followed. "I will go with you."

Word of the council meeting had spread, and villagers glanced furtively at Antelope as she passed. They whispered.

"Look at that robe!"

"Where did she get it? I wonder."

"Where do you think? Look who is with her."

"Far Walker? The Healer? Do you suppose—"
"Of course. She is beautiful and his mate has gone."
"And you know his man part is hungry."
"But she has powers. . . ."
"A Healer has powers of his own."
"Perhaps she will live with him. I heard—"
"But what if his mate returns?"
"Or Chomoc?"

Antelope knew they talked about her but she did not care. Anger and shock boiled in her. And fear. What would become of her and Skyfeather? Maybe she should move in with Far Walker, but she could not, not yet. . . .

Would she ever be able to mate again?

As they walked the paths of Yala, Antelope wondered what she would say to Red Leaf and Poqua. *Dear old Poqua . . . how could she blame me?* Antelope swallowed her tears.

When they reached Red Leaf's home, no one was there, not even the dog. But a neighbor would know who had Skyfeather.

Far Walker said, "I will remain here while you look for Sky-feather. Maybe Red Leaf and Poqua will return."

Antelope went to the nearest neighbor who sat outside, forming a pottery jar with coils of clay rope. The woman saw Antelope coming and rose.

"I greet you," Antelope said, trying to smile.

"I greet you also." The woman looked uncomfortable.

Antelope felt a stab of alarm. Something was amiss. She said, "I come for Skyfeather. Can you tell me who has her?"

"The warriors. They came and took your baby away." The woman wrung her hands. "I tried to make them stop, but they said the Great Sun ordered them to bring the baby to him." She shook her head and wrung her hands wretchedly again. "I think they want her for the Green Corn sacrifice."

Antelope felt as if a lance had slashed open her chest, as if her heart were shredded. She gave a great, sobbing cry.

"Skyfeather!"

▲19▼

Lipoe, younger wife of the Great Sun, sat in their luxurious dwelling on the mound and cradled Skyfeather in her arms. Her long, dark hair fell loosely around her thin face, which glowed now with pleasure. She held the baby close and whispered so Kala and Manimani would not hear.

"Warriors brought you for sacrifice but they shall not have you. No."

Her dark eyes brimmed. She caressed the round cheeks and the soft drift of dark hair. She held small fingers that curled around her own and felt they curled around her heart as well. Resolve welled up in her soul.

You shall be mine.

"Beautiful little baby!" she crooned. "Beautiful one!"

"A perfect offering for the Spirit Being," Kala said, crossing her plump arms over her stomach. Lipoe knew that since Kala was the elder wife, her opinions counted.

She watched Kala fastening a shell ornament into her hair while she regarded Lipoe with poorly concealed disdain. As usual.

Lipoe thought, *Yes, I am barren. But now I have the child I*

160

always wanted. A child much more beautiful than yours, Kala.

Kala had a son, Patu, and she never ceased to remind Lipoe of her birthing achievement.

But it was Manimani, the Great Sun's sister, who would be the next Great Sun; the descent was through the women of royal blood.

Manimani was there and she bustled about, ordering slaves to empty the night pots, sweep the stone floors, and rearrange the furs and finely woven covers on the Great Sun's bed. He would return soon; he was communing with Long Man.

Loud hous from below indicated the Great Sun was returning now. Manimani hurriedly ordered the slaves to bring fruits and pemmican for him; he would be hungry.

"Bring him also herb tea," Kala said. "He will wish refreshment." She gave Manimani a sharp glance.

It was true that Manimani had certain rights as sister of the Great Sun, but Lipoe knew that Kala resented Manimani's overreaching her authority. True, it was the right of the Great Sun's first wife to order his food, but Kala assumed authority she did not possess in presuming to dictate to her, the second wife, and to regard her with contempt because she was barren.

Lipoe gazed into Skyfeather's face, then at Kala, who ignored her. As she often did, Lipoe spoke only in her thoughts.

My child's heritage is far greater than yours. She is daughter of She Who Remembers and will have powers of her own, as you will see.

There were footsteps outside, and the Great Sun strode in with a swirl of scarlet robe and a slap of scarlet moccasins on the polished stone floor. His lips were tense and his eyes triumphant. He saw Skyfeather and reached for her.

"Give her to me."

Slowly, Lipoe handed the baby to him, although it was obvious that she did not want to.

The Great Sun held Skyfeather at arm's length, turning her this way and that. His eyes glittered under a slash of heavy brows. The child did not cry; rather, she smiled and made happy baby noises, waving her arms and legs.

"Ah!" Lipoe sighed. "So sweet, so beautiful!"

"A perfect offering," Kala said again. "Our mate chose well." She glanced smugly at the Great Sun. "It will be the best Green Corn ceremony ever performed."

"Of course." The Great Sun handed Skyfeather to Manimani as if the child were a bundle of sticks. "Tell Waikah to find a nursemaid. Care for her well until time for the sacrifice. The Spirit Being will be pleased." His full lips parted in a smile, displaying perfect teeth. "And so shall I." He gestured dismissal. "I wish to be alone now."

When they were gone, he growled in exultation. That Towa woman would learn what it meant to debase the Great Sun. Ah, yes!

Remembering Antelope as she stood naked before him, he experienced a sudden erection. What power did She Who Remembers possess to haunt him, to make him ravenous for physical solace?

But such a hunger could easily be fed. He strode to the doorway and summoned another slave, and another.

And still another, but the hunger lingered like a poisoned arrow deep inside.

Antelope sat on the ground in the neighbor's garden, spent from weeping. Far Walker squatted beside her, his arm around shoulders that felt small and vulnerable.

"Come," he said. "We shall talk to Peg Foot; he can help us. He has wisdom." *Wisdom I need.*

Antelope rose abruptly. "I am going to get Skyfeather back." She strode purposefully down the path.

Far Walker strode after her, gripped both her arms, and turned her to face him. "Remember this. You escaped death once. If you confront the Great Sun you will not escape it again. How will that save Skyfeather?"

She stared at him, great eyes searching his soul. He continued, "If there is a way to save Skyfeather, Peg Foot will know." He released his grip. "Come now. We shall find a way." Softly, he added, "Be courageous, my small one."

Silently, her face tense with suppressed emotions, she followed Far Walker down the path. Her head was high and her eyes dry; no tears were left.

Waikah, the midwife, wrapped her cloak close about her scrawny frame as she hurried through the darkness toward the Temple of Eternal Fire. Waikah's sister, Firekeeper, had summoned her to come to the temple at once. As was her custom,

Waikah talked to herself when burdened with distress.

"She has heard about Antelope's baby. She is afraid something bad will happen if the child of She Who Remembers is sacrificed. But Antelope is She Who Remembers no more. Ha! But what can we do about it, eh? Nothing. Nothing, I say."

A cool breeze swept from the river, hinting of a change of seasons. The plaza was deserted but for a few couples strolling arm in arm, oblivious of all but themselves. There was no moon, and stars burned cold, flickering as if touched by distant winds.

The Temple of Eternal Fire loomed ahead, a finger of smoke curling over it. Waikah's sister was busy as usual, mollifying Red Man.

"Why has she dragged me out at this time of night? I get little enough rest as it is, with babies arriving at all hours. And I have yet to find a nursing mother for Antelope's child." Waikah jerked her robe angrily about her. "I knew that Towa woman would bring trouble. I *knew* it. But would they listen to me? No. Now there is trouble, just as I said. Or why would my sister summon me this way, eh?"

When Waikah reached the temple, she had to pause and rest halfway up the steep steps. No light shone from the extended doorway, but she had been there before and reached it without stumbling. As she made her way through the tunnel-like entrance, she saw firelight inside the temple room where Firekeeper sat waiting.

Firekeeper rose, extending both arms. "I welcome you, my sister."

Waikah accepted the embrace without comment. She removed her cloak and flung it aside.

"Why have you called me here? At this hour? Eh?"

Firekeeper gestured Waikah to sit. "I have seen She Who Remembers. I was here when she reached sanctuary."

Waikah settled her aged frame on a fur-covered stool. "So? Continue."

Firekeeper leaned close, whispering as though to thwart an unseen presence. "She knows!"

Waikah's bony hands clutched her breast. "She knows? She knows what?"

Firekeeper glanced around as if the unseen ones might become visible. She leaned closer. "She knows he is not the true Great Sun."

"Ay-e-e-e!" Waikah's hands trembled. "How does she know this?"

"She has powers." Firekeeper rocked back and forth. "I don't know how she knows, but she does. I wish that the High Priest were here to advise us, but he has not returned, as you know. What will Antelope do if her child is harmed? What will she tell? Think about that."

"Ay-e-e-e-e-e!" Waikah wailed, remembering.

Remembering what had happened that cold winter night long ago . . .

How young Firekeeper was then, and how beautiful! Although the High Priest longed for her, she had mated foolishly with a powerful priest from a distant city who had returned to his home, leaving her to have her child without him.

Firekeeper was giving birth now, at this moment, in the temple so that her child—a son, she hoped—would be sanctified. But another midwife attended Firekeeper because she, Waikah, the most esteemed midwife in the City of the Great Sun, was assisting the current Great Sun, a woman, who was giving birth at the same time.

The two sisters had a plan, a secret plan discussed endlessly—if it happened that both babies were boys.

Prayers and many sacrifices brought results. The Great Sun's child was a boy.

"You have a son, a fine heir," Waikah told the Great Sun and her consort, who stood beaming at the tiny person in Waikah's arms. "Shall I take him to the temple to be sanctified?"

"No!" the Great Sun replied. "Give him to me. Now."

Waikah bundled the infant in a soft blanket, laid him in his mother's arms, and glanced up at her consort. "It would be well if Red Man could intercede with the Spirit Being for your son's safety, my lord."

"Cannot that be done another time?" the Great Sun pleaded. "There will be a birthing ceremony—"

"Witches and evil ones do not wait for ceremonies," her consort said. "It should be done now." He looked down at the beautiful woman who lay with a wealth of dark hair strewn about her on the pillow. "Please reconsider, my love."

"Perhaps you are right. It shall be done."

He reached down and took the little wrapped bundle from

her arms and handed the baby to Waikah. "Slaves and a warm litter will take you both to the temple and bring you back afterward. See that our son is properly presented to Red Man. Here." He removed a bit of conch shell, intricately carved, that hung on a cord among many necklaces. "He shall wear this. Red Man shall know our son's royal heritage." He draped the cord around the tiny neck. "Go now."

Waikah could barely conceal her gratification. All was going according to plan.

"I shall do as you wish, my lord."

The night was bitterly cold, and the nearly naked slaves shivered as they trotted with the litter carrying Waikah and the baby wrapped in furs. When they reached the temple mound, they stopped; they were not allowed to climb the mound unless ordered to do so by the priest on duty.

"Wait here," Waikah ordered. "You may use this." She indicated a fur robe. "I shall return soon."

Waikah hurried up the steps, her heart pounding with excitement. Was her sister's child also a boy? Their plan . . .

Firekeeper lay on a low bed covered with furs, a baby in her arms. She was alone, and smiling.

"I sent the midwife away. I needed her no more. Look."

Firekeeper parted the furs to reveal a baby boy, perfect in every detail. A beautiful male child.

"Ah!" Waikah sighed. "A boy!" She laid the baby she carried beside Firekeeper's son. "See? Both boys!"

The sisters looked into each other's eyes for a long moment.

Firekeeper said, "You are sure you are willing to do this?"

"You promise me special intercession with the Spirit Being?"

"I can and I will. For the rest of my life. And you shall want for nothing."

"Very well," Waikah said, her voice tense with excitement. "Let's do it now."

Quickly, Waikah removed the cord and shell from the Great Sun's baby, placed it around the neck of Firekeeper's child, and wrapped him in the royal blanket. The child of the Great Sun lay naked in Firekeeper's arms.

Firekeeper looked at him carefully. "He doesn't look the same."

"His mother held him only a few moments and his father

won't know the difference. He will see the shell and the blanket and that will be enough."

"Let me hold my son one more time."

Waikah laid the boy in his mother's embrace. She held him close, kissed him, and whispered, "You shall be the Great Sun, the Spirit Being's brother. Be worthy of that."

She handed the baby to Waikah. "Present him to Red Man. Then take my son to his royal home."

Waikah stood by the fire and chanted supplications as hurriedly as she dared. Then she kissed Firekeeper, said good-bye, and returned to the litter. The two slaves reluctantly removed the warm fur robe they had huddled beneath, wrapped it around Waikah and the Great-Sun-to-be, and trotted them back to the royal residential mound. The guards allowed her to enter without questioning.

The Great Sun's consort was asleep in bed; she lay awake beside him. Waikah entered quietly and laid the baby in her arms.

"He is sanctified," Waikah whispered. "He will be protected."

"I am grateful." She removed a bit of blanket from the baby's face and gazed at him in firelight for a long moment. She touched the bit of shell. Then she brought the little mouth to her breast and sighed, content, as the tiny mouth suckled.

"You shall want for nothing," the Great Sun said.

Waikah bowed her way out, murmuring farewell. Both Firekeeper and the Great Sun had assured her she would want for nothing. How fortunate she was!

But complications were not over. Firekeeper found she could not bring herself to assume responsibility for the Great Sun's child, said now to be her own. Her priestly conscience gave her no rest.

"I cannot keep this child," Firekeeper told Waikah. "He is a constant reminder of the wrong thing I have done. Give this child to someone who does not know who he really is." She gazed at Waikah with tears in her beautiful eyes. "Help me, my sister. I beg you. Find him another home. Ease my heart."

"You will remember your promise?"

"Always."

"I know a woman who may suffice. . . ."

*   *   *

It had all happened long, long ago. Now they were old, she and Firekeeper. Old and afraid.

Waikah sucked her lips over her toothless gums. "Why did you have to tell him? He would never have known—"

"I had to. I was his priest, and it was the New Fire ceremony when he came, as the Great Sun must, to purify himself. He said he had dreamed. A puzzling dream that made him wonder if he was two people. He was worried and unhappy. . . ." Firekeeper looked away, her soft voice trembling. "He was my son, you know. So I told him. But I lied about the other baby, the Great Sun's child. I said he died."

"Yes, you told him. And what did he tell you, eh? That if his secret is ever discovered, your head and mine will be impaled on stakes for arrow practice in the plaza. Our spirits would roam homeless forever. *That* is what your son said. Now the Towa woman knows, and now her baby is held for sacrifice. What shall we do, eh? Tell me!"

Firekeeper's deep-set eyes locked into hers. "Do what you must. Find another baby for sacrifice and return Antelope's child to her."

"Ha! You think the Great Sun will permit that? What sort of fool do you think I am?"

"Maybe the Great Sun does not have to know. He will see a baby sacrificed—"

"Antelope's child is no ordinary baby, as well you know."

"True. But at a distance, who will know? A baby is a baby—"

"This I cannot do. No."

"You will because you must, my sister. Unless you want the Towa woman to tell what she knows."

"Maybe she will anyway."

"Not if you tell her you will trade the safety of her child for her silence."

"So I must switch babies again, eh?"

Firekeeper smiled. "You must admit you do it well."

Waikah sucked her lips. "I *knew* that Towa woman would bring trouble. But nobody would listen, nobody. Especially the men. They pant after her like dogs."

"Of course. They are men and she is beautiful."

Waikah sighed. "We were beautiful once, eh?"

"Yes. A long time ago. I no longer remember being beautiful. I have forgotten passion. I have forgotten. . . ."

"But we do not forget what your son said. I shall find another baby for sacrifice and return Antelope's child to her."

"The Spirit Being will reward you." Firekeeper glanced about and hunched forward, whispering. "When I see him who is the real Great Sun living the life of a commoner in Yala, deprived of his heritage, my kia tells me I shall be punished for the terrible thing I have done. This I know."

Waikah shrugged. "But he is a man now, and no harm has come to you during all these years." She rose and wrapped her warm cloak about her aching bones. "Obviously, you are forgiven. Grieve no more." She turned to leave.

Firekeeper said, "I shall give Red Man many gifts, many prayers, to assure your safety and success, my sister."

They embraced and Waikah left the sanctuary. When she entered the night, darkness enfolded her as one of its own, dissolving her into itself.

Would gifts and prayers protect her from what she had done? And for what she now must do?

She was old.

And afraid.

▲20▼

"This is Peg Foot, my Teacher," Far Walker said. "He is known to all as the best Healer that the City of the Great Sun has ever had."

Antelope looked at the bent old man, leaning on a staff, who returned her gaze with a penetrating one of his own.

"I greet you," Antelope said politely.

"You are welcome in my house," he said without enthusiasm. He gestured. "Sit."

Antelope looked around for something on which to sit. She wore the new robe Far Walker had given her, and there was nothing to sit on but worn and dusty mats. She stooped, lifted a mat, and made her way through the extended doorway to the outside where she shook the mat vigorously.

Far Walker heard the flapping and his face reddened. "She is Towa and female," he apologized. "Her robe is new. She wants to protect it."

Peg Foot snorted. "The usual female bad manners. My mats are clean enough."

"Your eyes cannot see what they used to," Far Walker said gently. "The mats are dusty. A woman notices these things—"

"I need no woman, if that is what you are here for," Peg Foot

169

said irritably, and sat down, crossing his bony legs. "You know very well that I prefer to live alone."

Far Walker did know. Peg Foot's insistence on living alone had caused no small amount of hard feelings among those relatives he had left. It was customary for families to live together, and for him to refuse was insulting and unthinkable.

"But this woman needs you," Far Walker said carefully. "The Great Sun has taken her only child for sacrifice. She has no home and owns nothing but what she wears—the new robe she protects. Chomoc has not returned; she is alone." Far Walker glimpsed a look in Peg Foot's eyes, a look he tried to conceal. "She needs you."

Peg Foot turned away without reply, but Far Walker knew the secret tenderness of Peg Foot's heart and was encouraged.

Antelope returned, spread the mat, and sat down, carefully arranging her robe so that it did not touch the dirty floor. She regarded the old Healer, who sat cross-legged, absently rubbing the peg where one foot should be. Far Walker smiled inwardly as Peg Foot self-consciously avoided her gaze.

Far Walker watched as Antelope looked around the cluttered room. He looked at it again himself, trying to see it as she did. Baskets and bowls lined shelves and stood in profusion around the floor and on benches protruding from the walls. Strings of herbs and various pods, leaves, and twigs hung from the high beamed ceiling and wafted a potent odor, not unpleasant. Part of the wall bench served as a bed and was covered with a rumpled buffalo robe. A small altar held two bowls and an assortment of unrecognizable objects. There was no fire and few cooking utensils.

Antelope looked again at the old man. Did she see how thin he was? His crest of gray hair held a few tired feathers, and the sparse hank of hair hanging down in back was unadorned. His worn robe was not very clean, and it had a torn place.

Did she see how he needed her?

She said, "I cook well. I make good pottery. I tan hides, I make garments, I mend, I keep things clean. I sing."

Peg Foot shot her a quick glance. "You sing?"

Antelope leaned back, looked up at the beamed ceiling where the hanging plants stirred a bit in a breeze from the doorway, and she began to sing a wordless song. Her voice, high and sweet, filled the room. As she sang, Far Walker thought of

Chomoc and his flute; her song echoed his music. She sang of longing and loneliness, of sorrow and joy and springtime.

When she finished, there was silence in the room. Far Walker was too moved to speak. Peg Foot pretended there was something in his eye. He said, "It has been many winters since song filled my house."

Far Walker said, "You shall have it often, whenever you wish."

Antelope looked at the old Healer for a long moment.

"I would be proud to sing for you. And to cook for you and clean for you, if you will permit me to share your home." She glanced about. "It needs cleaning." She wrinkled her nose.

"Humpf!" he snorted, rubbing his peg. But he did not refuse her offer.

Far Walker said, "Honored Teacher, we need your wisdom." He turned to Antelope. "Ask him."

Antelope hesitated. Far Walker sensed her indecision.

She thinks he doesn't want her here, and who can blame her?

Antelope swallowed. "Esteemed one, please allow me to share your home. But most of all, please help me save my child. The Great Sun's warriors took her for sacrifice. . . ." Her voice choked. "My Skyfeather. Please."

Peg Foot's eyes looked into hers, and his glance softened. He said gruffly, "I have never abided a woman in my home since my last mate died. Never." He shifted position, rubbed his peg, and avoided her gaze. "But I suppose I could make an exception. You cook well, you say?"

"I do."

Far Walker said, "Will you help Antelope save her child?"

"I cannot know what is best to do until I get information from the slaves. They know everything."

"But you will try to help?"

"Perhaps. I can try only. I cannot promise success."

"Thank you!" Antelope cried. "Oh, thank you!"

"I thank you also, revered Teacher," Far Walker said.

Waikah found a nursemaid for Skyfeather, a slave girl of about fourteen winters who had been raped by warriors and whose child had been stillborn only days ago. She was slender as a willow but her breasts were full to bursting.

Waikah hoped that the wives of the Great Sun might not be

jealous of a slave girl, pretty though she was. She brought the girl to Manimani's dwelling since Manimani was responsible for Skyfeather.

Manimani and Kala were not there, but Lipoe walked the floor with Skyfeather, who yelled lustily.

"She is hungry," Lipoe said.

"I bring a suitable nursemaid." Waikah gave the slave girl a push forward. "Her name is Chipmunk. See how full her breasts are." She squeezed a naked breast; milk squirted.

"Here." Lipoe thrust Skyfeather at the girl. "Feed her."

Chipmunk sat on the floor and held Skyfeather, who nursed hungrily, her small mouth clamped to the girl's large, dusky nipple.

Waikah watched Lipoe lean forward, yearning. Now was the time to say what she must. But not with a slave listening; slaves whispered.

"I must speak with you alone, mate of the Great Sun."

Lipoe looked surprised. "Why?"

"I shall explain." She gestured to an adjoining room. "May we go in there?"

Lipoe rose reluctantly, still watching Skyfeather. "For a moment only."

Waikah followed Lipoe into the royal bedroom. Her heart rattled against her ribs.

What if she refuses? What if she orders the guards to throw me down the steps?

Lipoe sat on the royal bed and left Waikah standing. The dark eyes in Lipoe's thin face regarded Waikah regally.

"Speak."

"Skyfeather is a beautiful child."

"Yes." Impatiently.

"Eminently suitable as a gift to the Spirit Being."

Lipoe regarded her inscrutably. "Of course."

Waikah squirmed. This was going to be more difficult than she had anticipated.

"It occurs to this humble one that the city has other beautiful babies whose death would honor the Spirit Being."

A look flashed in Lipoe's eyes, and vanished. "So?"

"This humble one has heard of the powers of She Who Remembers and of the powers of her brother in Cicuye. The sacrifice of one of their own would assuredly be regarded as cause for confrontation—"

"Stop!" Lipoe raised her hand as though to push Waikah away. She glanced at the doorway where an elaborately painted deerskin hung for privacy. She leaned forward, whispering.

"This child will not be sacrificed."

Waikah gasped in relief. The gods were with her! Her lips parted in a wide, toothless smile. "How wise—"

"I shall keep this child as my own," Lipoe interrupted, glancing again at the doorway. "Find another for sacrifice."

Waikah was stunned. She clasped her bony hands. Questions scrambled frantically in her mind. How could she, or anyone, make Lipoe return Skyfeather to Antelope?

I know what will happen to me if I suggest such a thing. What is left of me at the bottom of the mound will be fed to vultures. What shall I do? What shall I do?

Lipoe rose, her pale face firm with resolve. "I shall expect you to bring another baby tomorrow."

She gestured dismissal.

Waikah bowed out, walking backward.

The family of Turkey Tail, famed pipe carver, was agog with excitement. Turkey Tail's young mate, Blue Wing, had given birth to her first child, a boy, who lay in his mother's arms wrapped in the finest blanket the family could provide. The family was planning a naming ceremony when Waikah, the midwife, arrived with gifts of corn, copper, and salt—and an announcement.

"The Great Sun has chosen your baby to be a gift to the Spirit Being during the Green Corn ceremony," Waikah said with great dignity. "These gifts I give you are from the family of the Great Sun in recognition of the honor bestowed you."

This was a lie. The valuables were her personal belongings, which she could not spare, but she was desperate.

Waikah continued, "On behalf of the Great Sun and his family, I congratulate you all." She placed the gifts on the family altar. "Now I shall take the child."

"No!" Blue Wing cried. "No, no!" Eyes wide with terror, she clutched the baby to her breast.

Turkey Tail swelled with pride. This would make him an

important personage. He might even be allowed to play chunkey with the elite. "We are chosen! We are honored! The Spirit Being will reward us well!"

Family members crowded around the mother, babbling. "Think what that means. Your baby will be with the Spirit Being forever!"

"No!" Blue Wing sobbed. "Not my first, my only one!"

Waikah edged her way to where the mother lay. She thought, *I cannot do this. But I must.*

She reached down but Blue Wing turned away, clutching her baby close. "No!" she screamed.

Turkey Tail pulled the tiny body from the screaming mother's arms and handed the baby to Waikah with a flourish.

"Please express our gratitude to the Great Sun for this marvelous honor," he said, beaming.

"I shall," Waikah replied.

She hurried from the house, escaping. But Blue Wing's anguished cries followed like a curse.

It was early afternoon. Workers were busy in the plaza building arbors from which the elite and their important guests could watch the ceremonies. A dugout canoe with traders and their wares had arrived, and traders entered the plaza carrying bowls and baskets of trading goods. There was loud discussion about where they could spread their merchandise. A crowd began to gather; arguments were always of interest.

Waikah avoided them. Holding her tiny bundle carefully, she made her way to the Great Sun's dwelling mound. The guards watched her coming, two guards on each step. Waikah swallowed nervously. She had delivered some of those men when they were born, and she was entitled to respect; but this young generation did not respect their elders as her generation had.

She paused at the bottom of the mound and looked up at the warriors looming above her. She stood as straight as she was able and spoke firmly.

"I have a gift for Lipoe, mate of the Great Sun. Tell her I am here. She is expecting me."

A warrior stepped down and reached for the blanketed bundle. "Show me what it is."

Waikah jerked away. "It is not for you. It is for Lipoe, mate of the Great Sun. I told you she awaits me. She will not be pleased at your delay." She stepped boldly up the first step. "Inform her I am here, or take the consequences when she learns her wishes have not been obeyed."

That gave the young warrior pause. He stood uncertainly for a moment, then gestured to the men at the top of the stairs.

"Inform Lipoe, mate of the Great Sun, that Waikah, the midwife, is here, and ask if Lipoe wishes to see her," he called.

Waikah watched with satisfaction as one of the guards entered the royal dwelling. *That will teach him respect,* she thought.

The guard came out almost immediately and gestured for Waikah to come in.

The stairs were steep and Waikah was old and tired. She had to pause several times to rest. The baby began to cry and Waikah tried to hush him without success. At last she reached the extended doorway and entered.

"Hou! Hou! Hou!" she cried, kneeling on one painful knee while the baby cried louder.

The Great Sun strode forward. He was bare from the waist up, and the ornate shell gorget, symbol of his status, glowed against his broad chest. Waikah did not presume to look into his face. Instead, she gazed at his red moccasins, waiting to be invited to rise and hoping it would be before her knee gave way and she toppled over.

"What gift is this?" the Great Sun demanded loudly.

Lipoe's voice. "I asked her to bring another child. Give it to me."

"Rise," the Great Sun said.

She did so with difficulty, holding the crying bundle.

Lipoe came and took the baby from Waikah's arms. "Go now," she said imperiously.

Waikah was outraged. She expected and deserved a reward. She turned toward the Great Sun. "It was my pleasure and honor to bring a gift to the mate of the Great Sun. As I was requested to do," she added pointedly, gazing at his moccasins.

Amusement flickered in the ruler's black eyes. He removed one of his bracelets and tossed it on the floor toward her.

"Take it and go."

"I thank you, holy one."

Waikah snatched the bracelet and backed out the door, bowing low.

When she had gone, the Great Sun strode to where Lipoe sat with a naked newborn boy in her arms. He watched her inspecting the child dispassionately, examining nose and ears, fingers and toes.

"Kala and Manimani will be pleased," Lipoe said matter-of-factly. "The child is perfect."

For a moment he did not reply. Rather, he stood looking down at her, thin and pale and barren, and felt a stab of irritation. He was frustrated again in trying to understand this mate of his. It was mandatory for Great Suns to marry commoners, but sometimes this woman seemed more royal than Manimani.

"Whose child is this and why is it here?" He scowled. "Why was I not consulted?"

Lipoe's dark eyes caressed him. "The Great Sun is not to be burdened with trifling matters." She held the baby for his inspection. "Look at him. A commoner's child and perfect for sacrifice."

"But we have one. Antelope's child."

"Of course. A girl. Are not females of any age forbidden in the Green Corn ceremony?"

"Who presumes to forbid the Great Sun whatever he desires?"

"Not I, my beloved."

Lipoe laid the baby down and rose, allowing her robe to fall, exposing delicate breasts and body; she was thin but shapely. She wrapped both arms around his waist and pressed herself to him. She was soft and smelled of flower petals.

This woman knew what he liked. He rubbed himself against her, then lifted her in his arms and carried her to his bed. As he savored her smooth skin and her knowledgeable, expert caresses, she paused a moment to look at him.

"May I ask a present of you, my handsome one?"

How like a woman, he thought. Choosing this moment when he was fully aroused and ready.

"Later." He parted her slim legs.

She smiled teasingly, resisting. "Please?"

Her woman part, pink and enticing, was moist with invitation. She smelled of woodland flowers and of woman's essence, infinitely seductive. He could force her, but her skill was such that he preferred her cooperation.

"What do you want?" he sighed.

"Skyfeather," she whispered, caressing him maddeningly

with delicate fingers. "I want her for my own. Sacrifice the other child."

He could wait no longer. He plunged into her, growling with pleasure. He loved the way she grabbed him deep inside. She could have anything she wanted.

Lipoe pulled him close. "May I have Skyfeather?"

"Yes," he groaned. "Yes."

·21·

It was midmorning in early autumn, unseasonably hot. Red Leaf and Poqua worked in their garden, harvesting beans and sunflower seeds in preparation for the Green Corn ceremony. The High Priest had not yet returned to announce the day when the ceremony would commence, but everyone knew it would be soon; the corn was ripening.

All worked feverishly in preparation. Ambassadors and other important guests would arrive from distant places and must be fed and accommodated, as well as people from the surrounding villages. Ceremonies took place nearly every moon, but the Green Corn ceremony was when the New Fire began a new year and was the most important ceremony of all.

Red Leaf paused and rested on the wooden staff of her bone hoe. She wiped perspiration from her round face and looked at Poqua with concern. Since Antelope and Skyfeather had gone, something in Poqua seemed to have gone with them. She was older, weaker, and her songs with the singing stick were sad. Now she sat on the ground, her hoe beside her, and gazed into the distance as if seeking what was not there. The eyes in her withered face did not sparkle anymore.

She is thinking of Antelope and Skyfeather.

Red Leaf thought of them often, too. Their names were never mentioned, but sometimes she wondered secretly if Antelope had really caused the death of Many Bears. Maybe the Spotted One was to blame. And when Red Leaf had rummaged through Chomoc's pack and found the treasures there, she knew in her heart that they belonged to Antelope—who had nothing now, not even her child. Skyfeather had been taken for sacrifice.

Now, as Red Leaf heard the shouts of Ringtail and Bobcat as they played with Hoho, she was glad they were safe and that they seemed happy at last. They had cried when Antelope and Skyfeather left. Even now, little Bobcat did not sing with Poqua as he used to.

Poqua sighed and pulled herself upright with her hoe. She glanced at the sun. "The boys will be hungry soon. I'll get corn cakes."

Red Leaf watched her mother hobble inside. The Spotted One had done more than kill Many Bears. He had wounded Poqua's kia, and hers, also. Only Red Leaf knew how she lay sleepless often.

I lost my mate. But Antelope lost everything.

Antelope floated on the river at the women's bathing place. It was early evening, when most women were busy with meals and family, and no one else was there. No one, that is, but a kingfisher diving for its dinner.

"I greet you," Antelope said.

The kingfisher soared away, a fish in its beak.

Antelope watched the bird disappear. She wished her heartbreak would fly away like that, with sorrow clutched in its grasp.

The movement of the water stirred the necklace she always wore. Antelope touched the scallop shell pendant and fingered its sacred turquoise insert. She pressed the shell to her and remembered the words of the Ancient Ones, all those who had been She Who Remembers before.

We are of all womankind and must endure much.

But she had endured, and her heart was breaking.

She submerged herself to cool her swollen breasts. She yearned for Skyfeather's sweet mouth. If Chomoc were there, he would drink from her, love her, and heal her with his music. . . .

She sat in the water and looked up at the sky where the bird had flown. Her anguish would not fly away. She sobbed with loud, agonized cries.

Gradually, she realized someone was in the water with her. Someone pulled her close, crooning in a deep man's voice. Far Walker's voice.

"Long Man accepts your tears. He will wash away your sorrow."

He pulled her gently to her feet; the river swirled around them. "I have news of Skyfeather."

She clung to him, unmindful of their nakedness. She felt almost as if he had saved her from drowning. Her sobbing eased.

"Tell me!"

"She is safe."

"Ah! Where is she?"

"With Lipoe, mate of the Great Sun. Come, I'll tell you more."

Antelope's heart surged with hope. She knew Lipoe was barren; she had heard it mentioned often. Maybe Lipoe would take pity on the mother of such a beautiful little girl. . . .

Far Walker led her to the sandy bank where her robe and his garment were draped on a bush. Dusk had deepened; it was nearly dark. The bank was uneven and rocky, with tall grasses hiding the rocks. Antelope stumbled on a hidden rock and fell to her knees.

Far Walker knelt beside her, but instead of helping her rise he looked deep into her eyes as if to strengthen her for what he must say.

"Peg Foot has talked with a slave. Lipoe will not allow Skyfeather to be sacrificed."

Antelope gasped in relief.

"Another child will be sacrificed instead. Lipoe will keep Skyfeather as her own."

Antelope's heart lurched. "No!"

"She will become a royal child. She will be given total protection and have the best of everything."

"She will not have me! Nor her mother's milk." Antelope pressed both hands to her breasts. "*I must nurse her, I and no one else.*" Tears choked her voice. "Who feeds her?"

"A slave."

Antelope bent low, so that her long hair touched the ground.

Grief, anger, fear, and a terrible loneliness raged in her; she made small noises like a wounded animal.

Gently, Far Walker laid her down in the grasses and stretched out beside her. He did not embrace her but crooned softly, wordlessly, his deep voice enveloping her like a healing balm.

Antelope listened. Something inside her listened. She heard Long Man's song and the whisper of grasses. She felt Earthmother cradling her in the sand, welcoming her.

Claiming her.

Was it the Healer's voice that unlocked a secret place inside her, allowing her to become one with Earthmother, to sense and to feel the mysteries?

A hawk wheeled overhead, its *skree* shattering the silence. Somewhere a rabbit trembled, and Antelope felt its fear. Somewhere leaves trodden underfoot cried out, and she heard their tiny cries. And in the sigh of the wind in the grasses, Antelope heard the words of the Ancient Ones. Kwani's voice spoke.

"The bond between us, mother and daughter, is eternal. And so it is and will always be between you and Skyfeather."

Memories seeped from Antelope's soul like water from the stones of an ancient spring. When she was a child, sometimes Antelope had seen what was far away, such as the terrible time a buffalo killed her father. She had *seen* that.

Now, as Far Walker's voice enveloped her, Antelope reached deep into her kia to see Skyfeather.

There she was, in a beautiful little bed, with adoring Lipoe leaning over her!

Skyfeather was unharmed and loved.

Antelope's heart lightened. Skyfeather was safe, and the bond between them was eternal. Gratitude tempered her anger against Lipoe, but the loneliness would remain always.

Always.

Far Walker stirred beside her. Antelope became acutely aware of his hard body against hers, but she did not push him away. She needed his strength, his protection, his comforting.

He drew her close, whispering. But she did not hear his words; she listened with all her senses to his touch. It had been long since a man embraced her with loving tenderness. She had thought she could never respond again.

He caressed her, lingering at her breasts, kissing her with

his fingers. Drops of milk oozed out. He bent and licked the milk as Chomoc used to do, teasing the nipple with his tongue to release more, while his hands kissed the rest of her.

Antelope felt a stab almost of pain. Her young body craved, demanded what he offered. Convulsively, she pulled his head harder to her breast.

"Drink from me!"

As he sucked from one breast while fondling the other, Antelope moaned with desire. It had been long, long. . . . She wanted him, needed him. Deeply. She pulled him close and rose to him, clutching his back, parting her legs to receive him.

He delayed, caressing her lingeringly until she moaned again. Then he thrust, gently at first, then masterfully, stronger and deeper, until she exploded inside in a burst of constellations.

The rising moon burned bright, and stardust drifted down.

◂ 22 ▸

Firekeeper swept the temple floor as vigorously as her aged arms permitted. With her was the young priest Wak-Wala, who carefully dusted the High Priest's star wall. Everything must be in perfect order when he arrived. He had been away on a pilgrimage and would return this day.

"Be very careful with those diagrams," Firekeeper admonished. "The High Priest will be angry if any of his stellar calculations are disturbed."

Wak-Wala frowned with impatience. "I *am* careful, esteemed one."

Firekeeper glanced at his handsome young face and at his muscular arms wielding the duster, and she remembered another face and other arms, long ago. Arms that had lifted her and swept her away. She turned aside; the past was past. She said, "Look to see if the High Priest approaches." She knew the High Priest still loved her hopelessly. He never spoke of it, but it revealed itself on rare occasions when he allowed himself to be a man rather than the High Priest.

A boom of the thunder drum and the shrill cry of flutes announced the arrival of an important personage.

"He comes!" Wak-Wala said, hurrying out the doorway.

Firekeeper glanced around to make sure all was in order. The fire was properly laid and burned low, the wall with the High Priest's mysterious inscriptions was dusted, and the tiny opening on the opposite wall was clear of cobwebs. The walls were splendid with bright feathers and tapestries and shining ropes of pearls. The altar with its sacred objects awaited the High Priest.

The temple was in perfect order. Everything was ready—except herself. Although she had fasted and prayed, she did not feel equal to a meeting with the High Priest. Antelope's revelation had overturned a stone of the past, revealing things hidden. Firekeeper wiped her brow with both hands as if to erase squirming memories.

The boom of the thunder drum, the cry of flutes, and the howls of homage grew close. The High Priest approached. Firekeeper braced herself, waiting.

Footsteps sounded in the doorway, and the High Priest entered.

Firekeeper was awed, as usual, by his presence. He was short, twisted, and stooped, so that he had to raise his head to look at her. Great, luminous dark eyes enveloped her with a calm, lancing gaze that left her feeling internally exposed. Beneath shaggy black brows, his beak nose rose majestically, giving authority to an otherwise benign face with ornate tattooing on forehead, cheeks, and chin. He wore a tall, domed headdress from which strange objects dangled and a woven cotton breech-clout, pointed in front and back. His bony back was painted with a circular design in blue, white, and black. A similar design on his chest and a great shell-and-copper gorget on a turquoise chain proclaimed his status as High Priest, astronomer, and diviner of mysteries. The gorget swung to and fro as he walked, bent over.

He approached Firekeeper with his slow, lurching gait, swinging from side to side, his arms twisted before him. As he looked at her, Firekeeper felt the magnetism of his penetrating gaze.

She bowed low. "Hou!"

He smiled, and it was as if light shone from within. "I come to read the signs." His voice was deep and musical.

"All awaits you, honored one."

Did he see my secret? Does he know my burden?

The High Priest approached the wall that was covered with

signs and diagrams only he understood. As if summoned by his presence, sunlight suddenly pierced the small opening in the opposite wall and thrust a bright lance against the wall opposite, illuminating a point in a diagram. Firekeeper knew that the markings mysteriously revealed the equinoxes, the times for planting and harvesting, and when important ceremonies were to be held; she was fearful of the power and depth of the High Priest's vast knowledge. She wished he did not love her.

Can he read signs within me? When he sees, in the village, the one whom I robbed of his heritage, does he know who that man really is?

For some time, the High Priest stood gazing at the wall. He nodded, and the sacred objects dangling from his headdress swung.

"It is time," he said. "Summon the Crier."

Firekeeper stepped outside and signaled a guard. "The High Priest summons the Crier."

Footsteps approached and the Crier entered. He prostrated his skinny frame before the High Priest.

"Hou! Hou!" he bellowed.

"Rise," the High Priest said, not flinching at the booming sound that came from such a meager source.

The Crier rose, his thin, old-young face awash with pride to be in the temple in the presence of the High Priest. He stood proudly waiting, his angular body stiffly erect, his eyes reverently downcast.

The High Priest said, "Make it known that the Green Corn ceremony will take place at the time of the full moon twenty-two days from today."

"Hou!" the Crier thundered, backing out the door.

The High Priest's luminous gaze rested again upon Firekeeper. "I must be alone here now," he said gently. "The temple must be purified."

Firekeeper was relieved. His all-seeing scrutiny was difficult to endure.

"I understand."

Because she was a priest she did not back out as she departed, but she did bow low, avoiding his gaze.

When she was gone, the High Priest stood motionless, his head bent.

"Ah, Firekeeper . . ."

*   *   *

Excitement surged in the city as the Crier made his rounds, preceded by a young drummer who tried manfully to make his drum as loud as the voice of the Crier.

"Hear all citizens!" the Crier boomed. "The High Priest has spoken."

Rat-a-tat-tat.

"The Green Corn ceremony will take place on the next full moon, twenty-two days from this day."

Rat-a-tat-tat-tat.

"Counting sticks will be sent to other towns and to ambassadors elsewhere so they will know when to arrive. Prepare your homes. Prepare the food. Make ready the temporary dwellings on the old plaza for those who have no clan or family here."

Rat-a-rat-a-rat-a-tat.

"Prepare for the fasting. Prepare for the black drink. The day of the Green Corn ceremony draws near."

Rat-a-tat-a-rat-a-tat-a-tat-tat-tat.

Antelope was outside grinding corn as the Crier passed, followed by a horde of squealing children. Since the night with Far Walker by the river, Antelope found herself seeking opportunities to be closer to Earthmother, and she spent as much time outdoors as possible. It seemed that her senses had become more alert and she felt more at one with trees and grasses and Long Man, and even with small woodland creatures, hidden. Sometimes, Antelope felt a drumming in her blood like the time she called the buffalo, and it was good to be alive.

Skyfeather is safe.

Antelope had been with Peg Foot for seven days and had been so busy cleaning and making the place more livable that she had forgotten about the Green Corn ceremony. Each day the slave Chipmunk stopped by with news of Skyfeather and was rewarded with corn or whatever was available at the time. Those who came to Peg Foot for healing paid him well, so something was always available for Chipmunk. The girl's thin face had filled out a bit, and her alert dark eyes missed nothing.

A young man was with Peg Foot now, seeking a cure for pain in his chest. Antelope heard the murmur of their voices and assumed they would be going to Long Man as Peg Foot and his visitors usually did. Peg Foot and Long Man seemed to be on intimate terms, helping one another.

As Far Walker helps me.

Since the night by the river, Far Walker had come often to ask how he might assist her in becoming established in her new home. He did not stay the night, but casually mentioned that she had never been in his dwelling and that she would be welcome there. Only his gaze and his embrace pleaded.

So she went. Eagerly.

His home was much like that of Peg Foot except that it was immaculately clean, and women's things were about, reminding Antelope that Far Walker had a mate.

"Where is she?" Antelope asked.

He shrugged. "I heard she was with Beaver Tail on a journey to the southeast. I do not think she will return. If she does, I shall divorce her."

Antelope looked at a woman's garment on a peg, and a comb, and a partially finished pottery jar. "Why do you keep these, then?"

He smiled. "I guess I like women's things in my home." He drew her to him. "I like having you here. Stay."

He kissed her and her knees became wobbly.

"I cannot."

"Why?"

She looked up at him, at his strong face and his direct, commanding gaze under a sweep of dark brows. How handsome he was!

"You know why. You have a mate, and so do I. Chomoc will return."

A long moment passed. "Do you still love him?"

Did she? From somewhere a flute played a brief tune, teasing, and Antelope remembered the times Chomoc had played for her, made love to her. She remembered the first time. It was spring.

Far Walker tilted her chin. "Do you?"

"Yes." How could she explain? "Yes."

He stretched out on the furs covering his bed. He raised his arms, clasped both hands under his head, and regarded her again with that commanding gaze that was a part of him. His face, with its high cheekbones, aquiline nose, and square chin, would have seemed severe but for the sensuality of his mouth, with its full, finely molded lips turned down slightly at the corners.

Looking at that mouth, and at the muscular body so gracefully at ease, Antelope wanted him. She wanted him. Could she,
indeed, love two men?

He read her glance and sat up, smiling. He rose, swept her
in his arms, laid her on his bed, and stretched out beside her.
Crooning deep in his throat he slipped his hands inside her garment, exploring, caressing. Caressing.

Soon she lay naked and beautiful, receiving him.

From somewhere the flute played again, and a teasing melody lingered on the breeze.

Almost it seemed like spring.

The caddí consulted the knots on his record strings and was
satisfied. The small bundles of twenty-two sticks had been given
to runners to distribute to other towns in the region. Recipients
would discard one stick a day until but one was left—which was
the day the ceremonies would begin. Swift canoes were sent to
notify ambassadors elsewhere. The plaza had been swept clean
and was being covered with new sand brought by the basketload.
Temporary structures were ready, and villagers' dwellings were
being cleaned, patched, and painted. Harvesting continued in
preparation for the fasting, the feasting, and for the winter to
come.

It was a busy time. Above all, it was the time of the New
Fire, a time of renewal and spiritual rebirth. During the Green
Corn ceremony, all wrongdoing except the crime of murder
would be forgiven, and disagreements, once settled, would be
settled permanently.

As governor of the city, the caddí would coordinate activities
for the Great Sun, the shaman, and the High Priest. The War
Chief would be responsible for order and activities among the
citizens and visitors and would supply guards for the plaza during the fasting and purification.

There was much to be done. The caddí laid down his counting strings and bustled outside.

The days passed quickly and visitors began to arrive. The
sentinels along the river were busy checking arriving canoes to
determine if the occupants were invited guests. If not, tribute
was required. One Who Watches, on the entrance mound west
of the city, was equally busy. It was said that more visitors than

ever before would be present for the Green Corn ceremony this year.

New ceremonial robes were made, new headdresses were fashioned, and the sacred shell cups and medicine bundles were readied for display in the plaza.

Thunder drums boomed as visitors continued to appear. A long canoe appeared in the distance, one richly carved and painted, with ten paddlers on either side and a canopy concealing occupants and contents. There was a babble of excited curiosity. Twenty paddlers! People waited for the canoe to draw near. It did not approach the city, but anchored at a distance downstream.

Nobody knew whose canoe it might be.

The Great Sun stood on the terrace of his dwelling mound and gazed over his city. All was going well. The shaman had consulted his crystal and communicated with the spirits and with Long Man, and the signs were propitious. The gods would be pleased. A great crowd would witness the sacrifice. The City of the Great Sun was the only one that included human sacrifice in the Green Corn ceremony—which might be why so many came to see. The Great Sun stood proudly; his city was the most sacred, the most powerful of all.

No one, not even the High Priest, knew his secret. No one, that is, but Firekeeper and old Waikah, and they were not about to donate their heads for arrow practice.

He smiled.

Antelope's child was growing more beautiful daily; a perfect gift for the Spirit Being. Lipoe would be displeased, of course, to discover that Skyfeather had been sacrificed, but after all he had not told Lipoe that she could keep Skyfeather permanently.

A switch would be made at the last minute; Skyfeather would be sacrificed instead of the other child. No one would know the difference—a baby was a baby.

He, the Great Sun, would have his revenge on the Towa woman at last.

·23·

It was very early in the morning and Peg Foot was still asleep. His bone peg lay on the floor beside him, attached to the wrappings that fastened it to his leg. The wrappings were soiled and the peg was grimy.

Antelope lay awake, thinking of Far Walker, thinking of Chomoc, and longing for Skyfeather. The pain of separation was hard to bear. She had to do something to ease the longing; keeping busy helped. Her glance fell on the peg and its wrappings. Peg Foot never allowed her to touch his peg while he wore it, but now he was asleep.

Quietly, she rose and tiptoed to his bed. He slept fitfully. Without the ornaments on his crest, or the garments and handsome gorget signifying his rank, and without the vigorous spirit that animated him when he was awake, he was a frail old man, snuffling in his sleep.

She felt a surge of affection for him. They needed each other and he had been kind to her; she would reciprocate. She dressed quickly, picked up the peg with its smelly wrappings, and slipped outside.

It was still dark, not yet *pulatla* when Sunfather appears to cast his golden mantle, but it was light enough for Antelope to make her way to the clothes-washing place at the river. She waded to the scrubbing stone, a smooth, flat-topped stone near the river's edge. She dipped the peg and wrappings in the cold water, rubbed the wrappings on the stone, then scrubbed the bone peg clean with sand.

It was pleasant there alone in the early morning with the river singing its water song. How could the people here believe that a monster lived in the river's depths? Of all their strange beliefs, this was one of the most outlandish. Nobody had ever seen it, of course, but the creature was supposed to be part serpent and part bird. Originally, it was said to have been a man who tried to kill the sun, but failed and was transformed into a jealous monster who would snatch people in the river or even on the riverbank and drag them down, never to be seen again.

As Antelope scrubbed the peg, she longed to be home again with her own people who knew that no monsters lived in rivers, and that the river itself was not a deity, but a gift from Massau'u to be respected. But while she lived here, she must be considerate of people's beliefs—no matter what they were.

Pausing, she glanced upstream where visitors' canoes were beached on the bank. In the far distance, one canoe by itself was anchored near the river's edge, tied to a tree. It seemed to be a very long dugout covered by a canopy. Important visitors, no doubt; probably ambassadors, waiting to enter the city in the morning. Far Walker had said ambassadors would arrive for the most important ceremony of the year.

Antelope waded ashore. Peg Foot would have a clean peg and wrappings for the events. She wrung the wrappings as dry as she could; they would finish drying by the cooking fire.

When she returned, Peg Foot was up and hopping about in a rage.

"Where is my peg?" he shouted.

"Here. I washed it, see?"

He snatched it from her and waved it in the air. "Who gave you permission to take my peg?"

She snatched it back. "You could not give permission in your sleep. It was filthy and now it is clean. I shall dry it by the fire and polish the peg so it shines." She smiled. "You will look nice for the ceremonies. Sit down outside by the fire and I will prepare your porridge."

"Give me my peg."

She handed it to him. He examined it, turning it over in both hands. "Humph." He handed it back. "Dry it." His voice was gruff but his glance was gentle. He hopped outside with the aid of his staff and sat down awkwardly, bracing himself.

Antelope laid the peg and its wrappings on a stone near the fire, but not so close that the wrappings would be damaged. The stone was warm and the wrappings would dry quickly.

It was lighter now; soon Sunfather would appear. It would be a crisp, sunny day with clouds billowing. Fragrant smoke wafted from other cooking fires, and the city stirred to life. Babies cried, dogs barked, and the rhythmic sound of women pounding corn in their mortars of hollowed-out stumps mingled with busy sounds from the river.

Those who came to Peg Foot for healing were generous in payment and his dwelling was well stocked with provisions. Peg Foot liked hominy porridge cooked with doves, and Antelope had prepared a large portion the day before. She went back inside and used a gourd dipper to scoop some from a storage jar, and poured the porridge into a cooking pot to warm. She found a spoon Peg Foot had made from a gourd; it had a long, curved handle and was beautiful. She took it, his eating bowl, and the pot out to him where he sat cross-legged on a mat. Soon the pot simmered, wafting a tantalizing aroma.

"Isn't it ready yet?" Peg Foot asked. "I am hungry."

Antelope scooped a large portion into his eating bowl and set it on the mat before him. While he ate with audible relish, she waited for him to finish before she ate. It was the custom here—one she resented, but it was important to follow customs. So she sat quietly, thinking of Skyfeather and Chomoc, thinking of her home in Cicuye and of Acoya, her brother, wishing she could see him again, wishing she could go home.

Peg Foot smacked his lips and belched politely. "Good!"

Sunfather rose in glory and was greeted with shouts of "Hou!" by people facing the Spirit Being. Antelope greeted Sunfather with her own song, learned as a child in Cicuye. She brought a bowl of cornmeal from the house and offered it to Sunfather with outstretched arms.

Now this day,
My sun father,
Now that you have come out

Standing in your sacred place
From which comes the water of life,
Prayer meal here I give you.

She tossed a handful of cornmeal toward the sun. Her voice soared, high and pure, as she sang:

> *Your long life,*
> *Your old age,*
> *Your waters,*
> *Your seeds,*
> *Your riches,*
> *Your power,*
> *Your strong spirit,*
> *All these to me may you grant.*

Peg Foot stood beside her, bracing himself awkwardly with his staff.

"Who taught you that song?"

"It is the song my people sing to greet Sunfather."

"Ah. It is a good song, a good prayer. But it is a man's song." He poked at the bone and wrappings. "I need these."

He reached for his peg. The wrappings were not totally dry but they were dry enough. Antelope tried to help Peg Foot attach the peg to the stump of his leg, but he indignantly refused. He had done it alone all these years. Why did he need a woman's help now?

Antelope sighed. Men wore an invisible skin that bled when scratched, and it was scratched easily. She ate what was left of the porridge in the pot, and took the pot, bowl, and spoon to be washed in the river.

It was a fine day and smelled good with smoke from cooking fires and delicious aromas from pots. There would be much tasty food for the ceremonies. The river smelled good, too. Long Man ran swiftly and small fish ran with him. Antelope saw them, bits of shining color flashing by.

As she washed the utensils in the river, a commotion arose upstream. The huge dugout canoe with a canopy and ten paddlers on either side sped swiftly toward the city. The paddlers chanted in rhythm, bending forward and back, muscular bodies gleaming in the morning sunlight reflected on the river. The canopy was richly painted in brilliant designs and hid whoever, whatever was inside. Banners on the canopy flapped in the breeze.

Antelope stood staring. Could this be the queen returning? The one who had taken Chomoc away? But this canoe was huge!

A crowd gathered on a ridge overlooking the river's bend where the canoe would be stopped by sentinels in canoes lined up blocking the river. As a security measure, warriors were posted on both banks, weapons in hand.

Never had a canoe sped as swiftly as this, with twenty strong men chanting and bright banners billowing! The huge canoe approached so swiftly it seemed it would crash its way through the sentinel canoes awaiting it. But with a shouted command from someone beneath the canopy, the canoe slowed and stopped. Immediately, it was surrounded by guard canoes.

Someone emerged from beneath the canopy to confer with the sentinels. Antelope strained to see who it might be, but distance and the surrounding canoes made it impossible. Well, no matter, she would find out eventually. She picked up the clean pot and bowl and spoon and was about to return to Peg Foot when she stopped in her tracks.

A flute. A flute like no one else's.

Chomoc!

She glanced at her bare muddy feet, and the old, wrinkled garment she wore, which used to belong to one of Peg Foot's mates; she had been saving her nice one for the ceremonies. She smoothed her tangled hair.

He must not see me like this!

Heart racing, she ran to Peg Foot's dwelling. He was inside, working on a patient, a frightened young woman with a bleeding wound on her arm.

"He comes!" Antelope said.

Peg Foot glanced up, annoyed at the interruption. "Who?"

"Chomoc!"

Peg Foot nodded. "He comes for the ceremonies." He bent over the woman's arm, applying a poultice. Antelope was dismissed.

Hurriedly, she removed the tangles from her hair with a comb Far Walker had brought her, rubbed her feet clean with water from the water jar, put on her moccasins, and slipped into the beautiful white robe given to her by Far Walker.

The young woman looked up at Antelope as she prepared to leave.

"You look beautiful," the woman said wistfully. Her own robe was old and unadorned; Antelope's glistened with pearls and bright embroidery.

"Thank you." Antelope smiled and ran out the door.

The flute called, teasing, promising. Antelope ran toward the beaching place as swiftly as the crowd permitted. When she drew near, she stopped.

He has been gone long. I must not appear too eager.

She smoothed her hair with both hands, took a deep breath, and walked with grace and dignity to the canoe where Chomoc stood. She worked her way through the crowd and stood looking at him.

The great canoe was beached. Twenty paddlers, strong men all, were lined up before it. Each man wore a short deerskin breechclout; intricate tattoos covered the body. The hair was fashioned with a stiff crest on the crown and a long hank hanging behind. Large earspools, bracelets at wrist and ankle, and heavy necklaces made a splendid display. But nothing compared to the man standing behind them—Chomoc.

He stood on the bow of the canoe, one foot resting on the edge, playing his flute. A magnificent feathered cape, fastened at his shoulders, floated behind him in the breeze, undulating as if to his music. His bare, bronzed chest was aglow with necklaces of turquoise, copper, shells, and polished stones of many colors. Bracelets adorned his arms above the elbows, his wrists, his legs below the knees, and his ankles. His short breechclout of softest deerskin was beautifully beaded, and he wore a wide sash with a long, beaded fringe. His moccasins were beaded also, and handsomely fringed.

Chomoc was a magnificent sight, and aware of it. He stood at the bow of the biggest canoe anyone had ever seen, and rejoiced with his flute.

How wonderful it was to see him again! He wore his hair in his old fashion with one thick braid down the back, adorned with feathers; his tall headdress of green and white feathers stirred when touched by the breeze. His ears were pierced in three places, and jewels hung from each. He wore strange markings on his forehead and chin, and both arms were tattooed. Antelope found herself looking at Chomoc as if for the first time, as if he were a stranger.

If he saw her, he gave no sign as he continued to play, his eyes closed, his fingers dancing on the reed.

Gradually, his music changed. It became tender, reminiscent. His flute sang of days past, of childhood gone, of remembrance.

He is playing for me.

She was a child again, sitting among golden leaves in the forest while Chomoc sang to her with his flute. Tears welled in her eyes.

The music stopped. Chomoc looked at her, a smile in his amber eyes. "I greet you."

He held out his arms, and she went to him. He helped her climb into the canoe and led her inside, under the canopy, away from the murmuring crowd and curious stares. It was dim, almost like night, in there, but Antelope could see the piles of baskets and bowls, and the places where the men slept. He removed his headdress and feather mantle and laid them aside. Then he led her to a raised bunk, lay down, and pulled her down beside him.

She resisted and sat up. Was this the Chomoc she used to know, used to love? But of course he was.

"We must talk," she said.

"Why?"

"I must know why you left Skyfeather and me."

He sat up beside her. "I thought you knew. The queen kidnapped me." Was there a hint of smugness in his voice?

"Why?"

"She wanted me as one of her consorts."

"And you were?"

"I had no choice." He lay down again. "But I am here now and I have missed you. Come." He pulled her down beside him. "My beautiful one."

He kissed her, whispering endearments. In his embrace, listening to his rich voice, she knew he was the Chomoc whom she had longed for. They made love in the old way, under the painted canopy, while people crowded about outside.

Later, in the semidarkness, in Chomoc's arms, Antelope found herself experiencing mixed emotions. The man she had loved, the man she had married, was here at last. Loving her at last. But it was different from what she expected.

He was different, somehow.

"I must tell you what has happened," Antelope said.

She told him about Many Bears and the jaguar, and the decision of the council.

He was outraged. "Do you mean they gave *my* belongings to Red Leaf?"

"Everything but my necklace and the garment I wore."

"Red Leaf has my turquoise, my salt, my rainbow flint—"

"Everything. And they forbid me to teach; I am She Who Remembers no more. Now I live with Peg Foot."

"They had no right. Those valuables belonged to me. *To me!*"

Was he more concerned about his belongings than he was about her? She continued, "That isn't all. I must tell you about Skyfeather."

As she told him he grew excited. "She is a royal child! We are parents of royalty. Think how this will increase the value of my trading! I can make up for what was taken away—"

Antelope froze in stunned disbelief. Had he no concern for their child at all? Was trading his only consideration?

Now was the time to tell him. "I want Skyfeather back, Chomoc. And I want you to take me home."

There was a long silence. He sat up. "I cannot."

"You cannot get your daughter back?"

"No." His voice was harsh. "I will never return to Cicuye." He leaned over her and Antelope could sense the tension in him. "Come with me to the City of the North. You must see it. It is unbelievable! Bigger, better than the small village of Cicuye"— contempt withered his voice—"or this city. A huge walled metropolis, fortified, with many mounds, many dwellings. We will live like royalty from my trading—"

"Not without Skyfeather. Not without our child." Antelope sat up and faced him. "I want to return to Cicuye. I want to go home."

He rose abruptly, and stood staring down at her.

"Then you must go," he said coldly. "But you will go without me."

Antelope rose, smoothed her hair and the robe Far Walker had given her.

Chomoc is like his father, Kokopelli. Trading comes first. Always. And always his flute will sing its magical way, obtaining whatever, whomever Chomoc desires.

Except me.

She left without saying good-bye.

·24·

The night before the Green Corn ceremony was to begin, Far Walker stood at a sacred place on Long Man; it was a secluded spot upriver where willows bent low. The full moon glistened, enveloping trees and river in radiance. Far Walker stood naked on the bank, facing east, and sang his prayer:

I come, O sacred one, to beseech your protection of her who is called Antelope and her girl child, Skyfeather. I beg that you keep them safe from those who seek to harm them or to take them away. Away from me . . .

He had seen Antelope go to Chomoc when that magnificent canoe arrived. Far Walker knew well what had happened during the time that Chomoc and Antelope were hidden under the canopy. Jealousy raged in him, and fear. His love potion had worked—for a while. But now Chomoc was back with all his wealth and glory, and Antelope had gone to him—her mate.

Far Walker had made it a point to avoid Antelope since.

Never would it be said that he, Far Walker, was a discarded, grieving lover.

He grieved in secret.

I have fasted. I have purified myself in the sweat lodge. I go tomorrow to cleanse myself internally with the black drink. I beg your purification now, O sacred one. Give Antelope and Skyfeather to me alone. This is my prayer.

Far Walker submerged himself in the river seven times, and seven times he sang his prayer.

The morning of the Green Corn ceremony dawned cloudy and cool. The shaman consulted his crystal again. It was supposed to have been a clear, sunny day; that was what the omens had promised. Was the Spirit Being displeased?

The shaman had begun his fast last night. He had a strange dream, one he did not understand. He dreamed that a white buffalo confronted him, shaking its great bearded head, and stared at him with fearsome pink eyes. The buffalo spoke. Its voice was like distant thunder, but the shaman could not understand the words. Then the buffalo dissolved into mist and was gone.

What did the buffalo say? What did it mean?

True, Antelope had called the buffalo—which were approaching closer daily—and he, the shaman, had taken the credit. But after all, it was the shaman's responsibility to make buffalo accessible, regardless of the method used, and this he had done. Soon the buffalo would be close enough for hunters to obtain all they needed in a single day.

What did the white buffalo say?

The shaman stepped outside to inspect the sky. It was overcast; dark clouds billowed on the horizon. Perhaps it would rain—a blessing. But the omens had promised a cloudless day so that the Spirit Being could observe the ceremonies in his honor. Was the Spirit Being displeased?

Perhaps he should consult the High Priest.

But no. The High Priest had assumed certain responsibilities that he, the shaman, claimed as his own, such as supervising the digging of the pit for the sacred fire in the plaza. Consulting the High Priest would imply that his knowledge was superior, and the shaman did not care to give the High Priest more power than he already had.

The Crier and his drum called all men to the plaza. It was time to go. The shaman adjusted his finest robe and put on the rest of his jewelry, but he did not don his deer mask. He would be partaking of the black drink, purifying himself internally, and would not be able to expel through the small mouth of the mask. He would wear the mask later.

With a final glance at the threatening sky, the shaman strode to the plaza.

All the men, except those who were sick or otherwise incapacitated, or those who for some reason were unworthy, thronged the plaza, which was guarded by warriors. No children or females were permitted except certain women who were allowed to bring the black drink. If a dog wandered in, it would be met with arrows.

The men had fasted the night before and would fast this day and night, drinking a brew made of a species of holly and other plants with emetic qualities. Purification was essential. While the High Priest chanted and the shaman danced to the throb of drums, the men drank more and more, then vomited. Some were able to press their arms across the stomach and expel to a distance of five or six moccasins.

One Who Watches and a few other chosen women, including Poqua, brought more black drink and set the jars at the edge of the plaza. The young priest Wak-Wala distributed the drink among the men. Firekeeper remained in the temple, awaiting the arrival of the Great Sun for his personal purification.

Far Walker swallowed the bitter brew as he watched Chomoc, who swallowed more than anyone and seemed unaffected. Antelope's mate did everything in excess, it seemed.

I must clear my mind of these thoughts. I must purify my mind as well as my body.

But it was difficult. Every man wore his most beautiful ceremonial garment, but Chomoc's outshone them all. He was not the tallest man, but he stood as if he were; even sitting or squatting, he had an arrogant stance. With his high arched nose, wide sensual mouth, and slanting brow he was far from handsome, yet even the northern queen wanted him. Why?

Why?

I must clear my mind.

Far Walker mingled with ambassadors from distant clans who drank the black drink fervently. Medicine bundles hung from poles stuck in the ground, and sacred shell cups engraved with jaguar and armadillo designs were on display. Also on view were sanctified copper plates and ornaments that priests had washed and polished the night before. These were shown only during the Green Corn ceremony.

Drums throbbed, the High Priest chanted, and the shaman danced.

Horned Toad had been chosen to place a basket of old tobacco outside the plaza for Poqua to take to men who were ill or unworthy or otherwise unable to participate. Far Walker watched as she hobbled slowly to the edge of the plaza and took the basket. He knew the recipients would eat the bitter leaves to purify themselves, and would be sick afterward.

Far Walker noticed with concern how Poqua walked; she was hurting. Why didn't she come to him? He could ease her pain. Did she not come because of his friendship with Antelope? The Green Corn ceremony was the time to forget past wrongs and renew friendships. Perhaps he should mention this to Antelope. It would be a good excuse to see her again. . . .

At midday, men gathered in solemn groups for discussion. All disputes settled this day would be settled permanently.

A wind rose, unusually cool for the Green Corn moon.

Lipoe dressed Skyfeather in a new deerskin garment, a white one embroidered with tiny pearl beads.

"After Chipmunk goes, you and I will attend the Green Corn ceremony, little one," she crooned. "You will be the most beautiful little girl there. And I will be the prettiest mother." She laughed, tossing her long hair. "I have a new robe, too. See?"

Lipoe smoothed her white robe adorned with pearl beads, like Skyfeather's, but with more elaborate embroidery and little shell and copper ornaments.

There were footsteps outside and Chipmunk entered. She looked frightened, but then slaves were supposed to be frightened. "Hou! Hou!"

Lipoe held Skyfeather up for display. "Doesn't she look beautiful?"

"Yes."

Chipmunk took Skyfeather to nurse, bending her head over the baby so that her long hair concealed her thin face.

Lipoe watched in silence for a time. Something bothered

Chipmunk and Lipoe was curious. Finally, she said, "Have you been watching the ceremonies?"

Chipmunk darted a quick glance at Lipoe. "Yes." She paused and looked down. "The Great Sun spoke to me before he went to the temple. He told me to bring Skyfeather to him there for sanctification."

"That is ridiculous. Skyfeather is my daughter. She needs no sanctification."

Chipmunk cast Lipoe a wretched glance. "I must obey."

"Of course." Men could be so unreasonable, and the Great Sun was no exception. But at least it indicated his regard for Skyfeather, to take her to the Temple of Eternal Fire for consecration.

"Very well. You have my permission to take my daughter to the Great Sun when you leave here," Lipoe said graciously, thinking how many people would see Skyfeather's new robe, more beautiful than any seen before. Surely she, Lipoe, was a mother to be envied by all!

Later, Chipmunk hurried down the steps of the mound, holding Skyfeather tightly in both arms. Her heart thudded. She was a slave, captured in war, and was lucky to be alive, but now she wished she were dead.

She did not go to the temple. Rather, she did as the Great Sun had commanded and ran toward the plaza. Behind one of the mounds near the plaza, a man would be waiting. The executioner. With a baby for sacrifice—a baby to be traded for Skyfeather. Beautiful little Skyfeather would die in the other baby's place.

Chipmunk choked back tears; she felt her heart would break. This child, whom she had nourished from her own body, deserved to live. Skyfeather's blue eyes saw things, Chipmunk knew—things others did not see. Would she see her executioner for what he was?

Almost, Chipmunk decided to disobey and let the other baby die. But disobedience brought torture as well as death. She did not want to die. Nor did she want to be stretched naked on a rack and be pierced with burning pokers in sensitive places.

Sobbing aloud, she reached the place where the executioner waited, handed Skyfeather to him, and took the other child, a boy. The Great Sun had ordered the boy to be presented to Lipoe as a gift from him, since she had produced no son of her own.

The sacrifice would take place tomorrow after the New Fire ceremony. What would happen when she brought the other baby to Lipoe?

Chipmunk trembled.

Fasting ended on the third day. Women cooked big pots of food, placed them outside the edge of the plaza, and returned home. Men who had fasted two nights and a day ate, but they ate slowly; it would be improper to break so solemn a fast in a hasty manner.

By noon, all the food was eaten, and vessels were cleared from the plaza and taken by women to be washed in the river. Dark clouds hung low and anxious eyes watched. Rain was needed, but the finest garments and headdresses were being worn. Some people had already changed to other raiment. Ambassadors and other honored guests huddled under arbors and temporary dwellings and watched the sky.

Thunder spoke over distant mountains.

The High Priest glanced skyward. He knew where the Spirit Being was, even though the sacred one was clothed in clouds. He summoned the Crier. "It is past noon. Announce the New Fire."

The Crier strode through the city. He carried his own drum this time, a large pottery one he had made, with a deerskin stretched across it. It had a deep, reverberating voice that accompanied his own very well.

"It is the time of New Fire!" he boomed, and his drum boomed with him. "It is the time of New Fire! Every spark of old fire must be extinguished. Stay inside your homes. Extinguish all fire, all sparks. Break no sacred law. The time of New Fire has come. New fires will be lit from sacred temple fire carried to the plaza. Prepare!"

The High Priest stood by the fire pit in the plaza. Dark clouds cast an eerie light on his twisted figure, clad in white. His white buckskin moccasins were painted red across the toes, and were adorned with a tufted pair of wild turkey spurs. The moccasins and robe were worn only for the Green Corn ceremony.

He peered at the sky and signaled the shaman. The shaman approached and stood beside the High Priest, who was totally aware of how the tall, lean figure emphasized the deformities of his own.

The High Priest said, "A storm approaches that will surely quench a fire."

The shaman nodded. "It is an omen. We must delay."

The High Priest thought, *At least there is something on which we agree.* Again, he inspected the sky. "Where is the Great Sun?"

"In the temple."

"Good. He will be safe there."

A chill wind gusted. Distant thunder rolled over the hills. A few drops of rain fell, then more. The High Priest hurried for shelter to protect his precious garments. His slow, lurching gait did not get him there soon enough and his fine white robe and moccasins were dampened. He stood with some of the ambassadors in a temporary shelter, watching the storm as it approached, listening to the storm's mighty voice. The storm carried the scent of rain, of growing things drenched, of dry earth saturated, and the metallic odor of air lacerated by lightning.

Darkness gathered. The black clouds, with august majesty and power, moved slowly forward, threatening destruction. Abruptly, all was still. Not a whisper was heard, but total inactivity and silence enfolded the earth. The birds did not utter a sound, but took leave of each other, seeking cover and safety. Even insects were silent. Then, suddenly, the storm's tremendous roar was upon them, bellowing its power.

The mighty clouds now expanded their sable wings from east to west, driven irresistibly by a tumultuous wind. The city vibrated with the fury of thunderclaps. Fiery shafts of lightning flashed and hissed. Trees bent beneath the storm's fury, tossing their limbs and boughs in wild convulsions. The arbors in the plaza were swept away, leaving people exposed to a raging downpour, and the roofs of some of the temporary dwellings were blown away.

"Seek shelter!" the High Priest shouted. The shaman and the Crier echoed the order, and people ran frantically to the nearest dwelling. The High Priest headed for the Temple of Eternal Fire. The force of the downpour slowed his progress as rain pounded down.

Once more thunder boomed in terrible power; once more lightning seared the darkness.

An explosion followed, and the earth shuddered.

The High Priest stopped and gazed in unbelieving horror.

The Temple of Eternal Fire was split open. Walls lay in crumbled piles. The temple's sacred and beautiful contents were strewn about, battered by the downpour.

The High Priest stood alone, drenched and grieving. This was a terrible omen. What had taken place here? What had his people done to merit such a catastrophe?

Where was the Great Sun?

Slowly, the High Priest became aware of people shouting, screaming, sobbing. Some ran up the temple steps and stood staring in shock.

Painfully, the High Priest dragged himself to the temple steps. His fine white robe, his white moccasins, were sodden and would never be worn again. Ducking his head in the rain, he dragged himself up the steps one at a time. More thunder boomed, more lightning hissed, but still the High Priest climbed to his temple.

A temple no more.

The High Priest stood among the rubble, gazing at the ruins. He groaned.

The sacred fire was extinguished.

His star wall of diagrams was gone. Baskets of hallowed objects lay scattered about, drinking rain. The altar was split; it had been hit squarely in the center. Pipes and other sacred articles were buried in the debris, and the feathers and pearls that had adorned the temple walls lay sodden in the ruins.

All this the High Priest saw. But his appalled gaze was riveted on the broken body of the Great Sun, which lay sprawled by the altar, and the crumpled form of his cherished priest, Firekeeper.

▲25▼

Chipmunk hugged herself in joy. The Great Sun was dead. She had seen him in the stricken temple with her own eyes. Soon he would be buried, and his mates would be buried with him; that was the custom.

Soon Lipoe would be dead, and Kala also, killed to accompany their mate to the Afterworld. Because Lipoe believed that Skyfeather had been in the temple with the Great Sun, she would assume the baby was dead, too.

Again, Chipmunk hugged herself. Never again would she have to endure Lipoe's arrogance, and never again would the Great Sun make demands of her. Never! He was dead, dead, dead.

Chipmunk stood in the pounding rain, rejoicing. In her arms was the baby boy she was supposed to give to Lipoe in exchange for Skyfeather, but now she would not have to endure that confrontation. The baby was not an attractive child, but he was healthy. However, after having Skyfeather, Lipoe would have been outraged at the substitution. She, Chipmunk, would have had to bear the brunt of Lipoe's fury.

No more, no more. The body of the Great Sun would lie in

state for four days, then he and his mates would be buried. Lipoe would be gone. Forever.

The ceremonies had come to an abrupt halt with the destruction of the temple and the death of the Great Sun—a fearsome omen; there would be no sacrifice. Chipmunk knew the Great Sun and Firekeeper would be sent to the Afterworld with proper ritual. But how could the city survive without its sacred fire?

The little boy squirmed and cried.

"Hush, small one. You will have your mother again."

A woman hurried by, and Chipmunk stopped her.

"This is Blue Wing's child. Please give him to her."

Accosted by a slave and battered by rain, the woman hesitated.

"Please," Chipmunk pleaded. "I cannot, and he needs his mother."

She thrust the crying baby into the woman's arms and ran away before the woman could give the baby back.

I must find Skyfeather!

She ran to the place behind the mound where the executioner had waited. He was not there. Skyfeather lay on the ground, battered by the downpour. She had crawled away a little distance from the mound and lay on her side, covering her face, trying to protect herself.

"Poor little baby, poor little one!" Chipmunk crooned, and picked her up.

Skyfeather whimpered and cuddled in her arms.

For a moment, Chipmunk thought of keeping Skyfeather for herself. She would love to! But no, that was impossible. She must return the child to Antelope. Surely a reward would be offered.

The City of the Great Sun was in turmoil. People wept and shouted and ran for their homes. Ambassadors and visitors from distant places left hurriedly to avoid contamination from whatever evil it was that had stricken the city. Of the visitors, only Chomoc remained.

Antelope returned to Peg Foot's dwelling to find him alone and grieving. "Our city is cursed. Something evil has happened here." He wrapped his arms around his knees and rocked to and fro. "Trouble comes. Aye."

Remembering the Great Sun, Antelope was not sorry he was dead. She wanted to make Peg Foot feel better, but didn't know how. Finally, she said, "Rain was needed. That, at least, is a blessing."

He kept rocking. "We are cursed."

Footsteps hurried through the extended doorway, and Chipmunk entered.

"Look!" Chipmunk handed Skyfeather to her mother, beaming.

Antelope gasped. Skyfeather! She couldn't believe it. At first, she thought her child was dead because she was so limp. Heart thudding, Antelope clasped Skyfeather close. Having her again was a miracle, too much to accept.

"Ah!" She could say nothing more, but gazed at the wet little form that clung to her.

Chipmunk leaned close, whispering. "Keep her here until after the funeral. Lipoe thinks Skyfeather was with the Great Sun in the temple and that she died with him."

Peg Foot said, "Are you sure about that?"

Chipmunk glanced furtively about as if for eavesdroppers. "The Great Sun commanded me to tell Lipoe that I was to take Skyfeather to the temple for sanctification, but secretly he ordered me to take Skyfeather to the executioner." She leaned closer. "For sacrifice."

"No!" Antelope gasped, clutching Skyfeather closer.

Chipmunk continued, "After the Great Sun was killed, I ran to where the executioner had been, but he was gone. Skyfeather was there all by herself. Lying on the ground. In the rain. So I brought her here."

"Thank you!" Antelope said with tears in her voice. "I thank you!"

"I knew you would be happy to have your baby back." Chipmunk glanced pointedly around the room, taking inventory.

"I have nothing to offer in reward but my gratitude," Antelope said.

Peg Foot crossed the room to a large basket. He lifted the lid and removed a length of fine cotton cloth given to him by a patient as payment. He offered the cloth to Chipmunk. "With my thanks also."

Chipmunk snatched the cloth and held it close, her eyes

brimming. "I have had no new garment since—since your people made me a slave." Without another word, she turned and ran from the room.

Antelope looked at Peg Foot with blessing in her gaze. "That was kind. And generous."

Skyfeather whimpered, and Antelope held the baby to her breast, hoping milk remained, but Skyfeather refused to nurse.

"She is wet and uncomfortable," Peg Foot said.

Antelope laid Skyfeather down and removed the soiled, sopping robe with its little pearl beads. Skyfeather's body seemed unusually warm, and she looked sleepy. Her blue eyes had no sparkle, and she was listless.

Antelope's heart constricted. Something was wrong with her child. "I'm afraid Skyfeather is sick."

Peg Foot bent over the baby, examining her eyes, poking a finger into her mouth to open it wide. Skyfeather cried and jerked her head away. Peg Foot ran his hands over the small body, prodding it gently, and bent his head to listen to her heart.

He nodded. "Something has harmed her. Witches, perhaps."

Antelope wanted to shout, to scream. She had her little daughter back at last, but an evil presence had taken possession. She trembled as if she, too, were sick. "What can we do?"

"I must learn who or what has harmed her. Then I will know what to do."

The storm was abating; thunder was a distant growl.

Peg Foot rose, his eyes intent, his manner professional—the Healer and Teacher, famed up and down the river.

"I go now to Long Man. I shall need burning coals and hot ashes when I return. If anyone questions you about building a fire, inform them that I ordered it for a medical emergency." He gave Antelope a kindly glance. "I shall do my best."

The rain had stopped; the storm was over, but dark clouds still hung low. Peg Foot headed for the river and saw that Far Walker was there with a patient, a young girl. He was using a conch shell cup to pour water on the girl's head and chest.

Peg Foot was surprised. A conch shell cup? That was not what he had taught Far Walker; a Healer should use his hand for such treatment. Conch shell cups were reserved for ceremonial occasions or for sending engraved messages to ambassadors. However, the girl was Far Walker's patient, it was his treatment, and he should be undisturbed.

Peg Foot made his way downstream to a favorite spot and stood on the bank. Long Man had increased in width and strength with the storm; leaves and twigs and branches swept by. This was good—it added potency to the water. Perhaps that was why Far Walker used a conch shell cup, to further increase Long Man's effectiveness.

A teacher may learn from a student, Peg Foot thought. *Perhaps I should ask Far Walker's assistance with Skyfeather. But only if the beads fail me.*

From a pouch at his side, Peg Foot removed two beads, one red and one black. These would determine whether or not he could discover who or what was harming Skyfeather. Chanting, he faced east and commanded his kia to master the beads.

He held the black bead between the thumb and forefinger of his left hand, and the red bead between the thumb and forefinger of the right hand. Still chanting and facing east, he extended both hands over Long Man. Concentrating with all his strength, he waited for the beads to move of their own accord in his hands.

Gradually, the red bead in his right hand began to stir. This was good; it meant his efforts would be successful. But then the black bead moved. It came to life like a tiny black beetle, slipped from his fingers, and crawled in his palm. The red bead moved no more.

Peg Foot groaned in despair.

I am too old. I cannot master the spirits as once I could. Skyfeather needs me, but she needs Far Walker more.

Carefully he replaced his precious beads in the pouch on his belt and followed the river to where Far Walker had been. The girl was gone but he was still there, praying, holding the conch shell cup in both hands.

Peg Foot stood silently, waiting. Far Walker finished his prayer, turned toward shore, and saw Peg Foot. He smiled in welcome. "What brings you?"

"Skyfeather. Bad spirits possess her, make her weak and feverish." Peg Foot swallowed; he had to say it, but it was not easy. "My beads tell me I will not discover who or what causes this. I request your help."

Far Walker gave Peg Foot a proud and solemn glance. "I will try, honored Teacher." He tucked the conch shell cup into a bag at his waist.

"Why did you use the cup?" Peg Foot asked.

"She was threatened in dreams. I changed her name."

Peg Foot nodded. A person's name was part of the physical being like an arm or leg, and sometimes it was necessary to change the name to deceive a vengeful spirit.

They walked in silence for a short distance. Then Peg Foot stopped and said, "I fear for Skyfeather. I think the Little People may be after her. Maybe the storm brought them."

Far Walker looked thoughtful. He knew that the Little People, no taller than a man's knee, lived in colonies in the mountains, in the rocks, and in forests. They were invisible (except to witches) and were kindly as a rule, helping hunters find their arrows or caring for lost travelers. But they also caused disease, and usually chose children as victims.

"That could be," Far Walker said reflectively. "Do you think we should search for witches?" Witches could assume any form, including that of Little People.

"Yes. I ordered Antelope to have hot ashes and burning coals ready for us. A medical emergency."

Far Walker hoped there would be no repercussions. No fires were to be lit until the sacred fire was renewed. But hot ashes and coals were necessary if Skyfeather was to be saved.

Peg Foot noticed with interest how pleased Far Walker seemed to be. Was it because he had been asked for professional assistance? Or was it because he would be with Antelope again? Far Walker had not been around since the storm and that had surprised Peg Foot. He had expected Far Walker to come to learn if they were safe. Perhaps Far Walker thought Chomoc might be there.

Peg Foot looked at Far Walker, who had adjusted his stride to match Peg Foot's slow limp. A thoughtful gesture, typical of him. This student of his was a superior person, a good man, a true Healer.

Chomoc had not come, not even to see his daughter.

While Peg Foot had gone to Long Man, Antelope was left alone with Skyfeather. She cradled the baby in her arms, rocking and crooning, trying not to be afraid of what was happening. She still stung from Chomoc's rejection. What had become of the Chomoc she knew? Or was it she herself who had changed?

Where was Far Walker? Why hadn't he come to see if they

were safe from the storm? Perhaps he was hurt somehow. If so, Peg Foot would know, but he had not mentioned it.

Skyfeather whimpered and Antelope held her close.

There were footsteps outside; perhaps Far Walker was coming. Antelope waited eagerly.

Red Leaf and Poqua entered. Antelope gazed in astonishment as they stood hesitantly inside the doorway.

"We greet you," old Poqua said, her voice wavering.

"My heart rejoices," Antelope replied in the traditional response. She was pleased and curious; why were they here? She had missed them. "Come in, come in."

Red Leaf said, "The Green Corn ceremony is when old wrongdoings are forgiven. We hope you will forgive ours."

Antelope was taken aback; she had not expected this. She said, "Of course. I have missed you. Please sit down."

They did not sit, but came closer to look at Skyfeather. Poqua touched the baby's face and glanced at Red Leaf, who was gazing intently at Skyfeather sleeping fitfully.

"What has happened?" Red Leaf asked.

"Sit down and I will tell you."

Antelope was comforted to have them there; it eased the burden on her heart. Red Leaf and Poqua sat on mats around the small fire Peg Foot had ordered so that coals and hot ashes would be ready for him.

Poqua and Red Leaf glanced at the fire uneasily, and looked at each other. No fire was to be built until the new sacred fire was lit and consecrated. What if the High Priest found out?

Antelope knew their concern. "Peg Foot said it was a medical emergency, so a fire was permissible." She laid Skyfeather down and brought sunflower seeds and dried persimmons for snacking.

"Tell us what happened," Poqua said.

As Antelope told her story, Poqua shook her gray head in agitation. "My singing stick spoke truly. It told me bad things would happen." She looked at Red Leaf, who had listened to Antelope's story in shocked silence, twisting tattooed fingers. "Remember?"

"Yes." Red Leaf wiped her forehead. "We want you to come back and live with us. The boys have missed you, too."

Antelope was surprised and touched. "I have missed them also; I missed all of you. But Peg Foot needs me. I must remain here."

There was silence as they nibbled on persimmons, dried and sweet from the sun, and hesitated to speak of the unspeakable—the death of the Great Sun and Firekeeper.

Antelope said, "Did the storm damage your dwelling?"

"No," Red Leaf replied, "but it ruined what was left of the garden."

"Most was already harvested," Poqua added.

Red Leaf twisted her fingers again. Finally she spoke. "Firekeeper and the Great Sun are being prepared for the Afterworld. It is said they will look beautiful."

"Aye," Poqua added. "And many fine things will go with them. Lipoe and Kala and Striped Serpent will make the journey also."

Antelope was shocked. This was not a Towa custom. "What about Firekeeper? Does she have a family that will be killed to go with her?"

"Only Waikah. But Waikah does not have to go with her sister unless she chooses to."

"After the funeral, the temple will be burned and another built upon the same place," Red Leaf added. Now that the unspeakable was being discussed, words tumbled out. "The new Great Sun will probably be Manimani, the Great Sun's sister, if she does not go with her brother to the Afterworld. The High Priest will decide, I think."

Skyfeather began to cry, and Antelope picked her up and held her to nurse. But the hot little body squirmed and she refused the breast.

"Give her to me," Poqua said.

Antelope handed the baby to her. Poqua cradled the child to her bony breast, poked a finger into Skyfeather's mouth, then put the finger in her own mouth, tasting it. She nodded.

"Her spittle has turned sour. She needs a potion. Where is Peg Foot?"

"Gone to Long Man. Coals and hot ashes will be ready for him when he returns."

Skyfeather cried weakly, turning her head away from Poqua.

"She wants me," Antelope said, and took the baby in her arms. She rocked back and forth. "Hush, little one. All will be well." But gazing into her daughter's face, Antelope felt the sorrow in her heart was more than she could bear.

All is not well. My baby is dying.

·26·

Hours passed but Peg Foot and Far Walker did not return. Red Leaf and Poqua sat silently, hands in their laps, offering comfort by their presence.

Antelope held Skyfeather close as if to absorb into herself the evil that was making the baby sick. Skyfeather's eyes were closed and her breathing was rapid and shallow. The little body seemed heavier somehow.

"Wake, sweet one!" Antelope said, touching Skyfeather's cheek. "Drink!" She held her breast to the baby's lips, trying desperately to give her child nourishment and strength. "Drink!"

Skyfeather sucked weakly, and stopped, her eyes still closed.

Antelope wanted to sob, to scream, but she must soothe her child. She rocked Skyfeather in her arms, crooning. The pressure of the scallop shell against Antelope's breast reminded her of who she was, and who Skyfeather would be someday. Antelope closed her eyes, reached deeply into her kia, and strained to reach her mother and the Ancient Ones, those who had gone before.

"Help us!" she cried silently, tears streaming. She visualized Kwani enveloping her with the loving blue gaze so well remembered. "Save your grandchild, who will become She Who Remembers—this child with your blue eyes. Heal her! Heal her!"

Did Kwani hear? Antelope could not be certain, but Sky-feather stirred, whimpering.

Poqua rose, straightening her old bones with effort. "I go to get my singing stick." She hobbled away, bracing herself on a staff.

Red Leaf's round face was clouded with concern. Her pudgy, tattooed fingers brushed a loose strand of black hair from her cheek. "You must eat to give strength to Skyfeather. I will pre-pare acorn bread and squash soup with raccoon—"

"Acorn bread is over there." Antelope swallowed her tears and pointed to a basket. It was true she needed strength for Sky-feather. "There is no raccoon but you may use venison." She indicated a bundle of jerky hanging from the ceiling.

Red Leaf rose, smoothing her garment over her stocky frame, ready to take charge. Antelope knew that because Red Leaf was of important lineage, one whose ancestors had been renowned hunters and warriors, she relished authority. Antelope welcomed assistance; she felt drained, as if the evil devouring Skyfeather devoured her, too.

It is because we are in a foreign place—with foreign medicine. What can Peg Foot and Far Walker do for Skyfeather? What she needs is a sand painting to invoke the powers of her Creator.

Red Leaf said, "Peg Foot will need boiling water, and I need some for soup." She pulled her stocky frame erect. "I will get water to heat on the fire. The fire . . ." Her voice trailed off. "Peg Foot is our chief Medicine Man, our Healer. Whatever he wants is permissible. I know he will want to make a brew." She came close to look down at Skyfeather. "Maybe the spirit of a lonesome relative calls her to the Afterworld." She glanced around the room. "Maybe the spirit comes to show the way."

Antelope's heart jerked. Was Kwani calling her granddaugh-ter to Sipapu? But no, that could not be. Skyfeather must be-come She Who Remembers. She would be needed.

"I go now." Red Leaf took a water jar and balanced it on her head. She had to squat a bit as she left to keep the jar from being knocked off by the low roof of the extended doorway.

Antelope watched her depart. She laid Skyfeather down on soft furs and knelt beside the small fire she had built on the sod floor in the center of the room; coals and ashes would be ready for Peg Foot. She was not sure how people here searched for witches, but she was willing to do anything that might help Sky-feather. If only she were home, Acoya would cure her; he knew magic with medicine.

There are different kinds of magic. I must give Peg Foot and Far Walker fair consideration. I must believe. . . .

There were steps outside and Poqua entered, carrying her singing stick. She did not speak but hobbled to the fire and sat down with the aid of her staff. She propped the notched stick between her knees, rubbed the smooth stick up and down the notches to make a rasping sound, and began to sing in her wavering voice, rocking to and fro. Her eyes were closed and her wrinkled face was rapt with concentration.

Much of Poqua's song was in an old language Antelope did not understand, but she did know some of the words. Poqua was pleading with the spirits of the tree from which the sticks were made to lend their strength and curative powers to Skyfeather.

Antelope's heart went out to her. Poqua was trying as best she could to help.

Red Leaf returned with a full water jar. She set the jar down, shaking her head.

"It is bad. People are leaving the city; it is cursed. The High Priest and the shaman will burn the temple and purify the plaza, but it is believed witches have come, and Little People—"

Poqua stopped singing and regarded Red Leaf calmly; her intelligent black eyes, encased in wrinkles, were serene. "We shall keep them away, you and I and the Healers. We shall spend the night here—"

"But you know witches steal the life force, the *orenda,* of sick people to add to their own. They put their mouths over the mouth of the sick one and suck the breath—"

"Stop!" Antelope cried. She bent over Skyfeather to see if her child was still breathing. She touched the small mouth and felt the breath. No other mouth was there. . . .

The entrance darkened and Far Walker and Peg Foot came in; Peg Foot carried a length of bark. They exchanged greetings. It seemed to Antelope that Far Walker filled the room when he glanced at her.

Peg Foot said proudly, "This bark is from the east side of a tree struck by lightning. It has powers." He handed it to Far Walker. "For the brew."

"Give me a cooking pot," Far Walker said to Antelope.

Antelope gave him the best pot, a good-sized one with handles she had made herself. Far Walker broke off pieces of the bark and dropped them into the pot. Peg Foot took the remainder of the bark and placed it in one of the baskets on shelves lining the wall.

Red Leaf indicated the water jar. "From Long Man."

Far Walker nodded and removed the conch shell cup from the pouch at his waist. Chanting softly, he dipped the cup into the jar four times and poured the water into the cooking pot.

"It is ready," he said. "Boil it until the water turns dark red."

Red Leaf set the pot on the coals. Peg Foot went to the altar and removed his most powerful pipe, one carved like a water serpent. Antelope's people treasured pipes of one kind or another, and she understood the importance of tobacco in ceremonies and in healing. She was grateful that Peg Foot used his best pipe now.

Peg Foot filled the pipe with aged tobacco from an incised pottery bowl with a lid; the lid's knob was a turtle, intricately carved. He glanced at Poqua and there was a moment of unspoken communication. Holding the pipe skyward, he began to chant. He held the pipe high for some time, then straight in front, toward the east, and toward the ground. Poqua accompanied him with the rasping rhythm of her singing stick.

In the dim light of the interior, Antelope felt she was another person, outside of herself, watching. The old Healer stood by his altar, invoking the spirits, while Far Walker stood beside him—the aged and frail, and the young and vigorous—in contrast but in spiritual harmony. This was a place of power, this Healer's lodge, with bowls and baskets and strange smells and bundles of mysterious herbs. Tobacco smoke drifted and filled the room with sacred essence. Poqua's singing stick coughed and whispered, and Antelope prayed.

Heal my child!

Peg Foot completed his chant and handed the serpentine pipe, stem first, to Far Walker. He accepted it reverently, smoked a puff, then blew the smoke over Skyfeather. He sang to her—words in an ancient tongue—blew smoke over her again, then handed the pipe back to Peg Foot, who replaced it upon the altar.

Far Walker turned to Antelope with a comforting gesture. "Now we search for witches." His attitude said, *Do not be afraid. I shall allow no witches here.*

Far Walker knelt by the fire, which had burned now to coals. Using a clam shell cooking implement, he scraped ashes aside into a small heap. Meanwhile, Peg Foot brought a gourd bowl of finely ground aged tobacco from a shelf and handed it to Far Walker.

"From the Great Serpent Mound of the east."

"Ah." Far Walker took the bowl carefully.

This was potent medicine, Antelope knew. She had heard of the Great Serpent Mound and its medicinal powers. She watched Far Walker take a tiny pinch of tobacco and drop it into the hot ashes.

"What does that do?" she asked.

He glanced up at her, pleased that she asked. "The center of the heap, here, represents this room where Skyfeather is. Any particle of tobacco that catches fire in the hot ashes to the right or left tells us from what direction a witch approaches. If the tobacco catches fire in the middle, a witch is directly overhead."

"I saw no spark."

"When there is no spark, there is no witch."

"Not yet," Peg Foot added.

Antelope wanted to shout, "Skyfeather needs a sand painting!" but these Healers used other methods; perhaps these methods were good. She remained silent.

Red Leaf stirred the contents in the pot. "The water is red."

"Good. Put it aside until it cools."

While the brew cooled, Antelope listened as Far Walker and Peg Foot quietly discussed possible causes of Skyfeather's illness.

Far Walker said, "As a baby, she could not have offended the spirit of some animal as hunters might."

"True," Peg Foot agreed. "But how about the *tsqalyá*, the insects and worms of every kind? When she was out there on the ground in the storm, maybe she crawled on some insect or worm whose spirit seeks revenge—"

"I think it is more likely the Little People. I heard them last night in the forest."

"Aye," Poqua said. "Singing, they were. I heard them, too. It sounded like wind in the trees."

"Tell me about the Little People," Antelope said.

"This tall," Far Walker said, indicating his knee. "With long hair falling down to their heels. They live in the mountains, in the rocks, in the water, and in the forest."

"Aye," Peg Foot added. "They have villages, clans, and houses, hold dances and councils just as we do. Travelers hear their music and dancing sometimes, especially if they are alone and lonely."

"Have you seen them?"

Peg Foot shook his head. "They are invisible. Except to witches."

"Then how can you know—"

"We know. They help hunters find their arrows, and sometimes they feed a lost traveler. But they can make children sick. . . ." He glanced at Skyfeather asleep on the furs. "We don't know why they do that."

"Maybe because children are small, like them," Far Walker said. "Maybe they feel threatened."

Skyfeather stirred and whimpered.

"Is the brew cool enough now?" Antelope asked.

Far Walker felt the bowl. "Yes." He picked up Skyfeather and held her carefully in one arm. With the other, he removed his conch shell cup and dipped it into the brew.

"Now, little one," he said, "you must drink."

Peg Foot produced a gourd rattle, which he shook, making a hissing sound. Far Walker propped Skyfeather in a sitting position and touched the cup to her lips.

With the sound of the rattle, Skyfeather opened her eyes and looked at him.

"She does not drink from a cup," Antelope said. "She drinks from me."

Far Walker's dark eyes regarded Antelope thoughtfully. He handed the baby to her and turned to Peg Foot. "May I use your blowing tube?"

Peg Foot nodded, rummaged in his medicine bundle, and handed Far Walker a reed tube as long as his middle finger.

"I will help her drink," Far Walker said. "Hold her steady."

As the rattle spoke, Far Walker lifted the cup, took a bit of brew into his mouth, put the tube to his lips, and leaned over Skyfeather. He inserted the tube into her mouth and ejected the brew into it.

Skyfeather choked and squirmed and swallowed and cried.

"She does not like that!" Antelope said, turning the baby away.

"No matter. She must have it. Here, little one, try again."

This time, she swallowed a bit more, still screaming. Again, Far Walker forced her to swallow.

"She has had enough. Hand her to me now."

Antelope gave him the baby and he held her a moment in his arms, looking down at her.

"Be healed, little one."

The rattle spoke. Skyfeather looked up at Far Walker as though she understood what he said. She had stopped crying and lay weakly, looking at him.

Far Walker laid Skyfeather down. Again, he dipped the tube into the conch shell cup, sucked up some of the brew, then expelled it on her small body. To the sound of the rattle he rubbed the brew all over her in a gentle circular motion, chanting meanwhile. Still she did not cry, but she did whimper when he turned her over to rub her back.

Antelope watched Far Walker's gentle touch and she saw his concern. She was comforted by his calm professionalism. His medicine was not the medicine of her people, but surely it was good. He was doing his best for Skyfeather.

Her heart warmed to him.

When the baby's body was completely covered with brew, Far Walker said, "The tree that survived the lightning will give its strength to her. Let her sleep, but watch for witches during the night. She is still weak."

Poqua said, "Red Leaf and I will spend the night here, helping Antelope and Peg Foot."

Peg Foot gestured with his rattle. "If we see a spark we will send for the shaman immediately. Go now and take care of your other patients. I will watch Skyfeather."

"Good." Far Walker took his cup and poured what was left of the brew back into the bowl. He glanced at Antelope. "You must drink a little of this brew also. It will give both of you strength when you nurse Skyfeather again."

His smile, sudden and intimate, took Antelope by surprise.

"Thank you" was all she could say.

He left, and it was as though the room became empty for a time. The four of them—Red Leaf, Poqua, Peg Foot, and Antelope—huddled around the small fire. The cooking pot was removed, and Peg Foot scraped together another small heap of hot ashes. He sprinkled ground bits of aged tobacco into the ashes. There was a sigh of relief when no spark appeared.

Red Leaf said, "We shall take turns during the night. I will watch first while the rest of you sleep."

Antelope shook her head. "I must watch—"

"You need sleep," Poqua said. "Red Leaf and I will take turns watching with Peg Foot. You lie down with Skyfeather and sleep now."

"Aye," Peg Foot said firmly, gesturing with his rattle again. "And drink some of the brew."

The rattle gives him authority, Antelope thought. She took a swallow of the brew; although it had a strange taste, it was not bitter. Skyfeather's breathing seemed more natural now and she slept again. Antelope lay beside her and cuddled close.

The murmur of voices, Poqua's chant with her singing stick, and the fragrance of smoke and tobacco blended into a soothing ambience.

She drifted into sleep.

▴27▾

Several times during the night Antelope woke to the sound of Poqua's chanting in rhythm with her singing stick. Skyfeather slept, breathing more easily. In the darkness, faintly illuminated by the small fire, Antelope saw Red Leaf or Peg Foot peering calmly into the ashes. Obviously, no witch was near. Reassured, Antelope floated back into sleep.

She woke to the sound of Skyfeather crying and the city's howls of welcome to the Spirit Being. Red Leaf and Poqua were gone, and Peg Foot slept nearby. Skyfeather waved her arms and legs and her little mouth was stretched wide.

She sounds as if she is hungry! Antelope thought. She picked up Skyfeather and held her to nurse. The baby suckled eagerly.

Skyfeather was getting well! Far Walker and Peg Foot had defeated the attacker, whoever or whatever it was. And Red Leaf and Poqua had helped to keep witches away. Joy and thankfulness flooded Antelope's heart. She held her baby close, feeling the warmth of the soft, small body in her arms, smoothing the drift of fine, dark hair on Skyfeather's cheek.

She needs a bath. I will take her to the river and we shall bathe. That will make us both feel better.

Peg Foot stirred awake. He sat up, his gray tuft in disarray and his wrinkles etched more deeply. He saw Skyfeather nursing and did not seem surprised. He nodded matter-of-factly.

"Aye. She will now be well."

Antelope felt a surge of love for her old benefactor. "I am grateful to you."

He wiped his sleepy face with both hands, yawned, stretched, and scratched himself.

"It is Poqua you should be grateful to."

"I am. I am grateful to all of you—"

"Did you hear Poqua during the night?"

"Yes, but I did not understand the words."

Peg Foot regarded her solemnly. "She commanded the evil that made Skyfeather sick to leave your baby and enter her, instead." For a moment, he watched Skyfeather nursing. "She will be well."

Antelope felt a sharp pang of concern. "Do you mean that Poqua will be sick now that Skyfeather is getting better?"

He shrugged without reply and used his staff to help himself stand up. He had slept with his peg on as he sometimes did when he was weary. Now he headed for the door. Antelope knew he wanted to relieve himself at his usual secluded spot, but she needed an answer to ease her heart.

"Poqua will not be sick now, will she?"

He left without reply.

Antelope swallowed her foreboding. Maybe Peg Foot had not heard her last question; he did not hear as well as he used to. Skyfeather still nursed, and Antelope rocked her, crooning.

When Skyfeather would nurse no more, Antelope carried her out into the morning; it would be a bright, cloudless day. But the city was unusually quiet except for the distant sound of drums and rattles and chants in preparation for purification. Slaves were re-covering the plaza with fresh sand from the riverbanks. No canoes were on the river; all visitors had departed. Except one—Chomoc. Antelope saw his huge canoe banked upstream. Where was he?

Remembering the Chomoc who used to be, Antelope felt tears sting her eyes. What had happened to the boy she grew up with, the one who called a rabbit for her, the boy who sang to her with his flute? She had loved him. . . .

Long Man ran colder than usual; snow must be on distant mountains.

The baby squealed as Antelope dipped her in the cold water. But she did not cry. Antelope used a handful of moss to wash her all over, and Skyfeather's blue eyes sparkled as they used to.

Antelope scrubbed herself, her hair, all of her, washing sorrow and fear away. The city might be cursed, but Skyfeather was getting well! She was not as strong yet as she would be, but the sickness was gone.

Antelope's heart overflowed. A song soared from her throat:

> *I thank you, holy ones.*
> *Thank you for taking the evil away.*
> *Thank you for allowing Skyfeather to live.*
> *Thank you for giving her back to me.*
> *I thank you, holy ones!*

Antelope parted the reeds, preparing to return to the bank, when something floating on the river caught her eye. It was a small bundle, like a little raft. As it floated closer, Antelope saw it was Poqua's singing stick, the notched piece and the smooth one tied together. It floated by serenely, accompanied by the first bright leaves of autumn.

Apprehension pierced Antelope like a lance. "Poqua!" she cried. "Poqua!"

Was that Poqua's voice singing a reply as her stick floated away toward the distant sea?

The High Priest sat with the shaman in his dwelling. They had been talking for some time. The Green Corn ceremony had been interrupted with appalling consequences. What must be done?

The High Priest regarded the shaman, who sat on a carved wooden stool not tall enough to accommodate his legs, which were crossed, pushing his bony knees waist high. What was it about the shaman's long, thin face and his long, thin nose that was so alienating? The High Priest said, "Of course we shall fast, seek a vision, and purify the city with prayer and sexual prohibition until new fire may be obtained. I assume you agree?"

The shaman nodded, his face expressionless as usual. "From what city should we obtain the new fire?"

The shaman was being routinely courteous, the High Priest thought. It was the duty of the High Priest to determine matters regarding the sacred fire. He shifted his position uncomfortably on the wooden bench; he must tell the shaman what he might not want to hear.

"Chomoc, son of Kokopelli, came for the ceremonies, as you know, and he is still here. He has offered to obtain sacred fire from the City of the North. His canoe and paddlers will have the fire here within three weeks."

The High Priest did not add that he knew Chomoc's offer was a bribe for special trading privileges. But fire from the temple of the City of the North would have great potency; its sacred power was needed here.

A spark flickered in the shaman's eyes and was gone. He wrapped long arms around his knees and stared over the High Priest's head. "New fire may be obtained from the temple of a city nearby within two days."

"Of course. But will it have the power of sacred fire from the City of the North?"

"I shall consult my crystal," the shaman said tonelessly, his left eyelid twitching.

"Of course." The High Priest smiled inwardly; he knew the crystal was a face-saving device.

The High Priest rose, lifting his twisted body with effort. He hunched over the seated shaman, whose face was almost on a level with his own. "I leave you now." He departed with his lurching gait.

He would fast, purify himself, commune with Long Man and the spirits, and seek a vision. He knew the shaman would do the same.

The city and its people must be saved.

Antelope hurried down the path toward Red Leaf's dwelling. She carried Skyfeather in the cradleboard on her back, and a basket of dried squash and dried persimmons in both hands. Her heart beat hard. She wanted, needed, to find that Poqua was well.

The day had turned cloudy and a chill wind blew from the mountains. Few people were about. Some huddled in small groups, discussing the disaster. They greeted her briefly as she passed.

As she neared Red Leaf's dwelling, Antelope heard a commotion, a keening wail. There was the sound of pounding; a platform was being erected. People crowded the house and yard, gathered around something Antelope could not see. They covered their faces, wailing.

Someone saw her coming. "She is here! Antelope is here!"

They turned and watched in silence as Antelope approached. Some of the people Antelope recognized; they were relatives of Red Leaf and Poqua. Others she had not seen before; their faces were not friendly.

"I greet you," Antelope said hesitantly. "Where is Red Leaf?"

Silently, they stood aside. Red Leaf was kneeling beside Poqua, who lay on a blanket upon the ground. The old woman was drenched; her soaked, lifeless body was a grotesque caricature of its former self. Keening, rocking to and fro, Red Leaf tried to dry her mother with a bit of cotton cloth, patting the wizened face with its open, toothless mouth, rubbing the bony arms and legs, wiping the feet with one moccasin gone.

Bobcat and Ringtail hunched beside her, crying.

Bobcat nudged Poqua's shoulder. "Wake up!" His crossed eyes peered tearfully at Red Leaf. "Why won't she wake up?"

"She can't. She drowned," Ringtail said, being the strong older brother. But tears choked his voice.

Red Leaf looked up at Antelope. For a moment she was motionless, expressionless. Finally, she said, "Skyfeather is well?"

"Yes."

Red Leaf's gaze returned to Poqua. Again, she rocked to and fro, futilely drying her mother's body with the bit of cloth.

A young man Antelope did not recognize stepped from the crowd. He was short and stocky and resembled Many Bears—a relative from another village, perhaps. He said, "Red Leaf told us what happened. Poqua took your baby's sickness into herself. She knew she would die so she gave herself to Long Man. They found her tangled in the reeds."

"She gave her life for your child," another said. This was a shriveled, middle-aged woman Antelope recognized, another relative who lived nearby. "Red Leaf lost her mate, and now her mother—"

Unspoken words were evident in sharp glances shot at her like arrows from one and then another and another.

They blame me!

"Our Great Sun and Firekeeper are dead and the eternal fire

extinguished. We are cursed," the young man said bitterly, staring at her. "Now Poqua will rest upon a platform—an offering to the Spirit Being—until only her bones remain for the Mortuary House." He scowled at Antelope. "She sings for us no more."

Antelope stood straight and looked him in the eye. "I grieve with you. With all of you. Especially you, Red Leaf, and the boys. Poqua adopted me as her daughter; I loved her."

She stepped forward and laid the basket of squash and persimmons on the ground beside Red Leaf. She gestured a Towa sign of blessing over Poqua and rose to leave.

Skyfeather saw the boys and made cooing sounds. Ringtail, who had always considered himself her brother and protector, came and reached to touch her in the cradleboard. "Stay here; don't go away again."

Antelope put an arm around his shoulders. "I live with Peg Foot now. He needs me, so I must go."

There was stony silence as she left. She felt their eyes like stinging insects as she followed the path. When she was out of their sight, she sat down on a big rock to grieve.

Now Skyfeather will be blamed for Poqua's death. I must find a way to take her home to our people.

But how? Chomoc and his men had gone, their big canoe skimming the river like a water bird. He was gone; she could not plead with him again. He had left her and Skyfeather alone in this foreign city, a city in turmoil, whose people blamed her. . . . She felt adrift in a raging current, floundering.

No.

She would be strong.

To whom may I turn to take me home?

Horned Toad knew the way, but even if he was willing, he was too old. Would Far Walker do it? Would he leave his people and his patients to take her on the long and dangerous journey to Cicuye? Warriors would be necessary to accompany them for protection. . . .

No. It was impossible.

A day passed, and another, while preparations for the funeral of the Great Sun and Firekeeper were under way.

The burial mound consisted of one great mound and three

smaller ones joined together. Antelope saw slaves leveling the tops of the mounds, and she wondered why. She asked Peg Foot.

He concealed his shock at her ignorance. "That is where the Great Sun will lie and all who go with him. The tallest mound is for the Great Sun and Striped Serpent and their mates and all they take with them to the Afterworld. Firekeeper and all the others who go with the Great Sun will be on the other mounds."

"They just lay the bodies on top?"

"Of course. Then they are covered with this much earth." He indicated the length of two moccasins. "Each time a burial takes place, the mounds grow a little taller." He peered at her over his peg, which he was polishing with a strip of buckskin. "Tomorrow, the Great Sun and Firekeeper will be waiting in the Great Sun's dwelling for people to come and pay their respects." He gave his peg a final, decisive wipe. "You will go."

Antelope shook her head. She rejoiced at the Great Sun's death, and she did not want to see the dead body of Firekeeper, whom she hardly knew.

"I don't want to go."

"I know." He flashed her a discerning glance. "But it will be dangerous not to."

Antelope did not reply. She thought of Poqua on the platform, waiting for her bones to be stripped and placed in a basket in the Mortuary House. She remembered the hostile stares and words of Red Leaf's relatives.

I do not belong here.

It was midafternoon. Outside, the Crier was announcing the lying-in-state of the Great Sun and Firekeeper; his voice and the sound of his drum faded away. A fly buzzed in the room, then all was silent. This city, this room, this good man, were foreign. She was, and always would be, an outsider. Suspect.

Now she would ask Peg Foot what she had always wanted to ask but felt she should not; it might indicate a lack of appreciation for all he had done for her. But she had to ask someone. She swallowed. "Healer, please tell me how I may take Skyfeather home to my people."

Peg Foot was fastening the peg to his leg, but he stopped abruptly to look at her. He gazed at her in silence for a long time. Finally, he said gruffly, "You are unhappy here?"

Antelope knew the gruff tone hid his emotion. What could

she say? She looked at Skyfeather who lay on her stomach, happily playing with a little gourd rattle that Peg Foot had made for her.

"You are kind to us, Peg Foot. Far Walker—" She stopped. She realized with a pang she did not want to leave Far Walker.

He said, gruffly still, "He has not been kind?"

"Oh, yes. He . . . he has been more than kind. It is just that Skyfeather and I are Towa and belong with our people. I want to see Acoya, my brother. . . ." Her voice faltered. She would not mention her vision.

"Ah." Peg Foot busied himself fastening the peg to his leg before he looked at her again. "It is a long way to Cicuye."

"If we traveled here, we can travel back—if someone will take us."

Peg Foot finished with his peg, then sat back on his heels and looked at her. "You must face the situation as it is. I doubt if anyone here cares to make that journey. They prefer to go by canoe to cities along the river, or go by foot to trade with rich cities of the east and the south. Many traders come here from the west, bringing what we need from them. There is no reason for them to go west."

"Maybe Far Walker—"

"No. He is needed here." Peg Foot rubbed his wrinkled cheek and his chin, and Antelope noticed how swollen his knuckles had become. They must hurt, she thought.

Peg Foot continued, "I am old, and I have taught Far Walker well. He will not leave us."

Antelope felt hopelessness and frustration well up in her. "I am not wanted here, Peg Foot. Red Leaf's family blames me for Poqua's death. . . ." She could say no more. She covered her face with both hands and sobbed.

Peg Foot came and sat beside her. He put both arms around her and held her close, making comforting sounds deep in his throat. She smelled his clean old body and felt his gentle touch. That unleashed all the tears she had not shed before, and she sobbed even more.

"Chomoc . . . refused. . . . He loves me no more."

Peg Foot let her sob for a while longer, then he removed both hands from her face and made her look at him.

"Others love you."

"But—"

"I love you. Far Walker loves you."

Antelope looked at him with tears dripping. "He has not told me so."

"Women!" Peg Foot snorted. "Must everything be expressed with words?"

That made Antelope feel better. She wiped her nose and cheeks with both hands. "I love you, Healer. I loved Poqua, also. . . ." Tears threatened again, but she swallowed them down.

"She knew she was going to die and she wanted to do this one fine thing. Do not begrudge her that."

Antelope looked at Skyfeather, who was rosy and happy. "How could I? But it is a burden on my heart."

"Yes. But it will pass. And you have Skyfeather."

"I must take her home, Peg Foot. Help me!"

He sat back on his heels again and looked thoughtful. "There may be a way."

Antelope leaned forward eagerly. "How?"

"There are a number of villages between here and Cicuye, are there not?"

"Yes."

"As I said, many traders come here bringing rainbow flint and other things to trade for the things brought to us by traders from the east and south. Our warehouse is full of these valuables. Now, when a trader comes from one of the western cities, perhaps he will take you back with him to his village. Then, when a trader from a city farther west comes to his village, perhaps that trader will take you with him when he returns home. And so on, village to village, until you reach Cicuye."

Antelope looked at him gravely. "Should I do this?"

He shook his head. "Too dangerous. You and Skyfeather would be alone, among strangers, at their mercy. They would expect to be paid well. But it is for you to decide."

"I don't have anything—"

"I do. If you need it, it is yours."

She put both arms around his scrawny neck and kissed his cheek. How could she leave him? In her heart, Antelope knew she could not leave Far Walker. Not if he loved her.

Did he?

If he really loved her, wouldn't he be willing to take her home?

But what if he could not leave his people?

Antelope pondered this for three days, then went looking for Horned Toad. Perhaps he would be willing to take her to the next village on the trading route west. She would go home, warn her people, see Acoya, her brother, and her friends for a short while, then return.

She found Horned Toad under a big old cottonwood tree. He was happily gambling with cronies and ignored her as she approached.

She watched a moment as he threw the smooth stones incised with markings. He chortled and the others exclaimed in their Caddoan tongue. He gathered the stones and prepared to throw them again.

Antelope stepped closer. "I must speak with you, Horned Toad."

He glanced up. "What about?"

"May we speak privately somewhere?"

He frowned impatiently. "Why?"

"Because it is necessary."

He spoke with the others in the language Antelope was still learning. They talked for a moment, glancing at her now and then. Finally, Horned Toad gathered his stones reluctantly, poured them in a small buckskin bag with beaded fringe, and rose. "Come."

She followed him to a cluster of small boulders by a stream, and they sat there, looking at each other.

Horned Toad sat jiggling the buckskin bag; the stones made a little clicking sound. "What do you want to tell me?"

Antelope looked into the shrewd old eyes she had known so long. She blurted, "I want to go home."

"Ha!" He shook his head. "Why?"

"I have had a vision." She told him of Kwani's warning that terrible beings from the Sunrise Sea would come to enslave and brutalize her people. "They are in danger and I must warn them. If you will take me to the first trading village going west, perhaps traders going west will take me home. . . ." She faltered, visualizing the dangerous journey, alone with strangers.

Horned Toad rubbed his grizzled chin. "No. I understand your concern, Antelope, but look at me. I am an old man. I came here to die and here I shall stay. I cannot, will not take you even to the next village." He rose, jiggling the pouch. "I return now to my friends and the game you interrupted."

Antelope rose with him, biting her lips. What made her think this old buzzard would help her? She said, "Very well. I shall find someone else and get Blacktail to pull the litter. Where is my dog?"

Horned Toad snorted. "He got mean, so we ate him." He strode away without a backward glance.

Antelope stared after him, shaking with fury.

How dare he!

Blacktail had been more than a burden bearer; he was a member of the family, a protector. To kill him, to devour him, was unthinkable savagery.

I cannot live in this place. Somehow, some way, I am going home.

▲28▼

It was midmorning and sunny, touched with the cool breath of early autumn. Antelope stood with villagers in a long line that reached to the residential mound of the Great Sun and led up the steps of the mound into the dwelling. Some people carried offerings of food, but Antelope did not. It was all she could do to make herself pay respects to a man she despised. She was doing it only because Peg Foot insisted—for what must be his good reasons—and she wanted to please her old benefactor. So she had left Skyfeather with him and joined the villagers. Peg Foot would follow later.

As people entered the dwelling where Firekeeper and the Great Sun lay in state, they uttered the death cry, a loud, wavering wail that chilled the blood and echoed throughout the city.

Slowly, Antelope reached the mound. Warriors remained on either side of each step. Antelope wondered if they were the same ones who had pursued and tried to kill her when she escaped from the Great Sun and ran to the temple mound for sanctuary. If they were, they gave no indication of recognition but gazed stonily at her and at other people passing by.

A woman stood in line ahead of Antelope. She was short and

stocky with long, black hair, unadorned. She had lived perhaps thirty winters and bore the effects of hard physical labor. She shuffled wearily and carried a basket of acorns on her head. From time to time she turned to look at Antelope and glance at her necklace. Several times she seemed about to speak, but did not.

After they had climbed a few more steps of the mound, the woman turned to Antelope again.

"You are She Who Remembers, are you not?"

"Yes."

"You should be teaching our girls the women's secrets."

"Yes, but—"

"Then do so," she said sharply, and turned away so abruptly that the basket nearly tumbled from her head.

Antelope stood looking at the woman's back. Tattoos embellished both shoulders in a design that squirmed down her arms. *She is right,* Antelope told herself. Now that the Great Sun was dead, perhaps a new order would evolve and she could become She Who Remembers again, become whole again. Perhaps all would be well. . . .

They made their way up the steps, one step at a time, until they reached the terrace and the extended doorway of the Great Sun's dwelling.

Inside, the Great Sun lay upon a large cedar litter. His face was painted red; a feather cloak of brilliant colors enveloped him. Around him, prized possessions overflowed from baskets and mats upon the floor. Antelope stared. He lay in splendor as if asleep.

Behind him, against the wall, Firekeeper lay on a smaller litter. She wore only a simple white robe, and her feet were bare. Her gray hair was unadorned but for a headband with a carved shell disk at her forehead. Her face, wrinkled and serene, seemed at peace.

The woman ahead of Antelope placed her basket of acorns on the floor among other food offerings beside the Great Sun's litter. She gazed at the painted face and said, "You no longer wish, then, to take what we present you? These things are no more to your taste? Our services please you no longer? Ah! You do not speak as usual. Without doubt you are dead. Yes, it is done. You are going to the country of the spirits and you are leaving us forever."

She threw back her head and gave a great, wavering howl. Then she turned away, leaving Antelope staring at the man who had attacked her and sent warriors to kill her.

His face beneath the headdress was arrogant still. Many necklaces and an intricately carved conch shell gorget lay upon his chest; carved earspools glowed with polished copper overlay. Arms, legs, and hands were adorned with pearls, and he wore new beaded moccasins for his journey.

Baskets of luxuries surrounded him: ornately carved pipes, copper breastplates and earspools and headbands, necklaces of pearls and turquoise and polished shell, lavishly painted and embroidered garments, fine pots and bowls (broken to release their spirits), engraved conch shell cups, painted shields, lances, banners, and many other objects Antelope could not see because they were hidden in the pile.

In contrast, Firekeeper seemed virginal. Antelope remembered her kindness and felt a pang of regret. She uttered no death cry, but she did make a sign of blessing for Firekeeper.

It was a relief to return outside. Warriors directed her down steps apart from the line waiting, and Antelope was soon back in the plaza.

As she turned toward her village, Antelope saw Waikah. The old midwife wandered aimlessly about, staring blankly ahead, babbling incoherently. A woman Antelope recognized as a neighbor stood watching.

Antelope greeted her and said, "What has happened to Waikah?"

"She grieves for the loss of her sister. Or so they say."

Antelope watched the wizened figure stumbling blindly this way and that, while death cries echoed and reechoed in the still air.

Carefully, the High Priest lifted the tall headdress of crimson feathers and placed it upon his head; it was time for the burial ceremony. The upper part of his stooped body was bare but for a copper-and-shell gorget swinging at his chest. Both arms were painted red and his belt was ornamented with red and black feathers.

"Your spirit caller," the caddí said, handing the High Priest a red baton in the shape of a cross with a cluster of black feathers attached to one end. Until the destroyed temple could be burned and rebuilt, the High Priest resided in the home of the caddí, who relished the prestige—even though it was an effort for the caddí to remain in the background. "Refresh yourself before you leave."

"I cannot break my fast, but I thank you. We must go."

"Very well." The caddí beckoned a slave. "Summon the musicians."

The High Priest inspected the four men with drums of different sizes, a young man hardly more than a boy who carried a gourd rattle in each hand, and three men with flutes. One flute was reed, another wood, and the third turkey bone.

Satisfied, the High Priest headed for the Great Sun's residential mound, his spirit caller in one hand and his staff in the other. The caddí followed, carrying a red-and-black pole with a banner. The musicians followed the caddí; they did not play but marched in solemn silence. As they approached the mound, people made way for them respectfully. Waiting on top of the mound was the shaman. He stood on the terrace, a towering figure in his deer mask and ceremonial finery. He raised both arms, chanting.

Slowly, painfully, the High Priest climbed the steps. Halfway up, he turned to look at the crowd of people below. So few! Usually, the funeral of a Great Sun would bring many thousands eager to do him and themselves honor by attending and by bringing the bones of their rulers and priests to be sanctified by burial with him. The High Priest felt a stab of grief. The Great Sun was cursed; no sacred bones would accompany him. No foreign dignitaries remained. His beloved city, like its ruler, was defiled.

When he reached the terrace, the High Priest greeted the shaman, who led him and the caddí into the room where the Great Sun and Firekeeper lay; the musicians lined up outside. As the shaman entered the room he gestured with his crystal, chanting commands to evil spirits to abandon the place forever.

The High Priest looked at Firekeeper, serene in her death sleep, and his heart paused in its beating. He had loved her, secretly, for many long years. He remembered the glory of her youth; how beautiful she had been! He gestured a blessing with his spirit caller, and turned to the Great Sun.

The ruler of the city was as imposing in death as he had been in life. The red-painted face was emotionless now, but the

High Priest knew it concealed secrets. Knowledge of what those secrets were would accompany him to the spirit world. Perhaps that was for the best. There was something about the Great Sun that had nudged the High Priest's innermost instincts. Sometimes, he had felt the ruler was but a shadow, and it had disturbed him greatly.

Now the Great Sun lay on his litter, surrounded by luxuries, prepared for his journey. The shaman continued his chanting as the caddí stepped outside to beckon the honored warriors who would carry the Great Sun to his burial place.

They entered, twelve strong men with faces and bodies painted red on the right side and black on the left. Their headdresses gleamed with a burnished copper plate over the forehead. Falcon markings embellished the outer corner of each eye: red on black, and black on red. Copper earspools gleamed, beaded forelocks hung to the nose, and wide copper bands encircled wrists and ankles.

The High Priest gestured. "Let the procession begin." He stepped through the extended doorway, followed by the caddí.

To the accompaniment of the shaman's chanting, eight warriors lifted the Great Sun on his litter and carried him out the door, followed by four warriors carrying Firekeeper, then more warriors carrying the baskets of luxuries. As they left the dwelling and stood on the terrace, the drums gave a great shout and the flutes cried out. From below, the death cry swelled, blending with the boom of the drums and the cry of the flutes. Only the rattles were silent.

The High Priest turned to lead the procession down the steps, followed by the litter bearers who carried their burdens sideways, a step at a time, keeping the litters level so the bodies would not slide off.

Still the rattles were silent.

Death cries continued, rising and falling. The High Priest and the procession reached the bottom of the steps and turned toward the burial mound.

Antelope stood in the crowd, watching. It was the first time she had seen the High Priest. She had heard he was crippled, but she was not prepared for his dignity. He leaned heavily upon his staff and his swinging, awkward gait made progress slow, but he had an aura of spiritual power that transcended physical limitations.

Behind the High Priest were the litter bearers, followed by the caddí and the shaman. After them came a line of men carrying baskets of belongings to be buried with their owners. These were followed by the musicians, playing solemnly in rhythm with the High Priest's lurching step. A long line of grieving relatives followed the musicians, sounding death cries.

Antelope remembered the simplicity of the burials of her people, and she was amazed. Never had she seen such resplendent garments as those in the procession. There were brilliant headdresses of feathers and fur, dazzling breechclouts painted and embroidered, large earspools, much jewelry on tattooed torsos. The shaman in his deer mask towered over all.

The litter bearers took ten steps to the command of drums and shrill of flutes. Then the music stopped. Slowly the bearers circled, turning the litters around.

Now the rattles spoke at last with a loud hissing, first one rattle then the other, each with a different supernatural sound.

When the turn was completed, the rattles were silenced and the drums and flutes cried out again for the next ten steps. Then came another turn and more rattles, and so on, as the procession made its way toward the burial mound. The heartbeat of drums, the sharp cry of flutes, the screeching hiss of rattles, the death cries, the High Priest with his twisted arms painted red leading the procession, the bodies upon the litters—it seemed unreal, a weird dream.

As the procession drew near to the burial mound, it encountered the stench of the nearby Mortuary House where baskets held the bones of ambassadors and other upper-class people waiting for the honor of burial in the same mound as the Great Sun. But none would be buried this time.

Again came the hiss of rattles as the litters were turned, and Antelope remembered Poqua and the rasp of her singing stick. Were songs with her little bundle floating out to sea? *Where is your spirit, Poqua? Has it departed, leaving you alone on the platform waiting for the Bone Pickers?*

Suddenly, tears stung Antelope's eyes, and for the first time she opened her mouth wide in a death cry.

Far Walker stood at the base of the mound, waiting for the procession to arrive. He was tense with expectation. As a Healer, he had devoted his life to keeping people alive; now he must help them on their journey to the Afterworld. It was a solemn responsibility, and he gloried in it.

All was ready. Those who would accompany the Great Sun and Firekeeper were seated, one above the other, on both sides of the steps leading to the top of the mound. Behind each one stood an executioner with a short length of rope looped around the throat of the seated traveler, waiting for the moment to jerk the rope so the journey could begin. The executioner was naked but for a breechclout, with half his face and body painted red and the other half black.

The Great Sun's brother, Striped Serpent, sat alone on the top step. Below him were the ruler's mates, Kala and Lipoe, elaborately dressed, and below them were relatives, and servants for the journey. The Great Sun's sister, Manimani, stood on the mound awaiting the High Priest. She would remain in this world to become the next Great Sun.

Far Walker watched the procession approaching and was proud. His city was cursed but his people persevered. The litters approached with impressive dignity, pausing, circling, advancing again. How awesome the drums, how commanding the voice of the rattles! His heart soared.

Antelope stood with Peg Foot and the crowd watching the procession. Peg Foot had brought Skyfeather and she was restless in her cradleboard, excited by the sounds and the people pressing close.

As always, there were murmurs and comments on Skyfeather's blue eyes, but Antelope ignored them. Her gaze was fixed upon Far Walker in the distance as he stood at the base of the burial mound, watching the approach of the procession. How handsome he was in his Healer's headdress of feathers and fur and a bright copper headband! His muscular, bronzed body was bare but for a red breechclout and a wide, embroidered belt with a fringe of black feathers. She wondered who had made that belt for him and surprised herself with a twinge of jealousy. Ever since her visit to his house she had wanted him again, but he avoided her. Why?

She wondered why he was standing there, and what he was going to do. She turned to Peg Foot, who was gazing at Far Walker, too, with pride glowing from him.

"Why is Far Walker there? What will he do?"

"Watch. You will see."

Far Walker signaled, and a warrior brought him a bowl, a shiny black one with incised designs. Holding the bowl in one hand, Far Walker mounted the steps to Striped Serpent, reached into the bowl, and withdrew what looked like a little wad of something dark. Striped Serpent opened his mouth and Far Walker gave him the substance, which Striped Serpent chewed and swallowed. Then Far Walker went to each of the Great Sun's mates and all the others seated and waiting, and to each he gave the substance, which they accepted eagerly.

"What is it that he gives?" Antelope asked.

"It eases the traveler's way."

Antelope wanted to ask more questions, but the procession was passing now. Amid death cries, the litter bearers marched and turned and marched again. Antelope watched the Great Sun go by to the tumult of flutes and drums, then the rattles, followed by honored warriors carrying the chests of valuables to accompany the ruler on his journey to the Afterworld. Then came Firekeeper on her litter, surrounded by flowers.

As Firekeeper passed, suddenly Waikah emerged from the crowd. She ran to the litter, grasped it, and tried to climb upon it.

"No! No!" she screamed. "She did not do it! No!"

Waikah was dragged away, still screaming, her eyes wild.

People shook their heads. Poor Waikah had lost her kia, grieving. But Antelope was shocked. That old woman had more than grief on her mind. What terrible thing had Firekeeper not done? Was a crime involved? One that Waikah herself had committed, perhaps?

Again, Antelope turned to speak to Peg Foot, but he had disappeared. She saw him making his way to the burial mound where Far Walker stood waiting for the litters to arrive. They stood together, the old Healer and the young one, facing the procession.

The drums grew more demanding, the flutes louder, and the rattles more feral as the procession approached the mound. The wail of the death cries rose and fell and rose again. The great burial mound with the three smaller mounds attached to it seemed like a giant, hunched animal waiting to be fed the bodies of the dead.

As the procession reached the mound, the High Priest greeted Peg Foot and Far Walker, then began to climb the steps.

Now the drums and flutes were muted, sounding to a different rhythm. Slowly the procession mounted the steps.

As the Great Sun passed, the executioners of the first pair of seated travelers on either side of the steps gave the ropes a hard, twisting jerk. Now the drums and flutes were silenced and the rattles spoke, hissing as the travelers writhed, convulsed, and collapsed. Then the executioners picked up the limp bodies, carried them in outstretched arms, and joined the procession.

Suddenly, Antelope felt sickened and wanted to leave, but she stood watching, paralyzed, as the procession mounted the steps, other pairs of executioners yanked the ropes, and writhing bodies fell while the rattles rejoiced.

At last the procession reached the top of the mound. To the chanting of the High Priest and the shaman, the Great Sun and his litter were placed in the center of the great mound, surrounded by his mates, Striped Serpent, and the woven chests of riches. Firekeeper and the others accompanying her and the Great Sun to the Afterworld lay on top of the attached mounds.

The music was silenced. Manimani, the Great Sun's sister, gave an agonized death cry, echoed by all below.

The travelers were on their journey.

Now the mourning relatives would bury their dead in a final, healing farewell. They filed behind the mound where baskets and buffalo bone shovels waited, filled the baskets with earth, climbed to the top of the mound, and poured the earth on those they loved who were no longer in this world, thereby securing their safety in the next. On and on it went, basket after basket, until the bodies were covered to a depth of two moccasins.

The mounds were taller now.

▲ 29 ▼

The moonlight glowed eerily through the trees, making ghostly shadows. Waikah stumbled blindly along a forest trail, ignoring a possible encounter with the jaguar; its cry had been heard recently, but no one had seen the Spotted One.

Maybe it was meant that the jaguar should find her. Maybe that would atone for her sin. She would die and nobody would learn what she had done, nobody would know that she had robbed the real Great Sun of his birthright and that the gods had taken revenge. It was she who was to blame that Firekeeper and the Great Sun had been killed, the temple destroyed, the city cursed . . . It was she, Waikah, the midwife, who was responsible for the death of her beloved sister and her sister's son—instead of helping life to be born as her kia demanded.

Her kia was defiled.

Waikah moaned, twisting in torment.

What must I do?

Was that a sound in the brush? She listened. Was the jaguar near?

"Come!" she called. "I am here!"

Let him take me.

She sat down on the ground and waited. Maybe he would come. It would solve everything.

But would it? What about the true Great Sun, living in ignorance of who he really was? What about his duty to his people? Her people?

No. I cannot tell. I cannot. I am cursed enough.

A cloud covered the moon and darkness hid the shadows, but it would not hide her from the Spotted One.

Perhaps it would be over soon.

The cloud passed, a breeze stirred the trees, and shadows swayed on the leafy ground. This way . . . that way . . .

Where was the jaguar?

An owl hooted, long and low. Was it calling her name? Was it now her time to die?

At last?

For a long time she sat there, waiting, listening. The moon rose higher and trees clung to it, yearning. From a distance came Long Man's voice, singing through the forest.

Is Long Man summoning me?

She rose with effort, grasping a low branch to pull her aching self up. In moonlight and shifting shadows, she followed the trail to the river. She stood on the rocky bank where reeds grew, and looked at the water. The moon's bright path shimmered, and Long Man's seductive song invited her along that path.

He would heal her, cleanse her kia.

Waikah removed her garment and worn moccasins and waded into the water. Its coldness shocked her; she had forgotten how late in the season it was, with snow on distant mountains. She lowered herself in up to her neck, feeling the cold water swirling around her. It revived her; it was as though part of her had been away since the storm. She rubbed herself vigorously with both hands and splashed water over her head.

"Heal me! Purify me! Heal me!" she cried aloud.

But she knew, yes she knew, that Long Man could cleanse her body but not her kia, her innermost being, which she herself had defiled. Only the High Priest could do that.

She must confess to the High Priest, obtain his absolution, and allow the real Great Sun to regain his true heritage. Only then would her kia be purified. Only then could her spirit enter the Afterworld—rather than wander aimless and alone, seeking sanctuary and finding none. Forever.

But could she face the High Priest? Could she endure his wise and penetrating gaze? He had always regarded her and her calling with admiration and respect. . . .

No. I cannot. I cannot.

But I must.

Wearily, she dragged herself out of the water, pulled her garment on her wet, hurting body, thrust her wet feet into moccasins, and returned along the moonlit path among the shadows.

The High Priest stood gazing at the ruins of his beloved temple. When Chomoc arrived with new fire and the Green Corn ceremony could be resumed, a flaming torch would be thrown into the heart of the temple so it could be purified, then rebuilt. But the High Priest would not watch it burn. Too much of himself was in there.

He turned away and started down the steps. It had been eleven days since Chomoc left, and the city was in mourning. No activity was on the river; no smoke rose from cooking fires; no fire at all could be lit. The city itself seemed to have been buried with the dead.

Nothing like this had ever happened before; how could he—and his people—cope with a catastrophe of such magnitude? Manimani would become the Great Sun now—if the council agreed. A meeting would be held to decide. But until new fire arrived and the Green Corn ceremony—the time of new beginnings—was concluded, no important decisions could be made.

Slowly, he made his way down, step by step. He should return to the dwelling of the caddí, but the noisy activity of the caddí's mate and children and relatives and their dogs robbed him of inner quietude. His own mate had died years before, and they had but one child, a girl who had married a stone carver from a distant village and lived there with him. Now the High Priest preferred to live alone in his temple with priests for company and a group of women who came each day to do domestic chores. His twisted body held no allure for women, and he had taken no other mate. He wanted no other—only Firekeeper.

Had she suspected how much he loved her?

Bracing himself on his staff, he paused to gaze across the plaza to the burial mound.

Ah, Firekeeper . . .

*   *   *

It had been twenty-three days since Chomoc departed to bring new fire for the Green Corn ceremony. For twenty-three days only cold, raw food was allowed. Those who had relatives in other cities went to visit to enjoy stews and porridge and roasted meats again.

It was during this time that a number of babies decided to be born, and Waikah was so busy trying to deliver them safely with no hot water available that she kept postponing her confession to the High Priest. She would do it tomorrow, but when tomorrow came another baby demanded birth, and she postponed again. Guilt gnawed at her, but she was so weary at night that she collapsed into troubled sleep—and another day had gone by.

On the twenty-fourth day, the thunder drum boomed at last. A canoe approached on the river. People rushed to see.

"Look! The canoe from the City of the North!"

"See the new banners! Blue and white!"

"The paddlers are blue and white now, too. Look!"

"I wonder if they are painted all over."

"Including their babymakers?"

"Ha! Blue-and-white babies!"

Laughter, obscene remarks, and more laughter.

Chomoc's flute sang out, rejoicing, as the canoe approached shore.

Antelope was with Peg Foot, helping him treat a young boy who had fallen into a thorny gully. Peg Foot's vision was not as good as it used to be, so she pulled out the small thorns one by one, while Peg Foot applied a healing ointment. When the thunder drum sounded and the flute sang out, Antelope knew immediately who had returned.

"It is Chomoc!" In spite of herself, Antelope's heart beat with the old expectation. She was a child again, waiting for him to bring her a surprise.

"Now we shall have the new fire," Peg Foot said. "The Green Corn ceremony will resume. At last."

The flute sang invitations, wonderful promises.

The boy squirmed impatiently. "I want to see."

Peg Foot gave him a nudge. "Very well. Come back later and we will finish."

The boy was off in an instant.

Antelope felt Peg Foot's wise gaze as he sat looking at her. He knew her too well. But did he know how much she missed

Far Walker, how much her young body longed for him? Far Walker had not been there since he treated Skyfeather; she had seen him only at a distance during the funeral.

"When will Far Walker come?" she blurted.

"Not until after the Green Corn ceremony is ended." His wrinkles deepened in a grin. "Men cannot have women until then, and he stays away so he will not be tempted too much."

He knows! Antelope thought, and she was embarrassed. She said matter-of-factly, "Chomoc has probably brought many things to trade. Shall we go to see?"

Far Walker will be there.

Maybe Chomoc has changed. Maybe he still loves me after all. Maybe he will be willing to take us home.

"Of course we go to see," Peg Foot said. "But there will be no trading until after the ceremony is completed."

Antelope scooped up Skyfeather, who was growing fast and getting heavier, and they left to join the crowd at the river.

When they arrived, the canoe was beached with the twenty strong paddlers lined up before it. Their muscular arms and legs were painted, one blue and one white, and blue and white lines radiated from the nose like cat whiskers. They stood with arms crossed and legs spread, gazing sternly ahead. They were an impressive sight—not lost on girls and young women who ogled them, giggling and whispering behind their hands.

The curtain in front of the canopy parted, and Chomoc stepped out holding a large clay jar with a lid. The lid had a hole from which a faint wisp of smoke curled up.

He wore his brilliant feather cloak and assumed the stance Antelope knew so well. "I, Chomoc, son of Kokopelli and consort of the queen of the north, present you with this sacred fire. It is a gift in friendship and expectation of many years of good fortune."

A shout went up from the crowd. "And years of good trading," he added.

How like him, Antelope thought. Trading was the important thing.

The High Priest stepped forward, followed by the shaman and the caddí. To more shouts from the crowd, the High Priest accepted the jar in his twisted arms, then handed it to the shaman, who held it high overhead so all might see.

The caddí announced loudly, "Proceed to the plaza. Prepare for the continuation of the Green Corn ceremony."

A procession formed, led by the High Priest bracing himself on his staff, followed by the shaman carrying the jar overhead. The caddí marched beside him and beckoned Chomoc to follow. Chomoc stepped inside the canopied area and emerged with his flute—and two beautiful young women wearing nearly transparent cotton gowns ornamented with glittering beads of many colors. Ropes of pearls and shells entwined their long, black hair, and their slender bare feet wore toe rings that sparkled in the sunlight.

"My concubines," Chomoc announced with a flourish, and motioned the women to join him in the procession. He lifted the flute to his lips and played a triumphant melody.

Antelope was shocked and angry. Jealousy boiled up. How dare he! Everyone in the city knew him as her mate and Skyfeather's father. Now look at him, flaunting those women, humiliating her! Ignoring her! He had not even glanced in her direction.

Seething, she followed the procession to the plaza. The High Priest stopped and motioned the Crier to step forward. There was a brief conversation and the Crier turned to the crowd. His loud, rich voice soared.

"The sacred fire will remain enclosed while the High Priest and the shaman purify themselves, then confer with the priests and others to decide when the ceremonies may continue. The fire will be guarded until then, and no fire is to be lit until the sacred fire is released. Women and children will leave the plaza. Men not purified with the black drink must leave also. All men will fast until the ceremonies continue. Pray for our city that the curse may be removed."

Antelope was gratified to note that Chomoc and his concubines were waved aside as the High Priest and others in the procession entered the plaza and went to a shallow hole that had been scooped out under a canopy as a place for a fire to be built. The High Priest gestured to the shaman, who knelt and placed the jar in the center of the hollow.

Where was Far Walker? She looked for him or Peg Foot but did not see either of them. Feeling bereft, she turned and left. Chomoc had not inquired about her evidently, nor had he made any effort at all to locate her. He was relishing the rapt attention not only of his concubines, but of young girls and women—men, too—who crowded close, thanked him for the fire, and urged him to play his flute again.

Antelope burned with embarrassment. It was as though she, his mate, and Skyfeather, his child, had never been.

A day will come when he discovers he cannot humiliate She Who Remembers and go unpunished.

The High Priest and the shaman were alone in the shaman's dwelling. The shaman's wife and two daughters had been sent to visit relatives so that the two men might prepare themselves for the new fire. Usually, the High Priest and the shaman would be in the sweat lodge, but since no fire was allowed to heat the stones, they sat before the shaman's altar in silence, appalled by the responsibility facing them. Nothing like this disaster had happened before; there was no precedent.

The High Priest concentrated on the altar, seeking inspiration. But he found it difficult for his kia to respond to the objects there, especially a bauxite pipe realistically carved in the likeness of a seated warrior resting his hands on his knees. The figure was strikingly lifelike, with a large, round copper plate on the forehead, great carved earspools, a heavy three-stranded necklace, and a feathered cape. Even the expression on the cruel face was uncomfortably real.

Such an object revealed something about the owner. The High Priest regarded the shaman covertly. His long, lean, straight body was an affront to one who was short and twisted like an ancient tree battered by storms. But it was the shaman's face that disturbed the High Priest the most—with a look about it of the bauxite warrior. Was a kinship there?

The High Priest forced himself to put his mind to the solemn responsibility they faced. He said, "We shall fast and commune with Long Man this night. When the Spirit Being shines forth in the morning, the new fire may be lit."

For a time, the shaman sat regarding his large, bony hands and did not reply. Finally, he cleared his throat and said in his rasping voice, "We must go to water."

The High Priest nodded. It was necessary to go to Long Man, to water, for final purification.

Neither mentioned his deepest concern, too painful to discuss.

This new fire was foreign. It would be forever suspect.
Their beloved city was doomed.

▲ 30 ▼

The morning dawned clear and cool, hinting of autumn to come. Antelope woke to the howls of the people greeting Sunfather. She sang her morning song.

Now this day,
My sun father . . .

This was the day the new fire would be released and sins of the past forgiven—a new beginning.

She finished her song and woke Skyfeather, who could sleep through any commotion.

"Come, little one. We shall begin this new day."

Skyfeather nursed vigorously, her rosy little mouth strong on the nipple. Her dark hair had grown longer all of a sudden; it drifted softly on her cheeks and clung to the back of her neck. Antelope's heart squeezed; how beautiful she was! This, her daughter, her mother's grandchild, was a link with all those Chosen Ones who had gone before and who would come after. Skyfeather would be She Who Remembers one day.

Antelope felt a pang of longing to teach again, to take her

place as She Who Remembers among her own people. Now that the Green Corn ceremony would make all anew, maybe this would be possible. She clasped the scallop shell of her necklace, worn smooth over the centuries by the touch of the Ancient Ones.

Help me become She Who Remembers again, to teach again. Help me to take Skyfeather home to her own people.

Skyfeather gurgled as if she agreed. She had finished nursing and wanted to play. Her blue eyes sparkled, and she waved her arms and legs, smiling a bewitching, toothless smile.

Antelope bathed Skyfeather from the water jar and dressed her in the garment Lipoe had given her; it had been washed carefully and looked beautiful. Antelope wanted to bathe in the river, but she might miss the ceremonies where Far Walker was sure to be. So she washed herself as she had bathed Skyfeather and donned her own beautiful white robe, which Far Walker had given her. The touch of it against her body was his touch that night by the river. . . .

Remembering, her body responded. It had been a long time. . . .

Antelope tucked Skyfeather into the cradleboard, looped the carrying thong around her shoulders, snatched a corn cake to nibble on, and entered the bright morning.

People thronged the old plaza where games and trading usually took place. The smaller plaza to the north of it was the sacred one; only men were there. Drums and chanting rose to the Spirit Being. Antelope edged her way through the crowd, and saw Far Walker. A group of men surrounded him, listening respectfully as he spoke. Antelope wondered what he was saying.

How commanding Far Walker was, how splendid in his ceremonial garments! As if sensing her gaze, Far Walker suddenly turned and saw her. He smiled, and Antelope smiled back—a mutual caress that made Antelope's heart skip a beat.

Chomoc saw, and Antelope was gratified to note his scowl. Ha!

Slowly, the High Priest approached the arbor where the jar of smoldering punk awaited. His ceremonial garments had been ruined in the storm, and he wore a plain, handsome white robe. On his chest lay a carved gorget made from a conch shell with two holes through which an otter skin thong was threaded and attached to two white buttons made of deer's antler. On his head he wore a piece of swan skin, doubled and wrapped around so that only the white feathers showed; a tuft of white feathers was on the crown.

The crowd fell silent as the High Priest reached the arbor and circled it three times. He gestured to the shaman, who knelt, removed the lid of the fire jar, and emptied the smoking punk upon chips and splinters of pitch pine that had been placed in the hollow. A young priest brought the High Priest the wing of a white bird. Chanting, the High Priest crouched beside the fire and fanned it with the wing while the crowd watched in reverent silence.

The shaman joined in the chanting, and the two voices blended with the thin wisp of smoke rising to the Spirit Being.

Still the people made no sound.

At last a flame flickered and was fed with dry wood stacked nearby. The flame grew, then leaped upward to exuberant cries from the crowd.

The High Priest rose with the help of his staff, and again he walked around the fire three times with a slow pace and grave demeanor, chanting prayers to the Spirit Being whom Red Man, the fire, represented.

Manimani brought him a basket of fruits from an assortment awaiting feasting. She walked with proud assurance, evidently confident that she would be selected as the next Great Sun. Antelope had never seen Manimani up close, but there was a subtle air of arrogance about her.

The High Priest threw each fruit, one at a time, into the fire and added a bit of button snakeroot from the medicine pouch at his side. Then he turned to face the people, who waited breathlessly.

"The new fire is born!"

A glad shout arose, accompanied by whistles and the frenzied barking of dogs, which were tethered securely so they might not enter the plaza and be shot. The High Priest gestured to the War Chief and the chief's assistant, who came running with torches to be lit at the fire.

"The Temple of Eternal Fire and the dwelling of the Great Sun will now be given to Red Man for purification."

He gestured again, and the War Chief and his assistant departed with flaming torches to the shout of drums and flutes.

Soon black smoke swirled upward from two sources, smudging the sky.

Antelope watched Manimani as she strode about, giving orders. Would the Great Sun's sister help her find a way to take Skyfeather home? Doubt poked a finger at Antelope's chest.

The High Priest stood by the fire and raised an arm for silence. Immediately, all was still. His rich, warm voice embraced them.

"It is the time of new beginnings."

Antelope listened impressed as the High Priest spoke to the warriors, reminding them of their responsibility to remain pure and carry out their duties bravely. Then he lectured the women, telling them that if any had failed to extinguish their old fires, or if any of them were impure, they must depart immediately or the divine new fire would punish them and their relatives. He told them to serve only pure food to their children, lest they get worms or fall ill. Sharply, he warned them not to break marital or sexual rules. Then the High Priest addressed all the people, telling them to ponder the meaning of the new, holy fire brought to them to purify their society.

Antelope remembered the old Crier Chief at the Place of the Eagle Clan, who lectured every morning from the high place in the cliff city where he climbed to reach the top. How long ago and far away . . .

The High Priest's voice rolled on. "If rules are not obeyed, we must endure drought, captivity, death from our enemies, and witchcraft and disease. Remember and obey the sacred rules of our forefathers so that we shall have good health, good crops, fine trading, and victory over our enemies." He paused, and his eloquent, dark eyes swept the crowd. "All past wrongs are now forgiven. Begin anew, cleansed and purified."

Slowly, with painful dignity, the High Priest left the plaza and headed for Long Man.

Now the shaman gestured, and one of the young priests called six old women dancers who had been waiting outside the plaza. They entered, each dressed in her finest ceremonial garments, each carrying a branch from a different variety of tree. Their arms and legs were anointed with bear oil, and tortoise-shell rattles encircled their ankles.

They were joined by six revered old men, each holding a

branch pulled from the arbor over the holy fire in one hand and
a wand decorated with white feathers in the other. To the beat
of pottery drums, the priest led the dance, circling the fire,
stamping his feet with short, quick steps, singing a sacred song.
The others followed, singing and dancing.

Antelope listened to the beat of the drums, the strong
voices of the old men, the shrill voices of the old women, and
the sound of the tortoiseshell rattles, and again she remembered the Place of the Eagle Clan, and their dances. . . .

Were the Anasazi still there? Or had they all departed to
continue their wandering as the gods decreed?

The dances of the old men and women ended. Now, at last,
everyone in the city might have fire. Burning branches were carried to a place in the plaza where people might come to ignite
fires of their own. Soon pots would be bubbling and meats ex-
uding tantalizing aromas.

Antelope went to obtain a fire of her own. As she poked
a branch into the flames to ignite it, a hand took the branch
from her.

"I shall bring it to you," Far Walker said. "Go and wait for
me." The look he gave her left no doubt as to what he had in
mind.

She laughed. "Yes. Bring a fire."

She hurried homeward, her heart beating hard. Chomoc's
flute sang in the distance, promising wonderful surprises. But
Antelope listened only to the drumming within her, the beat of
blood in her veins.

Soon she was back in Peg Foot's dwelling; he sat grinding
herbs with a stone pestle in a small bowl. Antelope put Skyfeather on the floor so she could crawl around; immediately she
went to Peg Foot.

"I greet you, small one," he said to her, smiling. Love for
Skyfeather softened his stern old face. "Here." He gave her a
wooden whistle he had carved for her to play with. She chewed
on it happily.

"Far Walker is coming," Antelope said. "He brings fire."

"Of course. His totem is Fire Bringer—the spider he wears
on his back. Do you know the story?"

"No. Tell me!"

"Very well." Peg Foot sniffed the ground herbs in the bowl
and was satisfied. He poured the contents into a gourd bowl with

a lid, placed the bowl on a shelf, and made himself comfortable on a seating mat. "In the beginning there was no fire, and the world was cold, until the Thunders—"

"Who?"

"The Thunders who live in the Upper World. They sent their lightning and put fire into the bottom of a hollow sycamore tree that grew on an island. The animals knew it was there, because they could see the smoke coming out at the top, but they could not get to it on account of the water, so they held a council to decide what to do. This was a long time ago.

"Every animal that could fly or swim was anxious to go after the fire. The Raven offered, and because he was so large and strong they thought he could surely do the work, so he was sent first. He flew high and far across the water and alighted on the sycamore tree, but while he was wondering what to do next, the heat scorched all his feathers black, and he was frightened and came back without the fire."

Antelope smiled; the Towa story of how the Raven became black was different, but she liked this story, too.

He continued, "The little Screech Owl volunteered to go, and reached the place safely, but while he was looking down into the hollow tree a blast of hot air came up and nearly burned out his eyes. He managed to fly home as best he could, but it was a long time before he could see well and his eyes are red to this day. Then the Hoot Owl and the Horned Owl went, but by the time they got to the hollow tree the fire was burning so fiercely that the smoke nearly blinded them, and the ashes carried up by the wind made white rings around their eyes. They had to come home again without the fire, but with all their rubbing they were never able to get rid of the white rings."

Antelope was intrigued. "I have not heard that before. Tell more!"

He grinned, pleased. "No more of the birds would venture, and so the little snake, the Black Racer, said he would go through the water and bring back some fire. He swam across to the island and crawled through the grass to the tree, and went in by a small hole at the bottom. The heat and smoke were too much for him, too, and after dodging about blindly over the hot ashes until he was almost on fire himself, he managed by good luck to get out again at the same hole. But his body had been scorched black, and ever since, he has had the habit of darting about and doubling back on his track as if trying to escape from close quarters."

"Yes, he does do that." Antelope hugged her knees with delight. Peg Foot was a good storyteller. His eyes sparkled with enthusiasm and he used gestures to illustrate events—like the little snake swimming in the water.

"When the little Black Racer came back, the great black snake, the Climber, offered to go for fire. He swam over to the island and climbed up the tree on the outside, as the black snake always does, but when he put his head down into the hole, the smoke choked him and he fell into the burning stump. Before he could climb out again, he was as black as the Black Racer.

"Now they held another council, for still there was no fire, and the world was cold; but the other birds, snakes, and four-footed animals all had some excuse for not going, because they were all afraid to venture near the burning sycamore. Until at last"—Peg Foot paused for effect—"the Water Spider said she would go. This is not the water spider that looks like a mosquito, but the other one, with black downy hair and red stripes on her body. She can run on top of the water or dive to the bottom, so there would be no trouble to get over to the island. But the question was, how could she bring back the fire? 'I'll manage that,' said the Water Spider; so she spun a thread from her body and wove it into a *tusti* bowl, which she fastened on her back. Then she crossed over to the island and through the grass to where the fire was still burning. She put one little coal of fire into her bowl and came back with it. Ever since we have had fire, and the Water Spider still keeps her tusti bowl. That is the little circle you see on the spider's back."

"Yes, I saw that and wondered what it was." Antelope was impressed. What a fine totem Far Walker had! "Thank you for that story."

"When Far Walker comes, look carefully at the spider he wears. It is a powerful totem."

"I shall do that. I want to be with him," she blurted. In her eagerness she could only be frank.

He shot her a glance from under shaggy brows. "Of course. He has not been here for too long; I want to be with him also."

Antelope fumed. "I think Far Walker wants to be alone with me—"

"You mean he no longer wishes to be with his Teacher? He

wishes to avoid me now?" Peg Foot shook his head in mock distress.

He was teasing her! Antelope laughed. "Go away, old man."

Peg Foot scooped up Skyfeather and stared solemnly into her blue eyes. "We go to play outside while your mother plays inside." Skyfeather cooed as Peg Foot carried her out the door.

Alone at last, Antelope smoothed her hair and wished she had bathed in the river that morning. She slipped off her robe, scooped handfuls of water from the water jar, and splashed it on herself. She was still wet and shiny when Far Walker strode in.

He stood gazing, his face aglow. It was as though his whole being was lit by inner fire.

Antelope was suddenly self-conscious. She tried to wipe the water away with both hands, but he came close.

"Let me," he said softly.

Slowly, caressingly, he slid his hands over her wet body, beginning with the curve of her cheeks, down to her throat and shoulders, to her breasts. He cupped each round, rosy-tipped swell.

"Beautiful." His voice was husky. "Beautiful."

He pulled her close and bent to her breasts, flicking his tongue on the nipples, caressing.

Antelope pressed his head to her. "Now!"

Still he held her, sliding his hands down her sides to the curve of her belly, to the moist, sweet place between her thighs.

"Now!" she cried again.

He filled her at last, and she lay spent, while he still pulsed deeply within her.

"I love you, Far Walker."

"And I love you. Until I die."

·31·

That same afternoon the High Priest stood in the river shallows, facing east, communing with Long Man and the Spirit Being. Smoke from his burning temple and from the Great Sun's dwelling drifted, its acrid odor drifting with it. Consuming what had been, but would be no more . . .

The High Priest was surprised and vaguely annoyed when Waikah, the old midwife, approached him; he did not wish to be disturbed. But her look of quiet desperation gave him pause. She strode to the riverbank, greeted him with two hous, waded into the water with her moccasins on, and confronted him.

"I must tell you." Her voice trembled.

He looked into despairing eyes surrounded by deep wrinkles, and knew he must listen.

"Speak."

She told him, wringing her hands. It was like blood spurting from a wound.

The High Priest listened in dumbfounded shock.

Waikah continued, "So you see it was I who switched the babies, who gave Firekeeper's child to the Great Sun. And it was I who gave the Great Sun's child to a commoner's family." Her voice broke. "The gods punished Firekeeper and me with that storm that killed her and her son and cursed us all—"

Waikah began to shake uncontrollably. Her gaunt face under stringy white hair was convulsed, and her toothless mouth was agape as she tried to speak more, and could not.

The High Priest felt the cold of the river in his veins. His beloved Firekeeper! He grabbed Waikah's shoulders. "To whom did you give the Great Sun's child?"

Waikah's lips flapped but only grunts emerged.

His twisted arms shook her in a viselike grip. *"Who is the real Great Sun?"*

Her eyes rolled and her head wobbled, but she could not speak.

A group of women approached with water jars, talking and laughing. They wandered along the shore toward the water-taking place, a deep pool near the bank.

The High Priest released Waikah. He must control himself. He swallowed and looked eastward toward the Spirit Being's rising place. A flock of white birds soared against the blue. He must allow his spirit to soar. He must be the High Priest.

Waikah stood staring at him, her mouth working silently.

The High Priest was suddenly ashamed; he had been bullying her. He touched her arm. "Do not be afraid," he said gently. "Tell me. Who is the real Great Sun?"

At last the words came. "Far Walker."

Far Walker! Firekeeper, the only woman he had ever loved, had robbed that good man of his rightful royal heritage. And this creature, this midwife, had helped her. The High Priest tried to swallow his anger, but could not; it burned in him.

Waikah snatched at his robe. "The Green Corn ceremony has taken my guilt away. But I want—I need—your absolution." She jerked at his robe with both hands. "Tell me I am forgiven!"

He pushed her away. "You forget," he said coldly. "Firekeeper and her son are dead. There is no forgiveness for murder."

Waikah stood frozen. Her eyes pierced his in desperation.

"Please," she whispered.

"No."

Slowly Waikah turned away and waded to the bank. The High Priest watched her go. It was as if she took Firekeeper with her, away from him forever, leaving him hollow inside.

*   *   *

It was dark night when Waikah knew what she must do. The moon had not risen, but the fire from the burning temple glowed brightly in the distance, beckoning. The High Priest had refused her absolution, but Red Man would not.

As she left her dwelling among the trees, everything suddenly appeared in sharp relief—the silhouette of branches swaying in the breeze, the scents of earth and night and smoke from the burning temple; the sound of her own footsteps, her breath, her heartbeats soon to cease.

Waikah looked up at the sky ablaze with stars, and her spirit soared. By obtaining absolution she would eliminate the curse, and all would be as it had been before. She, Waikah, the old midwife, would give herself as a sacrifice to save the city and save the people. The gods would be pleased, the rightful Great Sun would rule, and a new temple would be built on the place where she died. She, Waikah, would do what no one else could do—obtain absolution for the city and its people as well as for herself.

Slowly, she climbed the steps of the mound to where the fire sent sparks and smoke into the night. It grew hotter.

Red Man danced, beckoning, beckoning.

"I come!" Waikah cried triumphantly. With bony arms outspread she flung herself into the flames.

The temple fire still burned when Waikah's body was discovered among the cinders. Some said she had wanted to join her sister in the Afterworld. Others said she had given herself to Red Man for purification. Only the High Priest knew that Waikah had done it for the absolution he had refused her.

Guilt, and sorrow for Firekeeper, bent him more. He leaned heavily on his staff, and his lurching gait grew painfully slower.

So much of Waikah's body was burned away that there was some discussion as to whether she should be placed upon an elevated platform for the remaining flesh to decompose, as was customary. It was decided that her spirit needed the procedure to ease her journey to the Afterworld; the Bone Pickers would be summoned later. She was covered with a mat to keep vultures away, and food and drink and a new garment were placed beside her for her journey. A small fire would be kept burning the first four days to provide warmth and light. She had no dog to accompany her, but she had a pet squirrel that was killed and placed beside her.

For four days, relatives gathered frequently at the foot of the platform to wail and mourn. Antelope heard them, and it dampened her spirit. She was making a new robe and was singing when she first heard their death cries.

"How long will they do that?" she asked Peg Foot.

He paused in the carving of a new peg he was making for himself. Since Antelope's arrival he had become more interested in his appearance.

"Until the Bone Pickers come."

Antelope remembered the stooped, smelly old men with long, black claws. She shuddered.

Peg Foot noticed. He said, "Dealing with death is dangerous; death can be passed to the living. That is why only those who have defeated death for many years are qualified to become Bone Pickers." He gave her a sharp glance. "They face danger bravely. They are respected."

Antelope looked at the old Healer. His gray crest was newly stiffened with bear grease, and his forelock held new, shiny turquoise beads. He looked quite handsome. She smiled.

"You are respected more, Peg Foot."

Four days passed. It was decided that Waikah was ready for the Bone Pickers.

They came, two old men with their identifying tattoos—scrolls on each cheek and down the arms. They were followed by a young priest with a turtle shell rattle fastened to an ornate rod with dangling eagle feathers. The rattle had a high, wheezing voice that sent shivers down Antelope's spine.

She had come with other villagers to pay her respects, and stood at a little distance upwind to avoid the odor. It was a cloudy day and cool, which helped. The group of Waikah's relatives stopped their wailing to greet the Bone Pickers, then resumed their cries as the old men used a stepping-stone to climb to the platform. One sat at Waikah's head, and the other at her feet. The priest stood beside the platform, chanting and shaking his rattle.

The Bone Pickers mumbled prayers—to their spirit protectors, Antelope guessed—and began their dangerous work, praying the while. Sharpened black fingernails scraped flesh from a bone, then handed the bone down to a relative who placed it in a woven casketlike basket, wailing.

Antelope watched in fascinated horror as Waikah's head was jerked and twisted loose. The hair had been burned off and the face was nearly gone. Black claws scooped out the eyes and the skull's contents as the Bone Picker murmured supplications to his guardian spirit.

The wails of the mourners, the Bone Pickers' prayers, the sound of fingernails scraping, the chant of the priest, the voice of the rattle, plus the smell of the corpse and the sight of Wai- kah's bones being handed down, one after another, were too much. Antelope felt sick, but she could not leave. It would be an insult to Waikah and her relatives.

At last all bones were in the cane basket. The Bone Pickers descended to the final chants of the priest, and the platform and its contents were set afire to speed Waikah on her journey.

Now a feast was provided by Waikah's relatives. With the smell of smoke and her burning flesh riding the breeze, they celebrated her release from this world to the better Afterworld.

Antelope was shocked to note that the Bone Pickers did not wash their hands before eating. She wanted to vomit, but this also would be an insult to Waikah and her relatives, so she swal- lowed it down.

If Far Walker loved her as much as he said he did, he would ask her to be his mate. If so, she would have to become one of these people, and believe—or try to believe—what they did. Could she do this?

She felt the touch of the scallop shell on her breast. She was, and always would be, She Who Remembers. A foreigner in a foreign place. She pressed the shell to her.

I love Far Walker. What shall I do? Tell me!

There was no answer.

During Waikah's last rites, the High Priest spent much time with Long Man, steeling himself for what would come. A meet- ing was scheduled to appoint the next Great Sun and he, the High Priest, must tell them what Waikah had revealed. His peo- ple would face yet another disaster—discovering they had been deceived by the one ruler they trusted most. And, yes, by their High Priest's most honored assistant, Firekeeper.

The High Priest moaned with the pain of it and splashed water over his head.

"Make me strong," he prayed.

The meeting took place two days later in the house of the caddí. The High Priest and Manimani, as the most important personages, sat on raised benches before the altar. Seated before them were the shaman, the caddí, the War Chief, the Crier, Peg Foot, Far Walker, several powerful warriors, and the most honored elders. Also present were One Who Watches, Red Leaf, and an influential group of esteemed old women. Antelope, a foreigner, was not there.

Manimani's round face was flushed. She fanned herself jerkily with a turkey feather fan, crossing and uncrossing her legs. The High Priest thought, *She sees no point in this meeting since she believes she is now the Great Sun. She is about to encounter a revelation.*

He forced himself to pay attention to the caddí's introductory announcements—long and wordy, as usual.

"Therefore," the caddí continued, "it is now our sacred duty and esteemed privilege—our great and happy honor—to decide among ourselves who will be our next great leader and royal personage, sister of the Spirit Being"—he paused, swallowed, and corrected himself hastily—"sister or brother of the Spirit Being, the Great Sun. I ask our revered High Priest to discuss this with you."

Wiping his brow, the caddí sat down.

Bracing himself on his staff, the High Priest rose. Gathering his inner forces, he faced the people looking up at him. He took a deep breath, and began.

"We, all of us, face a situation we have not encountered before. The gods disrupted our sacred Green Corn ceremony. They destroyed our Temple of Eternal Fire; our Great Sun and Firekeeper were killed. No such punishment—for that is what it was, punishment—has been inflicted upon us and our city since time began. Therefore, we must ask ourselves"—he paused, looking from face to face—"why?"

Manimani smiled, fanning herself. "Maybe the gods wanted someone else to be the Great Sun."

There was shocked silence. Manimani realized she had spoken with unforgivable irreverence, and her round face flushed.

The High Priest knew how certain Manimani was that she would be chosen as the next ruler. He braced himself. "Manimani is right. The gods do want another to be Great Sun—and who that person is has been revealed to me."

Manimani beamed and there were murmurs of interest as the High Priest continued.

"I communed with Long Man, seeking wisdom and knowledge as to why the gods afflicted us and our city. Long Man heard my plea. Waikah came to me and confessed."

Manimani stopped fanning. "Waikah, the old midwife?"

"Yes. She who gave herself to Red Man in the burning temple. She confessed."

"Confessed what?" Manimani asked sharply.

"It is a long story, so I shall sit down as I tell it."

The High Priest sat on a bench and gazed over the murmuring crowd. They returned his gaze with avid curiosity, especially the women who knew Waikah well. One Who Watches fidgeted, twisting the bracelet Chomoc had given her. Red Leaf whispered behind her hand to one of the old women dancers. The men sat stoically, trying unsuccessfully to conceal their interest; their eyes betrayed eagerness. Only the shaman seemed uninterested; he gazed into distance, his face expressionless. Manimani sat with her fan in her plump lap and a small frown on her face. Flies buzzed. Outside, a mockingbird called. Far Walker turned his head, listening.

What was the bird saying? The High Priest took another breath, and began.

"It happened a long time ago, when Waikah and Firekeeper were young. . . ."

The people sat in stunned silence as the High Priest's story unfolded. From time to time exclamations burst forth. Manimani's black eyes smoldered, and her mouth set in a grim line. Once she rose to leave, then changed her mind and sat back down, fanning herself vigorously, her face flushed.

"And so you see," the High Priest said quietly, "the baby who was to become the true Great Sun was given to commoners, and Firekeeper's child took his place. All these years, the true Great Sun has been robbed of his sacred heritage, thanks to Waikah and her sister, Firekeeper. . . ." The High Priest's voice wavered. "At last the gods took revenge—"

The shaman gestured to speak, with apparent boredom. "Who did Waikah say the true Great Sun is?"

"Far Walker."

There was astounded silence, then a babble.

Far Walker froze in shock. He turned to Peg Foot, who did not seem to be particularly surprised.

Manimani jumped up, her face twisted. "It is all lies! Lies, I tell you! Where is the proof?" Rage shook her voice. "Waikah lost her kia in grief for her sister, as we know well. How could she speak truly? She was old, she had delusions—"

"She spoke truly." The High Priest's resonant voice was calm, his luminous gaze steady. "You cannot deny we are cursed."

"We are cursed with lies! I demand proof of this dead woman's hysterical jabbering before you deny me—or anyone—of the right to rule." Manimani's fan flapped in agitation.

Far Walker rose. "I know nothing of this." He gave Manimani a sardonic glance. "Royalty does not interest me. I am a Healer; patients are waiting." His firm footsteps sounded through the extended doorway as he departed.

In the heated discussion that followed, Peg Foot sat in silence. Finally, he lifted his staff for attention, then leaned upon it to rise.

"You have known me as your Healer for many years. I have healed you of your illnesses and your wounds—not all of which were visible. Is this not so?"

There were murmurs of agreement.

"Therefore, consider this. It is true that Waikah lost her kia. But she did not lose her mind. She knew well what she said when she confessed. One does not lie to the High Priest."

He sat down to a moment of silence.

Manimani's face flushed scarlet. Her voice shook. "I demand proof!"

"As do I," the shaman said.

The High Priest looked at the shaman, who returned his gaze. Malice lurked in the shaman's eyes.

The High Priest thought, *He can never forgive me for being the High Priest, with prestige greater than his own.* He said, "Perhaps the matter should be discussed." He turned to the caddí. "I leave the discussion to you." Slowly and with dignity, he sat down.

The caddí fingered his jaguar robe nervously. He cleared his throat, looked over the assembly, and spoke with effort.

"It is true that one does not lie to the High Priest." He cleared his throat again. "However, in moments of great stress, perhaps it is possible for one to believe truth is being spoken when, in fact, it is not. Therefore, it is up to this council to decide whether or not Waikah's words must be proven true before a new Great Sun is chosen. I invite your discussion."

Manimani rose, her face a storm cloud over the mountain of her bosom. "I refuse to participate in this so-called discussion. Should you choose to summon me, I shall be in my dwelling." She marched out in a billow of beaded robe, her head high.

The High Priest sighed. Far Walker had an enemy.

Discussion proceeded, some for truth finding and some against. Finally, the caddí raised his feather-tipped staff.

"If there is no more discussion, we shall vote. The War Chief will count. All who do not want a truth-finding ceremony, please stand."

A number of people stood up including, the High Priest noticed, most of the women. The War Chief marked vertical lines on a strip of bark.

Again, the caddí raised his staff. "Those who do want a truth-finding ceremony, please stand."

More people stood, and again the War Chief marked a line for each person standing.

The caddí said, "The War Chief will bring the counting marks up here for all to see."

The War Chief, a burly man of middle age and many scars, stepped to the front and held up the bark. Each person was represented by a black mark—those who wanted the ceremony and, beneath them, those who did not. It was obvious that there were more marks for those who did.

The caddí thumped his staff on the floor three times. He turned to the shaman and the High Priest.

"It is now your duty and responsibility to determine the truth or falsehood of statements made by the midwife, Waikah, to the High Priest," he announced. "It is the decision of the council," he added with another thump of his staff.

The High Priest nodded. "It shall be done."

"Within four days," the shaman said.

The High Priest wondered how he and the shaman could discover truth when their objectives differed.

Far Walker had more than one enemy.

▲ 32 ▼

Antelope sat outdoors by her cooking fire, stirring a pot of porridge; Peg Foot enjoyed porridge and Skyfeather was old enough now to have a little. Peg Foot was still at the council meeting. Antelope wondered what was happening; the meeting had lasted for a long time.

It was a warm afternoon in early autumn with a brisk breeze from the river and great white clouds billowing. Neighbors worked their gardens, children shouted in their play, and somewhere a child was learning to play the flute. The notes rode the air tentatively, up and down.

Chomoc and his flute were gone, along with his concubines. He had lingered for trading, for socializing, for a night with other women, and had made no effort to see her or Skyfeather. Remembering her nights with Far Walker, Antelope was glad—except that she would have liked Chomoc to know. Perhaps Chomoc did know, and realized she did not grieve for him. But when Chomoc left, he took her childhood with him. She did grieve for that.

Antelope sighed and paused in her stirring. Would Far Walker be willing to take her and Skyfeather home? Did he love her enough to leave the place of his birth and live in Cicuye? A Healer was welcome everywhere.

A babble of voices indicated that the council meeting was over; news was spreading. Red Leaf came hurrying home, and paused. Her round face was flushed and her eyes sparked with excitement. "It is Far Walker!"

"What is?"

Several women came running to surround Red Leaf.

"Tell us!"

"It is Far Walker."

"Aye-e-e-e!"

Chattering, they swept Red Leaf away like a raft caught in floodwaters. Antelope stood staring anxiously after them.

What has happened to Far Walker?

Antelope removed the pot from the fire, scooped up Sky-feather, and ran toward the ceremonial center, her heart thumping. Was he hurt? Had something terrible happened to him? If she lost Far Walker, she couldn't bear it. Not now.

As she rounded a bend in the path she nearly bumped into Peg Foot. His face was aglow. "Have you heard?"

"Tell me!" She grabbed his arm. "What happened?"

He smiled. "Come home and I will tell you." He saw her worried frown. "It is a long story, an incredible story—"

Antelope stepped in front of him, blocking his path, suddenly afraid.

"I want you to tell me now. Please."

"Very well. It is possible that Far Walker will be our next Great Sun."

She stared, unbelieving.

"See? I told you it is an incredible story. Come, let's go home, and I will tell you everything."

It had been four days since the council meeting. Antelope stood with Peg Foot and the crowd of people in the sacred plaza where the truth-finding ceremony was about to be held. It was said that the High Priest and the shaman had fasted, partaken of the black drink, purified themselves in the sweat lodge, and communicated with Long Man; they were now prepared to discover whether or not Waikah had spoken truth in her confession.

It was not a hot morning, but Antelope felt perspiration beading her face and body. Tension was a lump in her stomach. What if Waikah had spoken truth? If Far Walker became the Great Sun, she, a Towa foreigner, could not be his mate as she had hoped to be—expected to be. What would become of her and Skyfeather?

She looked over the crowd to see Far Walker, but he was not there. She turned to Peg Foot.

"Where is Far Walker?"

"Gone to the Holy Mountain to seek a vision."

The crowd murmured restlessly, waiting for the ceremony to begin. Priests and elders sat in a wide circle, surrounded by a ring of fire to keep witches away. Within their circle, another ring of smoldering coals surrounded a small mound built in the center of the plaza. Topping the mound lay a handsome stone pipe long as a man's arm, with openings at either end, and two bowls, like small chimneys, toward the center. Circular insertions of bright shell ornamented the length of the pipe on either side.

The drum sounded for attention, and the caddí strode to stand beside the pipe. His stocky frame assumed a commanding stance as he gazed over the crowd. His penetrating voice rolled over the plaza.

"Behold the sacred pipe of double powers. The High Priest and the shaman will partake of it to seek the spirit of Waikah in the Afterworld. Then Waikah herself will speak." He looked at the crowd waiting eagerly. "There must be silence. If any woman here is impure, she must leave at once, or the ceremony cannot be effective."

Several young women left reluctantly, heading for the women's hut.

The caddí watched them go. "The ceremony shall now begin." He stepped gingerly over the ring of coals and sat with the priests and elders. Manimani sat apart on a small bench, regarding the crowd with regal assurance. She wore a fine white robe and white swan feathers in her dark hair. An engraved shell gorget rested resplendently on her bosom—as if she were the Great Sun already.

Antelope looked at the ring of fire surrounding the seated men and at the smaller ring surrounding the mound in the center. She remembered long ago when a Medicine Chief had used fire to call Massau'u in an effort to make her die. . . . Would these chiefs try to destroy Far Walker—to assure Manimani's position as Great Sun?

Now the drums sounded a great voice, and the High Priest and the shaman appeared. Both were painted white all over but for the face, which was painted black. The crowd parted respectfully as the two men entered, stepped over (or was it through?) the outer ring of fire, and approached the center.

Antelope gasped to see that the High Priest carried a skull painted vermilion. His black face, his bent, twisted body, and his thin, white arms holding the skull made him seem like a great white spider with a black head, clutching prey.

The shaman followed him, chanting loudly. His angular frame towered over that of the High Priest. The thin, black face perched on his long, white neck reminded Antelope of a malevolent being from a bad dream. In outstretched arms he carried an oblong lidded basket of woven reeds.

To the shaman's chanting, they stepped over the ring of coals and stood by the small mound where the pipe rested. To the throb of drums the shaman placed the basket on the mound beside the pipe. The High Priest held up the skull to the four directions; Antelope saw the jaw gape wide in a silent scream. The High Priest placed the skull upon the basket, then lifted the pipe, gestured a blessing upon it, and handed the pipe to the shaman.

The shaman offered the pipe to the four directions, then to the Spirit Being above and to the spirit world below, chanting meanwhile.

Now the flutes sang softly as the High Priest and the shaman sat cross-legged, facing one another, with the pipe between them. A young priest stepped forward to light the pipe for each. Solemnly, with closed eyes, the High Priest and the shaman inhaled Red Man's essence, seeking entry to the spirit world.

Time passed, and still the High Priest and the shaman sat smoking the same pipe, eyes closed, while the soft voice of the flutes continued on and on. Children became restless and babies cried. Some mothers left, taking crying babies and querulous children, but most stayed, watching and waiting.

Suddenly, the shaman dropped the pipe, threw both hands overhead and began to chant, babbling strange words. The High Priest caught the pipe, held it in outstretched arms, then laid it upon the mound beside the basket and skull. The shaman continued his babbling chant in a hoarse voice, his black chin bobbing up and down, and his eyes rolling so that the whites showed. His long arms flayed the air, white fingers clutching.

The High Priest lifted the scarlet skull and beckoned to the young priest who had lit the pipe.

Now rattles hissed as the priest poked a burning rod through the open jaw of the skull, lighting something inside. A thin finger of smoke drifted through one empty eye.

"What's in there?" Antelope whispered to Peg Foot.

"Rotted dry wood, slow-burning moss, and the like—punk. It smolders."

The voice of the rattles returned the shaman to this world. He sat motionless for a moment, as though waking from a dream. He leaned close to speak to the High Priest, who nodded.

The High Priest faced the people. For a time, only the rattles spoke. The luminous, dark eyes in the spider head moved from person to person, probing.

Finally, the rattles silenced. The High Priest stepped with his awkward gait over the inner ring to face those seated inside the large ring of fire. In a low, clear voice he said, "Our shaman found Waikah's spirit; you heard it speaking in the shaman's voice. She said she gave herself to Red Man, who will tell us whether or not she spoke truth."

The High Priest gestured to the skull where one eye smoked. "She is there, and Red Man is inside her head, inside her mouth. If Red Man lingers until the Spirit Being returns tomorrow, we shall know that Waikah spoke truly, and Far Walker is the Great Sun." He paused to gaze at the people, who listened breathlessly. "If Red Man departs, we shall know truth was not spoken, and Manimani is the Great Sun."

There were murmurs, silenced by a glance from the High Priest. "Warriors will stand guard this day, this night, and tomorrow until the Spirit Being is directly overhead. Nothing and no one will touch Waikah's head or Red Man inside it. Red Man and the Spirit Being alone will determine truth."

Manimani rose. "The truth is known already."

The High Priest silenced her with a gesture. "The ceremony is completed for this day." He turned to the crowd. "Return home and pray for wisdom."

Slowly, the crowd dispersed. Peg Foot and Antelope left the

plaza, following the path to Yala. Once home, Antelope placed Skyfeather on the floor so she could crawl and explore, as she loved to do. Peg Foot watched her fondly.

"She is strong," he said. "And she is curious—a sign of intelligence."

Antelope was not listening. She saw again the great white spider whose luminous eyes pierced hers like a lance. She saw again the skull's jaw opened wide in a mute howl as smoke drifted from one empty eye.

This was the old woman who had shouted, "You do not belong here!"

Waikah spoke truth then, yes.

Did she speak truly to the High Priest?

That night, Antelope dreamed. She was home in Cicuye, standing on the high place where Kwani had initiated her as She Who Remembers. A mist swirled, and Kwani appeared. She seemed younger and even more beautiful than Antelope remembered. Antelope's heart squeezed.

"Mother!"

Kwani's blue eyes looked deep into Antelope's so that Antelope felt her kia, her entire inner being, exposed.

Kwani came close and put both arms on Antelope's shoulders. Antelope did not feel it, but she knew her mother's loving touch.

"You cannot do it," Kwani said.

"Do what?"

"You know what. Take that man, Far Walker, as mate."

"I love him, and he loves me. He—"

"You have seen his people, what they do. You cannot live with that, nor can you allow Skyfeather to do so. His blood is their blood, not yours."

"But—"

Kwani's eyes grew more intensely blue, and her voice was wind in the grasses. "Remember who you are, my daughter."

The mist swirled, and Kwani was gone.

"Mother!" Antelope called. "Come back! Please!"

Only the mist remained for a moment, then vanished.

Antelope woke in tears, reaching out to what was not there. For a time she lay weeping in darkness, reliving her dream.

Remember who you are. . . .

*   *   *

Manimani paced her dwelling, watched by young Patu, her dead brother's son. Patu was a moody child of seven winters, given to long silences. He said nothing, but his alert, small eyes followed her every move. Ordinarily, this would have irritated her, but now she was too distressed to care.

Could it be that the old midwife had actually spoken the truth?

Was my brother not my brother after all?

The thought was intolerable. It would mean that she was not his sister and could not take his royal place.

What if the skull still smoked tomorrow?

Her world was crumbling about her. Something must be done!

She paused in her pacing to think. Patu's opaque gaze was upon her. What went on in that boy's mind? If Patu's father was an imposter, his son was no kin of hers and she owed him nothing. Perhaps there was a way she could use him to assure her place as Great Sun. Perhaps . . .

But no. He was too young, and what she had in mind was too dangerous. What if the High Priest found out?

She continued pacing, back and forth, round and round, with Patu's eyes following every step. If Red Man still burned tomorrow, what would become of her? If it was true that Far Walker and she had the same mother, she would still be the Great Sun's sister—to sit at his feet while he shoved food at her with his moccasins after he finished, and always, always do only what *he* wanted, no matter how humiliating. All her life, Manimani had waited for the time she would inherit the position of Great Sun. Secretly, she was glad when the Great Sun died; her time had come at last. Now the city's curse was hers also. If Far Walker became the Great Sun, he would have the power to make her life a torment.

A dangerous situation required a dangerous solution. If indeed Patu was no kin of hers, she owed him nothing. Besides, it was just as important to the boy that she be the next Great Sun. If she was not and his father was revealed as an imposter, Patu would become a commoner, subject to hard work and scant privilege for a lifetime.

She went to sit beside him. She said, "You know about the truth-finding ceremony in the plaza, do you not?"

"Of course. I was there."

"Do you know what it will mean if the skull still smokes when the Spirit Being is overhead?"

A look hid in his eyes; what was it? He said, "Yes, I know. You will not be the Great Sun." He scratched himself casually. "Far Walker will be, instead."

His voice was matter-of-fact, not at all concerned. That disturbed Manimani. She said, "If I am not the Great Sun, you will not be the Great Sun's nephew. You will no longer be allowed to accompany the men playing chunkey, nor attend their gambling, nor will you be permitted in their secret societies, nor ride on the royal litter—"

"Far Walker would let me."

"No. Not if he is the Great Sun. Only his own children will ride with him."

"But he has no children."

"Not yet. But he will. He certainly will."

She glimpsed the disappointment in Patu's eyes, and smiled inwardly. The gods had given her an idea like a pot with a hot handle; she must maneuver carefully. She took a bit of dried persimmon dipped in honey and offered it; it was Patu's favorite treat. He chewed, swallowed it in a single bite, and waited for more like a puppy.

"You may have all you want," Manimani crooned. "But first, there is a small errand to do for me."

They talked for some time. Finally, Manimani said, "Do you understand what you are to do?"

He nodded, frowning.

"Good. Remember you are child of the Great Sun; no harm will come to you. The Spirit Being protects his own."

Manimani watched Patu march out the door. She bit her lips nervously. It was a dangerous plan and he was only a boy. . . .

What if Patu told? What if the High Priest found out? But she was desperate. Once her position as Great Sun was secure, she could handle whatever problem came up. It would be her word against that of a seven-year-old.

It wasn't until later that she thought of the guards. When she had enjoyed them, she would be willing to have them as consorts—for a while, at least. But what if her plan failed? Would they tell?

Would they?

* * *

It was night, and Patu had never gone anywhere alone, especially at night. Usually, he rode with relatives in a litter, with slaves carrying torches; but now he must go alone, like any other boy. "Like a shadow," Manimani had said.

It was late and the plaza was nearly deserted. A thin moon hung low and stars glittered. It was quiet but for distant drums and a coyote's song far away. Dogs howled reply and then it was quiet again.

Patu stopped to rehearse what he was supposed to say. It had to be exactly right. But something inside of him made him uneasy. He really did not like Manimani at all, but if she was going to be the Great Sun he had better do what she told him. If Far Walker was Great Sun, then he would teach Patu the Healer's secrets, like how to use the red and black beads. Patu liked secrets.

But he liked dried persimmons and honey, too.

Patu felt under his robe to see if what he needed was still there. It was. Rehearsing words under his breath, he hurried across the shadowy plaza. Two burly guards stood beside the small mound with the basket and skull upon it. The men were fearsome creatures with their falcon eyes and thick forelocks dangling, with their big shields and long lances and bows and arrows, with flint knives protruding from wide belts. The guards saw him coming and spoke to each other. He wondered what they said.

Patu was suddenly afraid. No one was supposed to go near them when they stood guard. What if they did not know who he was and speared him with a lance or chopped off his head?

He saw the skull on the basket. It seemed to be staring right at him as if it said, "This is how your head will look."

Patu wanted to turn around and run home. But he was the child of the Great Sun, protected by the Spirit Being. He must do what he must do.

As bravely as he could, Patu marched up to the guards, who watched him coming. One said, "Why are you here, Patu?"

They recognized him! He was relieved, but frustrated, too. He had hoped nobody would know him.

"I have an invitation for you."

The men glanced at one another, amused.

"You do?" one asked in a bantering tone.

"Yes. From Manimani."

Again, the guards exchanged glances. The other guard's voice was a lot different when he said, "What invitation?"

"She greatly admires your courage and devotion to duty," Patu recited. "She wishes to reward you and invites you to her bedchamber. One of you must always remain on duty here, so you will go one at a time. Take turns," Patu explained.

There was a stunned silence. The guards stared at Patu and at each other.

"Should we go?" one man asked.

"It is Manimani."

"You mean we had better?"

"That is exactly what I mean."

Patu said, "I will take your place until you get back." He reached for a guard's lance.

The guard laughed. "This is not the lance I shall need in Manimani's bedchamber. Here, small warrior."

He shoved the lance at Patu, who had to brace himself and hold it with both hands. It was much taller than he, and heavy.

As the guard strode away, the other called after him. "Remember we take turns."

"Ha!" He disappeared in the darkness.

Patu stood proudly, holding on to the lance. But behind him the basket of bones and the skull with the wide-open jaw made him nervous. He had to relieve himself. He prepared to do so where he stood.

"No!" the guard said sharply. "Not here. This is a sacred place. Over there." He gestured.

Reluctantly, Patu laid down the spear and headed for the sidelines. It was scary to be alone out there in the dark. He finished as quickly as he could and hurried back.

The guard was waiting for him as if he had had time to think things over and wanted to talk. He squatted to look at Patu.

"Why did Manimani send you instead of a slave?"

The guard's big face with falcon eyes and big teeth like a bear's made Patu back away. "It's a secret."

"A secret, eh? Hm-m-m." He stood up. "Maybe I will learn the secret when it is my turn, eh?" He laughed like a dog barking.

Patu stooped to pick up the spear. But it was heavy, so he sat down to rest for only a minute before he stood guard, too. It was late, and dark, and quiet. He was tired. Hungry, too. He wished he had some persimmon under his cloak instead of what was there. He felt to make sure he still had it. Yes.

He was really tired. Maybe if he lay down for a minute he would get rested and could stand guard with a lance like a warrior—until both men were back from Manimani and he could do what he was supposed to.

The ground was hard, not at all comfortable to lie on, but he would rest only a minute. . . .

Patu's back was to the skull, but he felt the heat from it. It got hotter and hotter. What was that rattling noise? He turned to look. The basket of bones was shaking; the bones wanted to come out! The red skull with open jaw and smoking eye stared at him. The skull got bigger and bigger, rose in the air, then came at him. Patu wanted to scream but no sound came out. He tried to jump up and run away, but he could not move. The skull got bigger still, and came closer. The thin finger of smoke in the eye came all the way out—only it was a tall, thin creature wavering in the breeze. It had fiery eyes and a little, crooked mouth.

The mouth opened and a crackling voice said, "I am Red Man. Try to kill me and you will die-e-e-e. . . ."

The smoke creature slid back into the skull, and the skull began to whirl and float away. . . .

"Wake up, Patu!"

Patu sat up with a start. It was early dawn. Both guards were there, looking down at him.

One said, "Manimani said you may do it now."

"Yes," said the other. "Manimani will be the next Great Sun, and we shall be her consorts." The men glanced at each other, grinning. "You, small warrior, will be Chief of Guards—if you do what Manimani told you."

Slowly, Patu stood up. He reached inside his cloak for the big piece of buckskin with designs painted on it to keep witches away. He unfolded it carefully. The guards stood a little apart, not looking at him, pretending he was not there.

The red skull sat on the basket, staring at him. Patu was afraid of it, of Red Man, and of the wisp of smoke coming out of the eye and some out of the nose, too. But he had to do what Manimani wanted. He must make certain that Red Man would go, so Manimani would be chosen the next Great Sun.

Hesitantly, he approached the skull, held the buckskin over it, and tried to summon the courage to cover it, to smother Red Man.

Try to kill me and you will die-e-e-e-e. . . .

Patu's hands trembled and tears stung his eyes. He could not do it.

"You will be Chief of Guards," the man said again. "You will have your own litter to go wherever you wish."

"And all the persimmons you can eat," the other added.

Patu was hungry. Quickly, trying not to see the smoke, he covered the skull with the buckskin and wrapped it tightly over the front and at the bottom.

You will die-e-e-e-e. . . .

He glanced at the guards. They were making it a point to look the other way. Carefully, he loosened the buckskin just a bit and lifted a corner to see if smoke came out. It did not.

He had killed Red Man.

He removed the buckskin and stuffed it inside his cloak.

He was not hungry anymore.

▲33▼

It was noon of the following day; the Spirit Being was directly overhead in a cloudless cobalt sky. Antelope stood with Peg Foot and other villagers waiting for the High Priest and the shaman to arrive. She bit her lips nervously. Tension was heavy in the air; people murmured restlessly.

"I don't see any smoke from the skull," Antelope said to Peg Foot.

Peg Foot squinted anxiously. "There could be some too faint to see from here." He did not sound convincing.

Antelope experienced mixed emotions. She had hoped—yes, expected—to be Far Walker's mate, but if he became the Great Sun it would be impossible; she was a foreigner. However, he would be an excellent ruler; his people needed him.

But I need him more.

She searched the crowd for him, but he was not there.

"Is Far Walker still on the mountain?"

"I think so. Yes."

Manimani and Patu sat on benches near the mound where the skull and the basket waited. Antelope noticed with some surprise that both of them seemed unconcerned. Manimani wore another new robe, and a slave stood beside her, fanning with a leafy branch. The branch waved slowly up and down, stirring Manimani's dark hair, but not that of the boy who leaned close, trying to catch some of the breeze. Manimani ignored him.

The beat of pottery drums announced the approach of the High Priest and the shaman. The High Priest was splendid in a white robe and a high, domed headdress with swan feathers and scarlet tassels. The shaman wore his deer mask and carried a tortoiseshell rattle in each hand; the rattles hissed loudly. Four drummers followed in single file; they wore only breechclouts, long fringed belts, and much copper and shell jewelry. Their beaded forelocks swung in rhythm to the drums as the procession made its stately way across the plaza.

As he approached the skull, the High Priest began to chant, and the shaman joined him, accompanied by drums and rattles. Antelope was impressed with the dignity of the High Priest as his thin, twisted body swung to and fro with each lurching step. His domed headdress seemed too heavy for his head, which hung forward so that he had to look up, but there was no mistaking the power of his presence.

Antelope found herself wishing she knew him.

Four times the procession circled the small mound while the chanting, drums, and rattles continued. Antelope's anxiety increased. Was the smoke gone?

At last the High Priest stopped in front of the vermilion skull. Still chanting and gesturing over it, he lifted it. Turning it this way and that, he inspected it.

There was no smoke.

He handed the skull to the shaman, who looked at it through the deer eyes of his mask and handed it back, shaking his antlered head.

Holding the skull in both hands, the High Priest faced the breathless crowd.

"Red Man is dead."

There were shocked murmurs and cries.

Manimani stood triumphantly. "I am proud to be your Great Sun." She gathered her robe about her, preparing a dramatic departure.

"One moment." The High Priest peered into the skull's jaw. He shook it a little and held it up to the breeze. He shook it again, speaking to it. Commanding it.

A tiny wisp of smoke rose from the jaw like the ghost of words unspoken.

"Behold! Red Man lives! He lives!"

The shaman reached for the skull and inspected it unbelievingly. Smoke drifted through the skull's empty nose. He thrust the skull back at the High Priest, who accepted it and held it high overhead.

"Far Walker is the Great Sun."

There was a great shout. "Far Walker! Far Walker!"

Antelope shouted, too. "Far Walker!"

Manimani stood frozen. She bent, grabbed Patu's arm, muttered something in his ear, then shoved him away. He tried not to cry, but tears rolled down. Antelope watched as Manimani summoned her litter and was carried through the crowd and across the plaza, while Patu trotted behind, sobbing.

Antelope clenched her hands angrily. How cruel! She was glad that Manimani would not be the Great Sun. But how could she rejoice that Far Walker was lost to her forever?

I am a woman alone, with no mate, no dwelling of my own, no people of my own, adrift like a broken branch on the river.

Far Walker stood on the mountaintop, gazing at the western horizon. The Spirit Being descended in majesty to cross under the world and reach his rising place in the morning. Far Walker had fasted and prayed a day and night. Now another night was near and he had received no vision, no answer to his pleas for wisdom, for a sign.

He was a Healer and that was what he wanted to be. When he had heard the High Priest tell Waikah's story and realized that he, Far Walker, could be the Great Sun, it was as though he faced a precipice and teetered on the edge. Below were the jagged rocks of the unknown—the life and responsibilities of the Great Sun. Around him were those who needed his skills, those who depended upon him to heal their wounds and cure their illnesses. Doing so gave him deep satisfaction—made his life worthwhile. How could he abandon them?

Yet the words of the High Priest resonated inside him. Something surprised him, something intangible—a sense of rightness he pushed aside, hiding it from himself. As if there was something from the past that his kia had known all along but waited for him to discover.

The Spirit Being flung his golden mantle and disappeared. Far Walker lay down, crossed his arms behind his head, and watched the stars appear, one by one. The Seven Sisters stood in their appointed places. Beautiful.

Beautiful like Antelope. If he was the Great Sun, could he have her? She was Towa. . . .

The precipice waited.

Groaning, Far Walker rolled over onto his stomach and pressed himself against the ground. He stretched his arms before him and clutched the earth with both hands.

"Earthmother, grant me your wisdom."

With every pore he sought response. He could feel Earthmother's heartbeat—or was it his own? For a long time he lay there, listening. If Earthmother replied, he did not hear her words.

He turned again to his back and gazed at the Seven Sisters in all their glory. He willed his kia to plead for him.

"Tell me if this Healer is truly the Great Sun. If so, what must I do?"

The Seven Sisters walked their appointed path so slowly that Far Walker could not see them move, but he watched carefully, waiting for a sign.

Time passed—how much, he did not know. Then it seemed that the Seven Sisters loosened a golden strand that floated down. As it came closer, Far Walker saw a golden spider dangling!

The spider hung suspended, swaying back and forth with the breeze. Its legs moved as if treading the air, and its tiny, bright eyes looked at him.

"You are the Great Sun," the spider said in a clear, high voice.

Far Walker stared, enchanted and speechless.

The spider swayed on its golden thread and dropped closer. "You are the Great Sun," the high voice said again.

"I am a Healer!" Far Walker cried.

"Yes. A curse scarred your people and your city, and your fire is foreign. A Healer is needed."

"But the High Priest and the shaman removed the curse!"

Tiny eyes peered at him. "Perhaps. But the scars remain."

The spider began to ascend the strand, its golden legs working.

"Wait! Please do not go!" Far Walker called, sitting up and reaching after it.

The spider's voice drifted down. "Healer, cleanse your fire, heal your city, heal your people."

The spider disappeared, taking the golden strand with it.

Far Walker gazed in wonder. The Seven Sisters glittered in regal splendor; he closed his eyes, reveling in their glory.

Was it their voices he heard in distant chorus? "You are the Great Sun. You will heal your people and remove their scars."

"I will try!" Far Walker heard himself cry. "I will!"

When he opened his eyes, the stars were gone and the Spirit Being was already in his eastern house, gazing down at him.

Far Walker was filled with humble exaltation. He rose and reached both arms overhead. He sang his prayer.

> *Spirit Being,*
> *Behold your spiritual brother.*
> *Behold me, your Healer.*
> *Help me to heal my city,*
> *Help me to heal my people*
> *And cleanse our sacred fire.*

A hawk soared high overhead and disappeared. Far Walker knew it carried his prayer to the Spirit Being. Feeling like a creature who sheds an old skin to reveal a new one, he strode down the mountain.

The news about Far Walker as the next Great Sun spread fast. Official shell carvers inscribed it on conch shells for ambassadors to deliver to distant mound centers. Signal fires and drums announced the news to cities nearby. People gathered in clusters, discussing it avidly, and community fires burned late.

But where was Far Walker? A ceremony was being planned to initiate him as Great Sun; his participation was needed. It had been two days and two nights since he went to the mountain. Now it was the morning of the third day and he had not returned.

Antelope had finished feeding Skyfeather, who drifted into sleep. Later, Antelope would take Skyfeather to the river to bathe, but now she would care for Peg Foot. He liked her to brush his hair and pin it up in back.

"You have the soothing touch," he said. "With training, you would be a good Medicine Woman."

Antelope laughed. "All women have the soothing touch. They absorb it with their mother's milk."

She brushed his gray crest and stiffened it with bear grease so that it stayed straight up. Then she brushed his long back hair, rolled it in a bun, and fastened it with a copper hair pin the length of a woman's hand. The pin had been twisted into spirals that held his thinning hair securely.

"You look handsome," Antelope said, smiling. "You could have as many mates as you want."

"I've had three, and I don't want any more. Besides, you take good care of me. What do I need a mate for?"

"If I have to tell you, I guess you don't need any."

He grinned. "I don't need a mate for that, you know."

Antelope did know. Many a village woman considered it an honor to fulfill a Healer's need.

How many did so for Far Walker?

Antelope wanted to ask Peg Foot more about Far Walker, but she hesitated because they were like father and son. Peg Foot might not want to discuss personal matters. But she had to know.

"Will Far Walker's mate return one day, do you think?"

"Perhaps. Who knows? But he is the Great Sun now, and his mate has been gone so long that he has divorced her. She is his mate no longer."

She blurted it out. "Could the Great Sun marry a foreigner?"

He gave her an understanding glance. "A Towa, perhaps?"

"Yes."

"I remind you that you were adopted by Poqua into her family. You are a foreigner no longer." He smiled and held out his hand. She took it, and he said, "You are loved."

She hugged his bony old frame. "I adopt you as my esteemed grandfather, Peg Foot."

A commotion outside woke Skyfeather, who yelled her objection. Antelope picked her up.

"Come, small one. Let's see what is happening."

Antelope stepped outside and stared. Four slaves appeared, carrying a litter covered with flowers. They were surrounded by a curious crowd including shouting children and yelping dogs. No one rode the litter; Antelope wondered whom it was for.

She called to the slaves, "Where are you going?"

Amid laughter and shouts, the slaves carried the litter to where Antelope stood.

"It's for you!" children hollered, tugging at her. "See the flowers! It's for you!" They pushed her forward.

The four slaves lowered the litter before her, and gestured for her to sit.

Antelope hesitated. "But why? Where will you take me?"

Peg Foot had followed her outside; now he stepped forward.

"Don't spoil a generous gesture, Granddaughter. Waste no more time with stupid questions. Sit! Leave Skyfeather with me."

One glance at Peg Foot and Antelope obeyed. She sat upon fragrant flowers, the slaves lifted her, and away they went, followed by the noisy crowd and barking dogs.

It was the first time Antelope had ridden a litter. The slaves walked in unison so that the litter swayed gently from side to side.

The two slaves in front were young men, slender and well built. One had yellow hair; she wondered about that. Had he been captured as a child from some distant place? Perhaps he, too, was far from home.

Where were they going? As they followed the village path to the ceremonial center, Antelope searched for Far Walker but did not see him. Had he arranged this? If so, why? Where was he?

More people appeared from their dwellings and from the river and from garden plots to join the crowd. It was a beautiful morning with clouds running before the wind and hawks riding the updraft. Antelope was being honored by these people as one of them. Suddenly happiness bounced around inside her, and she had to sing. Her high, sweet voice soared as she sang a wordless song, letting it ride the updraft, too.

They reached the plaza where new buildings were being erected on the mound of the Temple of Eternal Fire, and on the mound of the Great Sun's dwelling.

"There it is!" children shouted. "Look! The Great Sun's new home!"

Upon the mound, the dwelling of the Great Sun was half finished. The posts were erected and the reeds had been woven between them, waiting to be plastered. The roof was not yet thatched; sunlight glowed upon the people gathered within. Antelope could not see who they were. But Far Walker stood outside upon the mound, waiting for her.

Antelope looked up at him in his fringed, white buckskin garment embroidered with dyed porcupine quills and shell beads, and she felt a pang of jealousy. Who had made that garment for him?

How handsome he was! He wore no forelock; a white shell disk, fastened to an encircling band, shone upon his forehead and glowed like his brother, the Spirit Being. A great shell gorget lay upon his chest among ropes of pearls. More pearls encircled his upper arms, his wrists, his knees, and his ankles. His earspools were of shell and copper with quartz inlay, and his headdress was of white swan feathers tipped with red. He was a glittering deity as he stood there, gazing at her.

Antelope was surprised to find herself shy. This was not the Far Walker she knew. She felt intimidated. Why was he bringing her here with this boisterous crowd?

They reached the base of the mound. The litter bearers began the ascent and Antelope was relieved to see that the crowd had to wait below. As they approached the mound's flat top, she saw the occupants of the unfinished dwelling: the High Priest, the shaman, several chiefs, Manimani—and a group of musicians. When the slaves reached the top of the mound, the flutes began to sing.

Far Walker stepped forward, smiling. "Welcome, beautiful one," he whispered. He lifted her from the litter, gestured the slaves away, and led her inside the unfinished dwelling where the High Priest and the others awaited.

"We greet you," the High Priest said, his luminous eyes glowing. "We welcome you to a ceremony to initiate Far Walker as our Great Sun."

"Thank you," Antelope managed to say graciously. An initiating ceremony! What was she expecting?

The High Priest gestured to a mat on the dirt floor. "Kneel, Far Walker."

He did so, and the High Priest began to chant, accompanied by the flutes. The shaman stood by, face expressionless. Antelope glanced at Manimani, who watched Far Walker with tight lips and sullen eyes. The chiefs stood respectfully, heads bowed.

The High Priest finished his chant and gestured for the flutes to cease.

"There is much to tell you, and I shall do so after the city's celebration to welcome you as the Great Sun. For now, I give you my blessing. You are a Chosen One."

From around his neck the High Priest removed a necklace with a large pendant shaped like a hand and carved from mica so delicate that light shone through. Upon it was painted an open eye. The High Priest held the necklace out to the four directions, then placed it around Far Walker's neck.

"This is your healing hand, with the eye of the Spirit Being."

Far Walker touched it reverently. His voice shook slightly as he said, "I thank you, High Priest. I shall honor it."

The shaman stepped forward. From inside his garment he removed a crystal as long as his little finger. One end of the crystal, the part that would be held, was wrapped with fine cords of red, blue, green, and white. The shaman offered the crystal to the four corners, chanting, and then held it before Far Walker.

"This is Earthmother's power. Allow the Spirit Being to enter it, and the power will be yours. Use it wisely."

Far Walker cupped the crystal in both hands. "I thank you, shaman. I shall request your wisdom to guide me."

"Rise now," the High Priest said.

Far Walker did so, standing proudly.

Remembering the former Great Sun, Antelope was impressed by Far Walker's dignity. Where was the bombastic arrogance of his predecessor? In the grave where it belonged.

Now Manimani spoke. "I greet you, my brother. Allow me to assist you in any way needed. I have no gift but my relationship as your sister."

How cold! Antelope thought. She looked at Manimani's closed face. As if she sensed Antelope's gaze, Manimani's eyes met hers. Antelope felt a chill. This was an enemy.

The chiefs prostrated themselves before Far Walker, howling their obeisance. Then each rose, and one at a time they approached the Great Sun. Each chief placed a hand over his own heart in a gesture of loyalty, looked Far Walker in the eye, and warmly wished him the blessings of the Spirit Being.

The private ceremony was over. Antelope knew a great celebration would follow for all people to enjoy. The High Priest would then officially proclaim Far Walker as the Great Sun. What would that mean for her?

She looked at him, the Great Sun, splendid in his royal garments, and she felt alone.

The High Priest and the others began to depart. Antelope's flower-strewn litter waited at the base of the mound, but Far Walker motioned for her to stay. When all had gone and they were alone but for the musicians waiting silently, Far Walker came and took her hand.

"Come." He led her to the mat. "Sit, beautiful one."

Already he was the Great Sun, expecting to be obeyed. She sat and looked up at him. He returned her gaze with one so warm and glowing that she caught her breath.

He gestured to the musicians, who began to play their flutes. One of them, the youngest, sang in a low, rich voice. Antelope did not understand the words.

She turned to Far Walker. His proximity made her voice shaky. "What does the song say?"

"It is the old language. It is a love song. It says that love is a river that sweeps one away to an endless sea." He knelt beside her. "That is what the song says, what I want to say."

Antelope felt a drumming in her blood. She searched the place behind his eyes where his spirit dwelt and saw nobility. He loved her truly.

He took both her hands in his and leaned close. The flutes' sweet voices and the singer's song enveloped them.

"Be my mate," Far Walker whispered, his eyes pleading.

Antelope's heart overflowed and tears welled up. "Yes! Oh yes!"

·34·

Manimani hung on to the sides of the canoe and watched the passing scenery in gathering darkness. It had been seven days and nights since the community celebration proclaiming Far Walker as the Great Sun. He and that Towa woman with her blue-eyed child—imagine!—were being worshiped almost as deities, while she, the Great Sun's sister, was practically ignored. If that wasn't enough, there was the matter of the guards.

Had the guards told? Had Patu told? Would they?

If it became known that she, sister of the Great Sun, had tried to destroy Red Man so that she might become the Great Sun instead, it would be an intolerable disgrace. Furthermore, she would be talked about—laughed about—at evening fires wherever traders traveled and told stories, to be retold by others.

Drastic measures must be taken.

A village approached and Manimani scrunched down in the canoe so she would not be seen. The canoe was an ordinary fisherman's craft, and the two paddlers were nondescript slaves; it would merit little notice.

Two more villages were passed; the slaves banked the canoe at a third.

"Are you sure this is the place?" Manimani asked anxiously.

"It is," a slave said. He was a big, muscular fellow who wore a raccoon pelt on one arm. "They said the sorcerer would be up there." He gestured. "You are expected."

"How does he know?"

"By the drums."

"Does he know who I am? I told you—"

"It is known only that you are a woman from my village." The slave glanced at her plain, soiled garment, worn moccasins, and drab head covering. "No one will know unless you tell."

Slaves had a way of communicating with one another; Manimani was not certain of how, but she had learned what she wanted to know—where a good sorcerer could be found.

"Very well. You shall be rewarded handsomely. Take me to the sorcerer."

They walked up the village path—two slaves and a woman of obviously meager means—accompanied by shouting children, yapping, growling dogs, and a few curious townspeople. It was dark now. Cooking fires smoldered, sending rich smells on the breeze, and a community fire burned brightly.

The sorcerer's hut at the village edge was surrounded by scraggly trees that assumed weird shapes against the dark sky.

Manimani said, "Wait for me outside, and tell no one who I am."

"We obey, sister of the Great Sun."

"Sh-h-h! Not so loud!"

Manimani entered the extended doorway of the hut. It was pitch-dark in there, but firelight shone from the inner room. She entered it and stood at the doorway, waiting to be invited inside. It was a strange room with objects hanging from the walls and ceiling, and shelves crammed with baskets and bowls. There was an odd smell, rather like that of a Healer's lodge. Most astonishing was the fact that the sorcerer was a young woman, a beautiful woman with a mass of raven hair and dark eyes that penetrated her own.

"Enter," a soft voice said.

Manimani entered uneasily. This was not what she expected; the sorcerers she knew were old men. Could this woman be a witch?

The woman gestured to a mat, and Manimani sat awkwardly. The sister of the Great Sun was accustomed to sit only on carved stools or benches.

Dark eyes inspected Manimani carefully. "Why have you come to me?"

"I wish for a spell."

There was a pause. "What kind of spell?"

"A death spell. For two men."

Silence, as Manimani was inspected again. "I believe it will cost more than you care to pay, old woman."

Old woman! How dare this creature call me an old woman!

Manimani reached inside her shabby garment and removed a pouch of fine buckskin embroidered with iridescent shell beads. She opened the pouch and poured the contents on the floor. A magnificent necklace glittering with pearls and turquoise and shining copper beads lay at the woman's feet.

She picked it up, held it in both hands, and leaned closer to the firelight to examine it. She looked at Manimani.

"Who are you?"

"One who wants a spell."

As knowing eyes regarded her, Manimani realized her hands were being scrutinized—soft, smooth hands with marks where rings had been. She hid her hands inside her robe.

The woman smiled. "Secrecy costs extra."

How dare she! "You will be paid."

The woman placed the necklace around her neck and fingered it with a sensual gesture.

"Very well. Now I shall tell you what must be done."

They talked for a long time. When Manimani left, the slaves lay slumped in sleep by the door. She gave each a kick.

"Wake, fools! Is this how you guard me?" Realizing she had spoken too loudly, she whispered, "Take me home. Now!"

"But it is dark. No moon—"

"The river knows the way. Go!"

Stumbling once or twice in the darkness, they reached the canoe and soon were on the river. Manimani could see the slaves silhouetted against the starry sky as they bent forward and back, forward and back, paddling upstream. Occasionally, they passed the distant glow of a smoldering fire, and that was all. It was still but for the splash of paddles on the water, and the occasional grunt of a slave as the canoe was manipulated around a small

island midstream. The cool breath of the river carried the fragrance of damp earth and distant places. She fingered the pouch
that now contained magical substances. In her lap was a yellow
stone slab the size of a moccasin, to be used as the sorceress had
directed.

Manimani was satisfied. The guards would not reveal her
secret. Never. She pondered about the slaves. What if they told
someone where they had taken her this night? Perhaps she
should use the same spell on them. She did not worry about Patu;
nobody would listen to him.

A thought whispered, *Use the spell on the Towa woman, as
well!*

Manimani smiled and fingered the pouch. Her problems
would soon be over.

Patu curled up under a tree. Gone was his fine bed with soft
fur pelts. Gone were his home, his father, his mother, and all the
good things he had grown up with. Now he was little more than
a slave, and hungry, too. As a child, he was welcome anywhere
and could sleep or eat in any dwelling, but he preferred to sleep
where he could see the stars, smell the good tree smell, and be
close to Earthmother.

He reached to touch her and clasped a handful of leafy soil.
He rolled it into a ball in his fist and held it close to his chest
with both hands.

"Good night, Earthmother."

There were no arms to embrace him, no soft voice to send
him on his sleep journey, but Earthmother was close. He was
comforted.

He slept, and when he woke, he lay there remembering a
dream, a wonderful dream. A raccoon had perched on a limb
and looked down at him from behind its little mask.

"I greet you, Raccoon," Patu had said.

The little animal scurried down the tree and came to sit beside Patu and peer into his face.

"You are a shaman!" Raccoon said.

"I?" Patu asked, much surprised.

"Yes. A shaman is inside you waiting to grow."

Patu was so astonished he could not reply, and Raccoon ran
back up the tree and disappeared among the branches.

Now, as Patu lay there remembering his dream and gazing

up into the tree, leaves stirred and a small, masked face peered down at him. Raccoon!

It was true, then! A shaman was inside him! How wonderful! He would never have known had Raccoon not told him.

"I thank you, Raccoon!" he called. The mask vanished.

Patu jumped up, brushed his leafy breechclout, and relieved himself against the tree. Happy for the first time since Manimani sent him to kill Red Man, Patu ran into the village to tell the shaman his news—that he, Patu, would be his apprentice and learn to become a shaman.

The shaman sat outside his dwelling while his mate shaved the sides of his head with a sharpened clamshell. The woman ignored Patu as he ran breathlessly to confront the shaman. Prostrating himself properly, Patu yelled "Hou!" and waited for response.

"Rise," the shaman said irritably. "You see I am busy." He looked at the scrawny, not very clean boy who had once been a member of royalty. "Why do you disturb me? Have you no respect?"

As Patu recounted his dream, the shaman studied this boy of seven winters whose eyes shone in a face strangely adult for a child. Something about him . . .

"—and that is why I come, honored shaman," Patu finished. He stood there, eager eyes pleading.

The shaman pondered. It was true that he could use an apprentice to assist in his more tiresome duties. As he had no sons of his own, perhaps this boy . . .

"There would be much to learn. It would not be easy, and it would be dangerous, as well."

Patu's eyes glowed. "I will do everything. Everything."

The shaman's mate leaned over to him and whispered in his ear; he nodded.

"You will empty the night pots?"

This was the duty of slaves. Patu was shocked. He stood up straight, looked at the shaman bravely, and said as politely as he was able, "Your slaves will do that, honored shaman."

The shaman laughed. The boy's royal upbringing showed; it would be useful. "I would not choose an apprentice who emptied night pots." He laughed again and said in his rasping voice, "That was a test."

Patu's dark eyes glittered. "You choose me?"

The shaman rubbed his head where a stubble remained. It would be important to know what prestige, if any, the former Great Sun's child might provide.

"Perhaps. On a trial basis, of course."

Patu's smile lit his face as if Red Man glowed within.

For three nights Manimani had watched the two guards at the Great Sun's dwelling. Even though it was still uncompleted, the Great Sun's spirit might be there and the place must be protected at night when ghosts and witches prowled. When the Great Sun and his family moved in, guards would be on every step; now only the two men who had guarded Waikah's skull and bones were on duty.

Had they told?

Manimani dismissed her slaves and covered herself with a concealing black shawl. Quietly, she slipped outside. The moon was thin and new and shed little light, but the mound was outlined against the starlit sky. It was late, and quiet but for a child's cry in the distance. Manimani crouched behind a bush and watched the guards on the mound. Sooner or later, she knew, one of them would spit or urinate. She fingered the beaded pouch at her waist. She was ready.

She heard them talking to each other and laughing, while she crouched behind a bush—she, royal sister of the Great Sun!—hiding like a commoner, a thief! How did this happen? A royal sister could order the death of anyone she chose. But these were the guards the High Priest had selected to watch the skull. What excuse could she give? What if someone learned the truth? She cringed, and tears blurred her eyes. Ever since that Towa woman arrived there had been nothing but trouble.

Manimani wiped the tears away purposefully. Soon this nightmare would be over. After all, she, Manimani, was sister of the Great Sun, and blood ties were stronger than marriage bonds. She would show that foreigner what royal blood meant.

At last one of the guards strode down the steps, hawked, and spit several times, then retraced his steps. The mound was sacred, but it was permissible to spit on the plaza ground. Urination would have to be done elsewhere.

The guards resumed their conversation, walking around the flat top of the mound. When they were out of sight, Manimani opened her pouch and removed a tiny stick, and a tube consisting of a joint of the poisonous wild parsnip. She hurried to the spot where the man had been. Bending low, she saw, by starlight, the darkened spot on the ground and scooped a little of the wet soil onto the stick. Holding it carefully, she scurried back to the bush and placed the stick inside the parsnip tube.

She sighed in relief. That would take care of one of the guards. Now she would wait for the other. She removed another tube and stick, and waited.

Still the other man did not come down. Manimani was stiff and sore, but she was determined. She waited.

Finally, the other guard strode down the steps and headed away from the plaza. Manimani could not follow; she might be seen. All she could do was watch and try to see where he went so she could go there later and get a bit of his body water to put into the tube. She tried to see where he went, but it was too dark; he disappeared in shadows. He was gone so long that she wondered if he had gone home, but at last he reappeared. As Manimani watched eagerly, he paused and spit on the ground before he climbed back up the stairs.

Biting her lips tensely, Manimani waited until the men were out of sight again. It took longer, but she found the damp spot at last and captured a bit of it for the tube. She replaced both tubes in her pouch, clutched the dark shawl close around her, and scurried through the darkness to her dwelling.

Overcome with relief, Manimani lay on her bed and gazed at the ceiling. She found she was trembling—like a weak, old woman.

I have forty-one winters. I have survived two mates and want no more. But I am not old. No. Anyone else would be, but not Manimani, sister of the Great Sun.

She rose, stirred the coals in the fire pit, and added kindling. As a small fire lit the room, she sat beside it and opened her beaded pouch. Carefully, she removed the two parsnip tubes and laid them side by side. Poisonous! Inside each tube, along with the stick, were seven earthworms beaten into a paste, given to her by the sorceress. These would devour the souls of the dead bodies—and they *would* be dead. Oh, yes. To these Manimani added six splinters her slave had obtained from a tree struck by lightning. She handled the splinters carefully; lightning made them dangerously potent. Remaining in the pouch were seven yellow and seven black pebbles that the sorceress had imbued with her powers.

Tomorrow, the deed would be finished. She would order her slave to dig a hole at the base of the tree. Later, under cover of darkness, she would retrieve the yellow stone slab hidden nearby and place it in the hole. Upon the slab she would lay the splinters, the two tubes, and the seven yellow and seven black pebbles, and she would cover all securely with dirt stamped down. Then she, Manimani, sister of the Great Sun, would build a little fire over it, letting it burn to ashes.

Both men would die within seven days.

▲ **35** ▼

Antelope stood beside her new home-in-the-making and watched women slaves plastering the outside wall. They worked fast and well, scooping wet clay from jars carried up the mound by other women. They smoothed the clay with both hands over reeds woven between the upright wall beams. Brown hands were caked with clay, and daubs of it were on bodies bared from the waist up, and here and there on intent faces. Several of the women were old and could not work as fast as the others; two of them were so young they could not reach high enough to plaster the top part and someone else had to help.

Antelope's instinct was to get in there and help, but she could not. She was mate of the Great Sun and should not even be there. She was accustomed to slaves—all tribes had slaves captured in war or purchased in trade; they were regarded as prized commodities, but faceless. To Antelope, however, these slaves were foreigners in this land, as she was, and her heart went out to them, especially a young girl standing on tiptoe trying to reach high enough to plaster the top part. The girl couldn't do it and was embarrassed because Antelope was watching.

The women were uncomfortable in Antelope's presence, and

they kept yelling "Hou!"—which made her more uncomfortable than they. So she turned away and descended the steps of the mound to her litter waiting below. The litter had a raised back that extended overhead to form a little canopy from which a fringe of pretty shells dangled. Two male slaves waited, howled their greetings as she approached, then offered the litter to her. She sat upon it; they hoisted her shoulder high and carried her away across the plaza toward Far Walker's home—which was her home now, until the Great Sun's new dwelling was completed.

Every person Antelope encountered—man, woman, or child—bowed low and yelled "Hou!" when they saw her. Groups of children and their dogs trotted behind with noisy enthusiasm. As they passed the shaman's dwelling, Antelope was surprised to see Patu sitting outside as if he lived there. Antelope had wondered what became of the boy after his parents were gone. Was the shaman a relative?

Far Walker's dwelling was surrounded by guards—as his dwelling on the mound would be. When Antelope approached, there was the usual bellow of greeting, which Antelope found difficult to accept; it made her ill at ease. The litter bearers carried her to the door, lowered the litter for her to dismount, and backed away.

Glad to be home, Antelope entered to find Far Walker surrounded by certain members of the council, deep in solemn discussion. There was no other room for her to escape to, so as unobtrusively as she could, Antelope edged along the wall to a small storage area and crept inside. This was where Far Walker had kept his healing supplies and gardening implements. It smelled of herbs and musty earth. Antelope squeezed herself down between baskets and jars and sat with her arms around her knees.

The voices of the men droned on. There was talk about two guards who had died suddenly. One fell dead with no warning, and the other tumbled from a cliff. Was this an omen?

Skyfeather was with Manimani, who seemed to enjoy having a baby girl around now and then. Antelope thought about Manimani. Something was amiss there, but Antelope could not be sure what it was. Jealousy, perhaps? Undoubtedly, Manimani wanted to be the Great Sun. Maybe she resented Far Walker. *Or perhaps she resents me,* Antelope thought. There were times when

Antelope caught a fleeting look in Manimani's eyes, a hidden look quickly concealed.

I should not leave Skyfeather with her so often, Antelope thought with sudden concern.

Talk among the council members continued. Far Walker's deep voice resonated inside her. He was a masterful lover, tender and compelling, and she wished those men would go home.

The shaman spoke in his rasping voice. "Yes, the buffalo are many, and they come closer. Our hunters will bring much to your warehouse, Great Sun." He paused. "The former Great Sun requested that I call the buffalo. No one in our city had done this before, but buffalo come now."

A pompous pretender, Antelope thought with contempt.

She remembered when she had stood with the tree, embracing it, beseeching its strength when she called the buffalo. She remembered the drumming in her blood and how it filled her with a sense of power. She had told Far Walker.

"It happens sometimes. My heart beats like a drum and I feel—" How could she explain? "I feel strong. . . ."

He smiled and said, "The drumbeat in your blood is the voice of your ancestors. Let the drum speak."

It was speaking now. She was mate of the Great Sun. She would be what he and his people expected her to be. True, she could not teach young girls the women's secrets, but she could teach Skyfeather.

One day Skyfeather would become She Who Remembers.

PART 2

▲▼▲▼▲▼▲▼▲▼▲▼▲▼▲▼▲▼▲▼▲▼

SKYFEATHER

A.D. 1297
Four years later

▲ 36 ▼

$\mathbf{T}$he High Priest stood in his beautiful new temple and gazed at the diagram on his star wall. It had taken him many moons to re-create it with the help of his priests—whose hands and arms were stronger and more steady than his own—and it gave him deep satisfaction. A small, round hole on the opposite wall facing east allowed the Spirit Being to enter and point a bright finger at a spot in the diagram where certain stars indicated the times of important occasions.

Today was the beginning of planting season.

He turned to a young priest in attendance. "Summon the Crier."

The young priest hurried to obey and the High Priest was left alone with his temple, his diagram, and his memories.

Firekeeper . . . her soft voice and sweet presence.

He shook his head; it was unwise to remember the dead. Their spirits could come and take one away with them to the Afterworld. He would be willing to go, but he was needed here. He must stay a while longer until an assistant was trained and ready.

Firekeeper . . .

He turned to the eternal fire glowing in the center of the

303

crossed logs and gestured a respectful greeting. He stretched out both arms in prayer.

"Burn the loneliness from my heart, sacred one. I beseech you."

Footsteps echoed, and the Crier bustled in. He was a new one, a scrawny young fellow with a big swallowing-bump on his throat that bounced up and down when he spoke or swallowed, which was often.

"Hou!" he bellowed in a voice that resounded from wall to wall.

The High Priest acknowledged the greeting with a nod. "The Spirit Being says it is the time for planting."

He gestured and the Crier backed out, bowing. Soon his thunderous voice echoed throughout the city, announcing the planting season.

Antelope heard him as she and Skyfeather rode the royal litter on the way home from their bathing place. It was a tumultuous spring morning, with great billowing clouds soaring, and Windwoman rushing about. Skyfeather, at four winters, was growing fast and interested in everything. She brushed the blowing hair from her face and laughed at children who came running to see her, yelling, "Hou!"

"Hou to you, too!" she called.

Antelope sighed. She had explained that a royal greeting was for royalty, but this daughter of hers had a mind of her own.

"They are like me," Skyfeather had said earnestly. "I want to greet them, too." And she did.

They entered a swampy, wooded area where leaves burst anew, and a tumult of birdsong and chatter filled the air. Skyfeather listened intently. She turned to look up at her mother.

"They don't want us here."

"Who?"

"The birds. They say go away."

Antelope smiled. It pleased her and Far Walker, too, that Skyfeather was so attuned to everything in the forest. It was as if Skyfeather were a flute that the forest made sing.

"Tell the birds we shall not linger here."

"All right." She gazed silently up into the trees.

"Won't you tell them?" Antelope asked indulgently, playing make-believe.

"I did," Skyfeather said matter-of-factly. "Wait!" She turned to stare at a clump of reeds nearby. "Stop!" she ordered the litter bearers in an excellent imitation of Antelope's voice and manner. "Put me down."

The slaves turned to Antelope for approval.

"Why do you want to get down, Skyfeather?" Leaning closer, she spoke in Towa, "Do you have to relieve yourself?"

"Mother!" Skyfeather replied in disgust. "That's not it." She pointed to the reeds. "There's a hurt bird in there."

Antelope looked and did not see any. "Where?"

"Over there." She leaned forward and nudged a slave. "Put me down."

Again the slaves looked to Antelope for approval. She nodded; she wanted to encourage Skyfeather's interests. Besides, there had been a few times previously when Skyfeather did seem to sense what others did not, especially in the forest.

Antelope said, "It's swampy here, with snakes. Be careful." She gestured to one of the slaves. "Go with her."

Skyfeather looked down her nose. "I want to go by myself."

"No. He goes with you or you stay right here."

Skyfeather's blue eyes grew stormy, but she said nothing. Turning her back on the big slave who followed, she walked carefully, carefully, to the clump of reeds. She paused there to listen. Then she parted the reeds, searching. She stooped and turned, holding a little chickadee in both hands. She cuddled it to her chest and brought it to Antelope.

"See? It has a broken wing."

Antelope gazed with mixed feelings at this child of hers. She was Chomoc's child also, and that evidenced itself frequently.

"How did you know?"

"I heard it."

Heard a chickadee? A wounded creature made no sound that might reveal its vulnerability to enemies.

"What did you hear?"

"It called me to come and help it."

Antelope gazed at the small girl who held the bird tenderly, protecting the broken wing. The bird seemed unafraid.

Had Skyfeather really heard it calling her?

Chomoc could talk to animals.

Still holding the bird, Skyfeather climbed back on the litter. "Let's take it to Father. He will make it well."

Skyfeather knew that someone named Chomoc was her

birth father, but Far Walker was her real father whom she admired and loved. Chomoc had left her and gone far away when she was a baby.

The two brawny slaves lifted the litter and strode under trailing branches toward the plaza. The air was sweet with the fragrance of damp earth and new flowers and growing things. From deep in the forest came the passionate gobble of turkeys calling mates. Far Walker had told her that sometimes warriors imitated that sound in war cries. How ridiculous! Antelope thought. A jaguar's cry would be more intimidating. But she did not reply. She had learned long ago that he and his people did things and believed things that made little sense to a Towa. Manimani especially went out of her way to try to make Antelope feel like an ignorant outsider, not worthy to be the mate of a Great Sun. It had been four winters since Antelope became Far Walker's mate, but Manimani still persisted. Often she would sit in on council meetings just to find something to object to, it seemed.

Much had happened in four years. Many people had left the city, thinking it cursed, but new arrivals and new babies took their places. Time was taking its toll on Peg Foot and the High Priest, who seemed to have grown older than the passage of four years demanded. Perhaps the undercurrent of uncertainty still haunting the city was a factor, Antelope thought. They knew the sacred fire was foreign. Did they fear it would not serve them well?

She, as mate of the Great Sun, lived a life of privilege, with anything she wished at her command—anything but what she wanted most: to become a Teacher, and to have warriors escort her home.

Far Walker had said, "The council refuses to allow you to teach our young girls because you are Towa, a foreigner with foreign beliefs."

"But my teaching is for all—"

"I know, my love. But I must listen to my people."

He made excuses about not allowing her to go home, even for a short while. He could not spare the warriors. The journey was too long and too dangerous. Or she was needed for an important ceremony. Or her advice was essential on a matter pending.

Finally, he admitted, "I cannot bear for you and Skyfeather to be gone from me for so long a time. I need you."

They would make love again.

She loved him. Dearly. If only . . .

The litter rocked gently as they rode. Skyfeather sat with her back to her mother. Her soft, dark hair was tied with a bit of bright red buckskin with pretty beads hanging down the back.

This daughter of mine will be She Who Remembers one day. She is Towa.

Far Walker sat in the sweat lodge with the shaman and the caddí. The lodge was a low, round structure covered with skins to hold steam generated by water poured over hot stones. The men hunkered down as good, hot steam billowed, enveloping them.

As sweat poured from him, Far Walker felt tension lessening. He had invited the shaman and the caddí to join him so they might talk freely as men did in a sweat lodge. Also, this was one place where Manimani could not be present. A relief. Manimani might be his blood sister, but he felt no kinship to her whatsoever. To the contrary. Her insistence upon being present at all council meetings, her subtle jabs at Antelope, and her attempts to influence Skyfeather in matters that were none of Manimani's business were increasingly irritating. There were times when Far Walker wished he were only a Healer again. But duty was duty, and except for Manimani, it gave him satisfaction to be able to help his people. And to give Antelope and Skyfeather the luxuries they deserved.

The caddí grunted and slapped himself with a willow branch to stimulate his circulation. His chunky body glistened. He said, "I am ready to go to the river."

The shaman reached for the gourd ladle in a water jar. "A little more steam first." He poured a ladle of water on the hot stones. More steam rose with a hiss and the men hunched forward.

Far Walker was interested to note that the lengthiness of the shaman's body did not apply to his man part, which was small as a boy's. Maybe that was why he had become a shaman, to exert power he could not exert in other ways. The caddí was suitably endowed; his part was chunky, like himself. As for his own, Far Walker was satisfied; it was generous and served him well.

But all was not well in his domain. Far Walker rubbed his

body hard with a piece of buffalo hide—as if to rub worry away. Buffalo were coming too close; hunters from neighboring tribes got all they needed for themselves rather than having to obtain it through trade. His warehouse used to be full of buffalo skins and bones and jerky and other buffalo products eagerly sought; it had been a profitable operation. No more.

It was time to discuss important matters, but it was necessary to ease into it.

"How is Patu doing? I see him around town now and then and he seems intent on his student obligations."

The shaman took another willow branch and swatted his legs briskly. "He is learning."

"Will he know how to call the deer?"

"Of course."

"And the buffalo?"

The shaman shot Far Walker a glance. His left eyelid drooped. "Perhaps."

"As you know, the buffalo come too close. Traders who used to come to us for buffalo now get all they need, and more, for themselves. Would it not be wise to send them away?"

The shaman paused in his swatting. He said carefully, "I remind you, sacred one, that I was ordered to call the buffalo, and I obeyed."

"If you called them here, cannot you call them away? Since we no longer obtain valuables in buffalo trade, our storage house is nearly empty. We sell corn, of course, and our shell carvers are famous, as you know. As are all our artisans. But without the buffalo trade our city grows poor."

The caddí wiped the sweat from around his eyes. "Maybe we should require additional gifts from nobles of other cities who wish to be buried in our sacred mound."

Far Walker considered this in silence. It was true that rulers and nobles from other cities considered it a rare honor to be buried in the sacred mound. Of course, rich gifts were always offered and accepted, but perhaps more should be forthcoming. The sacred burial mound in the City of the Great Sun was for the city's people, not outsiders, royal though they be.

The caddí rose. "Are you ready for Long Man?"

Far Walker nodded. The shaman unfolded his long bones, bending low to avoid the ceiling. They pushed the door flap aside, ran naked down to the river, and splashed in.

The water felt wonderful. Far Walker rolled in it, letting Long Man wash worry away. He would return to his duties revitalized.

"He can move his wing better, now. See?" Skyfeather held the chickadee carefully in both hands as she showed it to Patu. "My father is a good Healer. He put that little splint on it. The bird says it doesn't hurt anymore."

Patu snorted. "Birds can't talk." He grinned with the superiority of eleven winters.

"Not like we do. They think-talk."

Skyfeather and Patu played on the terrace of the Great Sun's dwelling mound under the watchful eye of the slave Chipmunk. She sat nearby mending one of Skyfeather's pretty robes and flirting with the guards posted on the mound steps.

Skyfeather needed playmates, and Antelope had invited Patu to come whenever he wished. The boy was well trained, well mannered, and accustomed to life in the Great Sun's family. Also, Antelope felt that Patu had been unfairly treated; it was not his fault that his father had been an imposter.

Skyfeather placed the bird in a little basket lined with moss that Patu had brought her, and set the basket beside her. She and Patu sat on the edge of the terrace, swinging their legs, watching the activity in the city below.

Skyfeather said, "The bird is hungry. Did you bring some worms?"

Patu reached into a small pouch at his waist and removed a long, slimy worm that still had some wiggle left in it. He held it up. "See? A good one."

"Isn't that too big?"

"No. Watch." He dangled it over the chickadee, which pecked at it, its little head darting this way and that.

Skyfeather looked at Patu fondly. He was a good friend even if he was a boy, and nearly grown up. She wished she had some girls her age to play with, but they were all commoners and the daughter of the Great Sun could not play with commoners. Patu was supposed to be a commoner now but he was really the son of the former Great Sun, so he was allowed. He smelled funny because he worked with the shaman and mixed smelly things, but she didn't care. He was fun to play with and he brought her nice things, like worms for her bird.

"Look who's coming," Patu said, scowling.

Manimani climbed the steps, ignoring the guards who howled their usual greeting. Chipmunk prostrated herself as Manimani approached. "Hou! Hou!"

Manimani ignored her, too, and strode inside the doorway. Almost immediately she returned outside.

"Where is Antelope?"

Chipmunk shook her head. "I do not know, honored one."

"It is your business to know," Manimani snapped. She came to stand by Skyfeather and Patu, neither of whom greeted her. Skyfeather was afraid of Manimani's bulk and strong voice, and her sharp, black eyes always looking.

"Where is your mother, Skyfeather?"

Skyfeather knew that Antelope had gone to the shell carver's, but she was not about to tell Manimani. "Maybe she is with Long Man."

Manimani looked down at Patu with an expressionless gaze. She beckoned. "Come, I wish to speak with you privately."

Skyfeather watched as they went inside. She knew that Patu disliked Manimani as much as she did. She wondered what they were talking about.

They came outside again, and Manimani said, "Remember what I told you, Patu."

"I will not forget."

Manimani glanced at the basket with the bird. She reached down and picked it up, examining it distastefully.

"A sick bird and a worm! Ugh!" She tossed it aside. It wobbled, but remained upright. "Can your mother find nothing better for you to play with?"

"My bird is not sick. His wing is broken, but it is getting well. He eats worms because he is a bird." Skyfeather's voice wobbled, but she assumed a regal stance. "You almost hurt him more. Go away!"

Manimani gasped at Skyfeather's rudeness. She glanced at Chipmunk and the guards who had trouble keeping a straight face. Her own flushed scarlet. She aimed a vicious kick at the basket and sent it soaring in the air, then down, down to the base of the mound. The little bird fell out and tried to fly, but could not, and plummeted to the ground far below, where it lay motionless.

Skyfeather screamed in shock and fury. "My bird! You killed my bird!"

"You are fortunate that is all that is killed," Manimani said coldly. "I will see to it that my brother will punish you for your insult to me." She cast a withering glance at Chipmunk and the guards, and strode down the steps and away.

"My bird!" Skyfeather sobbed. She started to go after it, but Patu said, "Wait. I will get it and bring it to you."

Skyfeather flung herself on the ground, sobbing in heartbroken rage. Her bird, her beautiful little hurt bird, would never fly again. Manimani, her father's sister, had killed it.

Chipmunk tried to hold and comfort her, but Skyfeather only wept more. Patu came and sat beside her, holding the basket.

"I have your bird, Skyfeather."

She stopped crying long enough to sit up and look. The basket was broken. Inside, upon the moss, lay a lifeless little creature with a wing all askew.

Skyfeather sat holding the basket in her lap while tears rolled down and dripped from her nose and chin. "Manimani says Father will punish me," she sobbed.

"Don't cry. Please don't cry, Skyfeather. Your father loves you. It is Manimani who should be punished." Manimani had told Patu that if he revealed what had happened during the truth-finding ceremony, she would use magic to destroy him. Ha! He was learning shaman's skills; he had magic of his own.

Carefully, he reached into the basket's tangled moss and removed what was left of the worm.

▲37▼

The shell carver bent low over his work. He seemed young to be so expert, Antelope thought as she watched him. He wore no forelock on his forehead, but a beaded one hung in front of each ear. As he leaned forward to carve a tiny line with his stone tool, the forelocks brushed his cheeks. He worked with intense concentration, his brown hands steady and strong on the delicate shell.

Antelope had requested a new gorget as a special gift for Far Walker. He had gorgets, of course, but not like the one being made for him now. It would be a surprise. She hoped that it would ease some of the tension he had been under lately, worrying about the buffalo trade and other matters. His all-encompassing responsibility as the Great Sun weighed on him— a responsibility begrudged by Manimani, who found ways to let him know she could handle everything better.

The carver lived in a modest dwelling in a village where other carvers congregated. They sat outdoors in pleasant weather, careful to save every bit of discarded shell for beads or other ornaments. Friends or family would pause to visit, and sometimes a boy with a flute would play a melody to ease the carver's hand.

It was a cool spring afternoon with dark clouds massing on the horizon. As she often did, Antelope thought of home and hoped much rain would fall there. Loneliness hid in a tiny place in her heart. She loved Far Walker dearly and their life was one of privilege—but ruled always by foreign ways, foreign gods. Officially, she was She Who Remembers no longer; she was mate of the Great Sun. But Antelope fingered her necklace, knowing that although she could not teach the young girls of the city, she would be She Who Remembers always. And she could teach Sky-feather.

The litter bearers stood patiently, waiting. But Antelope was intrigued with the mastery of the artist and wanted to watch.

"Place the litter here, where I may sit."

It was not proper for a mate of the Great Sun to linger thus, but the litter was placed upon the ground. She sat, and the two brawny slaves stood on either side, arms crossed, stone axes ready at their belts, eyes alert.

The young artisan flushed with pride and bent more eagerly to his work. A piece had been cut from the side of a large conch shell; the piece was perfectly round, and smoothed at the edges. Two holes had been drilled near the top edge for a cord to pass through. An ornate design had been traced on the surface, and the carver was using a sharp stone tool to scoop out the background, bit by infinitesimal bit, leaving the intricate design in sharp relief.

It was slow, painstaking work. Seeing Antelope seated there, a crowd began to gather, howling greetings, and she realized that the carver was distracted. Her presence was a handicap to him.

She gestured to the slaves. "I shall return now."

They lifted the litter easily with her seated upon it, and bore her swiftly away.

As they followed the path to Yala, Antelope heard thunder drums announcing an important arrival on the river.

"I wonder who that is?" she said.

"Would you like to go and see?" a slave asked politely. He was not young, but he was strong and well spoken.

"Yes. Thank you."

Antelope wished she knew his background, and that of all the slaves who served them, but Manimani had informed her that it was not proper for royalty to concern itself with the back-

ground of slaves. So Antelope asked Far Walker about it, and he
was surprised.

"No, I do not know their background. They have been here
for many years and serve well, so what does it matter?"

"It matters because they are people, not dogs who pull a
travois. Do any of them ever get to return home?"

"You don't understand. This is their home; some were born
here. Those captured in war would return home in disgrace. We
treat them well." He pulled her close, smiling. "Do not concern
yourself, dear one. You know, do you not, that I am your most
devoted slave?" Hands caressed her lingeringly.

Remembering, Antelope felt her body responding. She
wished she were with Far Walker right now.

Again the thunder drum sounded, closer this time. As they
approached the river, Antelope stared.

A giant war canoe approached, with many paddlers sweeping it swiftly along. Two warriors holding banners stood at the
bow; other warriors sat along the length of the canoe, gazing
stonily ahead. A drummer beat time for the paddlers; the deep
voice of the drum was echoed by the thunder drum ashore.

"Will they attack?" Antelope asked, trying to keep her voice
calm.

"No. The banners say they come in peace."

"But why so many warriors?"

The slave shrugged. "I do not know. I am a slave."

She watched the city's warriors go in canoes to meet the
visitors. More warriors lined the banks, bows in hand, arrows in
quivers, stone axes at the waist. The War Chief greeted the visitors and there was discussion that seemed to disturb him con-
siderably. He gestured the visitors' canoe ashore.

Expertly, the paddlers swung the big canoe around and
beached it. Then, to the shout of the thunder drum, Far Walker's
litter was borne forward. He signaled, and the litter was lowered.
He strode to meet the two men carrying banners.

Again, there was heated discussion. Antelope yearned to
know what was being said.

"Can you carry me closer?" she asked.

The older slave shook his head. "Too dangerous. Arrows may
fly."

He was right, of course. So Antelope sat on her litter at a
distance, watching Far Walker and the War Chief in strained

conversation with the visitors. She wondered what they were discussing. Would conflict result? She thought briefly of Sky-feather and was glad she was at home with Chipmunk; Sky-feather was safe there.

"Where is the canoe from?" Antelope asked.

"The City of the North."

Antelope swallowed. Had the queen come again on a political mission? Intending to seduce Far Walker as she had Chomoc? If so, she had a surprise coming. Ha!

The discussion continued briefly, then two of the visiting warriors disappeared into the canopied area. They emerged with a man whose arms were bound to his body with thick ropes, and whose eyes were covered with a strip of deerskin. The warriors dragged him forward and shoved him at Far Walker.

Far Walker stood looking at the prisoner for a moment, then removed the deerskin.

Antelope gasped.

Chomoc!

It could not be, but it was.

Far Walker gazed at the man before him, whose amber eyes burned with sardonic defiance. So this was Chomoc, son of Ko-kopelli, and Antelope's former mate! How strange he was, with his slanted brow, downturned lips, and hawk's beak of a nose! Ugly, actually. But there was something about him. . . .

"Remove the ropes," Far Walker said.

Stone knives slit the ropes and Chomoc jerked his arms free. He stood with an arrogant stance, saying nothing.

"Why did you do it?" Far Walker asked.

Chomoc looked down his beak nose. "You know very well why." He searched the gathering crowd. "I wish to see Antelope. My mate."

"Your mate no longer. She is mate of the Great Sun now."

If Chomoc was surprised, he concealed it well.

Far Walker said coldly, "The sacred fire you brought to us was stolen. Stolen fire is contaminated. You defile our city. You desecrate us."

"Cannot the Great Sun and his High Priest purify a fire gen-erously brought from the City of the North? A bigger, more pow-erful city than this, I remind you."

"Why are you here? Why did they not kill you?"

Amber eyes glittered. "One does not harm the son of Koko-pelli."

The men with banners—the visitors' War Chiefs—glanced at each other. One stepped forward.

"Chomoc is here because our queen divorced him. She wants you to know that she and her people are outraged. Unless the fire is returned, and with suitable payment, there will be war. Our warriors have come in peace. We hope to depart in peace."

Far Walker ignored the threat. He said graciously, loud enough for all to hear, "I invite you, all of you, to be my guests. A feast will be prepared and we shall discuss how this matter may be settled to the satisfaction of all. Chomoc is to be taken to the temple where he will remain for the time being." He gestured. "Follow me to the plaza."

He returned to his litter and the four bearers carried him regally up the path to the beat of the thunder drum, accompanied by his warriors marching on either side and visiting warriors following. Four local warriors surrounded Chomoc and led him to the temple.

Villagers stared, whispering behind their hands.

The son of Kokopelli had returned.

Antelope hurried up the steps of the dwelling mound. She had heard Far Walker's announcement; a feast must be prepared. For once, Antelope was glad for the presence of Mani-mani, who relished the opportunity to organize and supervise a feast. Soon pots would be boiling under her command. Meanwhile, Skyfeather must be prepared for the occasion—to meet her birth father for the first time since infancy.

Chipmunk met her at the door. As Antelope's personal slave the girl was not required to prostrate herself and howl greetings each time they met, but she was expected to bow low. She did so now.

"Honored one, your daughter grieves."

"Why?"

As Chipmunk explained what happened, Antelope felt rage and frustration boil up. How dare Manimani!

"Where is Skyfeather?"

"She sleeps."

Antelope stood by her daughter's small bed. Skyfeather lay

curled on soft furs, tear streaks on her cheeks. Beside her was a little broken basket, empty now.

Antelope beckoned to Chipmunk. "Where is the bird?"

"Patu took it. He said he would make a little grave for it in the burial mound."

Good Patu, Antelope thought. He must have had a fine mother. Did she know her mate was an imposter when she was garroted to accompany him to the Afterworld? What a strange and sad custom; she would have joined him eventually anyway.

Suddenly, Antelope realized that when Far Walker died, she would be expected to die with him.

It was a chilling thought.

Cooking fires burned throughout the city and delicious odors wafted. In the plaza, Manimani sat royally upon her litter, giving orders. The visiting chiefs and warriors sat in a semicircle facing Far Walker and his warriors seated behind him. Women and girls passed among them with bowls of corn cakes, jerky, sunflower seeds, and dried persimmons. The visitors helped themselves generously while ogling the girls, who returned their glances, giggling.

Manimani was gratified. All was going well—except that Patu was constantly underfoot, following her wherever she went, dark eyes watchful. She knew, of course, that he was eager to please her so she would not use her magic to punish him, but his constant dark gaze was unsettling. She beckoned a slave.

"Tell Patu to go away."

The slave spoke to Patu, who flashed her a glance and backed away. Later, Manimani saw him at a distance, still watching.

Something in that gaze . . .

Unease pricked her.

In the temple, Chomoc faced the High Priest, whose luminous eyes regarded him inscrutably. Chomoc felt the penetration of that gaze. Little could be concealed from this old man.

Finally, the High Priest said, "You are safe here. But you can stay only until the Great Sun and the War Chief decide what must be done."

Chomoc thought of the four guards outside the door. He

smiled sardonically. "I shall be more than willing to depart whenever the guards allow it."

The High Priest was not amused. "The guards follow orders—those of the Great Sun and the War Chief. And mine."

Of course, Chomoc thought. *This priest may be a cripple, but he has power. I must be adroit.* He reached inside his soiled robe for the only belonging he had left—his flute. He removed it from its fine deerskin pouch.

"I wish to atone to Red Man. I shall sing to him with my flute."

The High Priest did not reply. He sat on a raised bench by the altar and gazed silently at his star wall as Chomoc began to play.

His flute sang of loneliness and regret, of lost love and memories. Then, subtly, it began to change. The melody soared of its own accord, singing of adventure and far places, erotic conquest and triumphant freedom. Chomoc closed his eyes and let his music take him away.

Howls of greeting outside announced an approach, probably of Far Walker and his minions, Chomoc thought. He stopped playing and watched the door.

Antelope entered. With her was an exquisite little girl with sky-blue eyes. Like Kwani's.

Chomoc swallowed. He had not expected this. Antelope was not the girl he knew from childhood, nor the woman who had been his mate—how long ago? This woman was regal, more queenly than Tima-cha, more beautiful than he remembered. She stood proudly, gazing at him as if he were an intruder. She and Skyfeather greeted the High Priest, who bade them welcome.

Antelope did not speak to Chomoc, but turned to her daughter. "This is your birth father, Skyfeather. His name is Chomoc."

The girl stepped forward and looked up at him. He had the odd feeling that those blue eyes saw things hidden.

Unexpectedly self-conscious, he reached out a hand to her. "I greet you, Skyfeather."

"My heart rejoices," Skyfeather said politely. "Do it again."

"Do what?"

"Play your flute."

Chomoc was impressed. She did not ask, she demanded. This was indeed his daughter.

He played of time gone by, of children in the forest, of singing birds and a little rabbit scampering.

Skyfeather gazed up at him with shining eyes. When at last
the music ceased, Skyfeather smiled. "I thank you, birth father."
She looked up at Antelope. "He played for my bird."

Antelope nodded gravely. "I am sure the bird spirit heard."

Chomoc was moved. How could he have abandoned this
child, this woman?

How could he get them back?

The feasting was over. Far Walker stood before the visiting
War Chiefs and their warriors, and raised an arm for silence.
Immediately, all was still.

"As you know, Chomoc is in the temple awaiting judgment.
I invite your War Chiefs, and whomever they choose to accompany them, to come with me to the temple and discuss what must
be done. The rest of you are welcome to remain in the plaza for
games and trading. We are pleased to have you as our guests."

The men agreed. The food had been excellent and the girls
were pretty. Games and good trading were certainly in order,
and inviting glances from girls offered delightful inducement.

Far Walker summoned his litter. To the beat of the great
drum and howls of homage, he and his War Chief, and the two
visiting chiefs with several of their warriors, followed Chomoc
to the Temple of Eternal Fire.

Far Walker was proud as they approached the holy place. It
rose in splendor, shining in afternoon light, offering a gift of
sacred smoke to the Spirit Being.

But sacred no more.

Chomoc. What should be done with him?

The important thing is to get him away from Antelope.

As they climbed the steps where warriors stood on either
side, Far Walker heard Chomoc's flute—like no music he had
heard before. It seemed unlikely that he serenaded the High
Priest. Perhaps he was playing for his own amusement.

He turned to his War Chief. "Before our guests are invited
inside, I must confer with the High Priest. Please explain to
them."

"I shall, sacred one."

When Far Walker entered, he was surprised and not pleased
to find Antelope and Skyfeather there. Chomoc sat cross-legged

on the floor, flute in hand. Antelope and Skyfeather were close by with the High Priest.

When Skyfeather saw Far Walker, she jumped up and ran to him. "My birth father played his flute for my bird." Her eyes sparkled. "Mother says my bird heard. Do you think it did?"

Far Walker cast a quick glance at Antelope. She smiled her usual beguiling smile, so he said, "I am sure it did." He turned to the High Priest. "Our War Chief and the visiting chiefs are outside, waiting to be invited to enter. We must discuss the matter of Chomoc and the stolen fire."

The High Priest nodded. "I shall invite them myself."

As the High Priest made his lurching way to the door, Antelope said quietly to Chomoc, "I have allowed you to see the daughter you abandoned so you might realize your loss. We shall leave you now. We wish never to see you again. Never."

"But Mother—" Skyfeather protested, tears threatening.

"Come." Antelope took Skyfeather's hand and dragged her, resisting, through the door.

She did not look back to see Chomoc's stricken face.

▲ 38 ▼

Far Walker looked over the crowd assembled in the temple for Chomoc's trial. With Chomoc were the High Priest, the shaman, the caddí, the War Chief, and, unfortunately, Manimani. Also present were the two visiting chiefs and four of their brawny warriors—with lances, battle-axes, and bows and arrows. This was acceptable only because the guards outside on every step were also heavily armed.

A pipe was being passed and smoked in silence. Far Walker and the High Priest sat on raised benches; everyone else sat on the floor facing the altar and the eternal fire. Sounds from the city drifted in. A fly buzzed.

Far Walker glanced at Chomoc, who sat casually, expressionless. But Far Walker had seen his face when Antelope and Skyfeather left. Antelope had surprised him.

My secret fear of losing Antelope and Skyfeather was groundless.

When the pipe had been smoked by all, the High Priest rose, replaced the carved stone pipe on the altar, braced himself on his staff, and faced the group before him. Light from the Spirit Being entered through the small opening in the wall and illumined his bent figure. He had donned his white ceremonial robe for the occasion, and the top of his head was concealed by a hat of woven reeds with tufts of white feathers and dangling tassels. As he bent forward, the tassels swung against his wrinkled, tattooed brow.

"As we all know, a crime has been committed. Chomoc, an Anasazi, son of Kokopelli, from the Towa city of Cicuye, and recently from the City of the North, is accused of stealing their sacred fire to bring it to us when ours was destroyed in a storm. As a result, our fire is contaminated and our city is endangered."

"Desecrated!" Manimani said loudly.

The High Priest continued in his low, rich voice. "We are here to determine how this crime may be rectified."

A visiting War Chief rose. He was young to be a War Chief, but the notches in the eagle feather in his hair proclaimed his high status. Luxurious necklaces adorned his chest, and his arms and legs wore bands of shell and turquoise. A bear paw was tattooed under one eye. He regarded Chomoc with contempt as he spoke.

"My name is Blue Hawk, War Chief of the City of the North. My queen demands that this thief be executed and his head brought to her as evidence."

"An excellent idea," Manimani said.

Far Walker shot her a glance. "We are here to discuss the matter. So let us do so."

The High Priest nodded. "Proceed."

The second visiting War Chief rose. He was short and squat, but powerfully built. His round head sat on a neck so short that his chin seemed to rest on his collarbone. He squinted under shaggy, black brows as he spoke.

"My name is Rocks-in-the-River. I am second War Chief of the City of the North. My queen also demands rights to your pearl-digging places on the river. Our diggers will replace yours. We have spoken."

The two visiting chiefs sat down; the warriors shifted their lances.

Far Walker was outraged and struggled to conceal it. He said, "Let us consider these demands one at a time. Chomoc's decapitated head will not restore the stolen fire. As for the pearl-digging places, these are ours as they have been for generations. May I point out that it is a long journey to send your people here where they will not be welcome, and it is a long journey back where ambush is not unknown."

"Especially with valuable cargo," the caddí said.

"Most especially if the cargo rightfully belongs to us," the city's War Chief added.

Blue Hawk flushed and his eyes sparked. "Threats do not intimidate the people of the City of the North. They do not intimidate me and our warriors. We intend to honor the demands of our queen." He stared coldly at Chomoc, who looked down his nose at him.

The caddí fingered his robe nervously. "You must honor your queen, of course," he said smoothly. "But you may wish to consider an alternative method of recompense. Let us discuss the possibilities."

"I agree," Far Walker said. "I understand why your queen feels as she does. But there may be a greater benefit to her than Chomoc's head."

Rocks-in-the-River scowled. "Our duty is not to find an alternative to the queen's commands. We shall do as she wishes."

"Exactly," Blue Hawk said, resting a hand on his battle-ax. The four warriors with him did the same.

So far, the shaman had said nothing. Now he unfolded his long frame to stand, towering over them.

"I have consulted my crystal and conferred with Long Man. They inform me that if the son of Kokopelli is killed, disaster will befall the killers. Your queen will be endangered as well as yourselves." His gaunt face was solemn; one eyelid closed and opened again like an owl's. "For the sake of your queen, I advise you to consider alternative punishment."

Blue Hawk and Rocks-in-the-River shifted uneasily. The powers of this shaman were well known.

Far Walker turned to the High Priest. "What is your recommendation?"

The High Priest faced Blue Hawk in silence for a moment, his great, dark eyes intense. "The stolen fire must be returned."

The visiting chiefs glanced at one another. Blue Hawk said, "Of course it must be returned. But that will not fulfill the queen's desires. Chomoc must be punished, and rich tribute paid."

Far Walker was gratified to note that beheading and the pearl beds were not mentioned this time. The shaman's words had taken effect. He turned to his War Chief, whose responsibility it was to assess punishment for crimes.

"What do you advise?"

The War Chief regarded Chomoc with calm authority. "It is my recommendation that you become a slave to our people and remain so for the rest of your life."

"Excellent!" Manimani cried. "He can empty my night pot."

Chomoc flushed and assumed a regal stance. "I refuse. The son of Kokopelli will *not* become a slave. I prefer to die."

Far Walker regarded Chomoc with secret approval; he had spoken well. Could it be that Chomoc had stolen the fire for the sake of Antelope and Skyfeather, so that their city would have fire from a powerful connection—the City of the North? Or was he simply trying to promote a good trading alliance?

Blue Hawk grinned. "The thief prefers to die. We are ready to oblige." He fingered his battle-ax, a formidable stone weapon. His warriors murmured agreement.

Far Walker turned to the High Priest. "I await your opinion."

The High Priest was silent for a moment. He gazed over the heads of those present as though to see the unseen. Finally, he said, "Death would be no punishment. Slavery would be."

Blue Hawk and Rocks-in-the-River looked at one another. Blue Hawk said, "Shall we take him home as a slave?"

Rocks-in-the-River shook his head. "Our queen said the only way she wants to see his face again is on his severed head."

Blue Hawk asked, "Do you think she would approve of the thief becoming a slave?"

"Who knows the ways of a queen?"

"True." Blue Hawk turned to Far Walker. "Perhaps she has not thought of the advantage of slavery over death. Perhaps we should learn our queen's wishes in the matter."

Far Walker nodded. "A wise decision." He needed time to determine strategy. Remembering Skyfeather's reaction to Chomoc, he would not allow Chomoc to become one of their household slaves, always available—and near Antelope. But that was what Skyfeather would tearfully expect, and he, the Great Sun, found his small daughter's tears difficult to ignore. Perhaps there was another way to handle the situation. He would try.

He said, "Your queen honored us with a visit. Therefore, I shall return the honor." He turned to the War Chief. "Prepare a canoe for a voyage to the City of the North." He turned briefly to display the spider tattooed on his back. "As you know, my totem is Fire Bringer. I, personally, shall return the queen's stolen fire. The queen and I will discuss Chomoc's punishment and whatever else she wishes."

There was dumbfounded silence. Blue Hawk and his men stared in disbelief. Never before had a Great Sun left his city for any reason, and certainly not to accommodate another ruler.

The High Priest shook his head. "No, my lord. You cannot leave us. I shall go instead."

"No. I must be the one to meet the queen face-to-face and discuss what should be done."

The caddí cleared his throat. He said timidly, "Who will be the Great Sun while you are gone?"

"My sister, Manimani."

Manimani beamed triumphantly. She might present problems, Far Walker knew, but she was the only one left with royal blood; all the others were in the Afterworld. He wondered sometimes if they learned they had died to accompany an imposter.

He would be gone only a short time.

The War Chief stared at Chomoc, who stared back. "What should be done with this thief in the meantime?"

"Winter comes. There is much to prepare. Put him to work."

Blue Hawk and Rocks-in-the-River whispered together. The warriors shifted uneasily. Blue Hawk said, "We agree to postpone punishment until after the Great Sun and our queen confer. However, two of our warriors will remain with Chomoc to see that he does not escape." He rested a big hand on his ax.

Rocks-in-the-River added, "We will conduct you and your canoe to our city. It would be wise for you to have gifts—rich gifts—when you meet our queen."

"Of course," Far Walker said. He thought, *The former Great Sun gave her pearls. She will get few from me.*

Antelope stared at Far Walker in shocked amazement. "You are going to visit the queen of the City of the North? Why?"

"To repair the damage Chomoc did to the relationship between our cities. And, incidentally, to save Chomoc's life."

"Is his life worth saving? I ask you. He has debased us all."

"Perhaps he stole the fire because of you and Skyfeather; he wanted you to be safe. In any event, he is son of Kokopelli and is Skyfeather's birth father. He cannot be decapitated at the whim of the queen."

Antelope swallowed. "Decapitated?"

"Yes. And the head brought to the queen as a trophy."

Antelope turned away. The thought of Chomoc's head as a trophy for the woman who had seduced him—or vice versa—made her feel sick. The years of her childhood and his kindnesses to her rolled by in her mind like tumbleweeds blown by the wind. And the times they loved . . .

"Go, then, if you must. But take me with you."

"I cannot, dear one. It is too dangerous. Skyfeather needs you here."

"I shall take her with me."

"No."

Antelope looked at him, at the sweep of his wide brow over eyes that loved her, and at his fine, straight nose—so different from Chomoc's. She looked at the set of his shoulders, and the way he held himself as though his body had always known who he was even when he did not. Power was in this man—not the power of prestige or position, but an innate strength. It was Far Walker, not she, who wanted to save Chomoc. Antelope felt a twinge of contrition. Chomoc was, after all, Skyfeather's birth father and her lover of long ago. . . .

"Who will take your place while you are away?"

"Manimani."

"Oh, no! Not Manimani. She hates me. Can't it be the caddí?"

"It must be one with royal blood. There is only Manimani."

"Take me with you, Far Walker. Please."

"I cannot. You know that."

"But—"

"I shall be gone only a little while." He enfolded her in his arms. "But you will always be with me, beautiful one."

Antelope clung to him. She remembered Skyfeather's little broken basket and tears for the dead bird. She thought of the times Manimani had belittled her, and the secret glances of animosity.

And she remembered the seductive beauty of the queen.

"Come home soon, Far Walker."

·39·

Antelope and Skyfeather stood on the bank, watching the handsome war canoes head east to where Long Man joined the Big Strong River. From there they would head north to the great city. The two canoes were a magnificent sight with strong men paddling in unison to the beat of the northern drum, while Far Walker's men chanted, their voices blending with the drum. Blue Hawk's canoe led the way with banners flying, followed by Far Walker, whose canoe was carved and painted in brilliant colors.

Under the canopied area, wrapped in buffalo hide in one of the most beautiful jars from the temple, Red Man nestled in punk. The High Priest had placed it there with powerful prayers and incantations, and Far Walker himself would attend it, feeding it whenever necessary.

Good-byes had been said, tears shed, promises made, and now Far Walker was going away. Away to visit the queen of the north.

We are alone again, Skyfeather and I, Antelope thought.

It had been a tense morning. She and Far Walker had made desperate love during the night and slipped away before dawn to bathe in Long Man together.

Antelope had pushed the wet hair away from her face and looked at Far Walker, whose wet body gleamed in fading starlight. As she watched him, she felt a sudden sense of foreboding.

"I am afraid."

He smiled, white teeth shining in his dark face. "Why?"

"I cannot explain. It is just a feeling. . . ."

"All will be well, foolish one. I shall be here with you and Long Man again soon."

"Long Man will have you all the way there and back."

He laughed. "True. But here I have you and that makes it a place unlike any other."

They embraced in the water, wet bodies clinging.

Now he and his canoe were gone, disappeared around the bend. The sound of the drum and chanting voices trailed behind them like a wake.

Antelope gestured for her litter. "Take us home now."

As they headed for the plaza, Skyfeather said, "Where is my birth father?"

"I don't know. In the temple, maybe. Or working in the fields, perhaps."

"I want him to play his flute again." Her blue eyes pleaded.

Antelope thought, *I should have anticipated this.* She said, "I am sure he will play his flute at the evening fire."

"But we never go there."

"No. But you will hear him."

"I want him to play for me." Her round face in its cloud of dark hair was solemn. "I want to see him. He is the only father I have until my real father comes home."

Antelope looked at her daughter whose small face mirrored her own. And Kwani's. But Chomoc was in her, too, in mannerisms and personality—more than Antelope wanted to admit.

What she says is true. How can I handle it? What can I say?

Antelope smiled reassuringly. "We shall talk about it at home."

"All right." Skyfeather leaned over the litter and yelled "Hou!" at children yelling "Hou!" at her and laughed at dogs who jumped, trying to reach her to have their ears scratched.

Antelope was glad to arrive at her dwelling mound and get away from the howling crowd. But she was surprised to see slaves carrying bundles and a bed up the stairs.

She asked one of the guards, "What is happening here?"

"Manimani is moving in," he said flatly.

Antelope dismissed her litter, took Skyfeather's hand, and ran up the steps and through the doorway. Manimani was bustling around inside, telling slaves where to put things. Antelope and Skyfeather's belongings, and those of Far Walker, were piled haphazardly in a corner. Chipmunk huddled among them. When she saw Antelope she hurried over and whispered, "I tried to stop her, but she said the guards would throw me down the steps." She wiped her eyes with a shaking hand.

"Never mind, Chipmunk. It will be all right."

Antelope strode to Manimani, grabbed her arm, and jerked her around face-to-face. "What are you doing in my home?" Her voice was cold.

Manimani yanked her arm away. She was taller than Antelope and stared down at her; Antelope felt her gaze like a stinging insect. Her voice stung, too. "This is where the Great Sun lives, is it not? Must I remind you who is the Great Sun now?"

"Must I remind you it will be for a short time only?" Antelope took a deep breath. "Take your belongings and go. This is my home and you are not welcome here."

"No!" Skyfeather shrilled. "You killed my bird!"

Manimani's face became a livid mask. "This is the home of the Great Sun and as long as that is who I am, this is where I shall live." She crossed her arms and stared down at Antelope. "However, as Great Sun, I graciously grant you the privilege of staying in my other residence until I shall need it again." Suddenly, she shoved Antelope hard. "Go now."

Antelope staggered but did not fall. Skyfeather backed away, frightened, and the slaves huddled silently together in the background.

Antelope said slowly and distinctly, "I shall not leave my home. I demand that you go right now and take your things and your slaves with you."

Manimani paled in fury. "I shall do no such thing. This is my home now and will be until my brother returns. He will not be pleased with your insults to me." She thrust a pudgy finger at the door. "Go!"

Antelope gave her a frigid stare, then leaned to whisper to Skyfeather. "Do not leave this room. I shall be right back. Stay with Chipmunk." She marched out the door, ignoring Manimani's triumphant grunt.

Antelope knew the two guards at the top of the stairs; they had chatted from time to time. Both guards were grizzled warriors of renown, chosen to protect the Great Sun and his family, and were in charge of the other guards posted there. Antelope went to Weasel Foot, one of the top two.

She said, "My husband ordered you to protect me and Sky-feather during his absence, did he not?"

A smile creased Weasel Foot's tattoos. "He did."

Antelope returned his smile; he made her feel better. "It seems I need protection from Manimani. She has ordered Sky-feather and me out of our home because she is the Great Sun now."

Weasel Foot said, "I had to allow the slaves to bring her belongings up here because, as you say, she is the Great Sun. For the time being, that is. However"—he beckoned the other top guard over—"I personally feel obligated to obey the command the Great Sun gave me before he left." He turned to the other guard. "Do you agree?"

"Absolutely." The tone of his voice left no doubt. "The Great Sun would not be pleased to learn we had allowed his mate and daughter to be driven from their home."

"Very well," Antelope said. "Please come inside with me while I inform Manimani that she must go, not I."

When Antelope went back in with the two guards following, Manimani was arranging sleeping furs on her bed. She looked up in mock surprise, but her expression changed abruptly to shock when she saw the guards.

Antelope said, "Your slaves may take everything back to your dwelling, Manimani. The guards will help if need be."

Manimani's mouth set in a hard line and her small, black eyes darted from one guard to the other.

"I am the Great Sun. I refuse! I shall have you both beheaded for this insolence."

Weasel Foot grinned. "Who will do the beheading?"

Manimani stared in grim silence. The guards were the elite of the warrior class; it was they who were responsible for executions. If anyone else did it, it would be murder.

Antelope said, "You may conduct your business in the temple, but you will live in your own residence."

Weasel Foot gestured to Manimani's slaves. "Take everything back that you brought in here." He fingered his lance. "Do you need help?"

The slaves glanced at Manimani, who stood in stony silence, pale with fury. "I am the Great Sun. . . ." Her voice trembled.

"Then go to the Great Sun's temple," Antelope said. "Pray for your brother's safe journey. Your belongings will be returned and will be in your home when you get back."

Weasel Foot gestured with his lance and the slaves hurriedly began loading things in baskets and litter carriers.

"Wait!" Manimani commanded. She flashed a look at Weasel Foot. "No one but the Great Sun orders my slaves to do anything. Is that clear?" She turned to three men and two women who stood uncertainly, waiting, their faces tinged with fear. "I wish to confer with the High Priest. You may take me to the temple and return my belongings to my dwelling. I do not choose to remain in a place contaminated by a foreign presence."

Head high, she stalked out.

Antelope turned to Weasel Foot. "Thank you. The Great Sun will be grateful to you. As I am." She smiled.

He bowed, his grizzled face solemn. He stepped closer so the slaves would not hear and whispered, "It is not over. Be careful. She will seek revenge."

Antelope knew in the depth of her being that what he said was true. Manimani was a dangerous enemy.

We must be very careful, Skyfeather and I.

Manimani trembled with rage and humiliation. She did not hear the howls of greeting as the litter bearers swept her across the plaza toward the temple, nor did she notice Patu trotting behind.

How dare that Towa woman insult her, the Great Sun and the Great Sun's sister! How could Far Walker possibly have taken Antelope as mate when he knew he was the Great Sun? She had bewitched him, that was it. She was a witch, of course. That was why her child's eyes were blue; she would grow up to be a witch, too.

The High Priest would know what to do.

The High Priest was studying his star wall when Manimani swept in. They exchanged greetings. Manimani sat on the Great Sun's carved bench and watched the High Priest making astral calculations.

When it became obvious that he was not impressed by or interested in her presence, Manimani said, "I wish to confer with you."

"Of course," the High Priest said courteously, enveloping her with his luminous gaze. With the help of his staff he lowered his twisted body to a mat and sat looking up at her. "I am ready."

"Very well." Manimani settled herself and began, "As you know, I am the Great Sun now, at my brother's request."

"Until he returns."

"Whenever that may be. Meanwhile, as the Great Sun, I belong in the Great Sun's dwelling, do I not?"

There was a long moment of silence as Manimani felt herself encompassed by the High Priest's searching gaze.

"Perhaps. Perhaps not."

Manimani swallowed her irritation. This priest was a powerful member of the elite, and it would be unwise to antagonize him.

"Permit me to explain. In assuming the responsibilities of Great Sun, I want to do the solemn opportunity justice. I assume you agree it would not be suitable for me to reside anywhere but in the Great Sun's dwelling."

The High Priest did not reply but looked at her without expression.

She bit her lips with impatience. "Please honor me with your opinion."

"I must know all the facts first. How does Antelope feel about sharing her home with you?"

"I do not wish to share. I have offered her the use of my own residence until her mate returns."

"Did she accept?"

"No! She ordered me to leave and take my things with me—"

"You mean you moved your belongings into her dwelling?"

"The Great Sun's dwelling. Of course."

"Antelope agreed to that?"

"She was with my brother at the time." Manimani shifted uneasily. "After all, I am the Great Sun now."

"Temporarily." He looked down at his crippled hands as though pondering their form. "What is it you want of me?"

"I have told you. I want your opinion. Should I, or should I not, reside in the Great Sun's dwelling?"

His dark eyes penetrated hers. "Let us remember that although Far Walker has gone on a dangerous journey for the sake of us all, he is still the Great Sun. You, his honored sister, are but a temporary substitute."

Manimani clenched her hands. "Substitute or not, I am the Great Sun until he returns, and I demand that I be allowed to reside in the Great Sun's dwelling."

His voice turned cold. "If you presume to demand of me, I must remind you that I am the High Priest. My authority is spiritual, not political; nor do I become involved in domestic disputes. However, since you demand my opinion, I shall give it." Pause. "Because it does not agree with yours."

Manimani's face flushed crimson. "You don't—"

"Far Walker's absence on a pilgrimage does not eliminate his mate's right to their home. Therefore, the final decision in this matter must be Antelope's."

Manimani swallowed, speechless with rage and humiliation.

The High Priest pulled himself upright and stood with dignity. "Please allow me to continue my calculations."

Without another word, Manimani strode out the door.

Back in her own dwelling, she looked at her belongings placed here, there, or anywhere. Fury and frustration overwhelmed her, and for the first time in many moons she wept bitterly.

Remembering all that Antelope had said and the cold words of the High Priest, she felt resolve well up in a raging flood.

The final decision would not be that of the Towa woman. No! Now, while Far Walker was gone, was an ideal time to pay another visit to the sorceress.

That night Antelope lay sleepless. Chipmunk slept nearby close to Skyfeather, and the guards were on duty outside as always. But the confrontation with Manimani had left Antelope shaken. She told herself there was no reason to be afraid, but an inner voice whispered that danger stalked like the Spotted One.

She lay curled in furs that bore the faint scent of Far Walker. She pulled the furs closer for comfort. Where was he now? What would happen to him in days ahead?

What would happen to her?

She clasped her necklace in both hands and pressed the scallop shell to her, pleading for communication.

"Come to me, my mother. Come, Ancient Ones. I need you!"
There was no reply.

It was silent outside; not even a drum sounded. She heard
only the drumming of her heart. As she lay there in the furs,
breathing Far Walker's essence, she remembered his words:

The drumbeat in your blood is the voice of your ancestors. Let
the drum speak.

Antelope closed her eyes. Again, she held her necklace close
and willed herself to become one with the drumming in her
heart, in her blood. Slowly, a feeling of peace rose within her
like water from a sacred spring. It filled her with calm assurance.
An inner voice, like the voice of ancestors, spoke.

> *Time is a great circle;*
> *There is no beginning, no end.*
> *All returns again and again*
> *Forever.*

She was She Who Remembers, one with all those gone before, and she would become an Ancient One for her descend-
ants—as Skyfeather would become, and her daughter's daughter
. . . forever.

I must begin teaching her, Antelope thought. She rose in the
darkness to stand beside Skyfeather's small bed and leaned close
to hear her soft breathing. How she loved this little being!

Comforted, she returned to her bed and drifted into sleep.
Stars circled overhead and night deepened. Darkness, raven
spirit wings, folded down. In the forest, the jaguar prowled.

Antelope dreamed.

Years dissolved. She was Kwani, her mother, in a faraway
dreamscape—dark, ominous, strange.

She stood alone on the mesa. There was a sound like water
pounding the banks in floodtime and great animals appeared, run-
ning wildly across the mesa, long tails streaming behind them.
Some of the beasts were white, some black, some spotted, others
brown. All had flowing hair along the top of their necks; the hair
rippled in the wind as they ran.

She gasped. A god rode the back of each animal! Glittering
garments clothed the gods from head to foot. Beneath the coverings
on their heads, dark bushy hair concealed their faces from nose to

neck. Mouths opened, shouting fiercely in a foreign tongue.

Antelope woke, trembling. What a horrible dream! Had she received her mother's vision? She held the necklace close.

"Speak, my mother."

Antelope closed her eyes, straining with all her power to communicate. Gradually, it seemed that she entered another dimension, another place in her mind. Slowly, a swirling mist dissolved and Kwani appeared, wearing the necklace of four beads. She was old no longer, but radiant in the glory of her youth. Her blue eyes met Antelope's in loving embrace, but her voice was solemn.

"It is true, my daughter. They will come, as I have told you."

"No!" Antelope cried.

"But one man will save us, one whose ancestor you are. He alone will unite us and drive the foreigners from our homeland. The blood of She Who Remembers will be renowned forever. . . ."

The mist began to fade, and with it Kwani's voice. "Warn our people. Warn them. . . ." The voice was gone.

"Come back! Don't leave me!" Antelope cried aloud, clutching her necklace.

Soft footsteps approached and Chipmunk leaned over her. "What is it?" she asked with concern. "No one is leaving you. We are right here." Her soft, soothing voice was a balm. "You were dreaming."

"Yes," Antelope said. "I dreamed."

But it was more than a dream. It was a revelation, a warning of danger to come.

I must warn my people.

I must, I will find a way to go home.

▲ 40 ▼

Manimani sat on the Great Sun's carved chair in the temple and watched the caddí addressing the council. She tried to make herself listen to his droning account of who was to plant and harvest what, how much of the harvest would go to the storehouse, and the latest gloomy report on buffalo products, but her mind was on the Towa woman and the sorceress.

The Great Sun cannot go to a sorceress; she must come to me.

What would happen if she did come? Would it not cause discussion and concern—and curiosity? A Great Sun is expected to rely on the shaman for such matters, not an outsider.

No, she could not summon the sorceress; she must acquire the necessary ingredients herself: worms, spittle, a poisonous parsnip, a yellow stone slab, pebbles of the proper size and color, splinters from a tree struck by lightning . . .

Who could assemble such things? The worms would be no problem. Patu could do that. In fact, with his shaman's training, he could probably obtain everything needed. He had been tagging around after her ever since she became the Great Sun, probably hoping for an opportunity to serve her again in some way to regain his royal status. Yes, Patu would be the one. She would summon him when this boring council meeting was over.

Across the plaza, Antelope and Chipmunk sat on the mound terrace enjoying a beautiful spring day and watching the city activity below. Patu and Skyfeather were playing a game, manipulating strings looped around both hands to form various shapes. Skyfeather's quick fingers flashed among the strings, and she laughed when she outdid Patu.

After a time, Patu leaned close and spoke softly so Antelope and Chipmunk would not hear.

"Manimani eats here sometimes, doesn't she?"

"She used to but doesn't anymore."

"Did she ever spit?"

"Sometimes."

"When?"

"When she ate something bad—like spoiled sunflower seeds. Why?"

He shrugged. "I just wondered."

The guards shouted warnings to someone approaching; it was one of Manimani's slaves. Antelope watched him climb the steps and approach her while guards stood on either side. He prostrated himself, howled greetings, then said, "I bring word from the Great Sun." He remained facedown, waiting.

"Very well. What is it?"

He rose. "The Great Sun requests that Patu come to her dwelling."

Antelope glanced at Skyfeather and Patu. "Why?"

He cringed. "I do not know, honored one."

Antelope saw the slave's anxious face and downcast eyes, and she felt a twinge of sympathy. This slave had not been treated well. He was no longer young, and he bore recent scars on his back. She turned to Chipmunk. "Reward him."

Chipmunk nodded, went inside, and returned with a small basket of delicacies: nuts and seeds and dried fruits.

"For you," Antelope told the slave.

He was astonished and touched. He took the basket and held it carefully in both hands. "I thank you, honored one."

Antelope called, "Come here, Patu."

Patu hurried over, dark eyes alert in his oval face, Skyfeather trotting beside him.

"You are to go to Manimani's dwelling," Antelope told Patu.

Skyfeather jumped up and down. "I want to go, too."

"No. Patu only."

"But I wa-a-a-nt to!" Skyfeather wailed.

"No."

Skyfeather burst into noisy tears. Patu put an arm around her shoulders. "Don't cry. I will come back."

Skyfeather's tears abated to sniffles. "Don't forget."

"Go now," Antelope said.

The guards escorted Patu and the slave to the stairway and watched them descend into the spring afternoon.

Manimani saw them coming. The slave was bringing a basket of something—a peace offering from Antelope, probably. But too late. Antelope's life was about over.

Patu howled his greetings, lay on his stomach with arms outstretched, and waited for Manimani to acknowledge him. But she had thrust out her hand to the slave for the basket.

The slave bowed respectfully, but kept the basket. "Antelope gave this to me in thanks for bringing your message, sacred one."

"Of course. But I am sure she meant it for me." She thrust out her hand demandingly.

A look flashed in the man's face and was immediately concealed. Slowly, he offered the basket with both hands. She took it, poked around in it with her finger, and set it casually aside. She waved dismissal, and he backed away, face expressionless.

Patu had been on his stomach on the floor all this time. Now she nudged him with her foot. "Rise."

He did so and stood looking at her with a level gaze that Manimani found disconcerting. She gestured Patu to sit. He did so, and Manimani settled her ample frame comfortably, helped herself from a bowl of nuts, chewed, and swallowed thoughtfully. Finally she said, "You have wisely chosen to protect yourself by remaining silent about what happened at the truth-finding ceremony. Therefore, I shall reward you."

"Thank you, sacred one," Patu said politely.

He did not seem impressed, but of course he was intimidated by her presence—as well he should be. She said, "I shall allow you to help me in obtaining a number of objects I shall require to treat one of my slaves."

Patu's face came alive. "Your slave is ill? I can—"

"No. The problem is of another nature. Therefore, I must ask that you do not mention to anyone what I am about to tell you; it will jeopardize the treatment. Do you understand?"

"Yes."

"Very well. I shall need several splinters from that tree struck by lightning during the last storm. Do you know the tree?"

"I do."

"Of course. And you know where to find wild parsnip, do you not?"

"Yes."

"I shall need that. My slaves will obtain the rest. Except for the worms. Seven worms, mashed to a pulp. I know you are good at finding worms." She helped herself to more nuts.

Patu's face was blank. What was the boy thinking? He seemed old for eleven winters. She said, "Do you have any questions?"

For a moment, he did not reply. Then he asked matter-of-factly, "What is my reward?"

Manimani frowned. Such arrogance! "Your reward is your head remaining on your body. Do I make myself clear?"

"Yes." Pause. "Sacred one."

"Good. You may leave me now." She gestured dismissal.

He backed away, yelling "Hou!"

When he was gone, Manimani summoned the slave once more. "Bring me Chipmunk."

While she waited for Antelope's slave to arrive, Manimani rehearsed what she would say to Chipmunk; she must make it believable. She paced the floor, pondering. Now and then she stopped for more nuts; it helped her to think.

At last the girl arrived, trembling with apprehension. Manimani dismissed the slave and tried to put the girl at ease.

"Here, have some pine nuts."

"Thank you, sacred one." She took one tiny kernel and ate it nervously.

"You may sit down, Chipmunk. Over here."

Manimani motioned to a mat beside her chair and Chipmunk sat, crossing her legs. She did not look at Manimani but stared down at her trembling hands.

Manimani said, "I have summoned you because you are Antelope's favorite slave. Since I was ordered from my home there, I shall not go to her myself. Rather, I trust you to handle a matter of great importance."

Chipmunk looked up with immediate interest, and Manimani continued. "As you know, Antelope and I have had words. But she is, after all, my brother's wife and I do feel responsible for her welfare now that he is away. Have another nut?"

Chipmunk took two kernels this time.

Manimani helped herself generously and continued. "I have learned that Antelope is under a bad spell. This may be why she is so unreasonable. However, the spell may be broken with proper procedures. This is where you can help her."

"I will do anything," Chipmunk said fervently.

"Of course. What you must do is very simple, but it must be in secret or the spell will not be broken. Do you understand?"

"Yes, sacred one."

"Very well. All you have to do is wait for Antelope to spit, then put some of it on a little stick and bring it to me. But no one—not Antelope or Skyfeather or Patu or the slaves or the guards or anyone else—must know. Do you think you can do that?"

"I will try."

"Good. If you can do that, then I, the Great Sun, will be able to have the bad spell removed. You will save Antelope's life."

Chipmunk nodded with solemn resolve. "I will do it, sacred one."

Manimani nodded. "Must I mention what will happen if you fail, or if someone learns what you are doing?"

The girl gazed at Manimani mutely, fear shadowing her face.

Manimani patted Chipmunk's head. "Too pretty a head to lose."

Chipmunk paled; her lips trembled.

"Remember all I have told you. When you bring me Antelope's spittle I shall reward you well. Go now."

Chipmunk was so shaken she forgot to howl as she backed out the door.

Manimani's slave had a name. It was White Duck. But people seldom called him by name; he was "Manimani's personal slave." Therefore, he was pleasantly surprised when he and Patu were bathing in the river and Patu said, "I greet you, White Duck."

"I greet you, Patu." The boy had grown a lot lately. How old was he now? White Duck couldn't remember. He rubbed both his arms and splashed water on his sore back.

Patu said, "Let me wash your back. I will be careful."

Nobody had offered to wash his back before. White Duck nodded and Patu slid his hands gently over the recent scars, cleansing them.

"That must have hurt," Patu said. "Why were you beaten?"

White Duck was embarrassed. To be beaten meant that one was inferior. Even a slave needed self-esteem. He did not reply.

It was a cool spring morning and children whooped and played in the water while their mothers washed clothes. The birds of summer were beginning to arrive and the air was filled with loud territorial announcements.

White Duck lay on the water and let it carry him a little way downstream. Patu floated with him, and the two drifted companionably. White Duck knew that Patu was the son of the Great Sun who had died, and he wondered why a person of such rank wanted to be friends with a slave. Could it be that he was lonely, too?

They passed a spot where watercress grew, and stopped to gather some, nibbling the while.

Patu asked, "How did you become a slave?"

White Duck sat on a rock and dabbled knobby feet in the water. The sun was pleasantly warm and the boy wanted to be friendly. This made White Duck feel good, so he said, "It was when I was about your age. There was a big battle west of here, on the plains. Our village was burned, my family killed. Only I survived because I knew where to hide. . . ." He looked at Patu. "I was a coward, you see. Afraid to fight." He wiped his jaw in an ashamed gesture. "My people, my village, everything was gone." He paused, remembering. "One day I was out hunting, trying to stay alive, when some warriors found me and brought me here. I knew many songs, I could cook well, so they gave me to Manimani. . . ." His voice trailed off.

Patu said, "That was a long time ago, so she must have been young then."

He nodded. "Young and eager to be a woman. She made me teach her how."

Patu held a sprig of watercress in his hand and gazed at it as if it might reveal the past. "But she has you beaten. . . ."

"Yes."

A fish splashed, leaving ripples, and a kingfisher circled, watching. Trees stirred in the breeze.

Patu said, "You have been a slave for a long time."

"Yes. A long, long time."

"Perhaps there is a way you can be free."

White Duck cast Patu a sharp glance. "This is my only home. I am too old to seek a life elsewhere, even if I could." His mouth twisted bitterly. "I am afraid to fight, remember?"

Patu looked White Duck calmly in the eye. "You do not have to do battle. You do not have to leave this place. And you can be free."

They sat talking together, the naked, scarred man and the naked boy slim as an eel. Birdsong and the distant shouts of children drifted by.

They talked for a long time. Finally, Patu said, "Put some spoiled nuts in her nut bowl. That should do it."

A sprig of hope rose in White Duck's heart like the frond of a fern thrusting itself from the forest floor.

▲41▼

"**S**top here," Antelope said.

She and Skyfeather were riding their litter on the way to Yala to visit Peg Foot. It was a breezy morning with clouds piled on the horizon; Antelope loved being outdoors on such a day. She breathed deeply of the sweet air and gazed at a landscape she had not seen for a while.

Beyond the houses and their neat gardens, rich farm plots spread on either side of the river. Trees, newly arrayed in green, clustered in the background, and reeds grew tall at the river's edge.

Spring planting was under way. Digging sticks poked holes in the prepared ground and seeds were dropped carefully into each hole. Then the soil was stamped down—all to the music of an unmistakable flute.

"There's my birth father!" Skyfeather squealed, pointing.

Chomoc sat in leisure on the sidelines with a guard on either side. He sat cross-legged, eyes closed, playing his flute in the way Antelope knew so well. He swayed from side to side, his flute singing of harvest and plenty, of dreams fulfilled, and of first-time love in the spring.

Remembering her and Chomoc's first time, Antelope felt

tears sting her eyes. It had been long ago, another time and place, when she was someone else, and so was he.

Remembering the past could be painful. But thinking of the future could be painful, too. She had to talk to Peg Foot about that.

Antelope gestured the slaves to proceed.

"No!" Skyfeather cried. "I want to hear him play."

"Another day. We are going to see Peg Foot now."

They were carried away, Skyfeather protesting. But soon she was laughing with children who howled greetings, telling them all that the flute player was her birth father and that they were going to visit the Healer.

Word reached Peg Foot before they did. He was waiting for them outside, his weathered face aglow. His robe was clean and his peg foot polished. He flung both arms wide as the litter was lowered.

"Welcome, Antelope! Welcome, Skyfeather!"

Antelope flung her arms around his bony frame and hugged him close.

"I have missed you," she said.

"I miss you both every day. I was planning to come and see you." He bent to look into Skyfeather's face. "I have a present for you, little one."

She beamed. "What?"

"Come inside and you will see."

Following him indoors, Antelope was met with the familiar odor from bowls and baskets and plants hanging in bunches from the ceiling. Antelope noticed the place was not as clean or as organized as it had been when she lived there, but Peg Foot could not see as well as he used to. She knew how he insisted upon living alone, with women coming in to clean now and then.

"May I see my present now?" Skyfeather cried, eyes sparkling.

Peg Foot hobbled to a corner of the room with Skyfeather hopping beside him. From a shelf he lifted down a carved wooden bird's nest. Inside was a lifelike, painted little wooden chickadee.

"I heard," he said.

Skyfeather held it carefully, turning it this way and that, blue eyes glowing. She lifted the bird from its nest and held it tenderly. She looked up at Peg Foot. "It looks real. It really is my bird." She took his hand and pulled him down so his face met hers. She kissed his cheek. "Thank you, Grandfather." It was the first time she had called him that.

He was moved. To be called Grandfather was the ultimate compliment.

"Come," he said gruffly. "Let us see what my patients have given me to eat."

He brought a bowl of buffalo stew and a basket of corn cakes and placed them on the floor beside seating mats. Antelope and Peg Foot sat, but Skyfeather was too enchanted with her bird to eat. She walked about the room, showing everything to the bird and talking to it conversationally.

"See?" she said, holding up the bird for a good look. "That is my grandfather's medicine. He is a Healer."

Antelope smiled. She said to Peg Foot, "Thank you for such a thoughtful gift. Her heart was broken when the bird died."

"I heard that Manimani was responsible."

"Yes."

They dipped corn cakes into the buffalo stew and ate in silence. Antelope was immensely flattered that Peg Foot wanted her to eat with him, a male; it was the supreme compliment. She was hungry and the stew was good. Finally, she said, "There is something important I want to talk to you about. I need your wisdom."

The tattoos around his mouth arranged themselves in a grin. "You know that I cannot refuse you anything, especially my wisdom, as you call it. So tell me."

"I had a dream. A vision."

"Ah. And what was the vision?"

"My mother came to me. She said our people are in great danger. I must warn them, Peg Foot. I must go home."

"Does Far Walker know of this?"

"No. I had the dream after he had gone. I don't know how long he will be away. . . ."

Peg Foot rubbed his peg thoughtfully. "He is the Great Sun now and can arrange a travel party, whatever is needed, to send you home. So wait until he returns."

"He may not want me to go. So I thought maybe I could leave while he is away. If he is gone a long time, I could return before he does."

Peg Foot shook his head. "I think you have forgotten how

many moons it took to get here, how hard it was, how hazardous. He would return long before you did. What will happen if he finds you gone? Think about that."

"But my people are in danger. They need me."

"You are mate of the Great Sun. You are needed here."

"Manimani is the Great Sun now, remember? She would be delighted if I left."

He frowned, nodding. "Manimani . . ." He dipped a corn cake into the stew and scooped up a big bite. He chewed thoughtfully, his chin bobbing up and down. He wiped his mouth with the back of his hand.

"I must confer with Long Man about this. Do not tell anyone else what you have told me. They may not understand. Wait for twice seven days, and if Far Walker has not returned, we can discuss it and decide what to do. Will you do that?"

"I will."

Manimani counted the yellow and black stones. There were exactly enough; the slaves had done well. However, they could not find a yellow stone slab of the right size, so she had allowed Patu to find it. He had also brought the parsnip and the splinters from the tree struck by lightning, and the worms nicely mashed to a pulp. All that was needed now was Antelope's saliva. If Chipmunk did not bring it within the next two or three days, she would summon the girl again.

Manimani realized that Patu was learning to become a shaman, so he had to know that he was assembling materials for a death spell. But unless Chipmunk told, Patu would not know whom it was for. Since both Chipmunk and Patu were very well aware that the Great Sun could send their heads rolling, they would not be eager to invite it. So there was little problem in that respect.

There was a problem, however, with time. No word had been heard from Far Walker and the canoes. Perhaps Far Walker was already on the way home; if so, he could be back at any time. She must move fast while she still had a Great Sun's power.

Two days passed and Chipmunk did not come. Manimani paced the floor impatiently, nibbling from her nut bowl to soothe her nerves. She noticed that White Duck was more than usually attentive, keeping her nut bowl filled. Occasionally she encountered a bad nut, but in a mouthful it did not matter too much.

Since she had become the Great Sun, he was eager, obviously, to stay in her good graces.

On the third day she sent White Duck to summon Chipmunk.

Chipmunk was out on the terrace and saw him coming. She knew at once that she was being summoned, and her heart jerked in fright. Manimani wanted Antelope's saliva and there wasn't any; Antelope did not spit.

Chipmunk clasped her thin, brown hands frantically. Manimani had said she would take her head if she failed, and she had failed. What to do?

Antelope and Skyfeather had gone somewhere; Chipmunk was alone. She heard the slave being greeted by the guards as he climbed the stairs. Hurriedly, she went inside to find the little stick she had hidden. Holding it gingerly, she spit on it hard. Spit looked like spit; who would know the difference? Maybe it would not save Antelope's life as Manimani said, but it would save hers. She tucked the slimy stick in a little basket and went out to meet White Duck.

"I was getting ready to go to Manimani," Chipmunk said as casually as she could. "Have you come to take me?"

"Yes."

"I will go with you."

As they hurried across the plaza to Manimani's dwelling, White Duck stopped suddenly and looked down at Chipmunk with an odd expression. He said, "We who are slaves must help one another."

Chipmunk was not sure how she could help a slave of the Great Sun, but she was too scared to comment.

He said, "I will be close by. Do not be afraid."

That was comforting and Chipmunk smiled up at him. The knots in her stomach eased a little.

Manimani had ordered guards to surround her dwelling; White Duck and Chipmunk had to pass stern warriors with lances and with stone maces hanging at their belts. Chipmunk held her small basket in trembling hands as they entered.

Manimani wore a new robe with dazzling embroidery of pearl and shell beads that glittered as she moved. Her long, dark hair was in a bun in back, like a man's, and she wore the Great Sun's crown of white swan feathers tipped with red tassels. An engraved shell gorget rested on her ample chest.

Chipmunk prostrated herself, being careful with her basket. Manimani dismissed White Duck with a gesture; he left the room, but Chipmunk saw him peek around the door.

"You may rise, Chipmunk."

The girl sat up and offered her basket. "I bring you what you wish, sacred one."

Manimani snatched it and inspected it carefully.

"How do I know this is hers?"

Chipmunk was surprised to find her voice steady. "When you cure her, sacred one."

"Ah." Her smile was triumphant as she set the basket down. "I shall reward you." She removed one of her many bracelets and offered it. "A gift from the Great Sun for faithful service."

Chipmunk accepted it and slipped it on her thin arm. "I thank you, sacred one."

Manimani suddenly leaned forward, her gaze like a lance as she said, "But do not forget what will happen if anyone learns what you have done."

Chipmunk quivered inside. "I shall not forget."

"Now go."

Chipmunk scurried away, her heart thumping. "What have I done?" she asked herself over and over again.

Patu could hardly contain his triumph. Everything needed for the death spell was ready—all but Manimani's saliva. White Duck had said not to worry; he would replace all the nuts with bad ones if necessary. He said that Manimani had made Chipmunk bring a sample of Antelope's saliva and had given it to him to be included with the other ingredients for the death charm.

"She is trying to kill Antelope," White Duck said.

Patu smiled bitterly. "She will be surprised to find herself in the Afterworld instead of Antelope."

"I threw the stick away and put lots more bad nuts in her bowl. She was furious at getting so many, and spit out a mouthful, as you can see on the stick," White Duck said. "I think she was going to have me beaten again, but she was expecting a visitor—Chomoc. He came with his flute and played for her. Then they went to bed."

They chortled about that, and Patu asked, "Did the guards come with him?"

"Yes, but they had to wait outside."

They laughed again. Patu said, "That Chomoc has been with half the women in the city. What do they see in him?"

White Duck shrugged. "Who knows?"

Patu had made his way through the forest to the lightning tree. Now everything was ready. He dug a hole at the base of the tree. Chanting the words of the charm the shaman had taught him, he placed all the ingredients in the hole, covered it well, and lit a fire upon it.

The smoke rose, blending with the leaves of the old tree that had withstood time and storms. Patu visualized Manimani in the poisonous parsnip-root tube, and relished the thought that in seven days she would be no more.

Antelope and Skyfeather, lovely little Skyfeather, would be safe.

Manimani feverishly counted the days, waiting for the seventh when Antelope would be gone forever. There had been no word from Far Walker. If he were on the way home, runners would have brought the news, so he was more than two days away.

She planned how she would persuade Far Walker to allow her to move in with him to look after him properly. She would no longer be the Great Sun, but she was his sister and she deserved a position of importance, including living in the royal residence. She still stung from that Towa woman's insulting insistence that she, Manimani, leave the Great Sun's dwelling when she *was* the Great Sun.

Only two more days . . .

The wind turned cold and great, black clouds swept low. Thunder boomed and lightning flashed and hissed. Because of the previous storm, people were afraid and huddled in their homes while rain pelted down. Manimani summoned Chomoc to entertain her, and they dined in luxury while the storm raged outside, drenching the miserable guards. It was the sixth day.

The seventh day dawned gray, but Manimani knew it would be the most beautiful day of her life. She looked at Chomoc sleeping—how ugly he was!—and nudged him awake. She wanted to savor her triumph in private.

"Go now, Chomoc."

He roused himself and gave her a look from amber eyes that

was not the kind of glance a lover should give. But in her exultation, Manimani didn't care. She wanted to celebrate.

"You may come another time," Manimani said. "Good-bye."

When he was gone, Manimani dressed carefully. For a moment, she felt a little dizzy, but it passed. She summoned her litter. She wanted to be there when it happened; she wanted to relish every moment.

White Duck and another slave arrived with her canopied litter. It was raining again, but she and her finery would be protected. As they crossed the plaza, thunder rumbled in the distance and lightning lit the horizon; the storm was passing. People were out and about, farmers were back in the fields, and fishermen were busy with their nets. Upstream, diggers would be finding more pearls for her adornment. Children splashed in mud puddles, shouting with joy, and she wanted to shout, too.

As they approached the dwelling mound, the sun appeared from behind a dark cloud and a great rainbow appeared, a glorious, perfect arch. Antelope and Skyfeather ran out to see.

As the slaves carried her litter up the steps, they slipped on the rain-slick log steps, but they made it safely to the top.

"Put me down now."

As they lowered the litter, Skyfeather ran up. "Come and see the rainbow!"

Antelope stood at the edge of the terrace, gazing at the rainbow, the wonder of it. When she saw Manimani, she called, "Come and see how beautiful it is!"

Pretending she was welcome here! Well, she would be soon. As Manimani crossed the wet terrace, she slipped a bit but regained her balance. She went to stand beside Antelope, waiting to see what would happen. Manimani looked down the sloping side of the mound to the base far below. Would Antelope topple and fall, bumping her way down that steep slope? What an exciting thought!

"Look, Manimani," Skyfeather cried. "See the colors!"

Manimani looked, but the colors wavered and blurred. She grew dizzy. A fog enveloped her, and a strange sound like a distant wailing rang in her ears.

Suddenly, everything seemed to go around and around.

She felt weightless, as though she could float free.

She was floating! Flying like a bird, like a chickadee, swooping down and down and down to the ground below.

▲42▼

The storm swept into the great valley where Big Strong River, to be known one day as the Mississippi, rolled on its twisting, vagrant course. Trees flung their arms wildly about; branches broke and fell into the water to be swept away, bobbing and turning in the current. Birds were silent and animals burrowed in their dens or hunkered down for the storm.

Two canoes headed upstream. Blue Hawk's men rowed mightily in an effort to avoid floating logs, while Far Walker's men struggled behind. It grew darker, the river rose, and great drops of rain began to fall. Thunder growled and boomed, coming closer. Lightning flashed beyond writhing treetops.

Blue Hawk shouted to his men and signaled Far Walker. "We must stop for the night."

They beached their canoes and made camp on a forested bluff. Sharp stone axes cut trees and brush for a makeshift shelter for each group. Blue Hawk's men kept to themselves. They gathered around a small, sputtering fire under their shelter, and glanced now and then at Far Walker and his men.

Far Walker thought, *They resent us even though I am bringing their sacred fire home.* He cradled the fire jar between his knees.

351

He would not leave it in the canoe unattended; soon it would need to be fed again and he would do it himself.

Far Walker wondered what future storytellers would have to say about a Great Sun's leaving his people to carry stolen fire to another ruler. "Too fantastic to be true," some would say, and he would not blame them. Never had it been done before. Had he not been a Healer previously, one of the townspeople rather than the Great Sun, he could not have done it. But a Healer he was, with concern for his people; he was one of them.

Warriors built a small fire and the War Chief opened a pouch of pemmican. A bowl of water was placed over the fire, and when it boiled a handful of pemmican was tossed in. It would swell to three times its size.

The storm arrived in fury and rain beat down, leaking through the branches of the shelter. Far Walker huddled miserably by the meager fire, longing for Antelope and Skyfeather, wondering if the storm reached them, hoping all was well at home. Rain dripped down the back of his neck, and flashes of lightning revealed the War Chief and his men were getting soaked.

The fire sputtered but did not go out. When the pemmican was ready, the War Chief lowered a gourd dipper into the pot and handed the dipper to Far Walker. The men gathered around, dipped in the spoons they always carried, and took turns helping themselves.

There was little talk over the shout of the storm. With each crash of thunder, the ground seemed to tremble. No sound was heard from the other group.

The War Chief said, "I do not like the attitude of the queen's men. Here we are, returning the queen's sacred fire, doing them a favor, if you please. And they act like they are doing us a favor by letting us accompany them."

There were grunts of agreement. The paddlers, warriors all, fingered their battle-axes. One man said, "Perhaps we should watch that the queen's men don't sneak away and leave us stranded."

Far Walker said, "The river will take us where we want to go whether they are with us or not."

The War Chief wiped wet hair from his forehead. "Yes, but they know the river."

"And the villages along it," a warrior added.

"We must remember one thing," Far Walker said. "We have the queen's sacred fire." He patted the jar between his knees. "As long as we have this, will they abandon us?" He looked from man to man. "I don't think so. What we must do is keep the fire."

The men pondered this in silence. The storm raged, the shelter shook, and the ground quivered. A terrific boom of thunder was accompanied by the creak and groan and loud wailing of a stricken tree as it toppled over the bluff, followed by a splintering crash.

"The canoes!" someone shouted.

Every man ran out to see. Lightning flashes revealed the worst. The tree had fallen upon the canoes. The queen's canoe was crushed in the middle, and Far Walker's was badly damaged.

Far Walker's heart sank. It would be days before the canoes could be repaired and be on their way again.

With the death of Manimani, the city had suffered yet another catastrophe. Frightened people gathered in groups in the plaza and around fires at night, discussing possible reasons for such an inconceivable disaster. Surely their city was cursed beyond restoration! Not even the High Priest could remove such an affliction.

"It must be witches," a man said, peering beyond the shadows of the evening fire.

Witches were feared above all. People nodded, huddling close together.

"Yes," another said. "Someone among us . . ."

"An outsider, perhaps?"

Unspoken words filled the silence. People did not look at each other.

"They say Manimani was pushed," a woman said.

"But the guards were there. They saw Manimani get dizzy and fall."

Another silence.

"A witch could make the guards think anything."

"Skyfeather's eyes are blue. . . ."

Litters and travois piled with personal belongings began to appear on paths leading out of town as people abandoned the city to live with relatives elsewhere.

Another royal funeral was held and Manimani was buried beside the former Great Sun.

"Who will govern now?" people asked anxiously.

"When will Far Walker come home?"

The caddí, the shaman, and the High Priest sat before the sacred fire in the temple. They had been in solemn conference for some time.

"We must learn when our Great Sun will return," the High Priest said. He turned to the shaman. "What does your crystal reveal?"

The shaman shook his head. "My crystal is cloudy. Something is wrong."

"Begin the drums and signal fires, asking for reply," the High Priest said. "Once we know where Far Walker is, we will know better when he will return. Perhaps he is on his way back now."

"Not likely." The shaman's left eyelid closed, then opened slowly. "My crystal clouds. The Great Sun is in some kind of trouble."

The caddí twisted his bracelets. "There is talk of witches. . . ."

The High Priest nodded. "I know. Foolish talk. People are frightened."

"Of course they are frightened," the shaman said. "And they have good reason."

The High Priest gazed at Red Man in silence. The fire burned low. At last he said, "I shall ask the Spirit Being for guidance."

It was a cloudy afternoon four days after Manimani's funeral, the day when Manimani's dwelling would be given to Red Man. Antelope stood on her terrace, gazing down at Manimani's house, but as yet no smoke or flames were visible.

Skyfeather was with Chipmunk, playing some make-believe game. *My poor little daughter,* Antelope thought. *She needs playmates her own age. If we were in Cicuye, she would have many friends.*

I have been here four winters. Will I ever go home again?

It had been twice seven days since Far Walker left. It was time to talk with Peg Foot once more.

Antelope was about to summon her litter, but hesitated. Something had changed these last few days. Since Manimani's death, Antelope sensed a difference in the attitude of the townspeople. It was in the way they looked at her and Skyfeather and how they whispered behind their hands.

Do they blame me for Manimani's death?

A chilling thought. She had better not go out and about again until Far Walker returned. She sent the litter to bring Peg Foot to her.

The guards greeted him warmly as he climbed the steps with effort. When he saw Antelope, he scowled.

"I am too old to climb steps. Why do you summon me, eh?"

"I will tell you. Here, sit down and have some dove stew with hominy." Antelope had made his favorite meal herself.

Mollified, the old Healer settled himself on a mat. "Where is Skyfeather?"

"Playing with Chipmunk. Patu has not been here lately. My daughter needs friends her own age. If we were in Cicuye—"

"But you are here, and here you must remain until Far Walker returns."

Antelope lowered a gourd dipper into the stewpot and poured the savory contents into a pretty black bowl. She handed him the bowl with her best carved spoon—one he had made for her. She was gratified to note that her hand was steady even though her heart jerked at the thought of what she was about to say.

"What if Far Walker does not come home?"

The spoon paused midair. "Of course he will come home. He is the Great Sun."

"He is a man, Peg Foot. He can be wounded, or sick. . . ." She did not mention the queen, the seductive, darkly beautiful woman foremost in her mind.

Peg Foot ate the rest of his stew in silence, scooped out the last tidbit from the bowl with his forefinger, and belched his appreciation.

"I thank you, Granddaughter." He settled himself comfortably. "Now let us discuss what to do."

Far Walker sat in his canoe hunched over the fire jar. It had taken nine days to repair the canoes and they were on their way again at last. Far Walker added a bit of punk to the jar, blew on it, saw a spark glow, and sighed in relief.

It was not yet dawn. Mist hung low over the river. How wide it was, how strange! The banks were hidden in the mist. It was silent but for the splash, splash of paddles or the sudden flap of wings as a water bird was disturbed. As the canoes rounded a bend, Far Walker glimpsed a bear and her cubs drinking at the river's edge. There was a growling snort and a rustle as the bear whirled and disappeared, cubs running after.

"That would have been good hunting," the War Chief said. "If we were not so delayed I would stop."

"I know how you feel," Far Walker replied. "But we must stay with Blue Hawk. I did not realize how dangerous this river is. We need him and his men; they know the river, and we are delayed too long already."

Ahead, Blue Hawk's canoe was barely visible. The men stroked in rhythmic unison, their paddles whispering in the water. The fragrance of damp earth from the storm and the sweet breath of the river blended with the aroma of the mist. Far Walker breathed deeply, cleansing his inner being of uncertainty. He would return the queen's fire and all would be well.

The days of delay had been difficult. Blue Hawk's men had been sullen and quick to anger. Only Far Walker's presence and the War Chief's training of his men had prevented a confrontation. Yet the men did work together under stress and the damage, much of it severe, was finally repaired. At last they could be on their way again.

Far Walker wondered how much longer it would be. He missed Antelope more than he thought possible. Each miserable night he had longed for her and made love to her in his imagination. . . .

He wondered about Manimani. She was probably causing trouble, but he would take care of it when he returned. She might be his sister in blood, but she was foreign in mind. They were strangers.

The mist began to lift and the sky brightened. Far Walker gazed with curiosity at the distant, muddy banks interspersed with small islands formed by the mighty river as it flooded, then receded. Ahead, smoke rose above a bluff. A village lay beyond.

In the canoe ahead, the men began to chant to the beat of a drum.

"Why are they doing that?" Far Walker asked the War Chief.

"To let everybody know they are on the queen's business, I guess."

"Will we be delayed here, do you suppose?"

The War Chief shrugged. "Who knows?"

Far Walker fumed inwardly. He and the War Chief would be expected home soon, and they had not even reached the City of the North yet.

As they passed the bluff, four war canoes appeared ahead. With shouts of greeting they pulled alongside the canoes of Blue Hawk and Far Walker. After lively discussion, all the canoes headed for shore.

Far Walker ordered his canoe brought next to Blue Hawk's. He called, "Why are we stopping here?"

"To pay our respects," Blue Hawk replied curtly, his young face scornful at such ignorance.

"And replenish our supplies," Rocks-in-the-River added.

Days of delay had taken their toll; provisions were needed. Far Walker settled back with impatience. "We cannot linger here."

Blue Hawk smiled grimly. "You are free to go ahead by yourself at any time."

Far Walker speared him with a glance. "Must I remind you that I carry sacred fire to your queen?"

Rocks-in-the-River shook his grizzled head. "We do not forget, nor do we forget what must be done to get you and the fire to our queen safely. Be grateful for our assistance."

The War Chief leaned close and whispered, "He is right, Great Sun. We must follow their lead."

The war canoes pulled ahead and the others followed. Clouds had been swept away. It would be a clear day, Far Walker thought with relief.

Ahead, a village approached. Smoke curled skyward and cooking smells wafted over the river. People thronged the banks, eager to see the arrivals. Women wore only a deerskin skirt tied at the waist with a fringed belt. Tattoos were fewer than those at home, but the women were shapely nonetheless and wore many necklaces and ankle adornments. The men in their breech-clouts looked much the same as those at home except for their hairstyles, which were less ornate and ornamented. Yapping dogs and naked children ran back and forth excitedly along the riverbank.

When the canoes reached the village, people waded into the river to help pull the canoes ashore. There was much talking and laughing, and children were shouting as the canoes were beached. People crowded around Far Walker and his men, smiling welcome, while women and girls stole admiring peeks at Far Walker.

As he followed Blue Hawk into the village, Far Walker was interested to see that their dwellings differed from those of his city. There were no extended doorways, for example. The thatched dwellings were conical, pointed at the top. The only mound was a small one beside a level, smoothed area probably used as a dancing plaza and as a chunkey ground.

A dignified old chief with a feathered staff met the visitors in the plaza. There were greetings and explanations while Far Walker and his men were scrutinized.

"You are welcome here," the old chief said. "I invite you to dine with us and spend the night in our village."

Far Walker bowed. "We thank you, but—"

"Of course we accept with pleasure," Blue Hawk interrupted, casting a sharp glance at Far Walker. "Our men are hungry and weary and will appreciate your hospitality."

"We bring buffalo hides and copper," Rocks-in-the-River said. "We will trade for provisions for the rest of our journey."

Far Walker had loaded his canoe with buffalo hides as part of his gifts for the queen. Blue Hawk stood close by, and Far Walker spoke softly so as not to be overheard. "Are those my buffalo hides offered for trade?"

Blue Hawk said, "You need provisions, do you not?"

"Those hides are for your queen."

"They cannot reach her if we do not. Think about that."

So there would be another delay. Far Walker tried to swallow his impatience. When would they reach the City of the North, finish their business, and start home?

Another thought. Who would accompany them on the way back?

Patu and White Duck sat where they had met once before, nibbling watercress that grew by the river. It was late afternoon on a cool spring day.

Manimani was gone.

They gloated over their success. A squirrel sat on a limb, scolding them loudly, and was ignored.

"I had never done it before, so I wasn't sure it would work," Patu said.

"She tried to kill Antelope. I wonder if she is surprised to find herself in the Afterworld instead."

They chortled. The squirrel ran up and down the tree, chattering in agitation.

Patu looked searchingly at White Duck. "Does anybody know how Manimani died?"

"Not really. Some say Antelope pushed her. Others whisper that Antelope is a witch, and maybe Skyfeather, too." White Duck rubbed his creased brow. "I did not think they would be blamed."

"Neither did I." Patu frowned. "I hope Far Walker returns soon." In trying to save Skyfeather and Antelope, had he endangered them? Patu felt a lump in his stomach.

White Duck said, "I hear that drums and signal fires will send word that the Great Sun is needed at home. Maybe that will make him hurry."

"Maybe," Patu said. "Maybe not. Perhaps he is already on the way back." He paused. "What will you do now that Manimani is gone?"

"Find a place to live after her house is burned."

"Because you were Manimani's slave, do you belong now to Far Walker?"

"I don't know. He is not here, and I will be gone when he returns."

"Will you go to another village? Find a woman . . ."

"No. I think I want to be a runner. Carry news from village to village. That way I will always be welcome."

"And fed," Patu added.

The middle-aged slave and the young-old boy gazed at each other in perfect understanding.

"When you become a runner, I will go with you," Patu said.

"Good. We go together."

Secretly, each was appalled at the realization of what they had done. A Great Sun can do no wrong, and they had killed one who was the Great Sun at the time.

Would Manimani's spirit seek revenge?

What would be their terrible punishment?

It would be wise for them to go far away.

▲43▼

Twice seven days and four more had passed since Far Walker had gone, and there was no word of him. The caddí sat cross-legged on his mat by his eating bowl and found he was not hungry. Unease lurked in his stomach. Smoke signals and drums signaled that Far Walker's city was in trouble and he was needed at home, but as yet there was no reply.

"You do not want your porridge?" his mate asked.

"No."

"Very well." Men ate first, but since he did not want his, she sat down and ate it herself. More would be left in the pot for another meal.

The caddí watched her slurping; it did not help his stomach any. He rose to go outdoors into the cool morning. He was making himself comfortable in a sunny spot when Manimani's slave, White Duck, approached.

The slave greeted him respectfully and stood waiting to be invited to sit. There was something different about White Duck, the caddí thought. He seemed more . . . confident. What was he after?

The caddí gestured. "Sit."

The slave squatted on the ground and remained silent, waiting to be invited to speak, as slaves were supposed to do.

"Speak," the caddí said.

"I thank you, honored one. I wish to offer my services as a runner."

This surprised the caddí. Now that Manimani was gone, he thought White Duck might want to be a slave to the next in command.

"Why do you want to be a runner?"

White Duck looked away and was silent for a moment. Then he said, "I have been a slave since childhood. Now I am a man, and I want to become a man. To be free to help my people, to help you, to go where I have never been, to see what I have never seen . . ." His voice trailed off. Again, he looked away.

The caddí pondered. It had been suggested that another canoe be sent to find Far Walker, but since the queen's canoe was escorting him, sending another canoe to check up might be construed as an insult. A runner could be sent, but the terrain was impassable in places. Bears and jaguars hunted in wilderness areas, and people in distant villages might not be friendly. It was too dangerous.

A slave provided the perfect solution.

"Your wish is granted, White Duck," the caddí intoned graciously. "Report to the storehouse for a map and supplies."

White Duck's face flushed with joy. He swallowed, then asked, "Where will you send me, my lord?"

"To the City of the North to find Far Walker, our Great Sun. Then return and report to me."

White Duck was overcome with gratitude. He placed his hand over his heart and bowed low. "I promise to find our Great Sun, and I will report to you when I do."

"You shall be rewarded. Go now."

The caddí watched White Duck depart. He wondered if he would ever see him again.

Across the plaza on that same morning, Antelope and Sky-feather sat on the terrace in the spring sunshine. Sounds of the city drifted up: snatches of conversation, laughter, shouts of children, barking dogs, crying babies, drums, turkey bone whistles, the pounding of poles in mortars as women ground corn, the shouts of men playing chunkey, the soft thud of mallet on copper, and women singing to the spiraling notes of a flute—a flute poorly played in comparison to Chomoc's mastery.

Chipmunk had been sent on an errand to the temple to learn if Chomoc and his guards were there. If he was not, the High Priest or one of his assistants might know where he was. One priest or another was always in the temple tending the sacred fire. They discussed things with each other and little happened in the city that they did not hear about.

When Antelope visited Peg Foot, he had suggested that she talk to Chomoc and find out more about the City of the North and their queen. Knowing what Far Walker faced would make it easier to guess when he might return and to decide what she should do now. But Antelope hesitated; she did not want to ask Chomoc for anything, not anymore. She longed for Far Walker; anxiety about his safety gnawed at her. Perhaps Chomoc could provide useful information. She must try.

A flock of birds soared overhead like a plume of smoke. Skyfeather watched them swooping, circling, and flying swiftly away. She said suddenly, "Patu is gone. He came and said goodbye."

"Where did he go?"

"Away. With White Duck."

"Manimani's slave?"

"He is a runner now. Gone to look for my father. Patu said he wanted to look for the Great Sun, too."

"Did the shaman know he was leaving?"

"I don't know." Her eyes blinked tears. "I miss him."

Antelope put her arm around Skyfeather's small shoulders. "I am sure he will return." She thought, *My daughter needs friends and playmates. She is deprived. Being mate of the Great Sun is more of a handicap than a blessing. But I love him, I love him. If only he were Towa. . . .*

As they waited for Chipmunk's return, they watched activity in the plaza and beyond. Trees blocked a complete view of the river, but buffalo hunters came and went, their canoes loaded. Nearby, skins were stretched out and pegged to the ground, fur side down, while women used a clamshell or bone implement to scrape the hides clean.

Antelope thought, *The shaman did this city no favor by forcing me to call the buffalo.* No longer did traders come to barter for hides and pemmican and other buffalo products piled in the city's warehouse—products acquired by trading with villages near and far. Now hunters obtained all they wanted from the vast herd lingering nearby. The city's coffers grew lean. A good corn crop was essential now. Corn was a valuable commodity everywhere.

Skyfeather said, "What are you thinking, Mother?"

"About corn." Antelope smiled. "That reminds me. It is time for you to learn about She Who Remembers. I will tell you a story."

"But I thought we were going to see my birth father." Her blue eyes were rebellious, and she stuck out her small chin.

Antelope thought, *How much like me she is!* and her heart melted. She said, "We must wait for Chipmunk to return so she can tell us where Chomoc is. He may be in the fields somewhere. She will be back soon."

"Oh. All right." She settled herself for a story.

"This is how the Ancient One, who was She Who Remembers then, told my mother and my mother told me. This world we live in now is the fourth world; there were three before that when people lived in darkness. Then Massau'u brought us to this fourth world where Sunfather gives us day and Moonwoman gives us night. But when women entered this fourth world they were small. Men were bigger and stronger. They hunted and kept most of the meat for themselves; they did not like to share. They only gave women what was left over and sometimes there was none to give. Women were weak, especially when they had babies in their stomachs and couldn't run fast or fight for meat. So Earthmother taught women how to find good plants and roots and seeds and flowers to eat, so they would not be hungry anymore. When hunting was scarce, it was women who fed everyone with the food they gathered."

"I want to learn that."

"You will." Antelope thought, *You will if I can take you home.*

She continued, "When women found good things to eat and learned to cook them, the men wanted some. So the women asked Earthmother what to do, and she said, 'Trade your good things for what the men can give you.' 'Do you mean their meat?' the women asked, and Earthmother said, 'More than that. Men can give you protection, you and your children. They can provide a dwelling. Trade yourselves and the food of your gathering for what men will give you. Remember well what I have told you.'"

"Did they remember?"

"Yes, for a while. They grew stronger and wiser. They traded themselves and the food they gathered for protection for themselves and their children, and for meat. Years passed, and the memory of what Earthmother taught them remained in their blood from daughter to daughter. No man, however strong, could best a woman skilled in remembering."

"Does my blood remember?"

"Yes. The blood always remembers. It is the voice of your ancestors."

"But when I get hurt and bleed, my blood doesn't say anything."

"It's not that kind of a voice. It is something you hear inside of you, something you just *know*."

Antelope smoothed a wisp of hair back from Skyfeather's earnest face and continued.

"More years passed and women forgot they knew how to remember. Knowledge lay hidden in a secret place, waiting to be summoned. Even when the knowledge was used, women did not know they had used it; the precious gift lay neglected and ignored. Teachers were needed to instruct young girls so they would not forget, but there were none who could teach. Earthmother grieved. She said, 'I will make a teacher.'"

"How?"

"She took a grain of corn and made it grow tall. The tassel became a head with long hair, leaves became arms, the stalk became a body, and She Who Remembers was created. She pulled herself from the ground and walked."

Skyfeather's face was alive with interest and curiosity. "Where did she go?"

"To find young girls, girls like you, to teach the women's secrets so they would not forget again."

Skyfeather looked puzzled. "What secrets?"

"What her powers and abilities are and how to use them. You will understand when you are older." Antelope fingered her necklace. "Ever since that day, we who are She Who Remembers have worn this necklace because each of us is one apart, a Chosen One. When I press it close to me like this, I can reach those who wore it before and pray for help when I need it."

"Do they answer your prayer?"

"Sometimes. Not always. I guess sometimes I don't pray hard enough. Every teacher must teach another to follow her. I shall teach you, and you will teach another one day."

Skyfeather reached to touch the necklace. "Will I wear it?"

"Yes, when you become She Who Remembers. Because we are Chosen Ones, Skyfeather. It is a sacred responsibility."

Skyfeather thought about that for a moment. Then she said, "Why are you not teaching?"

"Because I am a Towa, as you are, and people here believe differently than we do. They do not want me to teach. So I will teach you—"

There was the sound of running footsteps up the stairs, and Chipmunk arrived breathlessly.

"Chomoc is at the temple with the guards. The young priest there says to come. Chomoc played his flute for me." She brushed her hair back with both hands, preening. "He said I am pretty."

"Of course you are." How like Chomoc, Antelope thought. But Chipmunk did have lovely breasts and an expressive oval face where emotions came and went like clouds on a spring day.

Guards summoned the litter and Antelope and Skyfeather began to descend the steps to where the litter bearers waited at the base of the mound. Usually, the litter was brought to the terrace, but Skyfeather liked to hop down from step to step. Today, Antelope's two top guards came with them.

"It is not necessary for you to come," Antelope said.

"It would be advisable," the older guard replied. "Please allow us to do so, for your protection. People are uneasy and restless since Manimani's death because there is no Great Sun here now."

Antelope swallowed. "Do they blame me?"

"It is said that some do."

Skyfeather tugged at Antelope's hand, eager to go. Her eyes sparkled and she jumped up and down with excited impatience.

Nothing would harm this child.

"Very well. Come, and thank you."

It soon became evident that things were not as they used to be. When people saw them coming, they pretended not to and hurried away. No children came running; there were no howls of welcome. Even dogs remained at a distance.

Antelope felt a pang of fear. What was happening here?

Skyfeather sat in silence. Finally, she turned to look up at Antelope.

"People don't like us anymore." Her voice quavered. "Why?"

"Maybe Chomoc or the priest can tell us."

When they reached the temple, the guards remained with the slaves and the litter. "We shall wait here for you."

As they climbed the steps, Antelope wished she did not have to do this. Chomoc was not the boy she had grown up with nor the man who had become her mate. He had changed—all but his lust and his arrogance. And his flute, silent now.

As they approached the temple, Skyfeather whispered, "Will my birth father play his flute for me?"

"We shall see. Come."

Chomoc paced the floor under the ever watchful eyes of the two foreign guards and the cold gaze of the young priest. Ever since Chipmunk had told him that Antelope and Skyfeather were coming, he had felt the past closing in. Remembering Antelope, her beauty and indomitable spirit and her passionate lovemaking, he wondered how he could have forsaken her and their child. He never intended to. It was just that he had been distracted by the queen. . . .

The young priest who kept the fire raised his hand as Chomoc strode by again. "Stop! You disturb the spirits of this place."

Chomoc looked down his nose. "It is not my desire to be here." He glanced at the guards. He was glad that the High Priest was away somewhere. That cripple with probing eyes made him nervous.

Voices were outside; Antelope was coming! He struck a casual pose and waited.

They entered, the woman more queenly than the queen, and the beautiful little girl who glowed when she saw him. She ran up to him, smiling.

"Will you play your flute for me?"

"Of course."

"Later, Chomoc," Antelope said. "We must talk first." She turned to Skyfeather. "Ask the priest to tell you about Red Man while Chomoc and I talk. Then he will play for you."

Skyfeather looked doubtfully at the dour young man in his

priestly robe, but he smiled and beckoned. "Come and sit by me. I will tell you a story."

Skyfeather loved stories, but she hesitated.

"Go," Antelope said, giving her a gentle push. "Chomoc and I have much to discuss."

Chomoc watched his young daughter as she walked reluctantly to where the priest sat on a mat beside the fire. As Skyfeather stood beside the priest, looking down at him, her stance was so much like his own that he felt a pang of . . . what? He did not know; he had not experienced it before.

Antelope turned to the two guards ogling her. "Ours will be a private conversation. You may wait outside."

The guards glanced at one another, and then at him. Chomoc had managed to do some trading and had bribed the guards to allow him various romantic escapades. He knew they wondered now if they would be paid again.

He said, "The Great Sun's mate wishes to speak with me. It will be to your advantage to wait outside. It is safe." He smiled sardonically. "Obviously."

They grinned and departed. Chomoc heard them laughing outside. He thought, *Let them laugh while they can.* He had plans.

Antelope sat on the raised, engraved stool belonging to the High Priest and regarded Chomoc with the deep and level gaze he knew so well. How beautiful she was in her white robe embroidered with pearls and shell beads! Her dark hair fell softly to her shoulders, outlining the planes of her face with its high curve of cheek and sweet curve of mouth. Beneath the robe— ah!—the lovely swell where the necklace lay, and the body, the beautiful body . . .

He had loved her since childhood. He loved her now. How could he have forgotten?

She looked at him without speaking for a long moment. Then she said, "As you know, the Great Sun has gone on a journey to return the sacred fire that you stole." She paused, her deep gaze enveloping him. "Why did you steal it?"

Chomoc had not expected a direct assault, and momentarily he was at a loss. But only momentarily.

"For you and our child, of course. To assure your safety and that of the city. I knew the queen would not permit her fire to be dissipated by sending some elsewhere, so I stole it."

Again, that gaze. He would drown in those dark depths.

She leaned forward slightly and the necklace stirred. "I assume trading opportunities did not suffer because of your heroism."

He squirmed inwardly. Sarcasm was unlike her—or the woman she used to be. "As a matter of fact, trading was excellent. As always. Have you forgotten?"

"No. I remember your trading skills well." She smiled slightly. "I am sure the queen was impressed."

"Well, yes. But what she wanted was my music. And me."

"And you obliged, of course."

"She kidnapped me, you know. I was a prisoner."

Antelope did not reply. She leaned back and looked away. The murmuring voices of Skyfeather and the priest hung softly in the air. The fire whispered.

Antelope did not look at him. She said, "Do you think the queen will want Far Walker?"

"Possibly. He is somebody new." Inwardly, Chomoc exulted. This was an advantage he could use—her fear of losing Far Walker.

"How long will it take him to get there?"

"Depends on the weather, and the river, and how long they stop at villages along the way."

"How long did it take you?"

"I don't remember how long it took to get there after I was kidnapped." He thought the queen probably did not remember, either; they had been occupied. "When they brought me back they stopped only once, and it took eight days, paddling from dawn to dark." Actually, he was not certain about the number of days. He had been forced to paddle and had lost track of time. But Far Walker had been gone too long. The river was treacherous. . . .

Chomoc saw the flicker of fear in Antelope's eyes. After a moment, he said casually, "I will arrange a search party to find him and bring him home, if you wish."

"Won't that offend the queen?"

It would, indeed, but he was not about to say so. "I doubt it. But there must be an official government order. The caddí could give me an engraved conch-shell cup explaining my journey as an ambassador from the City of the Great Sun. They have to welcome ambassadors, you know, whether they like them or not."

"I doubt if the caddí would consider you as an ambassador." Antelope rose and walked about, thinking. After a moment she sat down again and looked at him searchingly.

"I had a vision, Chomoc. Kwani came to me." She twisted her hands; her lips trembled. "Our people are in danger. Grave danger. They must be warned."

"What danger?"

"Terrible beings from the Sunrise Sea. They will come to enslave and destroy us all." She leaned forward, and again the necklace stirred. "Our people, yours and mine, will suffer. While Far Walker is away, I wanted you to take me home and warn them so they would be prepared; then I would come back. But it is too long a journey." Again, she twisted her hands. "Maybe when Far Walker returns . . ."

Chomoc could hardly believe his ears. This was the opportunity he had been searching for. He said, "Our people will be warned. But first, Far Walker must be found and brought safely home. Then I will make the journey to Cicuye."

Antelope's dark eyes shone with sudden tears. "Thank you, Chomoc. I will speak with the caddí and ask him to make you an ambassador." For the first time, Antelope looked at him like the warm, loving woman he knew. Had always known.

Skyfeather approached timidly. "I want to be with you."

Antelope held out her arms. "Come. Your birth father will play for you now."

Chomoc looked into the blue eyes, Kwani's blue eyes, and he wanted to take his daughter in his arms and tell her how lovely she was and how sorry he was that he had abandoned her. Instead, he lifted his flute and began to play a song from his childhood, the "Roadrunner Song."

It was a happy melody. Antelope smiled and began to sing.

> Roadrunner with the bushy head
> Is always crying, "Poi! Poi!"
> As he runs around the house.
> "Poi! Poi!" around the house.

Soon Skyfeather was skipping about, just as they had when they were her age.

The priest objected. "This is a holy place. Be respectful!"

Chomoc said, "It is not disrespectful to be happy." But he changed the melody to another, one his father had taught him.

> *Does one live forever on earth?*
> *Not forever on earth, only a short while here.*
> *My melodies shall not die nor my songs perish.*
> *They spread. They scatter.*

The notes floated in the room, a plaintive echo from the past.
"Play more!" Skyfeather pleaded.

Another old song flowed from Chomoc's flute, one that only Kokopelli had played before.

> *Time is a great circle;*
> *There is no beginning, no end.*
> *All returns again and again*
> *Forever.*

Yes, my father, Chomoc thought. *All returns, and so shall I— following your footsteps to Tula. Instead of heading north where Long Man joins the Big Strong River, I shall head south to the sea and to your homeland—which will be my homeland now.*

Cicuye, Far Walker, and his mate, who is mine no more, must do without me. My journey will be safe; an ambassador has safe passage everywhere. I will be welcomed in Tula.

If only I did not have to leave Skyfeather.

▲ 44 ▼

Antelope breathed a sigh of relief. Chomoc would find Far Walker! And then he would return to Cicuye to warn their people. A load lifted from her heart. Perhaps Chomoc had changed to become more as he used to be.

"I thank you again, Chomoc," she said.

He looked down his nose. "Of course."

Antelope took Skyfeather's hand. "We shall leave now."

"No! I want my birth father to play some more."

Chomoc smiled. "I'll play while you go, and you can hear me all the way down to the plaza. I shall play especially for you." He turned to Antelope. "The sooner you obtain the engraved shell naming me as ambassador, the sooner I can find Far Walker and return to Cicuye."

"I shall see the caddí at once. Come, Skyfeather."

The flute's sweet notes followed them as they left. Chomoc's guards seemed in no hurry to return inside; they watched women and girls passing below and commented loudly on their various attributes.

Antelope's warrior guards waited with the litter. A small crowd had gathered; some seemed to be arguing with the warriors or the litter bearers.

As Antelope and Skyfeather approached, a man shouted, "There they are!"

"Witch!" a woman yelled.

The warriors hurried Antelope and Skyfeather into the litter, ordered it to proceed, and marched beside it, bows in hand. More people gathered, surrounding the guards and the litter.

There was a low growl as people followed. Antelope looked down into a blur of hostile, foreign faces. Her heart jerked, and she gasped in alarm.

"Stand back!" the guards shouted. "The mate of the Great Sun passes!"

"Witch!"

Antelope held Skyfeather close, her heart thumping. She and Skyfeather were bounced up and down on the litter as the bearers struggled through the crowd. Antelope pressed her necklace to her. "Help us!" she whispered.

On and on they went, too slowly, as people pressed closer. Antelope's heart pounded. She and Skyfeather had done nothing to deserve this! Anger blended with fear.

"Witch! Witch!" the cry rose.

Antelope clutched Skyfeather's hand. She felt the small body tense with fear. The faces following them—faces of people she thought she knew—were masks with murderous eyes and open, shouting mouths.

"Stand back!" the guards yelled again. They fitted arrows into their bows, and the crowd backed sullenly away.

As they passed a dwelling, a boy on the roof yelled, "Witch!" and threw a stone. It hit Skyfeather; she cried out and held her forehead. Blood trickled through her fingers.

Instantly, arrows flew and the boy tumbled from the roof with an arrow in his arm and another in his shoulder.

The crowd muttered angrily, but stayed back.

"Hurry!" the guards hissed to the bearers.

Antelope looked at her small daughter, who sat whimpering, trembling, holding both bloody hands to her forehead. Gently, Antelope removed the hands to reveal a gash over Skyfeather's right eye.

"It hurts, Mother."

Antelope held Skyfeather in her arms, trying to comfort her. But anger, cold furious anger, boiled up. What kind of monsters were these to attack a child—the daughter of She Who Remembers and the Great Sun? Glaring in furious scorn at the people who backed away from the warriors' arrows, she continued on to the dwelling mound, comforting Skyfeather as best she could.

The guards on each step murmured with concern as Antelope carried Skyfeather past them to the terrace where Chipmunk waited, wringing her hands.

"What happened?" she cried. "Is she hurt badly?"

Antelope did not answer but carried Skyfeather inside and laid her on the bed. Gently she removed the trembling hands caked with blood. The gash oozed fresh red.

Skyfeather began to cry at last. All this time she had whimpered only. Now she sobbed. Finally, she cried, "Why did he do that?"

"I don't think he meant to," Antelope lied. "I think he just wanted us to go away."

"But why?"

"People are upset because there is no Great Sun here to lead them, and so they blame somebody for their troubles." She turned to Chipmunk. "Tell the guards to summon Peg Foot and the caddí. *Now!*"

At Antelope's tone, Chipmunk scurried outside.

Suddenly, Skyfeather sat up. She stopped crying and stared fixedly at her mother, blue eyes solemn. "I know now why he did that."

Antelope dipped a clean cloth into a bowl of water. Anger still shook her but she kept her voice calm. "You do?" She prepared to wipe the blood away.

"Yes. He is afraid of me. Of us."

Antelope was taken aback. For a moment, she did not reply but gazed into Skyfeather's eyes—Kwani's eyes. "How do you know?"

"I just know."

Antelope wiped Skyfeather's face, being careful not to touch the gash. She said as casually as she could, "Something inside tells you? Is that it?"

"Yes. It doesn't *say* anything. It just tells me."

Antelope's heart swelled. This was her daughter, her body and spirit. "It is your ancestors speaking. The way a drum speaks. A drum does not say words, but it speaks."

As Skyfeather looked up at her with wonder and understanding, Antelope's anger faded. How fortunate she was to have this child!

Footsteps sounded outside, and Peg Foot hobbled in, carrying his medicine pouch. One look at Skyfeather and he stopped short, scowling.

"Who did this?"

"A boy," Antelope said. "He threw a rock."

"It hurts, Grandfather."

"Never mind, little one," he crooned. "I will make it well."

Antelope watched as Peg Foot rummaged in his medicine pouch and removed a strip of fine white buckskin, a small lidded bowl, the crushed leaves of a plant, and a small gourd rattle. He handed the rattle to Skyfeather.

"Shake this while I work. It will make bad spirits go away."

"All right." Skyfeather shook the rattle, intrigued with its whispery sound.

Chanting softly to the sound of the rattle, the old Healer removed the lid from the small bowl and scooped up ointment with his finger. "This will hurt a little bit, but it will help you to heal."

Skyfeather winced as the ointment was applied, but Peg Foot's soft chanting and the fun of shaking the rattle made it hurt less.

Dear Peg Foot, Antelope thought. How could such a man be of the same people who threatened her out there?

Again she longed for Far Walker, his strength and comforting presence. And, yes, his masterful lovemaking; her young body starved for him. If only . . .

She remembered the growling mob. She remembered the Bone Pickers and all the differences between her beliefs and his. If only he were Towa.

Outside, the guards shouted greetings; the caddí was coming. He strode inside, his jaguar robe flapping, and surveyed the scene with concern.

"I heard what happened. The boy will be punished."

"Arrows punished him already," Skyfeather said, still shaking the rattle. "He is sorry."

The caddí looked at Skyfeather without speaking. Antelope thought he probably did not know what to say. For a long moment he watched Peg Foot bandaging Skyfeather's head with the strip of white buckskin.

The caddí shook his head. "I hope Far Walker returns soon. Our city flounders like a water-soaked log adrift in the current."

"Any response from the drums or smoke signals?" Peg Foot took the rattle and replaced it with the bowl in his medicine pouch. "What about White Duck? Any word from him?"

"None. I don't understand it. Unless . . ."

"Unless what?" Antelope asked anxiously.

"Unless they were delayed in the storm."

"Chomoc has offered to find him," Antelope said. "But he will need protection. He must go as an ambassador."

"Hm-m-m." The caddí pondered. "I don't know if—" He paused. "He is accused of stealing the sacred fire. I don't know if he can become an ambassador."

Peg Foot said, "He has traveled the river and knows its peculiarities, its dangers. Send him, by all means."

"Yes," Antelope pleaded. "How soon can the carvers finish his shell?"

The caddí fingered his robe nervously. "I must discuss this with the council."

Antelope said, "Since Manimani is gone and Far Walker and the War Chief are not here, you, as governor, are responsible for the city's safety and well-being, are you not?"

"But the council—"

"Look at my daughter. Look at her! We encountered a mob out there. Far Walker is needed to bring order to this city, to save it. People are leaving, and I don't blame them."

"That is true," Peg Foot said. "We must face the truth. Our city is falling apart. Meet with the council if you must, but get the shell carved meanwhile. We must know what has happened to Far Walker. We must know, and *soon.*"

The caddí rose, gathering his jaguar robe about him. He said stiffly, "I shall consult with the council." He bowed and departed.

Antelope fumed. "Why doesn't he just take charge?"

"He is afraid to," Skyfeather said.

Antelope and Peg Foot looked at her as she sat up on her bed in her bloodstained robe, her forehead concealed by the buckskin bandage, her eyes solemn beneath it.

"I think Skyfeather is right," Peg Foot said.

Antelope did not speak. Her dark eyes looked into the eyes of her daughter, and it was as if she could see Kwani and the Ancient Ones, all those who had gone before.

The storm had passed and clouds raced with the wind, but the *Michi-sipi,* Big Strong River, was still in flood; it took all of the paddlers' strength to force their way upstream. Far Walker gazed in disbelief at the muddy torrent writhing around bends, sometimes cutting across the narrow neck of one of its loops. In times past the river had swerved in its bed, leaving islands and small lakes where wild rice grew. Mallards, teal, wood ducks, and other waterfowl would swoop low for the rice. Today they circled, sounding alarms at the river's rampage.

In places, Far Walker could not see from bank to bank; Big Strong River was an inland sea in powerful motion.

As the canoes approached a forested bluff, there was a rumbling roar. Far Walker watched in stunned incredulity as half of the bluff slowly collapsed and slid, trees and all, into the ravenous river. Great oaks whirled dizzyingly around a swirling vortex that tried to suck them to the bottom. The canoes bucked and rocked wildly in an effort to avoid the blind power of a supernatural force, a monster lurking in the river's depths.

Far Walker wrapped his legs around his fire jar and hugged it to him, determined that Big Strong River and its water monster would not have it. Over the past five days, they had passed many towns and cities and would soon arrive at the great City of the North. The sacred fire was still safe.

Several times on the way Far Walker had heard drumbeats as word passed from village to village, and once he saw a relayed smoke signal saying he was needed at home. Fear nudged him. Were Antelope and Skyfeather in danger? But he could not abandon his mission; it was nearly completed. Soon he would present the sacred fire with rich gifts to the queen, save his city from retaliation, and hurry home. It would be much faster going downstream.

But worry nagged him.

A wooden island, a mass of floating timber and debris, sped toward them. Blue Hawk swerved his canoe toward the distant bank, and Far Walker's canoe followed. The canoes pitched wildly as the island lurched by, a huge mass.

As they neared the great city, Far Walker saw paths along the banks with people going to and fro, carrying packs. Traffic increased on the river to an astonishing degree. Never had he seen so many canoes, some as long as sixty moccasins! They were carved from enormous cypress logs and were engraved and painted; some had banners. One or two had what looked like very large banners fastened at top and bottom to an upright pole, so that when the wind blew, the banner billowed and propelled the canoe forward. Going downstream with such a banner, and with many paddlers, a canoe sped more swiftly than a running deer. Far Walker gawked as such a canoe raced by with twenty-five strong men on each side, chanting in unison to the splash, splash of their paddles and the quick beat of a deep-throated drum.

Blue Hawk motioned for Far Walker's canoe to come alongside. As it did so, Blue Hawk pointed a forefinger ahead. "The queen's city is near. Stay close to me and do what I do."

Far Walker and the War Chief agreed, grateful for the protection. The animosity of Blue Hawk's crew had lessened since they and Far Walker's crew shared mutual problems and discomforts, but Far Walker would be glad to bid them thanks and good-bye.

But who would guide them home?

▴ **45** ▾

The High Priest made his laborious way up the steps of the dwelling mound. He would not have come had Chipmunk not told him Antelope needed to talk with him. She was afraid to face a mob again while going to the temple.

Outrageous! he thought bitterly. The mate of the Great Sun accused of witchcraft, and her little daughter hit with a stone! How could this happen in his city? Evil spirits certainly abounded here, bringing the city to ruin. He must confer with the shaman about more purification.

Guards greeted the High Priest reverently at each step. When he reached the top, the two main guards escorted him inside. Peg Foot was with Antelope in the sleeping room, inspecting Skyfeather's wound.

"Welcome to this dwelling, honored one." Antelope smiled and gestured the High Priest to a bench.

"I greet you," Skyfeather said respectfully, not moving her head, which Peg Foot held in both hands as he inspected her wound.

"And I, also," Peg Foot added. "Have a look at my patient."

The High Priest acknowledged the greeting. He stood braced with his staff and looked down at the small girl, who sat up straight on the edge of her bed while the old Healer examined her. The High Priest stepped closer and inspected the wound. It was a shallow gash where a bruise from the thrown stone had already turned blue.

"I see the bleeding has stopped," he said. "Good."

"My grandfather is a Healer," Skyfeather said proudly. "He makes people well. Like my father."

"That is true," the High Priest replied. He looked into the blue eyes, and for a fleeting moment it seemed that someone else's eyes looked back. It was for only a moment, but it gave him pause.

While Peg Foot replaced the bandage, Antelope brought a finely woven basket of dried persimmons and plums, shelled walnuts, and roasted hickory nuts. Offering the basket to the High Priest, she said, "Please eat, and then I must talk with you, honored one."

The High Priest sat on the bench while he and Peg Foot nibbled from the basket. Antelope and Skyfeather sat side by side on the bed, a platform extending from the wall and covered with furs. They watched in silence as the men ate first according to tradition—which neither mother nor daughter seemed to appreciate in their restless fidgeting. But then they were Towa, who allowed women to eat with the men. A strange custom, the High Priest thought, relishing the tart and tasty plums.

He gazed in appreciation around the inner sleeping room. It was beautifully appointed with fine tapestries on the walls, and shelves and hooks for personal belongings. The Great Sun's ceremonial robes hung in brilliant display against the whitewashed clay walls, and headdresses hung beside them. The platform bed had carved legs on the outer edge, and was surrounded by a curtain of finely tanned deerskin painted with designs honoring the Spirit Being and elaborate ceremonial scenes.

The High Priest thought briefly of what took place behind that curtain, and felt the pain of haunting regret. It was not for an aged and crippled one such as he.

There were still nuts and some fruit left in the basket when the men were finished.

"May I eat now?" Skyfeather asked, bouncing impatiently.

"You may. I must talk with the High Priest."

Peg Foot said, "I leave you, little one. I shall return tomorrow."

"Good-bye, Grandfather." She held out her arms and Peg Foot hugged her tenderly. When he had gone, she settled with the basket; she loved walnuts and munched happily.

Antelope said, "You may remain here until the High Priest and I have finished speaking."

Skyfeather's mouth was full. She nodded.

Antelope and the High Priest went into the outer room. The altar was there with its ceremonial pipes and ritual objects, the carved benches, and shelves holding feathers, shells, and other treasures. Two upright beams reaching from floor to thatched roof held hooks from which hung bundles and baskets of paraphernalia from Far Walker's days as a Healer.

Once a Healer, always a Healer, the High Priest thought. That was why he was returning the stolen fire, to avoid confrontation and to heal his city. Where was he now?

As if reading his mind, Antelope said, "You know what the situation is since Far Walker has gone. I am afraid for Skyfeather, for myself, for the city . . ." Her voice trailed off. She looked at him, her great, dark eyes beseeching. "What shall we do, High Priest?"

For a time, he did not reply. It was silent but for the wind. It was a turbulent spring day and Windwoman rushed wildly about; he heard her whistling at the door. His inner eye saw her as she swept over the city toward the mountains beyond.

The mountains.

Antelope heard Windwoman's voice, and she wondered if the High Priest was listening. His luminous dark eyes gazed into the distance as though seeking something, someone. His twisted, stooped body hunched on the ornately carved stool seemed to be listening also.

She repeated, "What shall we do, honored one?"

From under shaggy brows his gaze enveloped her, calm and deep.

"I shall go on a vision quest. To the Holy Mountain. But first, all the people will be called to the plaza for an announcement. They must understand that you and Skyfeather are Chosen Ones of the gods. To accuse you of witchcraft, or to harm either of you, will only bring more disaster."

Antelope looked into the place behind his eyes where his spirit dwelt, and a burden lifted from her heart. This holy man would save them. But what about Far Walker?

His penetrating gaze, wise and serene, searched her face. He said, "You are concerned for Far Walker."

"Yes."

"Of course. On my vision quest I shall learn how he is and decide what to do until he returns."

Tears stung Antelope's eyes. "Thank you, High Priest."

At dusk, before evening fires were lit, the Crier passed through the city, preceded by a boy beating a pottery drum. The drum's staccato voice proclaimed an important announcement.

"Hear, all people!" the Crier called. "Tonight, before moonrise, everyone will assemble in the plaza at the command of the High Priest. It is a matter of utmost importance. Only those in the women's hut and those who are sick or unable to stand will be excused. Warriors will seek out and punish those who disobey the command of the High Priest. Hear, all people!"

When the time had come, people thronged the big plaza, waiting for the High Priest. Antelope could see them from the mound's terrace, talking, gesticulating in torchlight. She beckoned Chipmunk, who sat with Skyfeather, swinging her legs over the edge of the terrace, watching.

Chipmunk came reluctantly; she was engrossed.

"Go down there and listen, then come and tell me all about it afterward. Remember everything."

Chipmunk beamed. "Indeed I will!"

"I wish I could go," Skyfeather said wistfully.

Antelope put her arm around her daughter's small shoulders. "We have a good view up here and Chipmunk will tell us everything. You will keep me company."

Chipmunk was already gone, running down the steps.

"Look!" Skyfeather pointed. "There he comes!"

It was a small procession led by two slaves bearing torches, followed by six flutists, two drummers, and six dancers with a variety of rattles. Behind them came the High Priest on a litter, followed by the shaman and the caddí marching in time to the flutes, drums, and rattles. Guards followed in step with the drum's beat, accompanied by slaves carrying more torches high overhead.

Antelope was impressed. She knew the High Priest was influential, but she had not realized how much. Hope sprouted
tendrils in her heart. All would be well.

She watched avidly as the procession approached a platform
erected on the plaza. As six flutes sang out and drums chanted,
the bearers lifted the litter so that the High Priest could step
easily to the top of the platform. He stood in torchlight, a twisted
figure, strangely commanding. The dancers circled the platform,
chanting, shaking the rattles with their mystical, compelling
sound. Around and around they went to the rhythm of the drums
and shrill cry of the flutes. The High Priest stood immobile, looking over the heads of the people as if to a distant source of power.

Antelope felt a small thrill of—what? Recognition? She, too,
sought the source. She touched the necklace at her breast, the
symbol of where her power lay—her timeless bond to Kwani and
the Ancient Ones, all who had gone before.

"I greet you," she whispered.

Still the dancers circled the platform. The shaman and the
caddí stood at the base with a torch bearer on either side. Smoke
from the torches rose and drifted; Antelope could smell the pungent odor.

The crowd grew in numbers and filled the plaza. At last, the
High Priest gestured. The music ceased and the dancers stopped.
All was still.

Again, the High Priest gestured. The shaman handed him a
ceremonial pipe carved in the figure of a seated warrior. The
High Priest took the pipe and held it up to the Four Sacred Directions, chanting meanwhile. Then he returned the pipe to the
shaman, faced the crowd, and began to speak.

People stood in silence, listening. Antelope could hear his
rich, deep voice, but distance blurred the words. She strained to
know what he was saying, but only occasionally could she understand a word.

She turned to Skyfeather. "Can you hear what he is saying?"

She shook her head. "No. But I think he is talking about us."

"I am afraid you are right."

A murmur rose from the crowd. People looked up at them
standing on the terrace, silhouetted against the starlit sky. Antelope felt exposed and drew back. The murmur grew louder.

Now the shaman climbed the platform to stand beside the
High Priest. He, too, offered the pipe to the Four Sacred Direc-

tions. Then he began to speak, lifting and lowering the pipe at arm's length, turning this way and that. Again, a murmur rose like Windwoman among the trees, and people stared up at the dim figures on the terrace.

Antelope clenched her hands nervously. What was he saying?

The High Priest gestured, and the caddí climbed the platform to stand beside him; he raised an arm for silence. When at last the murmurs subsided, the caddí spoke, followed once again by the High Priest.

Antelope looked down at the three men on the distant platform and at the throng of people listening intently. Moonwoman rose in full glory, pouring golden light upon the mound and the two figures there, and upon the world below. As if it were a signal, the people looked up at Antelope and Skyfeather.

"Hou!" a deep voice cried. Slowly, powerfully, like a river in flood, howls of homage grew until the plaza resounded with "Hou! Hou! Hou!"

Antelope was shaken. Three howls were for the Great Sun only. She turned to look behind her to see if Far Walker was there. No one.

Were they acknowledging her as the Great Sun? That she could not believe; it was impossible. Only Far Walker was the Great Sun, brother of the Spirit Being. If they expected her to presume to try to take his place while he was gone, they were much mistaken. That she absolutely could not, would not do. A sacrilege! And too terrible a responsibility. What she really wanted was to go home to her own people.

Again, the drums and flutes and rattles sounded. The High Priest returned to his litter, the crowd parted, and the procession proceeded across the plaza toward Antelope's dwelling mound.

She saw them coming, gasped, snatched Skyfeather's hand, and dragged her, protesting, inside. She searched frantically for a place to hide. There was none.

Running steps sounded outside, and Chipmunk burst through the doorway, her face flushed with excitement.

"They are coming for you!" she cried, her eyes wide. "They will take you to the temple to be consecrated. . . ." She paused for breath. "Did you hear what the High Priest said? And the shaman and the caddí?"

"No, of course not. Tell me."

"The High Priest said you and Skyfeather are Chosen Ones of the gods, and harming you or accusing you of witchcraft will bring more disaster upon the city. Oh, he was wonderful! And then the shaman and the caddí talked about sending White Duck and Patu to find Far Walker—"

"I knew Patu had gone. We miss him."

"Yes. Patu went to help White Duck. And the caddí is sending Chomoc as an ambassador to follow them."

Chipmunk rushed on. "And then the High Priest—oh, listen to this!—he said that the Spirit Being demands that you, as Chosen One of the gods and as mate of the Great Sun, that you take Far Walker's place until he returns. So they are coming to take you to the temple to be consecrated. . . ." Again, she paused for breath, her eyes aglow. "Isn't it wonderful?"

Skyfeather bounced up and down. "I want to come, too!"

"No. You must stay here with Chipmunk and the guards." She clasped and unclasped her hands. "I do not want to—"

There were greetings outside, footsteps, and the caddí strode in, then bowed low.

"Hou! Hou! Hou!"

Antelope stood straight and looked at him with what she hoped was a frigid gaze.

I am trapped.

Fear nudged her; she swallowed. "You were not invited here."

"I come at the request of the High Priest." He tugged at his robe nervously. "He wants to take you to the temple—"

"I refuse. I am not willing to assume the Great Sun's place. That is your responsibility, caddí."

"But—"

"Tell the High Priest I refuse to go." She gestured dismissal.

The caddí's mouth opened and shut; no one had ever refused the High Priest anything, and certainly not the highest honor he could bestow. The caddí gazed about the room as if searching for a solution to this extraordinary problem.

"You may go now," Antelope said, hoping her voice was not as shaky as she felt.

The caddí bowed out in a state of shock. Antelope breathed a sigh of relief, but Skyfeather was not happy. She pouted.

"My birth father might be at the temple. I wanted to hear him play."

"Another time."

Antelope collapsed on a bench. Had she insulted the High Priest, that good and holy man? She did not intend to. It was just that she could not, positively could not take Far Walker's place, not even for a short while. A thought tiptoed into her mind. *What if he never returns?*

Skyfeather tugged at Antelope's arm. "He is coming."

"Who?"

"The High Priest. I hear the guards."

Oh, no. How can I face him?

She gathered her inner forces and rose. "Chipmunk, prepare a basket of fruits for the High Priest." She took Skyfeather's hand and together they faced the doorway.

He entered slowly, leaning upon his staff. He seemed even more twisted and bent than usual. His head, thrust forward from between hunched shoulders, rose to look at her. Antelope felt the penetrating power of his gaze.

"I greet you, High Priest."

She gestured him to a carved bench, but he remained standing, his luminous eyes piercing her own.

"Why did you not come as I requested?"

His voice was not accusing. Rather, he asked merely because he wanted to know.

"Because I cannot take the Great Sun's place, holy one."

"This you cannot know. Not until you seek answers." He hobbled to the bench and sat down with the help of his staff. "I believe you may have powers of which you are unaware."

"I have the powers of She Who Remembers—"

"Yes. Perhaps you will learn more from your predecessors."

Chipmunk brought a basket of fruits and offered it. He refused graciously. "I must fast for three days; then I shall go to the Holy Mountain to find answers there." He rose painfully. "Come with me now to the temple to communicate with Red Man. Your people are waiting, mate of the Great Sun."

"High Priest, I am Towa. I do not believe in Red Man as you do. I believe in the Creator. Must I pretend to believe what I do not?"

He smiled. "The Creator has many names. You will be welcomed regardless of the name you know." A warm, kindly gaze enveloped her like a comforting balm. "Come, and let us commune with our All-powerful One, by whatever name you choose.

We shall purify our kias and seek wisdom."

It was a reasonable request, and she needed wisdom. Maybe she would find solace there. "Very well. I shall come, but only to commune with my Creator."

Skyfeather said, "Will my birth father be there?"

"No, little one."

"Where is he?"

"With one of the ambassadors. To learn how."

"Oh."

Antelope bent to hug her daughter. "I shall return after you are asleep. Dream happy dreams."

She followed the High Priest through the extended doorway, to the torchlit terrace where his litter awaited. Hers was already waiting below. The High Priest sat on his litter and was carried down the steps. She followed to howls of homage, with an undercurrent of something more.

She reclined on the soft furs of her litter and was carried swiftly away to the music of flutes, the throb of drums, and the voices of rattles—followed by a crowd that was strangely silent.

She pressed her necklace close.

▲ 46 ▼

As the two canoes grew closer to the City of the North, Far Walker was impressed with the rich farmlands spreading inland on either side where the soil was tilled with sharp-edged hoes of stone, shell, and wood. Obviously, Big Strong River gave the loam excellent reproductive powers. Planting had begun about half a moon before; already young corn leaves appeared.

It was a cloudless spring morning. They had spent the previous night at a farming village and were on the river with the morning mist. Now the mist was gone and Far Walker could see the paths along the banks where many people trudged toward the city with loaded packs. More canoes than Far Walker had ever seen at once crowded the wide river; some blew conch shell horns or whistles, signaling one another.

Far ahead, beyond distant bluffs, a smoky haze hovered. The War Chief pointed.

"Smoke. A big city!"

"Yes." Far Walker hugged his fire jar where a thin wisp of smoke still curled. "Soon we shall return this." What a relief that would be! Then he and his War Chief and men could go home at last. Beautiful, beautiful home.

Ahead, Blue Hawk's canoe picked up speed and the paddlers began to chant to the beat of a drum. New banners had been raised and the canoe was polished and gleaming. It cut swiftly through the water, leaving a spreading wake. Horns and whistles from other canoes greeted Blue Hawk, who responded with a blast from his own shell horn.

Far Walker's paddlers had to strain to keep up. Dwellings began to appear, square and rectangular, with thatched roofs but no extended doorways. More and more came into view, and here and there a low, flat-topped mound, usually with a structure on top. And everywhere, throngs of busy people who paid little attention to activity on the river, except for naked children who waved and shouted and splashed on the shore, playing with their dogs and with each other.

As the canoes passed a small girl, Far Walker noticed how she modestly crossed her hands over her little woman part until they had gone. He remembered his own little girl at home and missed her.

He sat in the center of the canoe with the fire jar between his knees. The War Chief sat in front, sometimes facing the paddlers to give orders, sometimes facing ahead as he did now. Far Walker admired the chief's broad back with its ornate tattoos, and the muscular arms and shoulders, also tattooed. The War Chief was a strong man for one so elderly—forty-two winters. The hair in two buns on top of his head and hanging in back was still shiny black and ornamented, as usual, with bright feathers and strings of animal teeth.

A handsome man, Far Walker thought. The queen should be impressed.

As if sensing his gaze, the War Chief turned to look at Far Walker, and gestured to where a turn from the main river loomed ahead. "I think we will arrive soon." His eyes with their falcon markings sparked with anticipation. "It must be a huge city. Look at all the houses! I counted twelve mounds already, and we are not yet there." The beaded forelock swung against his nose with a flourish as he gestured to his men. "Stay with the beat and there will be feasting and women tonight!"

"Yes!" they shouted and paddled even harder as they entered Big Strong River's tributary.

Here the river's flow was more gentle, making the journey upstream quicker. They rounded a large bluff and the paddlers paused involuntarily to stare. Far Walker gazed with amazement at what appeared ahead. Wide paths through grass and farmland led from the river past many dwellings and small, flat-topped mounds to a high stockade of stout logs. It encircled a distant mound complex so vast that he could not see how far the wall went. What lay behind the wall was not visible from the river—except for temples on the highest mounds and a soaring temple on what had to be the largest mound ever built. Banners waved from its distant top, which gleamed in spring sunlight.

Far Walker's heart thumped. What a city this was!

Blue Hawk's canoe headed for the shore. "Follow me!" he called.

When the canoes were beached, Blue Hawk waved a muscular arm. "I shall escort you to our queen. Rocks-in-the-River and my paddlers will remain with the canoes."

Far Walker agreed. He had donned his finest ceremonial garments, his headdress of white swan feathers, his shell gorget engraved with the Great Sun's insignia, and his finest jewelry. The queen would know that the Great Sun was a personage to be reckoned with.

The War Chief gestured, and gifts for the queen were assembled: eight fine buffalo robes; four long necklaces of shell and quartz; six copper hairpins and ornaments; four bracelets of polished stone, copper, and shell; eight copper earspools; a buckskin pouch of medicinal herbs; a crystal long as a man's forefinger with the holding end wrapped in fine deerskin and tied with colored thread; six bois d'arc bows; a fine ceremonial pipe carved like a duck; two beautiful conch-shell cups elaborately engraved; and a glorious feather mantle trimmed with lace that had taken much skill and many moons to create.

All of Far Walker's paddlers would be needed to carry the queen's gifts now being arranged in pack baskets.

A crowd had gathered to watch, murmuring in astonished admiration. They were a handsome people, Far Walker thought, although the women's tattoos were strange—a black line from the forehead down to the tip of the nose. The women wore deerskin or rough cotton garments fastened at the waist with fringed belts of bright colors, and the men wore brief woven breechclouts and much elaborate jewelry. Children wore nothing but a necklace or two. All were barefoot.

When the paddlers produced Far Walker's litter covered

with rich furs, and with beads and feathers dangling around the edges, the people commented in a language Far Walker did not know. He sat regally upon the furs of bear, fox, and jaguar, and held the fire jar between his knees.

"I am ready," he said.

Blue Hawk, banner in hand, strode up a path, shouting, "Make way for the Great Sun of the south!" One man beat a drum and blew a whistle as he strode behind Blue Hawk.

People stood aside, gawking, as Far Walker approached, led by the War Chief with lance in hand, and a long line of men bearing gifts for Tima-cha, the queen.

It was late morning. Smoke from a thousand cooking fires smudged the vibrant blue of a cloudless sky and lent a welcome fragrance to city smells pungent with refuse. Everywhere was noise: the pounding of mallet upon wood or stone, the booming announcements of drums, the shriek of whistles, shouts of children, the yapping of dogs, the chatter of conversation in a foreign tongue, snatches of laughter and song, the bellowing proclamations of Criers—big city sounds blending into a single, commanding voice.

As the procession followed a wide path leading to the massive stockade, it passed a small lake. Far Walker knew that earth to build those mounds had to be dug and carried a basketload at a time to the site. His own city had similar mound-building depressions that filled with water eventually, but nothing on such a huge scale. How many winters, how many summers had it taken to dig that lake and build the massive mound looming ahead?

As they drew close to the stockade, Far Walker was impressed. Stout logs had been set upright in a deep trench and were plastered with clay mixed with grass. Where the plaster was worn away, Far Walker could see that the logs had been lashed together with heavy rope. It was a formidable wall, at least twelve moccasins high, made more awesome by guard towers set at regular intervals.

Warriors manned the towers, bows in hand. They shouted down at Blue Hawk, who shouted back, waving his banner. Far Walker sat erect, gazing straight ahead, ignoring the warriors and the gaping crowds. They would know that his was the City of the Great Sun, and the Great Sun was he, Far Walker.

After more shouted conversation, a warrior blew a long blast on a conch shell horn, and Blue Hawk led the way through the main gate's L-shaped vestibule, which would admit but one person at a time into the inner city complex. Passing single file through the narrow entrance, they nearly collided with an outgoing caravan of foreign traders carrying cakes of salt. Far Walker knew that salt, from salt springs not too distant, was one of the city's many exports; he hoped to take some home.

Once inside the inner city, Far Walker tried not to stare. Directly in front, obliterating the view behind it, was a large, square, flat-topped mound with a thatched building on the summit. Was it a temple? No smoke rose from it. To the left was a circular mound that rose to a point; he wondered what it might be for. Burials, perhaps. The path branched, leading to the left or the right of the square mound directly ahead. Blue Hawk led them to the right.

They passed clusters of square, thatched buildings where people milled about, and then they beheld, at last, the heart of the great City of the North in all its splendor.

An enormous plaza swept ahead, leading in the far distance to the largest mound Far Walker had ever seen—or dreamed of. It soared in majesty on four levels and was so wide that Far Walker could not estimate the distance from one end to the other.

A smaller, flat-topped mound stood in the center of the plaza. Clustered along the edges of the plaza were more flat-topped mounds of varying sizes, and Far Walker counted three more circular mounds with pointed tops. Imagine! he thought. Thatched dwellings with peaked roofs surrounded the plaza, crowded with traders and artisans.

Far Walker passed arrowhead makers, leather workers, potters, salt dealers, weavers, and others who bartered their wares for grizzly bear teeth, rainbow flint, chert, dyed porcupine quills, masks—more trade goods than Far Walker could see at a glance.

Men, women, children, dogs, thronged the place. The sounds, the odors, the pressure of crowds, were ignored as Far Walker gazed in awe at the enormous mound ahead. He guessed it was higher than ten times ten moccasins, and ten times that wide. Amazing!

To the left of the giant structure ahead was a tall, flat-topped

mound with three buildings upon it. Were they temples? Far
Walker wondered. Smoke rose from the center building. Perhaps
priests dwelt there.

Far Walker's men gazed in astonished awe at the great
mound. They spoke to one another in Caddoan.

"Look at those steps! Do you suppose we have to carry all
this to that big building up there on the top?"

"I wager my flint knife that is where the queen is."

"Of course. Look at all those guards on every terrace—"

"Fenced all the way around. To keep people out, don't you
know?"

"I can't believe how big it is!"

A ramp led up the sloping side of the mound to the first level
where a terrace stretched the entire width and length of the
mound. Where the ramp met the terrace, four armed warriors
stood guard between two tall poles where banners flapped in the
breeze. At the left, an elaborate structure stood on a little mound
of its own with steps leading up to it. Was it a dwelling? Far
Walker wondered. Perhaps the queen lived there.

As they approached the great mound, a warrior on the first
level blew a long blast on a conch shell horn. Immediately, a
swarm of warriors came running. The sides of the mound were
perpendicular in front and sharply sloping on the sides and the
back; the warriors blocked entrance to the steps leading to the
first level. More warriors appeared on the terraces of the higher
levels.

Blue Hawk did not pause in his approach. Holding his banner high, he strode purposefully ahead, shouting, "Make way!
The Great Sun of the south brings gifts for our queen."

Far Walker held his fire jar close. He had fed the fire that
morning and knew it still lived. As they drew near the mound,
people followed, gawking at the treasures being carried to Tima-
cha. Far Walker wanted to look at them but he gazed ahead, face
expressionless as dignity required.

When at last they reached the mound soaring above them,
a War Chief stepped forward from the group guarding the steps
and confronted Blue Hawk. The chief was a brawny fellow with
small, sharp eyes and a bushy crest with eagle feathers. There
was a heated conversation in their foreign tongue. The chief
strode to Far Walker.

"What is in the jar?" he demanded in sign language.

Far Walker continued to gaze straight ahead. "Tell him," he said to Blue Hawk.

"I did, but he refuses to believe it."

Far Walker's War Chief stepped forward. "Tell him again. The sacred fire is for the queen only. It will not be exposed to anyone else."

Abruptly, the chief's brawny arm swept up and his big hand touched the jar. Far Walker jerked the jar away angrily. His War Chief stepped between the litter and the foreign chief, whose small, black eyes sparked triumphantly.

"I learned what I wanted to know," he signed. "The jar is warm." He swaggered down the line of men bearing gifts. Far Walker fumed as the chief paused at each load, pretending to admire the contents while searching for hidden weapons.

Satisfied, he raised an arm, shouting to the guards who stood aside as Blue Hawk led the procession to the tall flight of log steps leading to the first terrace.

As they climbed to the first level, and then to the second and third, Far Walker could see far beyond the walls to the vast city spreading in all directions. Ruling such a domain required wisdom and fortitude; this queen would be one to reckon with.

At a distance to the west stood the city's famous Sun Circle. Far Walker had heard of it—a large circle of upright posts used by Sun Chiefs for many generations. Shadows cast by the posts during various times of the year indicated when planting and all other important events should take place. Far Walker thought of his High Priest's star wall—simple, elegant, and equally effective—and he was proud.

At last they reached the fourth level. Far Walker breathed in relief. Soon he would see Tima-cha, the queen.

Soon it would be over.

Tima-cha reclined upon her bathing mat; it lay on a raised platform strewn with sweet-smelling blossoms. Three handmaidens, each with a jar of sacred water, poured it over her in driblets, smoothing it with their hands while singing prayers of thanks to the water spirit. The water made tiny puddles on the flowers. Another handmaiden laid out the jewels Tima-cha had selected, and still others stood nearby, holding fine cotton cloths to dry the queen when she chose to step from the platform.

Sunlight shone through a high window on an altar where

bowls of corn pollen, ceremonial pipes, and other sacred objects lay. Nearby, a young man sat behind a draped deerskin curtain playing a reed flute. The notes rose and fell daintily.

Tima-cha tossed her head impatiently. Thief and braggart he might be, but Chomoc knew how to make love with his flute. It was he who had taught her that music could create a magical spell, delightfully sensual. This so-called musician was infantile.

She flipped a hand. "He bores me. Send him away."

An older handmaiden stepped to the curtain and spoke with curt authority. "You are dismissed. Go."

The young man darted away like a frightened turkey hen.

Tima-cha laughed and listened to the commotion approaching. One of her chiefs had sent word that the new Great Sun of the south was returning the stolen fire. She wondered if he was as arrogant an oaf as the previous Great Sun, who had sat her on the floor while he ate and expected her to part her legs at his whim.

She gestured to a slave, a thin young girl, who approached timidly.

"Go and look at the Great Sun and come and tell me what he looks like and how many bearers bring gifts."

She scurried away. After a time, she returned, her face flushed.

"Well?" Tima-cha said.

"There are ten bearers."

Tima-cha frowned impatiently. "What about the Great Sun?"

"He is . . . he is beautiful."

"What do you mean *beautiful*? Like a woman?"

"No, no. Like a god. Strong, powerful . . . something about him . . . I can't explain."

"Hm-m-m." Tima-cha pondered. Perhaps this might be interesting. A smile touched her lips, and she gestured the slave away.

Outside, a conch shell horn announced that visitors were entering her domain, a palatial dwelling atop the highest terrace. She heard them approaching to the sound of her War Chief's drum. They would be there momentarily.

She smiled again and stained her cheeks and lips with rosy petals.

* * *

Blue Hawk led the procession to the queen's entry. "You will walk humbly in the presence of our queen. The litter will wait for you here, and the gift bearers will wait here also for invitation to enter. You shall meet our queen face-to-face. That is her wish."

Far Walker had seen an older woman speaking to Blue Hawk at the door and had wondered what was said. Now he knew. Hardly a suitable welcome for a Great Sun, especially one bringing sacred fire and lavish gifts.

Holding the fire jar in one arm, he strode inside. The older woman waited for him there.

"Follow me," she said and led him through a great hall with a high beamed ceiling and walls intricately adorned with handsome weapons, feathered staffs, banners, headdresses, and luxuries too numerous to perceive at a glance. Slaves scurried about, disappearing as he approached.

"Where is Tima-cha?" Far Walker asked. He was annoyed. He expected to be met and welcomed, as she had been welcomed in his city.

The woman signed, "I do not understand your language."

He signed his question, and she pointed to a curtain hanging in the doorway ahead.

"Enter," she signed.

He, the Great Sun, should pull that curtain aside himself? Had this ruler no manners at all?

Forcefully, he jerked the curtain aside and strode in.

He stared. A shining wet, tawny-skinned apparition stepped from a blossom-strewn platform and stood looking at him, arms outstretched for her handmaidens to dry her magnificent body.

He was speechless. Besides, it was her privilege to speak first, so he watched in silence as she was patted here and there with fine cotton cloths. He noticed how the process deliberately accentuated certain parts of her body. She turned to have her back dried—and to display a staggering loveliness.

She spoke over her shoulder with a delicious accent.

"You may place the jar on the altar, Great Sun."

Far Walker was intrigued. This was an audacious ruler. He suspected she would be a force to reckon with in war. But this was an encounter of a different kind. He smiled, stepped to the altar, and set the jar down carefully. He stood watching Tima-cha with his arms crossed on his chest where the conch shell gorget gleamed.

Handmaidens brought a shimmering white garment to Tima-cha and draped it lovingly around her. It clung to each curve, moving as she moved. She spoke in her tongue to hand-maidens who hurried to bring two carved benches and place them beside a floor mat. Tima-cha sat on one bench and beck-oned to him to sit on the other.

As he drew near he smelled her fragrance.

"I welcome you," Tima-cha said, holding up one hand and then another as a handmaiden slid bracelets up her beautiful arms. "I thank you for returning our fire."

She spoke casually, as though it were of no importance. Re-membering what he had experienced to bring the fire to her, Far Walker was not pleased. He did not reply, and she gave him a look from under long lashes.

"I assume you had reasons for bringing it yourself?"

"Yes. You honored our city with your visit. I wished to repay the courtesy."

"Ah."

She stretched out one lovely leg for her feet to be adorned with jewels. The white robe fell from her tawny skin, inviting inspection of the graceful curve of her thigh.

"I bring gifts," Far Walker said. He was being seduced, and he knew it; he was a bird being enticed to a snare. "Shall the bearers enter now?"

She wiggled her pretty toes, making the jewels sparkle. "If you wish," she said casually and nodded to the older woman who stood by the door. The woman disappeared, and the bearers en-tered.

As each gift was brought before her, Tima-cha glanced at it, fingered it perhaps, then waved it aside for the next. Only when she saw a necklace of rare pink quartz and fine shell beads did she exclaim. She lifted it from its embossed copper enclosure and held it to the light.

"Very nice." She handed the necklace to Far Walker. "The Great Sun may put this on me." She turned to face him, her dark eyes aglow, and bent her head, waiting.

He slipped the necklace over her head, still damp and sweet-smelling from the bath. She reached to touch his hand on the necklace, pressing his hand against her soft breast. She glanced up at him, full lips parted invitingly.

In spite of himself, Far Walker felt an erection. He wondered if it showed and glanced down to see. It did.

Embarrassed, he beckoned the rest of the bearers to display the gifts. They filed by, and she glanced at each gift politely. She lingered at the feather mantle, fingering the lace. Then her glowing gaze returned to him, pulling him to her with irresistible command.

Far Walker made himself return her gaze with austere dignity.

Why is she doing this? For more than the pleasures of the body, that I know. She has plans.

What does she want of me, of my city?

He said, "I have come to return the sacred fire stolen by Chomoc. My people and I express our regrets and wish you and your people long life, much good fortune, and many blessings."

Tima-cha nodded casually, fingering her bracelets.

The jar could hold buffalo dung, Far Walker thought, remembering what he had endured to keep her fire alive. *I could have sent it by a slave, and I wish I had.*

He bowed politely. "I thank you for your gracious reception, and bid you farewell." He turned to go.

She smiled. "Of course. But first allow me to repay your generosity with some small refreshment."

She gestured, and slaves appeared with baskets and trays loaded with fruits and nuts, dried meats, and other delicacies. The slaves placed it all on the floor mat and backed away, bowing low.

The queen spoke softly to her handmaidens, all of whom departed, leaving Far Walker and Tima-cha alone.

"Sit and eat," Tima-cha said with a wave of a slender hand.

Far Walker was hungry and the food was inviting. "I thank you." He sat and helped himself to jerky and fresh berries. He ate with relish as Tima-cha watched.

She said, "I recall that it is your custom for men to eat first while women wait."

He nodded, mouth full.

"I also remember that it is your custom to push food at a guest with your foot. Like this."

A jeweled foot darted forward, hit a basket of plums and sent them rolling across the floor. She exclaimed in sweet distress and kneeled to gather them up. In so doing, it was necessary to lean close to the Great Sun and to reach across him to retrieve a plum. Accidentally, she touched his man part, then lingered there, caressing.

Against his will he rose to her touch. Her fragrance, her incredible beauty, her sensuality and expertise were overwhelming. He found himself drawing her close. He slipped the garment from her shoulders, exposing exquisite breasts. Hungrily, he laid her down, sucked at each delectable swell, and explored the silken realm of the rest of her.

Tima-cha purred, wrapping arms and legs around him.

Far Walker felt her fingering his spider tattoo—the water spider carrying a burning coal in her tusti bowl.

The Fire Bringer.

When the flame ignited in him was quenched at last, Far Walker was ashamed. Why had he allowed himself to be ensnared like a foolish bird or a rabbit? He propped himself up on an elbow and looked down at the one who had ensnared him.

"Now tell me what you want, Tima-cha."

She smiled through her lashes and trailed her fingers over his chest. "I weary of my mates. I choose you as my consort."

So that's it. I wonder why.

"I am honored, queen of the great City of the North. But I cannot accept." He pulled away.

She speared him with a gaze. "I choose you so that our hunting and trading areas may be united. Surely you do not assume that your physical attributes are all that qualify you as my consort." She laughed. "Surely even a Great Sun can visualize the advantages of such a union. Think of the power!"

"I think also of your enemies, Tima-cha. They are a burden I do not care to share. As for power, the City of the Great Sun is renowned for its spiritual power, as well you know. Rulers from distant realms choose to be buried in our sacred mound for that reason." He rose, gathering his robe around him. "As for wealth and military power, I think even a queen can admit that the City of the Great Sun is generously endowed. No, I cannot accept your offer."

She jerked upright, her face crimson. "Guards!" she shouted.

Immediately, warriors swarmed the room, staring at their queen naked on the floor and the Great Sun standing over her.

Far Walker glimpsed their faces and knew they thought he had assaulted their queen. He was about to call his own warriors when Tima-cha rose with imperial grace.

"Send this foreigner and his people out of my city! Now!" Realizing she had spoken Caddoan, she repeated her command in her own language, glancing at Far Walker with withering contempt.

He turned and strode to the door without a backward look, the guards marching beside him.

▲47▼

The moon hung low above the Temple of Eternal Fire, illuminating the crowd gathered quietly below. They knew the High Priest communed with Red Man and the Spirit Being, seeking approval for Antelope to become Great Sun until Far Walker returned.

Would the Spirit Being accept Antelope, a Towa?

Could their stricken city be saved?

They waited in restless groups for the High Priest's announcement.

Inside the temple a small fire, centered in crossed logs, glowed in the darkness. Fragrant smoke rose, wavering, and drifted out the smoke hole to rise into the Spirit Being's domain. It was silent but for the murmured prayers of the High Priest and a young assistant, and Red Man's occasional soft voice.

Antelope sat on the floor before the fire, gazing at the flames. The floor was cold, but Antelope did not feel the chill. Anxiety and resentment flooded her. She felt besieged by responsibilities the High Priest and his people sought to heap upon her, responsibilities she did not want and felt unqualified to assume. She probed her weakened kia, seeking communication with her Creator—he who had created the logs now burning, he whose flames they were.

"Heal me!" she prayed. "Grant me wisdom."

Red Man whispered. What was he saying? Would the Creator speak through a fire?

Antelope clasped her hands in supplication, listening with all her being to Red Man's voice. But there was only the quiet fire sound, sending up a spark to glow and die.

Antelope turned to the High Priest and saw his compassionate gaze.

"You seek your Creator," he said.

"Yes. But . . ." Her voice faltered.

"Allow me to help."

He began to sing a prayer in his low, rich voice. It was in an old language, one known only to those whose ancient blood flowed with the true and holy knowledge of generations of priests before them. His song filled the temple like incense.

Although Antelope could not understand the words, she felt their benediction. Her heart eased, and peace enveloped her. She closed her eyes, visualizing Kwani, and pressed the necklace to her lovingly. Their mother-daughter bond was eternal, defying death, time, and circumstance.

The High Priest's song ended and the young priest continued with soft prayers. Antelope visualized her mother, and the stories she had told of her mystical revelations in the House of the Sun. There Kwani had become She Who Remembers.

Time passed. How much, Antelope did not know. Wearily, she lay down and closed her eyes. She clasped the necklace and willed her kia to open and receive the Ancient Ones.

"Come to me, Mother," Antelope pleaded.

Red Man sighed; the High Priest's murmured prayers flowed over and around her, soothing, healing.

At last, it came—a vision! Or was it a dream? Antelope saw herself with Kwani in the Place of Remembering, a temple on a high mesa—the House of the Sun. Here Kwani had come home to die. The temple had no ceiling; all was open to Sunfather's holy eye, just as Kwani had described it long ago.

They knelt before a stone altar, and somehow Antelope knew that Kwani's mortal bones lay beneath that stone.

"Mother!" Antelope cried, rejoicing.

Kwani's blue eyes embraced Antelope, and she smiled—a radiant, loving smile. "You seek wisdom, my dear one?"

"Yes. Oh, yes." Antelope felt her heart would burst. "My mate, the Great Sun, is gone. . . ."

Antelope poured out her story while Kwani listened intently, her face suffused with understanding.

"I sympathize completely," Kwani said. "I waited long for Kokopelli."

"Did he return?"

"Yes. And so will Far Walker."

"What must I do until then?" Antelope cried. "I cannot become a Great Sun. Tell me what to do."

Kwani said, "You have powers of which you are unaware. Place your arms on the altar stone and press your cheek upon it. The stone will grant you wisdom. Heed it, my daughter. . . ."

Kwani's voice faded, and she was gone.

"Mother!" Antelope cried. "Don't go! Please!"

Faintly came her mother's voice, "Heed the altar stone. . . ."

In despair, Antelope stretched out both arms, palm down, upon the altar; it was waist high and smooth at the top, just as Kwani had described it years ago. Antelope pressed her cheek against the stone warmed by Sunfather. Would it bestow its wisdom?

For a long time she knelt there, waiting.

Antelope pressed hard against the altar. "Help me! Grant me wisdom, I pray."

Slowly, slowly, it came, rising from the stone's mysterious depths—a sense of *knowing*. Layers of consciousness dissolved one by one, until knowledge was exposed like a deep and shining pool.

"Time is like constellations that swing in a great circle in the sky's vast bowl. There is no beginning, no end; all returns again and again, forever."

It was as if the Ancient Ones spoke. Antelope felt a sense of serene power bestowed by her ancestors, a power that time would not diminish. All returns. . . .

Again, the voices spoke.

"You are She Who Remembers. To teach is your destiny. Yet you do not do so. You diminish us."

"I am not allowed to teach!" Antelope cried, and was ashamed.

"You are blessed with ancient powers. You are a Chosen One, protected. Yet you endanger your powers by allowing others to command you. Take your rightful place, daughter of Kwani. You are the Great Sun; no one commands you now."

"Ah!" Antelope whispered. "Yes!"

The voices of all who had been She Who Remembers blended in a great and beautiful chorus. Antelope's heart overflowed as they sang.

> *You are not alone; we are with you always. You are She Who Remembers wherever you may be. You are destined to teach as we did before you and as all will who come after you. You are blessed. . . .*

The voices faded and the vision vanished, but the sense of serene power remained.

Antelope opened her eyes. Had she dreamed? The room was dark but for Red Man's faint glow, but she felt suffused with Sunfather's light.

She would become the Great Sun until Far Walker returned. And she would become a Teacher once more.

Joy surged in her. She sat up and saw the High Priest watching her. His deep, luminous gaze probed her own.

He said, "You have reached a decision?"

"Yes. I shall take Far Walker's place until he returns. And I shall be She Who Remembers again. A Teacher."

He regarded her in silence, his face solemn. Then he smiled and it was as if Sunfather's glow shone within him. He rose. "I shall tell our people what they wait to hear."

Bracing himself on his staff, he hobbled out, still smiling.

Antelope heard his voice rising and falling in dramatic cadence, announcing that the Spirit Being accepted her as the temporary Great Sun. The excited reaction of the crowd was heartwarming. Soon the High Priest returned, beaming.

"Come and greet your subjects, Great Sun."

Four days later, the temple was filled with young girls, scrubbed and in their finest garments. The Crier had announced that the Great Sun herself would teach the women's secrets, and excitement ran high. Now they sat crowded together, Skyfeather among them, whispering and giggling, gazing at Antelope—the

Great Sun—with awe as she stood by the altar smiling down at them.

Their upturned faces, tender and young and eager, touched Antelope's heart. She fingered her necklace, took a deep breath, and began.

"This is the necklace of She Who Remembers. It belonged to my mother, and her mother, and to all who were She Who Remembers before her. We wear it because it helps us remember secrets only women know, and have known since the beginning. These are the secrets I shall tell you."

The girls wriggled in anticipation, glancing at one another with delight. Some whispered behind their hands. Skyfeather smiled smugly; she knew the story already. Some of it, anyway.

Antelope continued. "These are secrets, not to be told to any man or boy. They are for us only. Do not forget that."

"We won't forget!" the girls said eagerly.

"Very well. We shall start at the beginning, when people entered this, the fourth world."

Antelope paused. It had been long since she taught, and she had feared she might omit some of the story, but it poured out as if of its own accord. The girls gazed up at her raptly, drinking in every word as she told how Earthmother had taught women to survive and how to trade themselves and the food they gathered for meat, and protection, and a home with their own fire.

"Women developed a special kind of *knowing*, handed down from mother to daughter through the centuries," Antelope continued. "They *remembered* the wisdom of generations before them, even though they did not realize they were remembering."

"The great sky circle turned many times," Antelope said, gesturing. "Women forgot they knew how to remember. They had to be taught again."

Skyfeather squirmed restlessly; she wanted to tell the story herself, Antelope knew.

"Teachers were needed to tell young girls the things I am telling you, but there were none who could teach. Earthmother grieved. She said . . ."

Antelope paused and noticed Skyfeather was bursting with an effort not to interrupt.

"Skyfeather, tell us what Earthmother said."

"May I stand by you to tell?"

"You may."

Skyfeather squeezed her way to the front to stand beside her mother at the altar. She stood very straight and spoke in a clear, high voice.

"Earthmother said, 'I will make a teacher.' "

Sunlight pierced the hole facing the star wall. Its illumination reflected onto the altar and upon the small girl standing there telling how Earthmother created the first teacher from a corn stalk. Skyfeather spoke with proud authority, her blue eyes aglow. The girls listened breathlessly.

As Skyfeather stood beside her, it seemed to Antelope that an aura enveloped her daughter, a mantle bestowed by the Ancient Ones. She swallowed a lump in her throat.

Silently she spoke to Kwani. "Do you hear your granddaughter? Do you see her as she teaches?"

Skyfeather finished her story, and the girls clamored for more.

"This is the first lesson, the beginning only," Antelope said. "There will be more next time. You may go now."

The girls filed out quietly. Skyfeather watched them go. "I would like to have a friend," she said wistfully.

"You may invite whomever you wish to visit you."

Skyfeather beamed. "I may?"

"Yes."

"Oh! May I invite them now?"

"You may."

Skyfeather's smile was dazzling. "Thank you!" she called over her shoulder as she ran, almost dancing, after prospective new friends.

Antelope knelt for a moment beside Red Man. Her heart was full. She offered thanks to the Creator for granting her wisdom enough to take Far Walker's place. Now she had the authority to do what she wanted to do, whether or not it had been done before.

Remembering her joy at teaching again, and Skyfeather's happiness, Antelope waited for the High Priest to return. She would thank him and tell him about Skyfeather.

She wondered if Chomoc was still there or if he had already gone. Surely he would be pleased to know how Skyfeather had stood there teaching. One day Skyfeather would be the greatest She Who Remembers of all.

*   *   *

Chomoc had gone, and the two guards and four paddlers with him. It was midday, and their swift canoe skimmed the water toward the place where it joined Big Strong River. That was where the guards and paddlers planned to turn north toward the home of the queen whom Far Walker had gone to see. And where Chomoc was expected to go, seeking the Great Sun.

Chomoc sat in the center of the canoe, fingering his ambassador's shell. How beautiful it was! And how valuable. It would serve him well on his journey south to follow the footsteps of his father, Kokopelli. For a time, Chomoc had pondered how to persuade the guards and paddlers to discard their plans to go north after Far Walker and to turn south instead. Bribery might do it. . . .

He had few pangs of conscience about deserting Far Walker, who had taken Antelope from him. Remembering Antelope as she used to be, and as she was now . . . Was she the same person who had loved him under the cottonwood trees? Long ago . . . How beautiful she had been in the temple, how coldly beautiful, when she said she never wanted to see him again, then left and took Skyfeather with her.

Skyfeather. Like him she was. The way she held herself, the way she looked down her nose . . . She loved his flute. Those blue eyes, like Kwani's . . . they looked at him with love.

Chomoc swallowed and turned the shell in his hands. He cared nothing for Far Walker. To the contrary. But Antelope and Skyfeather loved Far Walker and needed him.

It would not be easy to betray their trust. But he was, after all, the son of Kokopelli.

· 48 ·

Three days had passed since Far Walker and his War Chief left the City of the North. It was early afternoon, cloudy and cool, with a breeze hinting of more rain. Far Walker, the War Chief, and their six paddlers sped with the current downstream, on the way home at last.

Far Walker thought briefly of his encounter with Tima-cha and was embarrassed. It had been like a sudden fever. Like the mating of animals.

It diminished him.

He pushed the memory from his mind, washing it clean with thoughts of home. How glad he would be to see Antelope, beautiful Antelope, and Skyfeather again! And Peg Foot and the High Priest and the caddí . . . Much city business awaited him.

Traffic on the river was heavy. The War Chief served as navigator in frequent conference with the paddlers. They followed other canoes familiar with Big Strong River's course. Sometimes they went from one side of the river to the other, skirting small islands or hidden obstructions. But the storm had changed the river's course in places, and now and then Far Walker saw canoes stranded on a sand bar or caught in underwater debris. There was loud discussion as men from other canoes helped to pull the stranded ones free.

When they reached the place where Big Strong River was joined by another large one from the east, the river grew stronger and more turbulent. Busy cities surrounded the area, bringing more water traffic. Horns shouted, whistles blew, men called to one another in various languages or signed. Every city or village had a different language, it seemed; signing was common.

Because of their unfamiliarity with the water course, Far Walker and his men beached their canoe each night at one of the many villages along the river. Far Walker preferred not to be exposed as the Great Sun riding in an ordinary canoe with only a War Chief and six paddlers; it was beneath the dignity of his office. He wanted only provisions, sleep, and an early start in the morning. Therefore, he was introduced merely as a traveler returning home.

The day passed quickly as they journeyed south, following other canoes whose paddlers knew the river's dangers. Now that he did not have to care for the fire jar, Far Walker enjoyed watching the paddlers manipulate the canoe, ever alert to hidden obstructions.

Another village appeared. It was almost twilight, so the War Chief ordered the paddlers to stop and make camp. As they approached, a crowd began to gather on the bank, including the usual noisy group of naked children and yapping dogs.

Far Walker watched the people watching him. "Do you think they are friendly?" he asked the War Chief.

"Curious, more than likely. I shall ask permission to land." He ordered the paddlers to pause as they drew near. Bracing himself in the rocking canoe, the War Chief stood and signed, "We are travelers on the way home. We request permission to spend this night in your village."

There was muttered discussion, glances at the War Chief and Far Walker, and more discussion. Finally, the crowd parted as a middle-aged man and a boy appeared.

Far Walker stared. He knew those two. Could it be?

The boy shouted, "I greet you! I am Patu!"

The man stopped midstride, gazing at Far Walker in shocked astonishment. Finally, he bowed in deference. "I am White Duck. Welcome to our village!" He spoke to young men in the crowd who waded into the water to help beach the canoe.

Far Walker was astonished. What were Patu and Manimani's slave doing here? How could it be that a slave gave orders—and was obeyed?

As Far Walker stepped to the bank, White Duck said apologetically, "I cannot greet you as usual, with hous, because I am the shaman here. It would not be proper."

The shaman? A slave? Far Walker said, "I wish to be known only as a traveler. Do not divulge my identity."

"But where is everyone? Where are your attendants?" White Duck asked, then blushed with awkward embarrassment when Far Walker did not reply to his presumptuous question.

"Please excuse me," White Duck said hastily. "Come to my dwelling, and I will tell you all that has happened to us."

Far Walker was impressed. White Duck carried authority; he was indeed a slave no longer. How had this come about?

Patu said proudly, "I am the shaman's assistant. The shaman taught me and I taught White Duck. We know spells."

They had been speaking Caddoan, which the villagers did not know.

Patu could not control his avid curiosity. "Why are you here? I could not believe what my eyes told me!"

People clustered close, listening, waiting for White Duck to speak in their own tongue.

"I was on state business," Far Walker said shortly. He signed to the crowd, "We are pleased to meet old friends. We look forward to making more friends here."

They smiled and signed, "We welcome you, travelers. Enter our village."

It was a modest village of earth lodges and a small plaza for games and ceremonies. A dignified elder awaited them.

White Duck said, "This is our chief, Raven Wing."

"You are welcome here," the chief signed.

Far Walker replied, "I and my men greet you and thank you."

Preliminaries over, children crowded around the War Chief with awe, gazing at the strings of animal teeth entwined in his hair. They admired his fine forelock with two large turquoise beads swinging against his nose and touched the battle-ax hanging at his side. Far Walker was ignored.

The chief spoke sternly and the children backed away reluctantly. Women gazed with interest and invitation at Far Walker, who pretended not to notice. Covertly, the paddlers looked the

women over, each man wondering which of them might warm
him that night.

"Come to my dwelling," White Duck said again, leading Far
Walker aside. "The chief's wives will take care of your men and
make them comfortable."

Far Walker followed White Duck to an earth lodge surrounded by a small garden. Patu followed, striding manfully. He
had grown since Far Walker saw him last.

A pretty woman met them at the door. She was small and
dainty, with a black line tattooed from her hairline down to the
tip of her nose. She smiled shyly.

"My mate," White Duck said proudly. "Her name is Rainbow."

"I greet you," Far Walker signed, hoping his surprise was
concealed. Manimani's slave with such a mate? Incredible.

The lodge was surprisingly comfortable. An altar with a shaman's paraphernalia stood against the back wall. Bunches of
twigs and leaves hung here and there, lending a pungent aroma.
Clothing hung from pegs; bowls and baskets surrounded the fire
pit in the center of the room where a pot simmered enticingly.

Rainbow gestured Far Walker to sit on a mat beside the fire.
He did so, followed by White Duck and Patu, who settled themselves in anticipation. Rainbow lifted the pot, using mat pot-
holders, and placed it before the seated men. With a flourish, she
reached into a basket and removed three carved wooden spoons.

"I made those," White Duck said proudly.

She gave each man a spoon and indicated they were to eat.

Far Walker, being a guest, dipped his spoon into the pot first;
then the others followed, taking turns. It was a porridge of squirrel meat flavored with juniper berries. Far Walker did not like it
much, but he was hungry and ate heartily. Rainbow sat aside
quietly, watching with satisfaction.

"When will you tell me what has happened?" Far Walker
asked.

"Now," White Duck said. He took one last mouthful, wiped
his mouth with the back of his hand, and belched in appreciation
of his mate's cooking.

"It was after Manimani died," White Duck began.

Far Walker was shocked. "Manimani is dead?"

"Yes. I thought you knew. She fell off your residential
mound."

"But that's impossible. She grew up on that mound and knew it well. The sides are sloping—"

"It had been raining and was slippery." White Duck paused uncomfortably. "Some say . . . some say she was pushed."

"By whom?"

White Duck squirmed, glancing at Patu. "They say it was Antelope. But of course that is not so."

Anxiety punched Far Walker in the stomach. Antelope could be endangered. "Tell me what happened."

"Manimani slipped," Patu said abruptly.

Again, White Duck and Patu glanced at each other, and said nothing more. Odd.

"Who is Great Sun now?"

"I don't know," White Duck replied uneasily. "They wanted a runner to try to find you, to tell you that you were needed at home. So I volunteered. And Patu came with me."

Far Walker guiltily remembered glimpsing a relayed smoke signal saying he was needed at home. But by then he had almost reached the City of the North and thought he would be returning soon. He should have left the fire with the War Chief and gone home.

Far Walker glanced around the lodge and at the pretty woman who sat aside quietly. "But you are here as a shaman."

"Yes." White Duck and Patu exchanged a secretive smile. "When we stopped here we learned that the chief had an enemy he wanted to dispose of. This is a small village and had no shaman. Patu had learned how to make a death spell, but because he was only a boy, we thought it would be better if Patu told me what to do and I became the shaman. So then I said I was a shaman, and we made the spell—"

"And the chief's enemy was killed by a wild boar in the forest seven days later," Patu said proudly. "So the chief asked White Duck to be their shaman. I am the assistant." He grinned. "I teach White Duck what your shaman taught me."

"And you forgot what my people sent you here to do," Far Walker said sternly. Secretly, he was amazed that White Duck and Patu were so resourceful.

"Well, no, I did not forget," White Duck said, twisting his fingers. "I came to find you, but there are places where no runner can get through—or so the people here told me. And the forest has snakes, big ones. I hate snakes. Besides, they relayed smoke signals and I knew you would see at least one. . . ." His voice trailed off and he twisted his fingers again.

"As a matter of fact, I did. But we were almost there, so I waited until I could return the queen's fire." He paused, gazing long at smoldering coals in the fire pit.

Are Antelope and Skyfeather safe?
Who is taking my place until I return?

Antelope sat with the elders in council. They had been in the temple for hours, and she had a headache. The caddí droned on about diminishing stores, problems with traders, and reports of ambassadors from distant places.

"The City of the North sends word," the caddí said, and Antelope snapped to attention. "Tima-cha, queen of the City of the North, acknowledges receipt of the stolen fire."

Far Walker had reached the city! Antelope thought, and breathed a prayer of thanks. He would be home soon.

The caddí continued. "However, the queen is not pleased with the gifts offered, and demands gifts more in keeping with the seriousness of the crime."

There were outraged comments from the council. The gifts they had sent with Far Walker were lavish indeed. Did the City of the North want war?

"As we know, the War Chief is with Far Walker. We can do nothing about this until he returns."

Heads nodded in agreement.

Antelope said, "We can ask the High Priest and the shaman to confer with Red Man, and seek Long Man's counsel."

"I agree," the shaman said. "We shall discuss the matter."

Antelope sighed. She did not feel well, she hated these long discussions about city problems, and she longed for Far Walker's return. He would find a way to send her and Skyfeather home. If he loved her enough.

Did she love him enough to stay?

She loved him. Dearly. And she loved being a Teacher. But Kwani's warning lingered in her heart. She must prepare her people for the coming of savage gods from the Sunrise Sea.

The Ancient Ones had warned her. Now she must warn her people. That was her sacred duty as She Who Remembers.

She shifted uncomfortably on her bench. She felt ill and had a sudden need to throw up. She rose.

"I must leave; I am sick."

She hurried outside and vomited on the terrace. Holding her stomach with both hands, she retched again. Slaves scurried to clean up. Wretchedly, Antelope signaled for her litter.

Peg Foot came to stand beside her. He put an arm around her. "Come home with me."

Antelope needed his calm presence, his comforting. She nodded.

Peg Foot commanded the slaves to hurry, and soon Antelope was in Peg Foot's familiar dwelling. He beckoned her to his bed and bent over her, murmuring reassuring words. He examined her eyes, poked a finger into her mouth, felt her pulse, looked at her fingernails, and pressed his head against her chest, listening to her heart.

Does it tell him I am afraid? Antelope wondered.

He poked gnarled fingers at her body, examined her breasts, kneaded her stomach, and laid his head against her abdomen.

He sat up solemnly.

"You have Far Walker already," he said, and his wrinkled old face beamed. "You are pregnant."

▲ **49** ▼

White Duck and Patu, with most of the village, gathered to bid Far Walker and his men farewell. Baskets of provisions—dried fruits, corn cakes, jerky—were tucked away in the canoe. There were lingering good-byes between the paddlers and the girls, especially the pretty ones, and Far Walker felt a pang of loneliness for Antelope.

But he would be with her soon.

The old chief drew Far Walker aside. "I must tell you," he said. "I had a warning dream last night. Something bad is going to happen. Danger awaits. Be cautious!"

"I shall, and thank you, honored one." Far Walker bowed and joined the War Chief and paddlers in the loaded canoe. He would not worry about the dream; everyone had bad dreams now and then. Sometimes ancestors got lonesome and wanted company; they hoped a relative would die and join them. Maybe they thought that a warning of disaster might bring it about.

But he could not totally forget the chief's words. There was something in the air this day that disturbed him. Was it his imagination or were birds acting strangely? And dogs were not as active as usual. They slunk about.

The Spirit Being was well on his path when Far Walker's

canoe pulled midstream. Traffic on the river was lighter, but the War Chief found canoes to follow, keeping a sharp lookout for dead trees floating in the current, trees lying on shoals, and wooden islands of floating timber and debris.

The men, refreshed after a night of tender attentions, began to chant in time with their paddling. Far Walker settled back, enjoying the ride on the swift current. His thoughts drifted to his city. Since Manimani was gone, the caddí would probably serve as Great Sun until he returned, so all should be well.

A painted canoe with banners sped by. A navigator crouched intently at the helm, scanning the river ahead, shouting instructions.

"Who is that?" Far Walker asked.

"A runner," one of the paddlers said. "They work in relays. Some go by land, some by water when the land is impassable. They carry messages for ambassadors. They are fast. Very fast." He paused briefly in his rowing and grinned. "My companion of last night told me."

The War Chief pointed to forested cliffs ahead that thrust high from the river, with gnarled trees, like a headdress, on top. "A runner would have a hard time on land here."

Far Walker agreed. The forest closed in on either side, dim and silent, thick with shadows. The river twisted and turned, passing small lakes where it had changed course over the years, cutting off loops. Beaver dams dotted the lakes, and otters darted among the reeds. Once he thought he glimpsed timber wolves, but it could have been a play of light among the trees.

A wind rose, and dark clouds billowed.

Far Walker inspected the sky. Was another storm brewing? His canoe was loaded with men and provisions and rode low in the water. Ahead, at a sharp bend in the river, a pile of debris was lodged between boulders, narrowing the channel.

"Careful here!" the War Chief shouted at the paddlers, who viewed the obstruction with alarm. No other canoes were visible to follow; the men had to navigate the channel by themselves.

The canoe sped forward, swept by the current grown swifter as the channel narrowed. Ahead, the boulders loomed, entangled with debris; dead trees thrust out scraggly arms. The men cleared the boulders and debris, and were almost past when the canoe hit a dead tree on the muddy bottom. The canoe spun sideways, rocking crazily. The paddlers strained with all their strength. At last, the canoe righted itself and sped ahead.

"Good work!" Far Walker called, thankful that the canoe had been well built. "You saved us."

They grunted acknowledgment, scanning the river. The channel had widened and the going was easier now. On either side the forest loomed, a secretive presence.

A few drops of rain fell.

The War Chief inspected the sky. "Maybe we should make camp before it gets dark. It may storm again."

Far Walker remembered the storm only too well. "I agree," he said.

The men searched for a safe place to beach their canoe in case the river flooded again. A hilly spot offered protection, and preparations were hastily made to spend the night. After a feeble fire and a quick meal, the men hunkered down in darkness to await dawn.

Rain fell for a while, then ceased.

Perhaps it is clearing, Far Walker thought, and was relieved. Nothing more should delay their journey home.

He drifted into restless sleep.

A thunderous roar awakened him. He was tossed into the air and flung down again as if by a giant hand. The earth heaved and shook in convulsion. Springing up, Far Walker confronted his terrified crew. Dimly, they saw the river boiling with foam and heard the screaming of wildfowl in the willows.

Far Walker tried to conceal a stab of fear. "Save the canoe!" he shouted.

The men tried to stand and were flung down.

"The canoe!" the War Chief yelled.

The men stared, momentarily stupefied, as the canoe slid toward the foaming river. As the earth paused in its paroxysm, the men managed to stand. Again, the earth shook and the men staggered down to where the canoe slid closer to the river. Before Far Walker and his men could reach it, another convulsion tossed the loaded craft into the water.

Three of the paddlers dived after it and disappeared instantly, as though captured by the water monster and dragged to the bottom to be devoured.

For a moment, the men stood gawking in disbelief. Far Walker felt as if he had been kicked in the groin. He stared unbelievingly at the river that writhed and foamed in grotesque savagery. His heart jerked crazily. The canoe and all its contents were gone. Three strong and good men were gone. He and the War Chief stood numbly; the three remaining paddlers moaned in fear and sorrow.

Again, Earthmother roared and heaved. A tree crashed down beside them, and they staggered and slipped on the muddy bank. Birds screamed, circling wildly. Far Walker lay facedown in the mud; its slimy embrace seemed to ooze inside him.

"Get away from the river!" he yelled.

As the men turned desperately toward camp, they saw that part of the hill had collapsed, leaving an open chasm between them and what was once their camp—now buried under earth and fallen trees.

The men groaned in despair.

Like an echo, Far Walker remembered the old chief's words, "Danger awaits."

Antelope woke to a strange sound, like distant thunder. Her bed began to shake as if it were alive and threatening. Alarmed, she jerked upright. Skyfeather often slept with her while Far Walker was away, but this night she was in her own small bed. She woke, and came running.

"Mother! Something is under my bed!"

Again, the fearsome shaking and the rumbling noise.

Antelope scooped up Skyfeather and tucked her in bed beside her. She tried to keep her voice calm. "Earthmother is giving birth. It's that time of year, you know."

"But . . . but she doesn't do this all the time."

"No. Only on special occasions."

The rumbling, the violent shaking, continued. Garments and objects hung on the wall swung back and forth.

"I don't like it!" Skyfeather wailed.

"Never mind. It will be over soon."

Antelope swallowed her terror. Never before had she experienced such a thing, but she had heard of it. Earthmother's spasms covered vast distances; sometimes they killed people.

Was Far Walker safe?

She hugged Skyfeather close.

*   *   *

The men huddled together, waiting for dawn. The earth shook, trees crashed, water birds screamed, and the river's roaring voice grew louder.

"The river is rising," Far Walker said. He kept his voice calm, but he felt that something inside him was about to break. Would their ordeal never end? What had roused Earthmother's terrible anger? What did it foretell?

The War Chief's voice shook. "We must find a safer place."

"To do what?" a paddler asked. "Our canoe is gone—" He retched miserably and was mortified.

Far Walker sympathized. He understood well the men's fear and shock and their reaction. He felt it, too.

"Let's go into the forest and find something to eat," another paddler said, putting on a brave front.

"Yes." The War Chief patted his ax. "I shall find us a meal."

"But how will we get home?"

"Make a raft, of course," Far Walker said. "It's downriver all the way back."

They looked at the raging river boiling with foam, and said no more.

Again and again Earthmother shook and groaned. The men stumbled, fell, rose, and stumbled again as they made their way deeper into the forest. Crumpled trees blocked passage; the men had to climb over or go around—only to encounter more fallen victims, torn roots protruding. It was swampy in places, and the men sloshed through muddy water, keeping a wary eye out for water moccasins. They panted with fear and exhaustion, ignoring their bleeding scratches and torn and muddy garments.

They reached a small lake, surprisingly peaceful and calm, reflecting bright sunlight. Earthmother had quieted for a time, and Far Walker wondered if this might be a good place to camp.

"What do you think of this spot?" he asked the others.

A paddler sighed in relief, wiping mud from his face. "The water looks good."

"At least it is calm," the War Chief said. "Let's stop here."

"And bathe," Far Walker said.

Not bothering to remove what was left of their garments, the men splashed into the water and wallowed like buffalo. Shouting and laughing, they scrubbed away the mud and sand and shale.

"I'm hungry," a paddler said.

The War Chief wrung water from his long hair. "We are all hungry. I will find us a meal."

Suddenly, Earthmother cried out. The ground heaved and swayed. Trees tottered.

The men staggered out of the water and scrambled frantically up the bank, their faces taut with terror.

With a sound like a thunder drum, gaps as wide as a canoe opened in the lake shore. The men gawked in paralyzed amazement as the lake ran dry. Water hissed and gurgled, sinking into muddy chasms as if swallowed by an underground demon. Then, with a rumbling growl, the chasms closed and spouted black shale higher than the treetops. Geysers jetted from the earth, spewing sand and water, drenching the men with wet sand and shale.

A stronger shock threw them to the ground. They lay there, gasping. A strangling sulfurous vapor filled the air. They coughed, tears streaming.

Was there no safe place? Far Walker pleaded with his brother, the Spirit Being. "Help us!"

Gradually, Earthmother quieted and her spasms ceased.

The men, still coughing, looked at one another. They were unrecognizable—strangers in disguise, wet bodies smeared black.

"Let's get away from here," Far Walker said. "We should be in sight of the river in case it calms enough for canoes to navigate. Maybe one will stop and pick us up."

All agreed that, hungry as they were, they were more anxious to leave. They made for the river, crawling through fallen timber, scrambling around fissures and sinkholes. They heard the river before they found it—a chaos of drowned forest and swirling water. However, the river seemed less turbulent than before. Staying close to the bank and dodging debris, the men washed again.

Far Walker saw their cuts and bruises. He saw, too, the discouragement and fear and grieving that wounded more deeply. He prayed to the Spirit Being, "Take these good men safely home."

The War Chief cut saplings for shelter, and logs were found for a raft. Night closed down. One of the paddlers found flint to start a fire. Others gathered kindling, and eventually a sputtering fire burned—but with nothing to cook.

Now and then, Earthmother trembled as if settling herself for sleep. Each movement struck secret terror into the heart of every man. Would there be another violent paroxysm? Would Earthmother rage again?

Far Walker swallowed dread, hoping it was concealed.

The night deepened and the forest came awake. There were rustlings, bird sounds, and a jaguar's hoarse cry. The men glanced at one another and inched closer to the flames.

It would be a long night, Far Walker knew. The men huddled in silence. Were they thinking of those who were gone? Were their lost companions in the water monster's lair?

Antelope lay quietly in her bed, being careful not to disturb the small girl cuddled beside her. Earthmother had quieted, but now and then she shifted a bit. Sounds rose from the city: terrified wails as Earthmother stirred again, reminding all of her potential powers. Drums and rattles shrieked defiance to those evil spirits that had angered Earthmother, and chants to the Spirit Being swelled with each diminishing tremor.

Antelope felt her bed shake gently and hoped it would not wake Skyfeather, who had been acting strangely all day—a natural reaction to Earthmother's convulsions, Antelope assumed. But Skyfeather seemed oddly moody and preoccupied. Antelope had found her sitting on the terrace gazing into space as though she listened to distant voices.

"What are you thinking?" Antelope had asked.

"About my father. He is not happy."

"How do you know?"

But Antelope understood. When she herself was a child she had seen her father killed by a buffalo; he was far away at the time. . . .

Skyfeather looked up at her mother and Antelope saw tears in her eyes. "He hurts, Mother. He hurts inside. He is sad." A tear rolled down. "Something bad happened to him. I am afraid. . . ."

Antelope swallowed. What could she say?

"We who are or will be She Who Remembers must be strong, Skyfeather. We cannot let ourselves be frightened. Far Walker is the Great Sun; he will be home soon. Come, now. Let's play the string game."

They had played for a while, pretending all was well. But tonight Skyfeather had abandoned her own small bed, which she prized, and crept into bed with Antelope, seeking solace in her mother's arms once more.

There was no moon. Stars glittered coldly, and night sounds in the forest continued their whisperings. Far Walker glanced at the War Chief and his men, huddled silently by the small fire, gazing into the flames. Were they wishing they did not have to confront the river, the savage river, again? Were they afraid, too?

It grew quiet but for the river's voice. Too quiet. The men glanced uneasily into the black darkness.

Golden eyes glowed.

Then more. Here, then there.

"Timber wolves!" the War Chief whispered, grasping his ax.

They are hungry too, Far Walker thought. *The turmoil of the shaking earth has violated them. They are desperate, like us.*

More eyes glowed.

"It's a pack," Far Walker said. "We are surrounded. We must do something. Make noise!"

They shouted, clapped hands, and whistled. One man picked a burning stick from the fire and flung it.

The wolves backed away but did not leave.

The paddler who had flung the burning stick grabbed another. "I'll get rid of them," he cried. Brandishing the stick he ran at one of the wolves, and flung the stick. It hit the animal squarely; it backed off. The man followed, yelling, "Go away!"

"Come back here!" the War Chief shouted at the man. "Come back!"

The burning stick lay where it had fallen. The paddler reached to pick it up.

"No!" Far Walker yelled.

There was a snarling growl, followed by agonized screams. The man's terrible cries seared the night, then diminished and faded as he was dragged away.

More snarls and growls followed, and snuffling sounds.

"They are eating him!" a paddler cried. "Stop them!"

"They are many and we are few," the War Chief said. "We must face that."

The man sobbed. "He was my friend!" He reached for the War Chief's ax. "I'll kill them!"

"No," the War Chief said. "They will kill you."

The man tried to wrestle the ax from the War Chief's strong

grasp, but could not. He collapsed with moaning cries.

Far Walker put an arm around him. "He tried to save us all. He will be safe and happy in the Afterworld." He pulled the shuddering body close, and the man leaned his head on Far Walker's shoulder, sobbing helplessly.

This is too much, Far Walker thought. *We must leave this place. Tomorrow we will build a raft and take our chances on the river.*

There were but four of them now: he, the War Chief, and the two remaining paddlers, one of whom cried like a child, mouth wide open, tears gushing.

The rest of us weep inside.

Morning brought swarms of stinging flies and mosquitoes. Miserably, the men bent close to the fire, hoping the smoke would discourage their tormentors. The river swirled by, carrying a dead otter, a bear cub, squirrels, rabbits, and masses of bushes and torn trees.

Overhead, vultures circled.

"I go to hunt," the War Chief said abruptly. Ax in hand, he strode into the forest.

Far Walker watched him go. Would he see vultures feasting on what the wolves left?

He shook his head to clear it and to brush away flies. Mosquitoes hummed and zoomed in to attack. He slapped them futilely. "Let's get that raft made."

The paddlers worked feverishly, glancing over their shoulders now and then.

They were afraid, Far Walker knew. How could he give them courage? They would all need courage in abundance if they were to return safely home.

I must seek wisdom from the Spirit Being.

He walked into the forest, opening his senses to the air, the sun, the breeze, and the devastated land. He stood gazing up at blue sky, drinking in the Spirit Being's glory.

A bird sang from a tattered tree, and Far Walker was amazed to see a little yellow butterfly zigzag by.

He did not see the snake.

Chomoc sat uneasily in the bouncing canoe, holding on to the seat. He had spent a frightening three days in a village attacked by Earthmother and was glad the river had calmed enough—barely enough—for him to leave the terrified village and be on his way again.

He squinted with displeasure at the backs of the two guards. He had stared at those sweaty backs before—all the way from the City of the North down to the City of the Great Sun—and he was heartily sick of them.

Now he was returning to the City of the North—as an ambassador, of all things—but with the same ugly guards. He sighed. True, he had reluctantly allowed his better nature to prevail. He had postponed his journey to Kokopelli's home so he might search for Far Walker, fulfilling his promise to Antelope and Skyfeather. Of course he would attend to political duties as well. Actually, he couldn't wait to see Tima-cha's face when he encountered her—with his head intact. As an ambassador, he must be received with honor. Ha!

He was glad Earthmother's convulsions were over. It was the first time he had experienced such a thing, and he hoped it would be the last. He looked about him unbelievingly; the damage was enormous, much greater than farther south. He wondered if Antelope and Skyfeather had felt it.

He fingered his flute in its deerskin pouch and thought to voice his pleasure that Earthmother had quieted. But the current was rough, bouncing him about, so he decided against it. He was glad for his fine ambassador's canoe and strong paddlers; the canoe was big enough to hold many trading goods. His flute and the carved ambassador's shell were the only valuables he had now. A temporary situation, of course.

It was a bright morning with a few puffy white clouds. It would have been pleasant but for the smell, a strange odor he had not experienced before. And dead creatures lay about or floated by. The forest loomed on either side with splintered and fallen trees scattered about like warriors after a battle.

Chomoc wondered about Far Walker. Remembering Tima-cha, Chomoc thought he could well be delayed. Or he could have been hurt or killed during Earthmother's frenzy; that was certainly possible.

As the canoe rounded a bend, Chomoc saw a deer drinking by a clump of reeds.

"I greet you," he said in silent communication.

The deer raised its head in acknowledgment but did not reply.

"Look!" one of the guards said, pointing.

A wisp of smoke rose on the other side of the river. Someone must be camped there, Chomoc thought. But no canoe was visible. Vultures circled overhead.

Chomoc watched the vultures. "I think we should investigate."

"Not in that swampy place," a guard said. "Bad spirits are there."

"Spirits don't have campfires. I shall investigate. The rest of you may remain with the canoe."

The guards grumbled, but now that their former prisoner was an ambassador—imagine!—they obeyed. They tied their canoe to a massive fallen tree.

"Come if I call you," Chomoc ordered, climbing the bank.

They nodded glumly.

As Chomoc headed for the camp, he paused. This was an isolated spot; he should be cautious. He would circle the area before closing in.

As he trod silently through the forest, he encountered fresh footprints. Someone had been here recently. Very carefully he followed, watching, listening intently.

He saw him! Far Walker! At first, Chomoc did not recognize the Great Sun. What was left of his royal garments was in tatters. His hair, devoid of ornamentation, was loose and matted, and he was covered with bruises and jagged scratches.

Chomoc was about to call out a greeting when he stopped abruptly. Far Walker stood by a fallen tree close to where a snake lay curled—a large water moccasin. Deadly. Its pattern of gray-on-gray markings made it nearly invisible against the tree and the forest floor.

If I call, Far Walker will move and the snake will strike.

Far Walker stared up at the sky. What was he gazing at? Chomoc looked, but saw nothing except a few little clouds. Very slowly and quietly, he approached.

The snake sensed his movement; Chomoc felt the snake's irritation. He spoke to him, mind to mind.

"We are friends. We will do you no harm."

The snake's head lifted. "Go away!"

Far Walker turned and saw Chomoc. He gazed in stunned astonishment.

"Don't move!" Chomoc shouted.

Too late. Far Walker had turned, and the snake prepared to strike.

"Stop!" Chomoc ordered the snake. A forked tongue flicked out, pausing, but Chomoc felt the moccasin gathering strength.

With a leap, Chomoc reached Far Walker and flung him aside. In a flash the snake's white mouth opened wide. Chomoc felt the fangs thrust deep into the back of his knee.

"Chomoc!" Far Walker cried. "Here, let me look."

He knelt to examine the puncture, and looked up. "It is in a bad place. A large vein." His voice choked. He grabbed a stick and turned to kill the snake, but it had disappeared.

"He would not listen," Chomoc said. He sat down on the log where the snake had rested. He knew he was going to die, but it did not seem real. He was Chomoc.

Far Walker sat beside him, clasping and unclasping his hands. "You saved my life, Chomoc. I have no medicine bundle. . . ." His voice choked again.

"You can do nothing."

"I can try." Far Walker knelt and cupped Chomoc's knee with both hands. With his entire being he beseeched the Spirit Being and all the gods to save one who had saved him.

Chomoc was moved, but he had seen men die from such a wound—a long, slow, painful death. "You can do nothing," he repeated.

Far Walker touched his forehead to Chomoc's knee, then looked up at him. "Why did you come? How did you find me?"

Chomoc felt the poison invading his veins. It was getting hard to breathe. "I promised Antelope and Skyfeather. . . ."

He fumbled with the pouches at his waist where the flute and the carved shell lay. He was shaking. "Here, remove these."

When the pouches were placed in his hands, Chomoc handed them to Far Walker. "The flute is for Skyfeather. Give the shell to Antelope."

"I shall. I promise. . . ."

Were those tears in Far Walker's eyes?

Chomoc braced himself on the log with both hands, and began to sing his death song, one he had created long ago for this moment.

His voice rose and fell as he rocked to and fro, singing for the last time.

▲50▼

It was dim inside the temple where a council meeting had been in session for some time. A young priest tended Red Man, whose quiet voice had been ignored during long—and sometimes heated—discussion.

The High Priest watched Antelope as she faced the council and listened to the report of the caddí. The High Priest shifted uncomfortably. Antelope's face was serene, but he saw her clenched hands and he sensed her tension. She had assumed the Great Sun's responsibilities well, but he knew it had not been easy.

The caddí continued. "As you know, this is Planting Moon, but more people are leaving." He paused to emphasize this incredible circumstance. "Our best shell carver and his family departed today." He fingered his jaguar robe nervously. "It is said that Earthmother is angry and shook to reject our efforts to make her give birth with the planting." He shook his head in disbelief.

"Why is she angry?" Antelope asked.

The shaman spoke. "Perhaps it is because the Great Sun— the true Great Sun—has deserted us."

Antelope's eyes sparked dark fire. "He has undertaken a dangerous journey, one no *true* Great Sun has braved before, to save our city. And us." She speared the shaman with a gaze. "I shall not allow you, nor anyone else, to speak thus of our Great Sun. When he returns he shall be informed of your words. He will be justified in having your head impaled on a stake and displayed in the plaza. Do you understand me?"

The shaman scowled. "I understand you well, as do all members of this council. I say only what some believe."

"Not this member." The High Priest rose with the help of his staff and stood beside Antelope. He faced the shaman with dignity. "Word has come that our Great Sun is on the way home. Have you forgotten?"

"Then why is he not here? It has been long—"

"I am told that the earthquake struck Big Strong River with terrible power. We should be praying for our Great Sun's safety. I shall do so—after you leave this temple."

"Thank you, High Priest," Antelope said. "I shall pray with you. Now the rest of you may go. All except you, shaman. You will stay."

The High Priest smiled inwardly. How regal she had become! He watched the council members file out silently, faces expressionless. He suspected they stung inside.

The shaman remained seated, staring down at his folded hands.

Antelope sat silently on the Great Sun's carved bench, staring at the shaman. He felt her cold gaze, the High Priest knew. Again, the High Priest smiled inwardly.

Finally, Antelope spoke. "Let us discuss the matter of the buffalo."

The shaman did not reply. One eyelid twitched.

Antelope said, "It is unfortunate, is it not, that we have lost our buffalo trade? And that our coffers have become so meager?"

Again, the shaman did not reply.

The High Priest said, "The Great Sun expects an answer, shaman."

The shaman glanced up at Antelope, hatred in his glance. "Of course it is unfortunate, as are all the bad things that have happened since we were honored with your arrival, Great Sun."

Antelope returned his gaze calmly. "You claimed to have called the buffalo, did you not?"

The shaman's face closed like a door slammed. He did not answer.

Antelope smiled. "Now that our city has suffered such financial loss, how noble it is of you to take the blame."

The High Priest glanced at Antelope with surprise. What was this all about?

The shaman squirmed. "I did what I thought was best for our people."

"Are you proud of the results?"

The shaman started to rise.

"Sit down!" the High Priest said sharply. "Answer the Great Sun's question. Are you proud?"

The shaman sat back down and wiped his face. "I grieve for our people."

"I see." Antelope regarded him for a long moment. "As I grieved for Skyfeather when you threatened me?"

The High Priest pointed his staff at the shaman. "You threatened her?" he growled softly. "Explain!"

Again, the shaman wiped his face, and did not reply.

Antelope smiled. "Tell him, shaman."

The High Priest listened incredulously as the shaman reluctantly related how he had forced Antelope to call the buffalo for him and threatened death to Skyfeather if Antelope told anyone, or if she failed. When he attempted to omit something, Antelope reminded him sharply.

"I wanted to help our people," he continued, clasping and unclasping his hands. "She was not one of us. . . ."

The High Priest jabbed his staff toward the door. "Leave us!" he demanded, his voice shaking with rage and contempt. "Depart this city! Go and never return."

The shaman rose, staring incredulously. "I am the shaman. I—"

"No longer," Antelope said. "You heard the High Priest. You are an outcast. Go."

The shaman shot Antelope a final burning glance. "I shall go and take many with me. This city is cursed—as it has been ever since you and Chomoc inflicted yourselves upon us." He stalked out, head high.

Later, Antelope lay exhausted on her bed. Council meetings wore her down. Outside, on the terrace, Skyfeather and a group of noisy girls played happily. At least that was something she had accomplished as Great Sun—given her daughter friends, and assumed her place as She Who Remembers, to teach again.

Far Walker, hurry home. Your city needs you.

I need you.

Antelope stirred uneasily. Of course it was not true that her coming—hers and Chomoc's—had harmed the city. Or was it?

The High Priest had confided that the city was, indeed, cursed. But it was because their sacred fire was polluted.

"I am trying to cleanse it," he had said, and a look of sadness lay deep in his eyes. "I am trying."

Antelope listened to the girls laughing and playing outside. Skyfeather would be She Who Remembers one day. Here, in this dying city?

Antelope rose abruptly and stood in thought.

I must take Skyfeather home.

But what of Far Walker? How could she bear to leave him?

Antelope pressed her necklace close, pleading for courage and wisdom. Like a whisper in her mind she heard Kwani's voice.

"Warn our people! It is your duty as She Who Remembers."

Antelope recalled her vision (or was it a dream?) of the terrible beings on huge, strange beasts; men who would kill and enslave. . . .

She closed her eyes, agonizing.

I shall do what I must. But how?

The canoe sped homeward. Far Walker watched the familiar landscape slide by. Once again they were on Long Man; soon Antelope would be in his arms. Far Walker had stopped at a village to obtain new garments and have his hair washed and arranged. He was not adorned as the Great Sun, but at least he would be presentable for Antelope and for his people.

He refused to look at the body wrapped in a blanket provided by one of the paddlers. It lay in the bottom of the canoe, motionless and silent—as Chomoc seldom had been. Far Walker tried to ignore it; it was a too-painful reminder of his own mortality. One day he, too, would be motionless and still. . . .

Beside him were the flute and the ambassador's shell; he would bestow them as Chomoc had requested. It still seemed incredible that Chomoc had saved his life at the cost of his own.

Far Walker gazed down at the wrapped figure. "I thank you, Chomoc," he whispered, and gestured a blessing.

*   *   *

The thunder drum boomed. It sounded like an announcement of an important arrival. Antelope ran out to the terrace to see. Could it be? Had Far Walker arrived?

Chipmunk and Skyfeather hurried over, surrounded by chattering girls.

"Is it Father?" Skyfeather asked excitedly.

Antelope felt her heart leap. "I don't know. Let's go and find out."

All of them—Antelope, Skyfeather, Chipmunk, and the girls—dashed down the steps between smiling guards and ran toward the river. A crowd had gathered, talking, laughing, shouting. Whistles blew, and again the drum boomed.

Antelope and Skyfeather made their way to the bank. The canoe was about to be beached; the paddlers manipulated it expertly. But the man standing—was that Far Walker in ordinary garments, and with bruises and scratches not yet healed?

"Father!" Skyfeather cried and waded into the water to meet him as he stepped from the canoe. He swept her into his arms.

Antelope swallowed. What terrible thing had happened to him? "Far Walker!" she cried, almost sobbing, and ran to meet him as he climbed the bank, Skyfeather in his arms.

He embraced them both, holding them close as laughing people surrounded them and slaves ran to get his litter.

Suddenly, a shout, then appalled silence.

Far Walker released Antelope and Skyfeather as the War Chief and the two guards carried a wrapped body to the shore. They laid it upon grass that was green with spring.

"Where shall we take Chomoc?" the War Chief asked.

"To the temple," Far Walker said.

Word passed through the crowd. "Chomoc. It is Chomoc."

Skyfeather went to kneel beside him. She reached out a small hand and placed it gently on his chest. She leaned over and whispered, "Your flute will always play for me, birth father."

In the darkness, Antelope and Far Walker lay with arms entwined, their passionate lovemaking having ebbed at last. Antelope had told him she was pregnant.

He was overjoyed. "A son!" he had cried, beaming.

"A daughter, maybe."

"If she is like you, I shall be a lucky man."

Now they spoke softly so as not to awaken Skyfeather. Far Walker had told her what happened, but it was too much to accept now, too much to believe. Chomoc . . .

Skyfeather stirred; beside her lay the flute. Antelope saw again how Far Walker had lifted Skyfeather to his lap and said, "I have a present for you."

She had squealed happily. "What is it?"

"A present from Chomoc."

"Let me see!" Skyfeather bounced with anticipation.

Far Walker reached for a bundle he had brought from the canoe. Unwrapping it, he removed a painted wooden flute, beautifully carved.

"Chomoc told me to give you this."

Skyfeather held it reverently with both hands. Then she ran a finger over the carving and touched the painted designs, her face solemn, her eyes aglow.

Antelope remembered Chomoc as a boy, playing his flute for the first time.

"Play it, Skyfeather."

Carefully, Skyfeather's fingers sought their places. She lifted the flute to her lips and blew. There was but a whisper of sound. She took a deep breath and blew again.

A sweet note trembled on the air.

Skyfeather smiled radiantly and looked at the flute, turning it over in her hands as though to find the music's source hidden somewhere within.

Now she slept, Chomoc's presence beside her.

Antelope touched Far Walker's cheek. How good it was to have him close once more! He had been silent for a while. "What are you thinking, dear one?"

"I did not want to tell you. I think I am jealous."

She laughed. "Good! Jealous of whom?"

For a moment he did not reply. Then he said, "Chomoc gave me something for you also."

"Tell me!"

"His ambassador's shell."

Antelope bit her lips. It had not kept him safe from the water moccasin. . . . "Give it to me in the morning," she said, snuggling close.

Far Walker said, "I think he wanted you to have it for safe passage home."

Antelope exclaimed in surprise. She propped herself on an elbow. "What are you saying, Far Walker?"

"He knew you wanted to return to your people. Is that not so?"

Antelope felt the touch of the necklace. She must tell the truth.

"I do not want to leave you. I love you. But—"

"But?" His voice was strained.

"I had a vision. Kwani came to me." The words poured out, telling her story. "I must warn my people," she finished. "It is my duty. But I cannot leave you!" Tears choked her.

He pulled her down to him and held her close. "We must see things as they are, my love. My city is dying, and so, inevitably, shall I. When that time comes, you will be forced to die with me—your throat, your lovely throat garroted—" He paused, and Antelope felt the beating of his heart. "Skyfeather, too . . . No. I cannot allow that to happen. You must return to your people. You will join me when your time comes."

"But—"

"I shall have the War Chief assemble a protecting party— warriors, everything needed—"

Antelope's heart overflowed with love for this man. Again they embraced, seeking to absorb each other, to keep each other always.

Chomoc was given a royal burial, befitting one who had saved the life of a Great Sun. Antelope shed tears for him, for the boy he used to be and for the man he ultimately became.

Now it was time to begin her journey home. Antelope and Skyfeather had gone to the temple for the High Priest's blessing and he had prayed for them, asking the Spirit Being's protection. He said, "This is my farewell. I cannot—" he paused, his deep eyes brimming. "I shall not be present when you depart for your home." Antelope swallowed, remembering.

Many had voiced sorrow that she must go. But because she was Towa, they understood the Great Sun's decision. She must return to her own people.

It was a fine day, ideal for a journey. But first, Antelope and Skyfeather wanted to tell Peg Foot good-bye. As the litter reached his door, Peg Foot stood waiting.

"Welcome!" He beamed. "I have been expecting you. Come in."

Antelope looked about the room for the last time. It had been her home; a part of her would remain here. A lump rose in her throat. "We come to say good-bye."

"I know," he said, and held out his arms.

Antelope hugged him and kissed his leathery cheek.

Skyfeather said, "My chickadee is going home with me, Grandfather. It will always remember you, and so will I."

Peg Foot pretended there was something in his eye. "Better not keep all those warriors and dogs and travois waiting. . . ." He blew his nose. "I wish you a safe journey."

Antelope kissed him again. "Farewell, dear Grandfather."

Far Walker awaited them outside. He had donned his royal garments and swan feather headdress, and he gleamed with a Great Sun's splendor.

How handsome he is! Antelope thought again. How she would miss him!

A crowd had gathered to see them off. Some brought gifts— food for the journey, new moccasins, small things they had made. Red Leaf brought an infant's winter robe.

"The baby will need it come birthing time."

How did she know? Antelope wondered. She had not told anyone but Far Walker. Women sensed things.

"I thank you, Red Leaf." But she was gone, disappearing into the crowd.

Far Walker dismounted from his litter and came to stand beside Antelope and Skyfeather.

"Good-bye, dear little one," he said to Skyfeather.

To Antelope he gave one final gift, a conch shell necklace engraved with a spider carrying a tusti bowl on her back.

"To remember your Fire Bringer." His dark gaze embraced her. "Good-bye, my love." His voice broke. "I must leave you. . . ." He turned abruptly as though he could bear no more. He gestured for his litter. "Take me to the temple."

"Good-bye, Father," Skyfeather called, her voice trembling, but the Great Sun was gone.

The War Chief strode up. "All is ready. You may go now." He waved an arm and shouted directions at warriors and impatient dogs. He turned to Antelope. "I wish you farewell and a safe journey."

"Will you keep Far Walker safe?"

"I will. That is a promise."

He strode away without saying more, but Antelope was comforted. The War Chief would keep his word.

It was the second day on the trail. All had gone well. The dogs were glad to be on the move, and the men were in good spirits.

Antelope spoke to the Ancient Ones. "She Who Remembers is coming home. The child within me will be born among our people."

Like a butterfly, like a spring breeze, a sweet note rose. Skyfeather held the flute to her lips, her eyes closed, her fingers finding their way.

> *My melodies shall not die, nor my songs perish.*
> *They spread, they scatter.*

▲ Epilogue ▼

When, at last, the long journey was completed and Antelope saw her home high on the ridge once more, she stood gazing. How beautiful it was, rising tier on tier against the blue sky!

"There is our home, Skyfeather."

Skyfeather was awed. She had seen many villages but never such a city as this. She said hesitantly, "Will they be glad to see us?"

"Of course. We are their people—and they are ours."

Skyfeather lifted the flute to her lips and played as Chomoc used to do to announce their arrival.

"Chomoc, do you hear your music?" Antelope whispered.

The entire party was received with celebration and rejoicing.

Antelope's brother, Acoya, Medicine and City Chief, welcomed them eagerly. "I have waited long for your return." Skyfeather received a special welcome. "How like Kwani you are!" he said softly, his voice deep with emotion.

At first evening fire, Antelope told of her vision and Kwani's warning. They listened intently.

"We must remember and tell our children and their children," she said. "We do not know when the evil ones will come. We must be prepared."

Acoya glanced at the people gathered around the fire. They nodded solemnly.

"We shall not forget."

Antelope's child was born, a boy who became a renowned Medicine Chief, a Healer. Skyfeather grew in beauty and wisdom, becoming one of the greatest She Who Remembers of all.

Meanwhile, people built homes in impregnable places—high cliffs, mountain hideaways, remote canyons. Kwani's warning was handed down from generation to generation.

Many winters, many summers passed before "terrible beings from the Sunrise Sea" invaded Pueblo villages. Spaniards on horseback killed, enslaved, raped, robbed, and brutally assaulted a noble people, just as Kwani had foretold.

A descendant of Kwani's—and Antelope's and Skyfeather's and all who came after—rose among his people. In cliffs and on high mesas, in remote kivas and around evening fires, plans were whispered, strategy discussed.

Never before had Pueblo tribes united against a single enemy. But this man brought them together for one purpose—to drive out the despised Spaniards.

"We shall regain our homeland. We shall plant our own fields, worship our own gods," he promised, and they believed him.

Up and down the valleys, from village to village, runners delivered knotted cords, each one marking a day before the planned attack would begin. Columns of smoke rose on that early summer morning, signaling.

The Pueblo Revolt, which began on August 10, 1680, is history. At terrible cost, the Spaniards were finally driven away like animals before a wildfire. The People possessed their lands, their homes, and their holy places once more.

The name of their leader, Kwani's descendant, was Popé.

Many Indian tribes no longer exist. But Pueblos endure on their mesas and wide-sky places to this day.

What of the necklace? Where is it now?

Antelope, Skyfeather, and all those who were She Who Remembers after them handed the necklace down from woman to woman. Years passed. White settlers came, more and more. The sacred beliefs of The People, their ceremonies and artifacts, were ridiculed and forbidden by white men in power. The People held to their old ways in secret until they could practice them freely again.

As the necklace passed from hand to hand over the centuries, gradually the knowledge of its powers was lost. It became a token, an artifact.

Today, it is elaborately framed, the prized possession of a woman in Dallas who inherited it from an unknown ancestor. It hangs on the den wall of a lavish home for visitors to admire. Its powers, long neglected, are unrealized.

One day the necklace will make its powers known.

> *Time is a great circle;*
> *There is no beginning, no end.*
> *All returns again and again*
> *Forever.*

▲ Afterword ▼

The places mentioned in this story still exist. The City of the Great Sun no longer stands, but the mounds are eternal. You may visit them at Spiro Mounds Archaeological Park in Spiro, Oklahoma, near the Arkansas border.

Centuries have taken their toll. The grassy mounds rise high against the sky; their temples are no more. Gathering places are silent and empty now—but for spirits lingering there, a presence sensed and remembered. Stand on the site of the vast plaza and see in your imagination the Great Sun sweeping by on his litter, and hear the shouts of homage, and the flutes, and the drums. . . .

The City of the North, Cahokia, near St. Louis, is a remarkable site. The city covered nearly six square miles and had a population of tens of thousands in residential sections. The biggest mound, Monks Mound, is the largest prehistoric earthen construction north of Mexico. It is a hundred feet high and a thousand long; its base covers over fifteen acres.

The inner city is being restored. Perhaps the restless spirit of Tima-cha is making itself known.

The future is only the past
Entered again by a different gate.
—SIR ARTHUR WING PINERO

439

▲ Acknowledgments ▼

A book of fiction based upon a prehistoric past with no written record demands input from archaeologists, anthropologists, and other experts if the place, the people, and the culture are to be presented accurately. I am indeed fortunate in having been given help so generously. However, experts differ, and there are times when a novelist must take dramatic license. Therefore, any deviation from facts known or presumed is my responsibility alone.

Dennis Peterson, manager of Spiro Mounds Archaeological Park, was more than generous in answering endless questions, making suggestions, and sending photographs.

I am indebted without measure to my daughter, Linda Lucretia Shuler, whose fine analytical and creative hand is evident throughout this book.

My thanks to Dr. James A. Brown and Dr. Richard Ambler for expertise graciously given.

Cheers and profound thanks to my super agent, Jean V. Naggar, and my incomparable editor, Liza Dawson.

To those scientists and scholars, past and present, whose books are listed in the Bibliography, I salute you. What an education you gave me! I am especially grateful to Walter Havighurst

440

for his book *Voices on the River,* giving eyewitness accounts of the great earthquake on the Mississippi River in 1811.

Writers need writers, and I appreciated the help and moral support of all the members of my writing group, The Circuit Writers of Brownwood, Texas. Especially helpful were Jo Anne Horn, Charlotte Laughlin, and Helen Perrin.

Above all, I am grateful for the support of my family, especially my husband, Bob, who cheered me on—month after month, after year.

Thank you, thank you all!

▲ Bibliography ▼

Beck, Warren A. *A History of Four Centuries*. Norman, Okla.: University of Oklahoma Press, 1962.

Beckwith, Thomas. *The Indian or Mound Builder*. Cape Girardeau, Mo.: Naeter Bros. Publishers, 1911.

Bell, Robert E., Edward B. Jelks, and W. W. Newcomb. *A Pilot Study of Wichita Indian Archaeology and Ethnohistory: A Final Report to the National Science Foundation*. August 1967.

Benavides, Fray Alonso de. *Benavides' Memorial of 1630*. Translated by Peter P. Forrestal, C.S.C. Washington, D.C.: Academy of American Franciscan History, 1954.

Billard, Jules, editor. *The World of the American Indian*. Washington, D.C.: National Geographic Society, 1974.

Blacker, Irwin R. *Taos*. Cleveland: World Publishing Company, 1959.

Bolton, Herbert Eugene. *The Hasinais*. Norman, Okla.: University of Oklahoma Press, 1987.

Brown, James A. "Trade and the Evolution of Exchange Relations at the Beginning of the Mississippian Period." *The Mississippian Emergence*, edited by Bruce D. Smith. Washington, D.C.: Smithsonian Institution Press, 1990.

———. "On Style Divisions of the Southeastern Ceremonial

Complex: A Revisionist Perspective." *The Southeastern Ceremonial Complex: Artifacts and Analysis*, edited by P. Galloway. Lincoln, Nebr.: University of Nebraska Press, 1989.

———. "The Search for Rank in Prehistoric Burials." *The Archaeology of Death*, edited by Robert Chapman, Ian Kinnes, and Klavs Randsborn. New Directions in Archaeology Series. Cambridge and New York: Cambridge University Press, 1981.

———. "The Southern Cult Reconsidered." *Midcontinental Journal of Archaeology*, Vol. 1., No. 2 (1976).

———. *Spiro Studies*. Vol. 1, *Spiro Focus Research*. Norman, Okla.: University of Oklahoma Research Institute, Stovall Museum of Science and History, 1966.

———. *Spiro Studies*. Vol. 2, *Graves and Their Contents*. Norman, Okla.: University of Oklahoma Research Institute, Stovall Museum of Science and History, 1966.

———. *Spiro Art and Its Mortuary Contexts*. Evanston, Ill.: Northwestern University Press, n.d.

Brown, James A., Robert E. Bell, and Don G. Wyckoff. *Mississippian Settlement Patterns*. New York: Academic Press, 1978.

Cadillac, Antoine Lamouth. *The Western Country in the 17th Century: The Memoirs of Lamouth Cadillac and Pierre Liette*, edited by Milo Milton Quaife. Chicago: The Lakeside Press, 1947.

Cather, Willa. *Death Comes for the Archbishop*. New York: Alfred A. Knopf, 1966.

Clements, Forrest E. *Historical Sketch of the Spiro Mound*. New York: Museum of the American Indian, Heye Foundation, 1945.

Davis, Hester A., Don G. Wyckoff, and Mary A. Holmes. *Proceedings of Seventh Caddo Conference*. Oklahoma Archaeological Survey. Norman, Okla.: University of Oklahoma, 1971.

Debo, Angie. *The Rise and Fall of the Choctaw Republic*. Norman, Okla.: University of Oklahoma Press, 1934, 1961.

Fergusson, Erna. *New Mexico: A Pageant of Three Peoples*. New York: Alfred A. Knopf, 1951.

Folsom, Franklin. *Red Power on the Rio Grande*. Chicago: Follett Publishing Company, 1973.

Gilbert, Claudette Marie. *Oklahoma Prehistory*. Norman, Okla.: University of Oklahoma, Stovall Museum of Science and History, and Oklahoma Archaeological Survey, 1980.

Griffin, James B., editor. *Archaeology of Eastern United States*. Chicago: University of Chicago Press, 1952.

Hackett, Charles Wilson. "The Revolt of the Pueblo Indians of New Mexico in 1680." *The Quarterly of the Texas State Historical Association*, October 1911.

Hamilton, Henry W., Jean Tyree Hamilton, and Eleanor F. Chapman. *Spiro Mound Copper*. Columbia, Mo.: Missouri Archaeology Society, 1974.

Hammond, George P. *Don Juan de Onate: Colonizer of New Mexico*. Albuquerque: University of New Mexico Press, 1953.

Havighurst, Walter. *Voices on the River*. New York: Macmillan Company, 1964.

Hewett, Edgar L., and Bertha P. Dutton. *The Pueblo Indian World*. Albuquerque: University of New Mexico and The School of American Research, 1945.

Holmes, Mary Ann, and Claudette Marie Gilbert. *Prehistoric Panhandle Farmers: The Roy Smith Site*. Prehistoric People of Oklahoma, No. 3. Norman, Okla.: University of Oklahoma, Stovall Museum of Science and History, 1979.

Holmes, Mary Ann, and Marsha Hill. *The Spiro Mounds Site*. Norman, Okla.: University of Oklahoma, Stovall Museum of Science and History, and Oklahoma Archaeological Survey, 1976.

Holmes, Mary Ann, and Donald R. Johnson. *Scenes from Spiro Life*. Norman, Okla.: Oklahoma Archaeological Survey, n.d.

Howard, James H. *The Southeastern Ceremonial Complex and Its Interpretation*. Stillwater, Okla.: Oklahoma State University, 1968.

Hudson, Charles. *The Southeastern Indians*. Knoxville: University of Tennessee Press, 1978.

Hughes, Jack Thomas. *Prehistory of the Caddoan-Speaking Tribes*. New York: Garland Publishing, 1974.

Jennings, Jesse D., editor. *Ancient North Americans*. San Francisco: W. H. Freeman and Company, 1978.

Johnson, Philip. "When the Pueblos Rebelled." *Westways*, May 1956.

Keating, Bern. *The Mighty Mississippi*. Washington, D.C.: National Geographic Society, 1971.

Maxwell, James A., editor. *America's Fascinating Indian Heritage*. Pleasantville, N.Y.: Reader's Digest, 1983.

Mooney, James. *The Swimmer Manuscript*. Bureau of American Ethnology, Bulletin 99. Washington, D.C.: Smithsonian Institution, 1932.

Peckham, Stewart. *Prehistoric Weapons in the Southwest.* Santa Fe: Museum of New Mexico Press, 1965.

Peet, Stephen D. *The Mound Builders: Their Works and Relics.* Chicago: Office of the American Antiquarian, 1892.

Phillips, Philip, and James A. Brown. *Pre-Columbian Shell Engravings.* Cambridge, Mass.: Harvard University, Peabody Museum Press, 1975.

Powell, J. W. *Seventh Annual Report: Bureau of Ethnology.* Washington, D.C.: Smithsonian Institution, 1885.

Robertson, James Alexander, editor and translator. *True Relation of the Hardships Suffered by Governor Fernando de Soto & Certain Portuguese Gentlemen During the Discovery of the Province of Florida.* Vol. 2, *1557.* De Land, Fla.: Florida State Historical Society, 1932.

Rogers, J. Daniel. *Spiro Archaeology: 1980 Research.* Norman, Okla.: Oklahoma Archaeological Survey, 1982.

Rogers, J. Daniel, Michael C. Moore, and Rusty Greaves. *Spiro Archaeology: The Plaza.* Norman, Okla.: Oklahoma Archaeological Survey, 1982.

Silverberg, Robert. *The Pueblo Revolt.* New York: Weybright and Talley, 1970.

———. *Mound Builders of Ancient America.* Greenwich, Conn.: New York Graphic Society Ltd., 1968.

Smith, Bruce D. *Patterns.* New York: Academic Press, 1976.

Southern Plains Lifeways: Apache and Wichita. Norman, Okla.: University of Oklahoma, Stovall Museum of Science and History, and Oklahoma Archaeological Survey, 1984.

Stuart, George E. "Who Were the 'Mound Builders'?" *National Geographic,* December 1972.

Texas Archeological Research Laboratory, University of Texas at Austin. *Caddoan Mounds: Temples and Tombs of an Ancient People.* Austin: Texas Parks and Wildlife Department, 1984.

Thomas, David Hurst, editor. *Columbian Consequences.* Vol. 1, *Archaeological and Historical Perspectives on the Spanish Borderlands West.* Washington, D.C.: Smithsonian Institution Press, 1989.

Verrill, A. Hyatt, and Ruth Verrill. *America's Ancient Civilizations.* New York: Capricorn Books, 1953.

Webb, Clarence H. *The Caddo Indians of Louisiana,* Second Edition. Baton Rouge, La.: Louisiana Archaeological Survey and Antiquities Commission, 1986.

Wedel, Waldo R. *An Introduction to Kansas Archaeology.* Bureau of American Ethnology, Bulletin No. 174. Washington, D.C.: U.S. Government Printing Office, 1959.

———. *An Introduction to Pawnee Archaeology.* Washington, D.C.: U.S. Government Printing Office, 1936.

Willey, Gordon R. *An Introduction to American Archaeology,* Vol. 1. Englewood Cliffs, N.J.: Prentice Hall, 1966.

Wright, Muriel H. *A Guide to the Indian Tribes of Oklahoma.* Norman, Okla.: University of Oklahoma Press, 1951.

Wyckoff, Don G., and Timothy G. Baugh. "Early Historic Hasinai Elites: A Model for the Material Culture of Governing Elites." *Midcontinental Journal of Archaeology,* Vol. 5, No. 2 (1980).

Wyckoff, Don G., and Jack L. Hofman. *Southeastern Natives and Their Pasts: A Collection of Papers Honoring Dr. Robert E. Bell.* Oklahoma Archaeological Survey, No. 11. Norman, Okla., 1983.

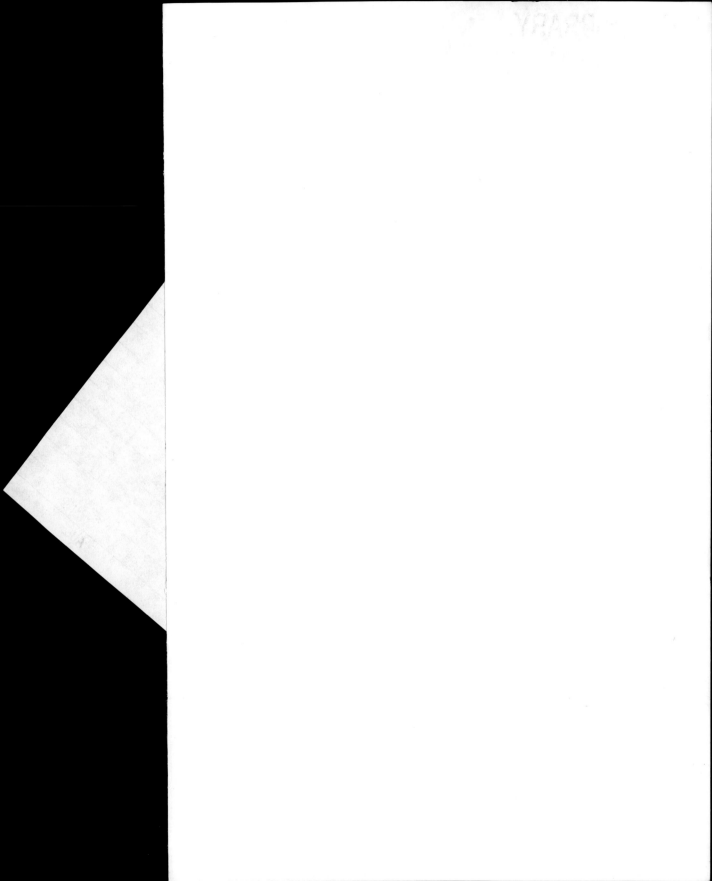

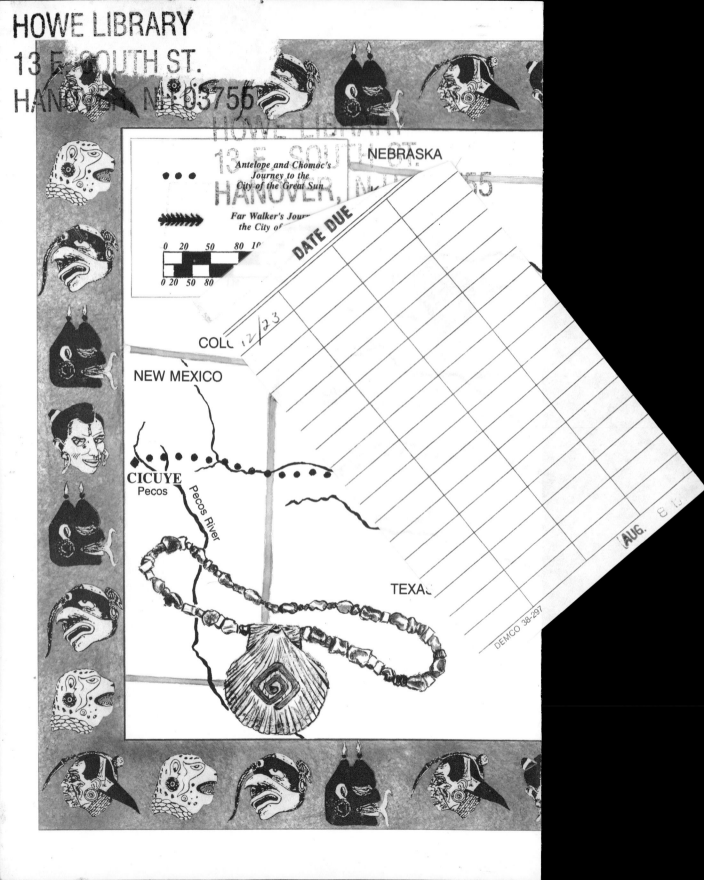

NEBRASKA

Antelope and Chomoc's
Journey to the
City of the Great Sun

Far Walker's Journey
the City of

0   20   50   80   10

0   20   50   80

COL

NEW MEXICO

CICUYE
Pecos

Pecos River

TEXAS